# CONCEALED

## BOOK TWO OF THE BEHOLDER SERIES

### CHRISTINA BAUER

# COPYRIGHT

Monster House Books
Brighton, MA 02135
ISBN 9781945723995
Second Edition

# DEDICATION

For All Those Who Kick Ass, Take Names
And Read Books

# AUTHOR'S NOTE

Dear Readers,

Here are some thingy-things to know about this special edition:

### Why I did this

Short answer: I'm changing distributors.

Long answer: Because of that switch, my first seven books need new back-end tracking numbers. In other words, I must deactivate the original PORTIA (as well as some other books) and then republish it.

As in, the exact same book.

So there will be two versions floating around.

Again, of the exact same book.

Which will be hella confusing.

Now for some context. My day job used to be in software, and we have a saying: *it's not a bug, it's a feature.* So, I figured that if I must have two versions, one of them might as well include new content.

The special edition series was born.

### What's in this special edition

An all-new honeymoon story! Boom. Mic drop.

### More special editions ahoy

As I mentioned above, my first seven books need new product numbers, so they're also getting extra content. Here's an overview of all seven new special editions (SE):

- ANGELBOUND SE, Angelbound Origins Book 1
- SCALA SE, Angelbound Origins Book 2
- MAXON SE, Angelbound Offspring Book 1
- PORTIA SE, Angelbound Offspring Book 2
- CURSED SE, Beholder Book 1
- CONCEALED SE, Beholder Book 2

So there you have it: why I wrote this special edition and some other semi-random stuff. Hope you enjoy this new special edition!

Thanks for reading and being you,

Christina

# CONCEALED

With a sigh, I rode deeper into the old forest. Here was a scene fit for a fairy tale. My elegant horse. Woods in the summertime. And me, a girl with pale skin, dark hair, and a flowing white gown: the innocent young maiden.

What a lie.

In truth, I was one of the realm's most deadly Necromancers. Mages like me wielded powerful magick over spirit and bone. Most people were terrified of us and for good reason. Necromancers were known for summoning ghosts and reanimating the dead. Not that I dabbled in that kind of thing personally. Ghosts whined for ages before doing even the smallest task. And decaying bodies? When reanimated, they became just as petulant as any ghost, only they smelled something awful. *Not worth the effort of casting, in my opinion.* There were other spells that I preferred.

My horse let out a high-pitched whinny. *My poor Smoke.* She so wanted to gallop. As did I, for that matter. But my plan called for me to ride slowly while looking innocent. The reason? I sought out sensitive information from the brigands who hid in these woods. Of course, I could just lure them to me with a spell. However, that meant projecting magick over long distances. Not too clever. That kind of casting could easily be detected by my enemies and used to track me down. I needed to be careful.

No, the scum of the forest had to approach me of their own free will. And that could only happen if I looked harmless.

*Please, let me look harmless.*

A weight of worry settled on my shoulders. I needed information and badly. My Sister mages from the Midnight Cloister were still missing. The desire to find them constricted my heart, tight as a vise.

As did my need for Rowan, if I allowed myself to think about him.

Suddenly, the tree branches rustled with extra force. I tilted my head, every sense in my body going on alert. Was someone finally approaching?

Seconds passed. No one appeared. I tried to hide my disappointment and kept riding along at an inching pace. *Clip-clop. Clip-clop.* The monotony made me wish to pull my hair out.

Images flickered through my mind. I pictured the Necromancer girls that I'd met in the Midnight Cloister. My Sisters. They'd all looked so wide-eyed and innocent as the evil Vicomte led them off to his secret prison. And these were no ordinary dungeons either. The Vicomte had a mysterious device that siphoned off Necromancer power. I shivered at the thought. My Sisters would writhe in agony as their magick was removed. And once their powers were fully drained, my young friends would transform into withered husks of skin. *Dead.* The thought made my stomach churn.

Sadly, the treachery against my people didn't end with my Sisters. Over the past five years, thousands of Necromancers had been imprisoned and marked for death. It was the Tsar who began all the abductions. Three months ago, I put that villain into exile, trapping him on a random magickal plane. Afterward, I assumed that our worries were over. How foolish of me. The moment the Tsar was gone, one of his main followers, the Vicomte, took up the heinous plans against my people.

Since then, things have only become worse.

The Vicomte has expanded the Tsar's program of abduction and murder, killing far more Necromancers than the Tsar ever did. No one has found any bodies, though.

*By the Sire, please let that mean some of my people are still alive.*

I could only hope that when I found my lost Sisters, I would discover some trained Necromancers along with them. So few of us remained. My Cloister, the Zelle, was the last of its kind, and it now held less than a dozen expert Necromancers. All were over ninety and could no longer cast any serious spells.

Footsteps rustled in a nearby thicket. *Someone's close.* My heart thrummed in my rib cage. Only certain travelers stole through the shrubbery.

*Thieves. How perfect.*

A hulking brute of a man lurched out from the trees and grasped my horse's reins with his meaty fist. Any other lady would have screamed. I could have cheered for joy.

"Afternoon, my lovely. I'm Bartley." His voice had the deep rasp of someone who enjoyed far too much whiskey. Like the other thieves I'd met, Bartley wore a mishmash of whatever clothing he'd claimed from his latest kills. In this case, Bartley donned a gentleman's long-coat over ragged pants and a patched-up shirt. He rubbed his thick hand over his bald head, a movement that showed off his small black eyes.

A warm sense of satisfaction bloomed through my chest. Someone this evil looking was certain to have good information. "Hello. I'm Elea."

"Call me Bartley. Are you alone?"

"Yes. And you?"

Bartley didn't say a word. The barest rustling in the trees answered for him. More thieves waited nearby, not that I cared. At close range, I could use certain spells without attracting attention. And since I was a Grand Mistress Necromancer, I didn't have to bother with reanimating the dead or calling on ghosts. Satisfaction warmed my blood. With any luck, I would cast my favorite spell today.

*Ah, the joy of conjuring skeletons from stone.*

After all, rock contained the concentrated remains of what had once been part of a living thing. It was an advanced form of cadaver, if you will. A Grand Mistress Necromancer could reform that raw material into a new skeleton.

I really loved casting these.

My skeletal servants had no personalities unless you counted mindless obedience. They smelled only of chalk if they had a scent at all. Best of all, a good Necromancer could give her skeletons some flair. I often covered mine with glittering gemstones. My teachers had frowned on this, but I was a girl, and we girls needed sparkly things.

Bartley took a half step closer. "Hand over your gold, and we'll let you go easy." He stared at my chest. "Yes, easy."

I stifled the urge to roll my eyes. Thieves always stared at my breasts and threatened my virtue. It was getting rather tedious. "I'll gladly pay you for information. Will you answer my questions?"

This was a rule of mine. *Always give the thieves an honest way out.* Not that any of them had taken it.

"By the Lady of Creation, you're a feisty one." Bartley grinned, showing a mouth full of yellow teeth. "Now, you've got me curious. Go on. Ask your questions."

"I'm searching for a child." My voice cracked as I pictured six-year-old Ada. She was a tiny wisp with a huge smile and an invisible friend named Wulf. "The Vicomte Gaspard took her."

Bartley's eye twitched, which came as no surprise. With the Tsar was gone, the Vicomte was the most feared man in the realm. "Never heard nothing 'bout the Vicomte kidnapping Necromancers."

*Of course, he hadn't.*

"I didn't say she was a Necromancer." My voice dripped with venom. "*You* did." Bartley knew something about my people—I could tell that without even casting a truth spell. "One last chance. Talk to me."

"I already did, wench." His thin mouth twisted into a snarl. He wouldn't answer any more questions voluntarily.

*Let's see what magick can do.*

Raising my left hand, I pulled Necromancer energy into my body. The power was everywhere, if you knew what to look for. Thousands of travelers had passed along this very road, their hearts filled with joy, dreams, and despair. That force was still in the ether, waiting for a Necromancer to transform it. I pulled the energy into my soul.

Magick rushed through me, energizing my body like a breath of fresh air. I focused it into my left arm. My bones there glowed blue as I whispered an incantation.

*Bones born in night*
*Honed by magick's light*
*Heed my call*
*Rise up for the fall*

The thief's piggy eyes narrowed. "You don't look like no Fantome."

Hope sparked in my chest. Fantomes were trained Necromancers who served the Vicomte. If Bartley knew about them, then he might be even more valuable. "I'm not a Fantome."

"Well, you can't be no free Necromancer. They're hardly none left." His mouth set into a determined line. "Is this some kind of trick?"

"No, it's more of a trap." I slipped off Smoke and stepped to the side. Pushing the power out of my hand, I set my spell loose. Blue mist appeared about Bartley's feet just as he lunged straight for me.

The man didn't get far. In fact, his feet stayed rooted to the spot.

Bartley shifted his weight, trying to break himself free. "What did you do?"

"Me? Nothing." I gestured toward the ground. Bartley couldn't know it, but more of my magick had whirled beneath the soil, shifting the stones into new forms. "The skeleton I conjured, though…"

Bit by bit, Bartley tipped his head down to peer at his worn leather boots. Skeletal hands had pushed through the earth and were now wrapped around his ankles. The white granite bones contrasted against the dark soil.

"You bitch!" Bartley reached under his longcoat. No doubt, he was searching for a weapon.

This wasn't my first battle, however. I still had plenty of ambient energy left to conjure more skeletal servants.

With a flick of my fingers, another set of bony arms burst through the ground nearby, followed by a third. Two new skeletons wiggled their way out of the soil and stood at attention. They were magnificent—seven feet tall with amber bones and glowing blue gems in their eye sockets. What a sight.

Bartley gasped and yanked a knife out from under his coat.

With a wave of my hand, I summoned more blue mist around me as Bartley tossed his blade at my head. My enchanted shield shattered his weapon before it got anywhere near. Metal shards burst in the air and fell in a glittering cascade to the forest floor. Necromancers weren't supposed to show emotion, but I allowed myself a small smile.

Four more thieves leapt out of the forest, a mixture of men and women in raggedy dress. While howling in unison, they all rushed toward me. Unfortunately for them, they hadn't counted on my skeletons. It was a common enough mistake. Most conjured skeletons were clumsy things that lumbered toward their enemies. Not mine. All my castings were whip-fast and deadly. The moment my skeletons saw I was under attack, they wrapped their bony arms around the thieves' throats, snapping their necks in quick succession. All except one.

Bartley gasped. "Who are you?"

"Someone who deserves answers." I rubbed my palms together. For extra effect, I allowed a small puff of blue mist to whirl about my hands. "Let's try again. What do you know about the Vicomte Gaspard?"

He lifted his chin. "Nothing. I swear."

"I see." This one wouldn't be easy to intimidate into talking. *He must be hiding something really important.*

I waved my left arm, and two more skeletons wiggled out of the ground. This time, I cast them to look extra frightening. Both were eight feet tall with opal-black bones and pointed teeth. Blue light shone about their bony hands, which meant they could not only fight, but cast spells as well. The pair loomed over Bartley, their jaws clacking with silent laughter. A wet spot appeared on his pants. *Excellent.*

"Tell me what you know, Bartley. If you don't, I'll be forced to ask them to cast a truth spell. You've heard about those? The skeletons squeeze information from your head. I'm told it's very painful."

"I can't tell you nothing." Little bits of spittle flew from Bartley's mouth as he spoke. "The Vicomte—"

"He's not here and I am." I snapped my fingers, and the two dark skeletons went to work. One held Bartley's head still while the other pointed its bony finger right above his eyeball. "Perhaps we'll work up to a truth spell. There are other ways to injure your skull, you know."

"No!" Bartley stared cross-eyed at the skeletal hand. "He's got Necromancers hidden away."

"Where?"

"On Royal lands."

"I've checked every inch of that man's estate." Or cast spells on his servants to do it for me. "My Sisters aren't there."

"I said Royal lands, didn't I? It's one of the nobility that has them."

My heart sank. I was afraid of that. There were hundreds of noble families. Searching all their lands could take years, even if I cared to use magick. "Which noble is hiding the Necromancers?"

"I don't know." Bartley was visibly shaking now. I believed he was telling the truth—the man didn't know anything more about where my people were being held. Still, I needed other kinds of information. "There's a machine that drains magick from my kind. Have you seen it?"

"I can't tell you 'bout that. He'll find out. He'll kill me."

"He *might* kill you." I snapped my fingers, and the skeleton twisted its wrist, bringing the pointed bone of its fingertip even closer to Bartley's eye. "But I definitely will."

Bartley howled with fright. "He's got a device. A small thing, no bigger than a skipping stone. I never got to see it close up, but it's made of metal. Them Fantomes put it on the prisoners. That's what drains 'em till they're dead."

I pictured little Ada, six years old and subjected to some kind of evil contraption. The thought made me ill. "Who made this device? How does it work?"

Tears streamed down his dirty cheeks. "I don't know. I swear."

I thought back to the single clue I had from Veronique, one of my Sisters from the Midnight Cloister. As she was dragged away,

Veronique spoke the name of a Royal. I'd been searching for that girl ever since. "What do you know of a Royal named Amelia?"

"You mean the Lady Amelia Masson?"

My pulse sped. I was hoping that Veronique was referring to the Lady Amelia Masson. Mostly because I'd already checked another dozen Lady Amelias already and had come up empty. "What do you know of Amelia Masson?"

"Lady Amelia lives near here. She's crazy. Locked herself up for years."

Worry weighed on my shoulders. I hadn't considered that one of the Amelias wouldn't be sane enough to answer my questions. "And that's all you know about her?"

"Bandits broke into her mansion a few months back. Took some silver and ran for the forest. After that, they all disappeared. No one knows what happened to them, but I'm guessing it wasn't good."

"Why do you say that?" I happened to know for a fact that those bandits were dead. I'd found the bodies myself, after I uncloaked the magick that concealed them. They lay in the forest not far from here.

"Lady Amelia is under the Vicomte's protection. One of his adopted children, you know?"

"I've heard." Amelia Masson was also said to be a genius with mechanics, not that I was about to volunteer that information.

"Well, them bandits had no business breaking into her house. Everyone knows what happens when you attack what the Vicomte sees as his property."

"Indeed." The Fantomes had tortured those bandits for days before they finally killed them. My chest tightened with rage. The bodies had been twisted and flayed almost beyond recognition.

Bartley was shaking more violently now. "That's all I know. I swear."

I believed him. Still, I needed to be sure. I nodded to the skeleton holding Bartley. "Test him."

All the blood drained from Bartley's face. "You said you wouldn't cast no truth spells."

"Forcing you to speak is different from testing whether you just lied. This one won't hurt."

The skeleton gripped the thief's head while blue light flared more brightly around its bony hands. "He's telling the truth, Grand Mistress."

"Fine." I couldn't hide the note of disappointment in my voice. "Erase his memory and set him loose."

"As you command."

The skeleton's hands flared blue once again. Bartley's eyes rolled back into his head, and he collapsed onto the ground. He'd sleep for an hour and wake up with a headache. Not to mention a lot of work to do if he chose to bury his friends.

One of the opal skeletons turned to me. "Will you need anything more?"

"No, you all may go." I waved my hand, and the skeletal servants settled back into the earth. Once they were gone, I tapped my cheek and thought through Bartley's news. There were two kinds of people on my continent. First, there were Necromancers, who had magick. Second, there were the Forgotten Ones, who had none. Of course, Forgotten Ones would say they had learning and machines, which were superior to mage craft. Personally, I'd rather have magick any day.

In turn, the Forgotten were divided up into Royals—like the Vicomte—or Commoners such as Bartley. Bartley just told me the lost Necromancers were on Royal lands. No matter how I turned over that information, it didn't narrow things down much. I shook my head. There was nothing to do but move forward. Crazy or not, perhaps the Lady Amelia Masson would have more insights for me.

I hoisted myself into the saddle and patted Smoke's neck. "Let's keep going, girl." I sat up straight, scanned the road ahead, and saw the man who'd haunted my thoughts for weeks.

*Rowan.*

My breath caught. Rowan and I had teamed together once. He helped me send the Tsar into exile. Afterward, we'd parted ways. I thought I'd forget him. That hadn't happened. Instead, every day I found myself listing the many reasons why Rowan could never be more than my friend.

It was a long list.

To begin with, Rowan was from a different continent than mine. Visiting each other meant casting transport spells, which wasn't easy to do. Plus, Rowan only visited my continent because he served his King as a master spy. Not exactly the kind of man you built a life with.

Then, there came the fact that Rowan was a kind of mage called a Creation Caster. That made him the exact opposite of a Necromancer in almost every way. His magick came from life and nature. Necromancers pulled from death. Casters were known for open displays of affection. Necromancers were schooled to control every feeling. So, although we'd successfully teamed in battle, chances were that Rowan and I weren't compatible in other ways.

To make matters worse, Rowan wasn't just any Caster. His uncle was their ruler, Genesis Rex. Everyone knew that the Imperial family only married for political gain. Meanwhile, I was a lone Necromancer who only owned a small farm.

Not exactly the ideal for an Imperial marriage.

On reflex, my fingers brushed the mating band that Rowan had given to me. I wore it on a chain that hung around my neck and under my clothes. It wasn't a real symbol of genuine affection, only something we'd been forced to exchange in order to fight the Tsar. Even so, I wore it every day.

It was a silly thing to do, but I couldn't help it.

"Hail and well met, Elea." Rowan gave me one of his crooked grins. Warmth spread down to my toes. He was leaning against an oak tree, wearing the loose green leathers, hooded cloak, and longbow of a Forgotten One and a hunter. Some kind of disguise, obviously. When Rowan had helped me fight the Tsar, he'd worn fitted Caster leathers.

Other than the hunting gear, Rowan looked as he always had: tall and strong-limbed with broad shoulders and tousled brown hair. A day's growth of beard rounded his chin. His green eyes seemed to pull me closer, and his full mouth looked delicious.

*A delicious mouth?* I needed to stop thinking this way about Rowan and quickly. Straightening my spine, I gave him a proper greeting, the way any Creation Caster would. "Hail and well met."

"I should say so." Rowan scanned the corpses. "Excellent work with the Band of Eight, by they way. Those are some of the most fearsome thieves around."

"Band of Eight? I only ran across five of them."

Rowan's smile broadened. "I might have helped a bit. Someone has to keep an eye on you."

A warm feeling spread through my chest. *Rowan watches over me.* "You didn't need to do that."

"I know." He nodded toward Bartley. "How long before he wakes up?"

"An hour."

Rowan offered me his hand. "Come down and walk with me. We need to talk."

Panic tightened up my spine. Touching Rowan was a bad idea. It always made me lose focus. "I'm fine up here."

"If you insist." Rowan raised his right hand, closed his eyes, and began an incantation. This man was the most powerful mage I'd ever seen. While Necromancers like me pulled their energy from the remains of the past, Casters like Rowan pulled in living power to make magickal animals.

A red mist hovered around the ground at Rowan's feet. Within seconds, the haze solidified into a massive black horse with a red saddle. That could only mean one thing.

*Rowan plans to ride alongside me. The thought made me giddy.*

"Nicely done," I said. "But where are your snow tigers?" Normally, Rowan rode either Radi or Umeme.

"I'm trying to keep a low profile." He winked. "You should try it sometime." He effortlessly hoisted himself onto the horse's back.

"What do you mean?" I had a fairly good idea, though.

"Your spells. I saw flashes of ethereal light from a league away."

I shrugged. "A girl has to cast sometimes. It may have been bright, but the power levels were low and at close range. No Fantomes would have detected anything."

His full mouth thinned to a determined line. "I still don't like it. The Fantomes are dangerous."

"I'm aware." At one time, the Fantomes had been the personal entourage of the Tsar. Now, they followed the Vicomte. For months, these mages had been scouring the continent and arresting anyone with Necromancer ability.

Mostly, they wanted to find me.

Officially, the Vicomte announced that he desired an audience with the brave Necromancer who sent the Tsar off into exile. I didn't believe that nonsense for a second. What the Vicomte really wanted was another Necromancer to drain.

*No, thank you.*

"Be careful, Elea. That's all I ask."

I gave him a sly grin of my own. "I suppose I'm not an expert at sneaking about, unlike some people."

"No, you're not." Rowan's gaze suddenly locked with mine. Once again, I felt pulled in by the intensity of his stare. "I like that about you. Quite a lot, as a matter of fact."

*By the Sire.* His words were making me feel all squirmy inside. I needed to change the subject.

"I'm off for Jaxminster."

"Still looking for a Lady Amelia?"

"Yes, unfortunately. The one in Jaxminster is my thirteenth attempt."

He let out a low whistle. "And what happened with the other twelve?"

"All dead ends." I wanted to scream with frustration. "The next one on my list is the Lady Amelia Masson. Does that name mean anything to you?"

"Not at all." Rowan's face became unreadable. I hated it when he did that. And since Rowan was a master spy for the Creation Casters, he did it quite a lot.

"Why are you *really* here, Rowan?"

He arched his right brow. "What if I said I missed you?"

"Liar. You're as single-minded about protecting your people as I am about rescuing mine."

"True. Even so, I still missed you."

I wasn't letting him off the hook that easily. "In other words, you'll tell me what you want when you're good and ready."

Rowan chuckled. "How do you read me so well?"

"Call it my gift." We followed a turn in the road. "How has your work been going?" Rowan also sought news of the missing Necromancers, but for a different reason. He feared the Vicomte gathering up their magick. If anyone wielded that much power, then they could attack Rowan's people. As a result, while I'd been hunting down Lady Amelias, Rowan was working on a diplomatic course between the Vicomte and the Caster's King, Genesis Rex. "Any luck so far?"

"We're seeing some initial success with diplomacy. Luncheons, balls, dinners. No word yet about the Vicomte's plans for the Casters."

"That's unfortunate."

"We've made allies with a few of the Royals, which is good. A handful are quite unhappy with the Vicomte. One in particular might be useful."

"Anyone I should know about?"

"Not at this time." His face became stony once more.

"You're doing it again."

"What?"

"Playing the spy."

"You know I'd tell you if I could, Elea." He gave me another one of his intense stares. "My first duty is to the throne."

I blushed and looked away. "I understand." And I did. When your uncle is your King, and that King orders you to keep a secret, then your follow those orders and keep your mouth closed.

We rode along for a few more minutes before Rowan broke the quiet. "Have you any ideas on how the Vicomte could wield Necromancer power?"

"I've been thinking about it." In fact, I'd been contemplating it quite a bit. "It would need to involve a totem ring." That was how we Necromancers stored spells. Totem rings enabled mages to cast lengthy incantations with a single word—there was no lighting up bones or creating colored smoke. Unfortunately, totem rings were incredibly hard to create and only stored one kind of spell at a time.

Rowan stared at my hands. "I notice you're not wearing any today." Normally, I had a totem ring on every finger of my left hand.

"Yes, I've had to set those aside. Wearing totem rings would be a clear sign that I'm a Necromancer. And the spells for creating new rings would attract too much attention." Sadly, I didn't have any old rings to use, either. They'd all been ruined during my last battle against the Tsar.

"The Vicomte using a totem ring." Rowan frowned. "It's possible.

Although, how would he get the magick into his body? The man isn't a Necromancer. Totem rings only work for mages like you, right?"

Excitement fluttered inside my stomach. I loved these chats with Rowan. There were no other free mages around that I could discuss new magick with. Sure, I could transport back to my old Cloister, the Zelle, and chat with Petra, my Mother Superior. However, Petra was almost a hundred years old. Her mind was sharp when it came to traditional magick. But when I needed to think through new uses of power, no one was better than Rowan.

"What do you think?" Rowan spoke again, snapping me out of my thoughts. "How could the Vicomte take in power from a totem ring?"

"I do have one idea."

Rowan grinned. "I knew you would."

My body warmed under his praise. "The Vicomte has a number of adopted children. All of them are experts in machines."

"And?"

"He's not bringing in orphans out of the kindness of his heart. I think he's putting them to work. They're creating some kind of device for him. It's a machine about as large as a throwing stone. And if my guess is right, that device could transmit magick into a non-mage."

"Quite possible." Rowan nodded slowly. "The Vicomte's been obsessed with machines for years. We'll focus our spy work in that area." His voice took on a deep tone that I liked very much indeed. "Thank you, Elea."

I looked away quickly. Even with the space between us, being this close to Rowan made me all distracted. I needed to refocus on my mission. "I learned some news about my lost Necromancers. Perhaps you can shed some light on it."

"I'll do my best."

"The Vicomte is hiding my Sisters somewhere on Royal land."

"Not his own property?"

"It's someone from court. The thief back there confirmed it."

"I see." Rowan grew quiet. It was what he always did when thinking through a problem. "Not a lot of places could be used for draining magick. After the Tsar took power, my team canvassed all the known dungeons on Royal lands. None of them would have worked for such a purpose."

"I'm sorry to hear that." A sense of emptiness filled my soul. My people had been disappearing for years, and yet there was no sign of them.

"Take heart. I'll check around. One of the old dungeons could have been adapted for draining magick. Or perhaps a new one was built since the Tsar took power." He pulled off his glove, reached across the distance between us, and took my hand. The shock of his touch moved through me. Confidence and care warmed my soul.

*Oh, you are dangerous, Rowan.*

"If anyone can find them, Elea, you can."

Rowan gave my hand a gentle squeeze and then released me. My arm went cold without his touch. I hated admitting this, but I dearly missed Rowan. That simply wasn't right. Necromancers like me shouldn't form attachments. Still, when it came to Rowan, I couldn't help myself somehow. I cleared my throat and tried to put on a casual voice. "If nothing comes of this last Lady Amelia, perhaps I could aid you in your diplomacy."

He gave me another crooked smile. "You might expose me with your spells."

"A likely story. You just don't want me involved."

"That's right." His gaze intensified once again. "I want you safe. If this last Amelia doesn't work out, then I want you to return to Brad-dock Farm."

Naming my old farm made my chest ache. The servants who were working on it were good people. They sent me regular missives, and things were going well. Even so, that farm was my only home. Some days I wanted my old rocking chair and fire-lit hearth so badly, I could hardly stand it. And if I failed with the Lady Amelia Masson, then I was sorely out of other options and ideas.

I stared at the western horizon. Braddock Farm was that way. Maybe it was time to regroup for a while. I could harvest some grain. Read a few spell books. Plan other ways to find Ada.

When I spoke again, my voice was dreamy. "If I went back to Braddock Farm—and I'm not saying that I would—would you alert me of any news?"

"I'd even let you cast a compulsion on me."

I scanned his features carefully. A compulsion spell was no small thing, and Rowan's face looked open and earnest.

"In that case, I'll consider it."

His eyes glittered. "That's all I ask."

We reached the edge of the forest. A small town stretched out before us. *Jaxminster.* Here the buildings stood no more than two stories high. All of them were made of white plaster and framed by heavy wooden beams. A tall clock tower stood at the far edge of town.

I stopped my horse. "This is the place. Lady Amelia Masson lives in the estate beyond that clock tower."

"How do you know?"

"Amelia was adopted by the Vicomte. All his so-called children have extraordinary gifts in science or mechanics. They must build their own clock towers as an early project for him."

A flicker of unease crossed Rowan's features. "I hope it goes well for you."

"I've nothing to fear from her. The worst rumor I've heard is that she's a crazy recluse. At least, she's not one of the adoptees who builds weapons."

Rowan frowned. "What about the Fantomes?" It was a valid concern. Almost every Royal had a Fantome in residence. That was how the Vicomte controlled his court.

"Amelia's out of favor. She doesn't have any Fantomes around. I'll ask her a few questions and hope she has answers. Perhaps she'll share something useful."

Rowan's frown deepened. I knew he was still worried about my safety.

I lowered my voice to a serious note. "I'll be fine, Rowan."

"Still, I'd rather that you could easily contact me without attracting attention." Rowan raised his right hand. The veins there glowed red as crimson mist swirled about his arm. Within seconds, the haze solidified into a little robin that sat quietly on his palm. "This bird is one of my familiars. If you need to get a message to me, call her name, Tamu. My magick will do the rest."

The little creature hopped onto my shoulder. Her tiny claws pricked my skin before she flew away. "I will. Thank you."

Rowan opened his mouth to say something and then closed it just as quickly. I glanced over to his hands. He was wearing his heavy leather gloves once more. I couldn't help but wonder... Did he ever wear his mating band? For one full day, our souls had been connected through those rings. Did that mean as much to him as it did to me?

My hand settled onto the base of my throat where my own ring hung under my gown. I knew it was weak of me. Even so, I treasured this band. Wearing it with Rowan was one of the few moments in my life where I felt truly linked to another person.

Rowan noticed my hand, and his features became unreadable. An itchy feeling moved over my skin. When we were talking just now, Rowan admitted to hiding something for his King. What could it be? Part of me wanted to press for a full answer, yet I held back. I couldn't afford to get any more involved with Rowan than I already was.

My mission lay elsewhere. I needed to save Ada and the other Necromancers. Straightening in my saddle, I nodded toward the town. "It's time for me to leave."

Rowan shifted his horse onto another path. "Be safe."

"And you as well." I clicked my tongue, and Smoke took off for Jaxminster.

## 2

*F*or hours now, I'd been shouting at the front gate of Lady Amelia Masson's estate. My hands ached from gripping the iron bars so tightly.

*No one seems to be home.*

Leaning forward, I rested my forehead against the iron bars and angled for a better view.

*Still, nothing to see.*

The courtyard beyond the gate lay empty. This was unbelievable. What self-respecting Royal didn't have any guards? Maybe this one really was crazy.

If I didn't know for a fact that Lady Amelia Masson still lived here, then I might have moved on a while ago. Especially since the darkening clouds threatened rain.

Finally, a light step sounded on the forecourt. A servant walked into view. She was older and petite, with a shrewd face and golden hair that had been pulled into a tight bun. "What do you want?" Her voice was clipped.

"Is the Lady Amelia Masson here?"

"Yes, she is."

"May I speak with her?"

She pursed her wrinkled lips. "Your name?"

"Lady Elea."

"No, it's not, girl." She used the pronunciation that the farmers did—gurl—which had a little twang to it. She knew I was lying.

*Here we go again.*

I gripped the skirts of my gown. This was supposedly the latest fashion. My hair was perfectly coiffed and styled. Still, something about me screamed *farmer.* I suppose it was better than screaming *Necromancer.* Still, it meant that I rarely got introduced to the various Lady Amelias I was trying to meet. Even worse, the few times I did greet them, they always had Fantomes in their houses, so I couldn't cast any spells for easy answers. Well, not without risking exposure, anyway.

My fingers itched to empower an incantation. This mansion was one of the few that didn't have any Fantomes in residence. Still, that didn't mean they weren't lurking nearby. The Vicomte was known for sending Fantomes to remote places on a whim. I couldn't take the risk.

All my previous Amelia encounters had ended with me being shown the door and quickly. Afterward, I always had to find house servants and secretly interrogate them. It was painstaking work, not to mention nerve-wracking. At every moment, I could have been detected.

The woman at the gate began to turn away.

*No, no, no.*

There was nothing left to do but say who'd sent me. Not that it had ever helped before.

I cupped my hand by my mouth and raised my voice. "I know Veronique."

The woman paused. "Who?"

"Mademoiselle Veronique Adeline Josephine de Haverville. She's the one who told me to find Amelia."

Seconds passed. The woman turned around and eyed me carefully. "How would you know our Veronique?"

A weight lifted off my chest. *Our Veronique.* This was the first time anyone had shown a glimmer of recognition when I mentioned that name. "She's in dire trouble." My voice wobbled. "Please. This is life or death."

The woman stepped closer and cracked open the gate. Leaning

out, she scanned the thin street outside the mansion. All the rickety wooden buildings appeared deserted. No one was walking along the rutted road. She stepped back inside. "You'd better come to the garden. My Lady will want to see you."

My knees turned rubbery beneath me. At last, a Lady Amelia who knew something and was willing to talk. I only hoped she wasn't as crazy as Bartley had claimed.

The servant marched off across the cobblestone courtyard. "I'm Clothilde, by the way. Close the gate behind you."

I slammed the massive thing shut and followed Clothilde toward a massive mansion made of rose-colored marble. Clothilde strode up the front steps and yanked the mighty door open with ease. The front entrance led to an elaborate reception room made of shining wood. The arched ceiling was painted with images of a family coat of arms—a longsword wreathed in red roses. *Strange.* I'd never seen a crest like that before. I scanned the space around me. It was even stranger. No other servants seemed to be about. A mansion this large should be full of them. "Is Amelia the only lady of the house?"

"Save your questions for her." Clothilde led me through a warren of passageways that led to a lush garden. Flowers burst from their small plots of ground, a riot of purple, pink, and green. Scaled trellises arched through the air. It couldn't have been more different from the gray, cramped look of the town.

Lady Amelia sat on an overlarge wooden swing. She had the face of a doll, what with her porcelain skin, wide eyes, and bow-shaped mouth. Long curls spiraled over her shoulders. Her dress was the large-skirted variety that all the Royals seemed to favor. Its pink satin was the perfect shade to highlight her bright red hair. She looked up from the small leather book on her lap. "What's all this?"

"Your Ladyship, someone to see you. Says she knows Veronique."

Amelia shooed the servant away with her fingertips. "Thank you. You may go." She closed the book, and a whirring noise filled the air. The volume was covered in tiny gears that had clicked into place, locking the book up tight. I'd known how Royals were obsessed with new machines and odd fashions, yet I'd never seen anything like that book before. Perhaps this contraption was of Amelia's making? She was a master machinist, after all.

"I'd like to stay at your side, my Lady." Clothilde shot a wary glance in my direction. "You'll want to be careful what you say to this new girl. Especially what you *show* her, if you catch my meaning." Her frown deepened with the word *"show."* What could Amelia have to share? I decided to save that question for later. "This one says she's a lady, but she's fresh off the farm."

I suppose I could be insulted. Even so, Clothilde's words made me feel a little more confident about Amelia. The girl had clearly inspired her servants to care for her welfare. That had to count for something.

Amelia waved her dainty hand. "I'll be fine."

"As your ladyship requests." Clothilde turned back toward the house.

Amelia scooted over, making room for me beside her on the swing. "You may have a seat."

"I'll stand, thank you."

Amelia stared at the path that led to the greenhouse. "Clothilde's not gone far, you know."

"Good."

Amelia narrowed her pretty blue eyes. "You fear for my safety?"

"No, I'm pleased to see that someone else does."

"Well said." She folded her hands neatly in her lap "Who are you?"

"A friend of Veronique's."

Amelia's eyes widened. "Do you know where she is? She disappeared."

"No, I don't. That's why I'm here. I've been trying to find her. Can you help me?"

Amelia drummed her fingers atop the metal gears of her book. Her mind seemed just as sharp and interlocked. She wasn't replying. Yet at least I could be certain she wasn't insane. She exhaled a long breath. "How could I help you? I don't know where Veronique is."

"You may know something that can assist. May I ask you a few questions?"

"If you must." The wary look in her blue eyes said she might not answer, however.

Still, I couldn't believe my luck. This was he furthest I'd gotten with any Lady Amelia. Sad to say, I hadn't planned much past getting through the front door. I eyed the girl before me carefully. Veronique's last words were for me to find someone named Amelia. Still, was this the person she'd really meant? And even if it was, how much could I trust this stranger?

"What you know about Veronique?"

"Almost everything." Amelia kicked her foot against the ground and began to gently swing. Her features softened as she talked about her friend. "Vee loved yellow gowns and handsome boys. She was clever with anything that had gears; not that she'd ever let you know it. The girl was selfish and shrewd. Even so, you'll never meet anyone with a stronger heart." Amelia looked up at me through long lashes. "Your turn. What do you know of how Veronique disappeared?"

It didn't feel right sharing too much. After all, I'd only just met Amelia. I decided on an answer that was both truthful and vague. "She was taken."

"Now that's an avalanche of information." Amelia rolled her eyes. "Perhaps this will free your tongue. I'm a Necromancer." She quickly lifted her arm. Her pretty features scrunched up in agony as a flash of blue light skittered across her palm. She shook out her hand. "Damn, that always hurts." She lowered her voice to what was supposed to be a menacing level. "But don't think I won't use my power if I have to. I'll get the truth from you, one way or another."

My mouth hung open for a moment before I was able to school my features again. I couldn't believe it. Was it only a day ago that I was threatening thieves with the same logic? *The gods have a sense of humor.* "I admire your spirit, but that wasn't Necromancy."

"That's what you think." Amelia lifted her chin. "Answer my questions or I'll strike you down."

I worked hard to hide my smile. *You want to strike me down? Get in line.* Still, her display did prove one thing. Amelia was desperate to find Veronique. I sat down beside Amelia on her swing. "You can't go around showing off blasts of blue light like that. You'll get dragged in by the Fantomes. In fact, I'm amazed they haven't pulled you in already. I thought anyone with Necromancer power was drained ages ago."

"I was adopted by the Vicomte, same as Veronique. All of us so-called children have Necromancer power. We use it to build things for him."

This supported my theory about how the Vicomte planned to take in Necromancer magick with a device. Having machinists with some Necromancer abilities would only help him figure out how to take in power from a totem ring. I leaned forward. "And you used some of your magick to build the clock tower."

"Precisely."

"It still doesn't explain the risks you're taking right now. I've heard stories about the Vicomte and his adopted children. Most of them came to a nasty end." *Like Veronique.*

"I'm the only child he actually adopted. His sole heir. And I have magickal wards that protect me from him. Otherwise, he'd have sent me away ages ago." Her gaze turned pleading. "That's what happened to Vee, isn't it? He sent her off."

The question hung in the air. *What happened to Veronique?* My Necromancer training was clear on this point. Evade all straightforward answers, even to another Sister. Yet I wasn't feeling very logical today. My heart wanted to trust Amelia. After seeing Rowan leave again, I desperately needed someone I could rely on in this mission.

*I'll tell her the truth.*

"I was once a captive of the Midnight Cloister. Veronique was imprisoned there with me. The Mother Superior at Midnight meant to kill us, yet she didn't. I escaped. The Vicomte took Veronique away."

Amelia's lower lip wobbled. "And what's he doing with Vee? Are the rumors true? Is he draining her?"

My soul ached for Amelia. She desperately wanted to find her friend. I knew just how that felt. "He's trying to. But we can get to her first."

Amelia fiddled with the gears on the cover of her book. When she spoke again, her voice was low. "But you don't know where he's keeping her."

"I was hoping you might know something that could help find her. How well do you know the Vicomte and his court?"

"I'm the Vicomte's first and only child, in the legal sense, anyway. He's my Daddy Dearest." The words *"Daddy Dearest"* dripped with venom. She leapt off the swing and paced a line on the garden path. "Veronique was my best friend until that heartless snake stole her away. I want her back. You've no idea how long I've searched with nothing to show for it. I'll do whatever is necessary." She paused and turned to me. "What else do you want to know? I'll tell you anything."

"How familiar are you with the lands of the Royals? I've learned that the Vicomte is hiding Veronique and other Necromancers on the estate of one of his courtiers."

Amelia's brows lifted. "Other Necromancers?"

"Of course. Veronique wasn't the only one taken."

That calculating look returned to Amelia's doll-like face. "That's why you're here, isn't it? You care for another Necromancer like I do for Veronique."

*She is a clever one, I'll give her that.*

"Yes."

"Who is it?"

I sighed. "Why do you want to know? I've decided to trust you. Isn't that enough?"

"No, I want to understand what you get from all this. Most people hate Veronique. The gods know I certainly did when we first met. Why risk yourself to save her?"

I pinched the bridge of my nose. This conversation kept digging me in deeper. Now I'd have to reveal everything. Taking in a long breath, I raised my left arm and pulled Necromancer power into my soul. The delicate bones in my left hand shone with sapphire-bright light. I made each bone glow in succession like fireflies. This was a trick only the most advanced Necromancers could manage. "I'm a Grand Mistress Necromancer. All Sisters and Brothers are my concern."

Amelia's face turned slack with shock. "I've heard of you. You're the one Daddy Dearest wants to meet. Everyone says you're in hiding."

"I don't want to be found. There's a difference." I lowered my palm and stopped the spell. "I wish to free as many of my fellow mages as possible. Some of them are my friends. Others aren't. One is a child. Above all, I wish to save her. She's an innocent."

Amelia nodded slowly. "All right. I understand. You said Veronique was being kept on Royal lands. What kind of estate are you looking for?"

"Someplace large with a great dungeon. It would be a newer mansion, something built or rebuilt within the last five years. Any ideas?"

"Two estates come to mind."

Excitement sped through my bloodstream. "I need access to look around those places. I can't seem to get past the front door of any Royal. Can you assist me there?"

She looked me over from head to toe. "I might be able to help."

Clothilde stepped back up to the edge of the clearing. "Would you like luncheon, Your Ladyship?"

Once more, Amelia made shoo fingers at her servant. "I'm quite well, and the farm girl hasn't tried to kill me yet. We'll go to the cottage when we're ready to sup."

I didn't bother to hide my smile. Amelia had a lot of spirit. I was starting to like her.

Clothilde curtseyed. "As you command."

Once Clothilde was gone, I returned my attention to Amelia. "How exactly will you help me?"

"I can take you around the estates."

Disappointment weighed heavily into my bones. "That won't work. The Vicomte has seen what I look like."

"As in, how you look now?"

"In a way. I was dressed in Caster leathers when I went after the Tsar. The Vicomte was there."

Her eyes sparkled with interest. "That sounds like quite the tale."

"It's the main reason the Fantomes want me, but it's a story for another day. In any case, I don't think the Vicomte could forget me."

Amelia laughed, and the sound was as lively as a bubbling stream. "You don't know Daddy Dearest like I do. He doesn't notice women, and if he did, he'd only have seen you as a Caster and an outlaw. Wait until I get you ready for court. You won't recognize yourself. And Daddy Dearest will certainly never put two and two together. He's not interested in people, you see. Only machines." She twisted a lock of red hair about her finger. "I didn't catch your name."

"Elea." My stomach growled, and I realized I'd been standing outside for longer than I thought. "How about we discuss it over luncheon?"

"I'd like that. Tomorrow, I can show you my laboratory. All of us children have one."

"You can't show me now?"

"It's boarded up and covered in sheets. Clothilde and I will need all morning to open it up. Don't worry. You'll see it soon." Her eyes narrowed. "In the meantime, there are a few taverns in town. Stay at the Autumn Arms. No one will notice you there."

"Are you certain?"

"Positive. I'd love for you to stay with me, but that would cause gossip. Best for all of us if we keep this quiet."

I scanned her carefully. *"Best for all of us."* Amelia was risking so much for Veronique and me. "Are you certain about helping me? I'm a wanted criminal."

"Daddy Dearest merely wants to chat with you."

"Amelia." I shot her a grave look. "He wants me dead."

"Don't be silly. He wants everyone dead at some point. Besides, you're my friend now. We're off on a great adventure. Nothing more." She slipped her satin-clad arm into mine and tugged me toward the house.

With that, it seemed I had become friends with the Lady Amelia Masson. And I liked that feeling far more than I should have.

Mother Superior would not be pleased.

## 3

*M*y tavern room held little more than a small cot, a side table, and my traveling trunk. The walls were made of rough-hewn wood. A small mottled window peeped out over a view of thin and winding streets. I'd come here right after my visit with Amelia, and the place was as discreet as she'd promised. The innkeeper barely looked at me when I registered. No one asked my name. It was perfect.

Now I had safely moved into my room with daylight left to burn. That meant one thing.

*Time to prepare for my regular spell casting.*

I began by closing the shutters over my window. Sure, this tavern looked out over a set of isolated streets. Even so, I couldn't risk anyone seeing the light as I cast my magick. I finished with the window, opened my traveling trunk, pulled out a collection of rags, and set about plugging up every crevice I could find. After that, I double-checked my work.

*This is as safe as things will get.*

I was ready to cast my spell. Every day, I used magick to try and see Ada. It was a tricky affair because this particular spell reached out over time and space. If I wasn't careful, it would act as a warning bell to the Fantomes. Casting it was risky, but I'd become desperate. I needed to see where Ada was kept.

Trouble was, even though I cast this spell every day, I had yet to see anything useful. Sorrow weighed down on my shoulders. How much longer could I keep going? At some point, I had to admit it was hopeless, didn't I? Rowan's words came back to me.

*"Don't give up. If anyone can find Ada, it's you."*

I straightened my shoulders and reminded myself of my power as a Grand Mistress Necromancer. The more I cast a spell, the better I got at it. Maybe this time, I'd see something that could help.

Closing my eyes, I reached out to the energy and memories that lingered in this room. The air was thick with the history of those who'd been here before. Determination, weariness, passion... I pulled all that energy into my body and focused it into my left arm. The bones there glowed sapphire-bright with magick. After taking in a deep breath, I spoke the words for a seeing spell.

*In all spirit, there is power*
*In these shadows, I find light*
*Heed my spell, the whisper's hour*
*From the darkness, give me sight*

With a flick of my wrist, I released the energy from my hand. A blue mist appeared around the floor. *Beautiful.*

The haze turned thicker until I was surrounded by an azure-colored cloud. With a snap of my fingers, the mist cleared away. Now, I no longer stood in the small tavern room, but in a long stone hallway that was lined with stout, metal doors.

I was in Ada's dungeon. Again. My heart sank.

The visions from my spell always took me to the same place and time. Here was the dank underground prison cells where Ada and Veronique were first kept. Condensation dripped down the dark and slimy stones. The air was rife with the scent of urine and filth. Soft cries echoed down the hallway, tugging at my heart. The voice was that of a young girl.

My eyes pricked with tears. *Ada's weeping.*

I stepped up to one of the closed dungeon doors. The first time my magick had taken me to this moment, I'd frantically searched up and down the passage until I found her. After so many visits, I now knew exactly what door to check. I moved closer, my limbs heavy with dread. It took a force of will to peer through the metal bars covering the small window-hole. The cell was small, dark, and empty, save for two figures.

Ada sat inside, her tiny six-year-old frame wearing the same gray Novice robes she'd had on when I last saw her in the Midnight Cloister. She was curled into Veronique's lap, her head buried in the older girl's shoulder. The child's high-pitched sobs rang through the air. Each one was like a lash against my skin, reminding me how I'd failed my young friend.

My throat tightened with grief. Ada's pale face was streaked with dirt, and her brown eyes were red from weeping. Veronique's long blonde hair was held back with a leather tie, and her once-smooth face was lined with worry.

"Shh," Veronique whispered. "Elea will find us. You heard the guards. Someone sent the Tsar into exile. That had to be our Elea. She'll come for us next. Mark my words."

It didn't matter how many times I saw this exact moment, it always chipped away at my soul just a little bit more. Ada and Veronique were imprisoned somewhere, and they needed my help. This scene had taken place months ago, and I'd seen it dozens of times since then. And what had I done for them in all those weeks? Nothing.

A shiver rolled down my back. I knew enough about magick to know why I was trapped in seeing this scene. Ada and Veronique could already be dead. That was how my magick worked. The energies of the past lingered in the present. The truth was, I may have spent months searching for people who were nothing more than bones.

The blue mist grew heavy around me once more, as it always did when I reached this part of the vision. Once the haze disappeared again, I had returned to my tavern room.

Another failure. I hadn't seen anything new.

My thoughts went back to my conversation with Rowan. If things didn't work out with Amelia, perhaps I would visit my farm. Harvest time was approaching. My fields would soon become a single sheet of shifting barley. After that, the first colors of autumn would reach the forest leaves.

*Perhaps if I transport back for just a day...*

I shook my head. As long as there was a chance of helping Ada and the others, I had no business taking breaks. Tonight, I needed to rest while I could. Tomorrow, I'd head back to Lady Amelia's mansion. Anticipation skittered across my skin. I couldn't allow doubt to make me feel hopeless. Success was still possible.

I couldn't wait to see what lay hidden in that laboratory.

## 4

*A*melia began the next morning with a tour of her mansion. As we walked along, she cheerfully described the purpose of each chamber, such as the study, conservatory, and library. All the rooms looked the same to me. Each place was filled with huge furniture covered in dusty sheets. Growing up in a farmhouse, I never imagined having this much space, let alone not using every inch. I tried to stay silent about it, but after the tenth room, I couldn't keep quiet any longer.

"This place is enormous." My voice echoed in strange ways through the deserted chamber.

"We never come to these parts of the cottage."

On reflex, I pulled my ear. *I must not be hearing her correctly.* "You call this place a cottage?"

"Only because it irks Daddy Dearest." She disappeared behind what looked like a bureau covered in a tarp.

*Daddy Dearest. That's the Vicomte. Good to know that her hatred of him seems consistent.* "Who helps you maintain this place?"

"It's only Clothilde and me. She keeps up our two bedrooms and a small kitchen. I mind my garden. Daddy Dearest sends in groundkeepers for the rest. They never set foot inside the house. The rest of the place can go to hell, for all I care." She waved her hand before her, shooing some cobwebs from her path. "The door to my old laboratory is this way." She paused before a wall that was painted with the crest of a tall sword wreathed in roses. "Ah, here we are."

I nodded to the image. "Is that your family coat of arms?"

"My mother's, yes." She pulled out a ring of keys from her pocket and began fiddling with the lock on the door. "Mother died right after I was born. My brother and I were promptly shipped off to an orphanage." She glanced at me over her shoulder. "Our father was a Commoner and a swindler, you see. When Mother ran off with him, her family disowned her."

My heart went out to Amelia. I knew what it was like to not have any family. My parents had passed away when I was only a baby. My guardian, Rosie, died when I was fifteen. "I'm sorry to hear that. Are you in touch with other members of the Masson family?"

"Not a one. The Massons still won't acknowledge my brother or me. They loathe the Vicomte and he hates them right back. All this" —she waved around the mansion— "was a way for Daddy Dearest to tweak their noses. My Mother's family doesn't have any mansions that are nearly as fine."

"And your father?"

"Died a year after he dropped off Philippe and me at the orphanage. I began building little toys for the children there... tiny mechanical dolls and the like. Someone told the Vicomte and he adopted me." She shook her head. "The things I have built for that man. You won't believe it when I show you."

Clothilde appeared in a nearby doorway. She was always lurking about. "Excuse me, my Lady. Would you like to have luncheon now?"

"I just ate breakfast." Amelia swung around to face her servant. "Why would you ask me about food?"

Clothilde straightened her stance. She looked stiff as a rail. "You seemed to be sharing so much with this stranger, I thought you might have become lightheaded for want of a meal. Surely, you'd rather have an early luncheon than share your secrets."

My eyes widened. Something important was in the basement laboratory. I knew it. Perhaps it was the Vicomte's machine. *No wonder Clothilde worries for her mistress.* My gaze flipped between Amelia and Clothilde. Would my new friend still show me what I needed to see? Or would I have to rely on darker ways to get the information?

Amelia's doll-like face stayed perfectly cool for a long moment. After that, her big blue eyes narrowed. "Remember your place, Clothilde."

Clothilde's prim features crumpled with despair. "Show her your secrets, and you risk too much. Please."

My heart sped so fast I felt it beat against my ribs. What could be down there that would scare Clothilde so thoroughly?

Amelia lifted her chin. "You are free to leave my employ at any time." Her voice gentled. "I have to do this, Clo. Not only for Veronique. For me. I won't be his obedient child anymore. I can't keep hiding. It's time to do something to stop him. I hope you can understand."

Clothilde's shoulders slumped. "I'll have luncheon at noon."

I could have sung for joy. I was getting closer.

"Thank you, Clo." Amelia returned her attention to the door and began jangling the keys again. "One of these has to work, blast it all." The door clicked. "Ah, here we go."

I fought back a cheer. Now, I might finally see whatever secret Amelia was hiding. Excitement prickled across my skin. Perhaps it could be some kind of totem ring wrapped in machinery. That would certainly be the obvious choice. And where better to build one than here? "I can't wait."

"Follow me." Amelia stepped across the threshold to descend a darkened staircase. I stayed close behind. At the base of the steps, there stood a thick door made from what looked like an intricate mass of tiny, interlocking gears. I'd never seen anything like it. I brushed my fingertips across the uneven metal. The thing reminded me of the mechanical book Amelia held when I first met her. "Did you make this?"

"Yes." Amelia beamed. "We had too many fires erupting from our experiments. One conflagration might have made its way up into the house." She patted the door. "This keeps everything out."

"I should say so. It looks sturdier than a castle wall."

Amelia's eyes brightened under my praise. "It is. Let's see my workroom." She twirled a few of the gears in an odd rhythm.

Suddenly, the entire door came to life. All the many metal disks spun and clacked. With a great thunk, the door swung wide open.

I took a half step backward. "That was amazing. I never thought I'd see magick without magick, if you know what I mean."

Amelia beamed again. "Thank you. Everyone said that I was the greatest of the Vicomte's chil—" Her face fell. "Of the machinists he put to work."

*Poor Amelia.* How horrible to be called someone's child and then be asked to serve them like a slave. I wanted to offer her some kind of comfort. I couldn't think what to do though. In the Cloister, I'd been schooled to hide my emotion. Still, a bad attempt was better than none. "I know I said this before, but I'm sorry for what happened to you. Truly."

Amelia's face lightened a bit. I took it as a good sign that I'd done the right thing. "I appreciate your concern." Determination hardened her sweet face. "Come along now." She moved past the clockwork door and into the workroom itself.

My breathing quickened. Clothilde had warned Amelia not to show me something. Now I might discover what that *"something"* was.

I trailed Amelia into the laboratory. The moment I entered the massive chamber, my mouth fell open. The place wasn't so much a basement as an underground cathedral. Heavy stone pillars lined the walls, the columns bending into arches that jutted up into the shadows. Small iron desks lined the floor.

I stepped around the maze of tables. The surfaces were piled high with tiny gears, bits of metal shavings, and odd-looking tools. "You worked here alone?"

"No, there were hundreds of us here at the cottage. Machinists, every last one. I was their leader. We worked on a secret project for Daddy Dearest."

I brushed my fingers across a line of tiny knives with wooden handles. "What happened to everyone?"

"I was told they went to work in other laboratories." Amelia shook her head. "That's the official story. Truth is, the Vicomte sent them off to be drained." Her voice broke. "They're all dead."

A weight settled onto my shoulders. "He spared you because you're his heir."

"I'm certainly his only heir, but that's not why I was spared. The Vicomte adopted me from a Cloister orphanage. That was…" She tapped her chin. "Oh, a few years before the Tsar took over and gutted the holy houses."

My stomach tightened at the thought. So many Cloisters and Monasteries were ruins now. The Cloister where I'd trained, the Zelle, was one of the few that remained standing. It was certainly the only one that was still inhabited. The thought seeped all the excitement from my soul.

Amelia stepped closer. "Are you all right, Elea?"

"I'm fine." It was a tribute to my Necromancer training that I could sound so calm right now. Controlling emotions certainly came in handy sometimes. "Please, go on."

"The Mother Superior at my orphanage was a strong leader. She wouldn't let the Vicomte finish his adoption until she cast protection spells on us. Long story short, the Vicomte can't hurt my brother or me."

"You spoke of your brother before. Is he here? I didn't see him upstairs."

"Most likely, you won't see him today. He travels much of the time." A small smile rounded her lips. "Philippe is a freeloader and a rogue, I'm afraid. And I mean that in the best way."

I stepped around the tables, eyeing the piles of mechanical pieces. Much as it helped to know more about Amelia, I had other reasons for being here.

*My Sisters are still missing. Time is running out.*

"I'd like to be honest with you," I said.

Amelia tilted her pretty head, making her red curls sway. "Go on."

"Here's what I think happened. You were building something for the Vicomte, and it included a Necromancer totem ring. You wish to show me the plans, but Clothilde disagrees. Am I right?"

Amelia took off toward one of the tables. After a few steps, she paused and worried her lower lip with her teeth. "Clothilde doesn't think I should trust you." She swung around to face me again. "That Necromancer trick you did with your hand… The way you lit up your bones was impressive." She didn't sound impressed. "How can *that* really help Veronique?"

"What you saw was only a small show of power. I can do far more. It was *my* magick that sent the Tsar into exile."

Amelia sniffed. "Just exile? Why didn't you kill him?"

"Would you believe me if I said that I made a bargain with the Sire of Souls and the Lady of Creation themselves?"

Amelia folded her arms over her chest. "The god and goddess? No, I wouldn't believe that in the slightest."

I held back a sigh. The Sire of Souls and the Lady of Creation really did forbid me from hurting the Tsar. *Who can account for a deity's logic?* "Let's just say that sending the Tsar away was hard enough. That's why the Fantomes are after me. If I can exile the Tsar, then I must be powerful. That makes me a nice source of magick for the Vicomte's collection. Or even worse, it makes me a threat to him. I might be the only mage who could kill the man in cold blood."

Amelia's eyes lit up. "You would murder Daddy Dearest? Truly?"

"He abducted a friend of mine, a child. Now he's torturing her. If I had the chance, then yes, I'll kill the Vicomte in a heartbeat."

Amelia nodded with her mouth hanging open. "You're a little frightening, Elea."

"I worked for five long years to become a Grand Mistress. I'd better be frightening." I stepped up to a table and ran my fingers over the collection of tiny metal tools. I didn't know much about machines, but even I could tell these were parts of a small watch. All of which made sense. The Vicomte was known for carrying multiple watches with him wherever he went. "Tell me about what you built here."

There was a long moment where Amelia stared at the tabletop. My hands turned slick with sweat. *Please, let her tell me willingly.* I didn't want to force her with a spell.

At last, Amelia broke the silence. "I built the Vicomte a device. I call it a vortex watch."

*Vortex.* "It pulls in power to one place."

Amelia nodded. "That's what I had everyone working on." She gestured across the room. "Some groups were dedicated to metallurgy, others to the conductive properties of coils. I focused on the gear that held a small totem ring."

Her words seemed to hover in the air. *Totem ring.* I knew it. "And who made this totem ring?"

"None other than the Tsar himself. The Vicomte's agents stole quite a few of the Tsar's totem rings over the years. It was all very hush-hush."

"Because the Vicomte had you secretly building this vortex watch." I rubbed my neck and thought through this new information. "What did the Vicomte say the vortex watch was for?"

"To drain the Tsar and send him off to prison. Officially, the Vicomte was the Tsar's greatest supporter. In secret, he loathed the man." Amelia gestured around the room. "All my people were excited to help in the project, myself included. We knew that the Tsar had agents rounding up those with some Necromancer ability and throwing them into dungeons." Her mouth set into a determined line. "People just like us. We wanted the Tsar out of power."

I rarely thought about the fear of living under the Tsar if you were an untrained Necromancer. It must have been terrifying, wondering if you could be abducted at any moment and unable to defend yourself. "So, you thought you were helping to overthrow a tyrant."

"Precisely. It wasn't until the Tsar went into exile that I learned the truth. The Tsar hadn't just thrown Necromancers into dungeons. He drained power from his prisoners. Tortured them." She shivered. "I should have known."

"You can't blame yourself."

Amelia scanned the room, her eyes glistening. "Everyone here looked to me for leadership. I thought we were overthrowing a tyrant. But the moment my vortex watch was finished, Daddy Dearest sent everyone away except for Clothilde and me." Her eyes flashed with hatred. "That's when I figured out the truth. Daddy Dearest never intended to overthrow the Tsar. He wanted to *become* him. He plans to use the vortex watch, soak in the power of a thousand Necromancers, and become the only ruler of the continent."

I thought back to Rowan's claim that the Vicomte was trying to kill Genesis Rex. *His plans could very well reach beyond our continent.*

Amelia thumped her chest with her fist. "The vortex watch was my work. My creation. It was meant to be something good, and Daddy Dearest twisted it into evil." Her blue eyes narrowed into angry slits. "So I created a second device."

Her words bounced through my consciousness. It seemed too good to be true. *She made another watch?* When I spoke again, it was an effort to get out every word. "Tell me what you built."

"Daddy Dearest had stolen a number of totem rings from the Tsar. When all my machinists left, there were still some bands left in the laboratory. Most were rubbish, yet one totem ring had possibilities. I tried everything I could to build another vortex watch from it. Nothing worked. The totem ring inside the first vortex watch contained unique spells. The Tsar never cast anything like it again."

I slumped against a desk. "So, you couldn't build another vortex watch. What did you create?"

"There was one totem ring with useful qualities. It was perfect for spying on what was happening with the vortex watch. So I built that into a device. I call it my witness watch."

The words echoed through my mind. *Witness watch.* My body felt numb. "Can it show us the location of the vortex watch? Because wherever that thing is, we'll be sure to find Ada, Veronique, and the others."

Amelia shook her head. "It's not that kind of witness. While the vortex watch stores Necromancer magick, the witness watch tracks how much power has been gathered."

"That could still be useful." *I think.*

"The witness watch also shows you exactly how much more power is needed before the totem ring in the vortex watch is fully charged."

I twisted my hands together at my waist. "I don't want to know the answer to this question. Still, I have to ask. Once the vortex watch is fully loaded, can it transfer that power to whoever wears it, regardless of whether or not they're a mage?"

Amelia stared at the floor. "Well, before it's fully charged, the vortex watch can only drain out power. But once it's full and ready? The vortex watch can transfer magick to anyone, mage or not."

The walls seemed to press in around me. "I was afraid of that." I scrubbed my hand over my face. *A vortex watch and a witness watch.* "Do you still have copies of the plans for either device?"

Amelia sashayed over to one of the tables, her dress rustling with every step. "I can do better than that. I have the witness watch right here." She pulled open a drawer, took out a small watch, and held it up on her palm. "This was my own secret project. Daddy Dearest doesn't even know the thing exists."

The world took on a dreamlike sheen. I stood here, in a laboratory, and about to touch my first clue about my Sisters. It didn't seem real. I walked up to Amelia. With shaking fingers, I pulled the device from her hand. It was a small disk on a leather wristband. "How it different is this from the vortex watch?"

"They look identical from the outside."

I brought the witness watch closer. On the device's face, there stood spindly hands to mark the minutes and hours. The image of a tiny moon peeped through a hole on the surface. "Is this supposed to tell the time?"

"Only as a decoy." Amelia plucked the device from my palm. "The watch doesn't show the true time, only how much Necromancer power has been pulled into the ring. When then hour reaches midnight, then the totem ring inside the vortex watch is fully charged."

My stomach sank. "This reads nine p.m. Only three hours to go until the Vicomte has enough power. What does that mean in terms of our schedule? How much time do we have left?"

"At this point, there isn't a lot of time remaining. By my calculations, every hour on the watch marks a day for us."

I paced a line on the floor and tried to organize my thoughts. "It's nine o'clock now. That give us three hours—I mean three days—until the vortex watch reaches midnight."

*Just three days. Amelia's right. That's not a lot of time.*

How I hated to ask this next question. "What happens when the vortex watch is fully charged? How exactly will the Vicomte get the power?"

Amelia turned several small gears on the side of the watch. Sharp metal prongs sprang out from the back of the device. "These go into your flesh and dig right into the bone. That transfers the magick."

I tilted my head. "But if that's a witness watch, why does it have transfer prongs?"

"It's a legacy from when I was trying to make that into a vortex watch. The prongs don't actually work." Amelia slowly handed the device back to me. "After I built the witness watch, I was so excited." Her voice didn't sound excited in the least. "I tried to find people who'd help me use it to defeat Daddy Dearest."

"I take it that didn't work."

"Clothilde's right that I'm not the best judge of character. One group of my so-called allies merely stole my silver and ran. At least they stole the goods before I revealed anything incriminating. Others tried sending me off to a madhouse. In the end, I'm afraid that I simply locked up the laboratory and went to my room."

*And she's been hiding out in this mansion ever since.*

A tear rolled down Amelia's cheek. I rested my hand gently on her shoulder. Touching was frowned upon among Necromancers. Still, Amelia looked so distraught, I had to make an exception. I locked my gaze with hers. "I'll find that vortex watch and wherever that device may be, I'm sure we'll find Ada and Veronique." I forced my voice to take on an encouraging tone. "You said there were two estates where our friends might be kept?"

Amelia stared at her hands for what felt like an hour. Finally, she spoke once more. "The first place we'll want to check belongs to the Havilland family." She looked at me and winced. "They won't let you through the door. I spent years in manners training. You're no lady. They'll send their Fantomes after you in a heartbeat."

"Perhaps I can sneak in as a servant."

"You don't act like one of them, either. It's no matter. I'll go by myself and look around." She gave me a small smile. "I can be quite sneaky when called for."

"Absolutely not. You won't go alone."

"Then I'll bring my brother."

"No, I'll accompany you. We'll simply have to come up with some story of how I'm a shoestring relation. A half sibling on your father's side, perhaps?"

Amelia began nibbling her thumbnail. "That might work."

"Of course, it will work. Plus, I'm a fast learner." I gave her shoulder a little squeeze. "If you want to rescue Veronique, this is how it will happen. We need to work together." The moment the words left my mouth, I knew they were true.

"I'll try to train you." Amelia winced. "But I can't make any guarantees."

"Not to worry." I straightened my shoulders. I could fake being Royal. After all, I learned how to be a Necromancer. How hard could it be?

"You'll need new clothes too."

"What's wrong with these?" I brushed my hands over my silver dress. "I was told this was the height of fashion."

"That's a traveling gown. You can't wear that to meet anyone. And that's just to begin with." She started counting off on her fingertips. "You'll need luncheon shifts, dinner dresses, and at least one ball gown."

I worked hard not to whine. "Those will take weeks to make."

"Not with my seamstress. Besides, we'll need time to train you up… *If* we can train you up, that is." She stepped around me, looking me over with an expert eye. "A day or two might be enough. *Might.* You'll still have to pass the Philippe test, just to be certain."

"Your brother?"

"Oh, yes." She chuckled, and I liked seeing the light in her eyes again. "He's somewhat of an expert on how women act in Royal society."

Just hearing the words *"Royal society"* made bile rise up my throat. There was no avoiding it, however. "Where do we begin?"

"First things first. Let's work on your posture."

Amelia might as well have offered to dip me in acid—the idea of posture training seemed that awful. But so little time remained to save Ada, Veronique, and my other Sisters. I would do whatever was necessary. "Why wait? There's no time like the present."

After all, only three days remained before my Sisters were good as dead and the Vicomte became a powerful Necromancer. There was no question about it. I simply had to appear Royal.

## 5

*J* sat at the edge of a board-stiff chair in a scratchy gown and tried to look pleasant. It wasn't easy. Amelia had dusted off some corner of the mansion for us to practice having a formal luncheon. The room was musty and dark. High above me, the arched ceiling stayed hidden in shadows. A single small window was propped open nearby. Flurries of dust motes shifted through the light.

I'd been working at it less than a day, and already I hated courtly life.

Amelia was seated across from me, her hands neatly folded in her lap. She had to be just as uncomfortable as I felt, and yet, you wouldn't know it by her sweet smile. We'd been practicing social manners all morning. Even so, it seemed like we'd been at it for months. Unfortunately, I wasn't improving.

*And only two days remain to save Ada.*

"How was your evening?" asked Amelia. She picked up a cup of mulled wine from the table between us.

"Noisy." I was proud of how I kept on my perky smile through this statement. When I learned Necromancy, we were trained to hide all emotions and speak in a monotone. According to Amelia, ladies were expected to practically jump for joy over a teaspoon. It was odd, but I was trying to get used to it.

Amelia shot me a blank look. It was the courtly face she showed when she was displeased. "What a very short answer. Why don't you tell me *why* the tavern was so loud?"

I fought the urge to wince. One-word answers were rude; I'd forgotten that rule. "There was screaming."

Amelia shook her head, and I wanted to punch something. *I'd gotten it wrong again.* I cleared my throat. "Did I say *screaming*? No, there wasn't exactly that."

Amelia brightened. "I see. What was happening then?"

"The innkeeper was preparing dinner." *There, that was a nicer way of putting it.* I felt rather proud of myself. This small talk wasn't so hard.

"I don't understand. How was that loud?"

"He was, uh, culling the meat." *Now, that had to be obvious.*

"I still don't follow."

She couldn't be this thick. Everyone knew why things got noisy at a culling. "Why the pigs, of course. They make an awful racket when you—" I shrugged.

Amelia set down her goblet on the tabletop with a thunk. Her blue eyes flashed. "Elea, that's the worst small talk I've ever heard. This is supposed to be a light and pleasant conversation, remember?"

It took everything I had not to growl. There was learning how to chitchat, and then there was wasting time while lives were at risk. Even the Royals couldn't be this shallow. "Please. Food is one of the most pleasant topics around. Surely, the Royals know how meat ends up on their tables? It can't come as a shock."

Amelia pinched the bridge of her nose. "Elea, there are things we don't say in polite society. Discussing how pigs squawk while their throats are cut is one of them."

I froze. *Gods-damn it. She got me again.* That comment was as good as wearing a sign that said, *farm girl here.*

"Let's keep going." Amelia's smile got larger, which I thought wasn't possible. "Did anything else happen last night?"

"I tried to reach out to a friend of mine who's a— Blast it! I was going to say *mage*."

"Keep going. You're doing better. Discussing a friend is good. We'll work on ridding the mage references later."

I inhaled a calming breath. *That was a better attempt at chitchat; I must focus on that.* Talking about Rowan also made me feel better, so I kept on going. "I'd called for my friend's silly bird about a dozen times. There was never any reply. Not so much as a tweet by the window. It was worrying, to say the least."

"Now, that won't do."

"I know. My friend must learn about this watch you gave me." I patted my pocket, which was where I kept the witness watch at all times. "Plus, I've been casting seeing spells for months. My visions of Ada or Veronique haven't changed a bit. They could very well be—" I stopped myself before saying *"dead,"* as I was certain that would cross some kind of societal rule. Not to mention the fact that it might upset Amelia. "They could be out of range of my magick." It was unlikely, but possible.

Amelia sighed. "When I said *"that won't do,"* I wasn't talking about contacting mages."

I leaned back in the chair. "Then what did you mean?"

"You." Amelia shook her head. "You told me the truth."

"So?"

"People never tell the truth at luncheon. We're here to play a part. Don't you remember?"

"No, you asked me a question and I answered it. If I were talking to the Havilland family, I wouldn't have said anything about magick."

"That's not what I meant. We're here to pretend that our lives are near perfection. The Havilland family needs to see us as people worthy of their time. We want to impress them enough that they take us on a tour of their property."

"Where the gallery is." Their portrait gallery was one of the few large places that had been recently built. Lots of odd stories surrounded the construction. It was precisely the kind of place that could have been created to drain magick.

"Yes, few people get invited to see that gallery. If we look like ho-hum blabbermouths, we won't get asked to go."

I rubbed my temples with my fingertips. No matter how many times Amelia explained the rules of society to me, I couldn't stick to them. It all seemed like so much random nonsense. "So we're to pretend that everything in our lives is flawless?"

"No, I said *"near perfection."* It's good to share that something is wrong. However, it must be some minor point that's only meant to give the illusion of honesty and intimacy." She glanced around the room, as if the answer would be written on the tapestries. "Such as having too many suitors. You can share that kind of issue because it's not really a problem, you see?"

I sighed. How much did I wish I could cast some spells and just break into the gallery? Quite a lot. But the Havilland family's Fantomes would swarm me in a heartbeat. "Right. Their property, their rules. I must impress them with my wit and beauty." I held in a groan. "You realize this is ludicrous, don't you?"

Amelia grinned yet again. "Welcome to courtly life. Why do you think I enjoy hiding out in this mansion? Once you step onto the game board, you can never stop playing. Not to a friend or a lover. Not even to your own family. No matter what, perception is reality. That's what I taught Veronique, and it's what I'll teach you."

I eyed her carefully for a long moment. Veronique was selfish and shrewd while Amelia was open and bubbling with energy. "I don't understand how you two became friends."

Amelia picked up her wine goblet once more. "Veronique has a good heart under that selfish veneer. We helped each other when we were both ready to give up. Do you know what that means when two people go through fire together?"

I thought about fighting the Tsar with Rowan. "I understand." I leaned back in my chair and took stock of the situation. Amelia was trying so hard to help me, and I wasn't the most appreciative guest. "I've never said thank you for all your aid. It really is kind of you to put yourself at risk for me."

"Kindness has nothing to do with it. I had only one honest friend in the entire world, and that was Veronique. The Vicomte took her from me simply because he could. Not to mention his other crimes." A steely look shone in Amelia's eyes. "I'll do anything to bring that bastard down."

My brows lifted. This harder side of Amelia was something to see. "Well, then. I'm glad you're not my enemy."

"We all cast magick in our own ways, Elea."

"So we do."

Footsteps sounded from behind us. Amelia's face lit up. "Philippe!"

Amelia's brother was exactly as she'd described him: tall and dashing with golden hair, intelligent blue eyes, and a white-toothed smile. I couldn't help but like him instantly, and that was an impressive feat, considering all the stories I'd heard. Amelia seemed to think I'd quickly fall for his courtly charms, so she'd told me what a womanizer and all-around rogue he was.

Philippe kissed his sister lightly on each cheek. I noticed how he wore a black velvet longcoat decorated with bright silver buttons. Plus, his leather shoes were so shiny I might see my face in them. He was a courtly animal indeed.

As Philippe strode closer, it felt like the very air around him vibrated with his presence. There were some people who exude energy and life. Philippe was one of them. Trouble was, he knew it. After pausing at my side, he bowed slightly at the waist. "You must be the lovely Elea. Amelia's told me all about you."

I rose and gave him a quick curtsey, just like Amelia had taught me. "And she's warned me about you."

"Has she?" Philippe rubbed his chin. The motion highlighted how he had the classic bone structure of an aristocrat—all high cheekbones and sharp jawline. "You're quite charming, Elea. You know that?"

"In more ways than one." I knew quite a few killing charms, but I decided not to volunteer that fact.

"Well done, sister." Philippe slipped into the seat beside me and drummed his long fingers on the shiny wooden table. "This new friend of yours is very clever."

Amelia folded her arms over her chest. "Well, what do you think?" The question came out like I wasn't even in the room. "Does she look like a lady?"

I sat up straighter in my chair. Clearly, this was a test to see if I was ready for a visit to the Havilland family. I forced on my most vacuous smile. "Do I?"

Philippe eyed me carefully. "You dress the part, but acting it? You're not a lady in the least, I'm afraid."

*I bit back a growl. This was beyond frustrating.*

Amelia smiled brightly. "Why don't we take a break?"

Philippe pulled up a chair next to our little table. "Don't mind if I do."

A flapping sounded from the rafters of the building. Philippe groaned. "I told you to get more servants. Another bird has gotten in."

Amelia didn't even look up from her cup of wine. "They fly around all the time. I don't mind it so much. Gives the house a sense of life."

Philippe's eyes narrowed. "I should bring my bow and quiver in here. Get some practice."

"You're a barbarian, Brother."

The bird swooped down from the eaves and out the open window. It was red with green eyes. My body froze.

*That's Tamu. Rowan's bird.*

The animal perched on a fir tree just outside the window. It stared at me, fluffed its wings, and chirped. There was no question. It wanted me to follow it.

"Excuse me," I said. "I'd like to spend the rest of my break by taking a short walk."

Amelia frowned. "Come back soon?"

I rose. "You can count on it." Turning on my heel, I marched off to follow the bird, wherever it might lead me.

## 6

*I* strode through the forest behind Amelia's mansion. Rowan's bird flitted from branch to branch, guiding me along a thin path through the fir trees. My heart thumped harder at the thought of seeing Rowan again. There was only one problem, though.

Philippe was following me.

Clearly, Philippe was a master at courtly conversation. But creeping silently through the forest? Not exactly one of his skills. As I walked along, I thought of ways to get him to abandon me.

The only good thing? I didn't need to follow courtly rules while I did it.

The bird led me deeper into the trees. Soon, even the breeze couldn't break through the thick canopy of leaves. *This is far enough away from the mansion to afford some privacy.* Pausing, I turned around. "Hello, Philippe." The steady trudge of his footsteps ceased. "There's no need to hide. I wouldn't mind some company."

Philippe stepped out from the shadows. "I should hope so. A lovely lady like you, all alone in the forest? Anything could happen." He winked. "Out here, dark creatures prey on helpless maidens such as you."

My brows lifted. I was many things. Helpless wasn't one of them. *Time to end this.*

Raising my left arm, I pulled Necromancer power into my body. The bones in my left hand instantly glowed blue. I sent a plume of sapphire smoke rolling across the forest floor. As spells went, this was a minor use of magick and nothing that would alert a Fantome. That said, it should be more than sufficient to inspire Philippe to depart. For extra effect, I made the smoke billow around us in waves.

All the while, Philippe stood with his mouth hanging open. It was a most satisfying reaction.

I snapped my fingers, and the mist disappeared. "Listen to me carefully. The dark creatures fear me, not the other way around. I'm a Grand Mistress Necromancer."

*That ought to do it.*

For a long time, Philippe said nothing. Seconds passed until a sense of worry curled inside my stomach. What had I done? I needed Amelia's help. Scaring the wits out of her brother was foolhardy. When I spoke again, I took care to keep my tone gentle. "Philippe?"

"You're a Grand Mistress Necromancer." He stood frozen for another moment. After that, he started to laugh. The sound was gentle and rolling. "That's brilliant."

"Really?" Most Royals feared Necromancers. "Thank you."

Philippe inspected me from head to toe. His gaze was so careful it was as if he were committing every detail to memory. "I'm afraid I misjudged you, Grand Mistress Elea." His tone became reverent. "My apologies."

My cheeks reddened. "Don't worry. Few suspect I'm a Necromancer since I'm not a Fantome."

"Let me try to make it up to you." Philippe sauntered up to my side. "I promise to inspire smiles on your trek through the forest. Would that be sufficient penance for my misdeed?" He kept right on speaking without giving me a chance to answer. "Have I ever told you about the time I saw the Vicomte fall in love? It was terribly silly."

"Your offer is kind." I watched Rowan's bird hop from tree to tree. "I'd like to be alone for a while, though."

Philippe lifted his once-shiny boot, showing how it was now covered in dirt and gunk. "But I've ruined a perfectly good pair of boots while trying to protect you. The least you can do is allow me to keep you company." He gave me a roguish grin. "Besides, the tale is a gossip's dream, if I may say so."

I narrowed my eyes. *Maybe I can turn this to my advantage.* "If you insist on coming along…"

"I do."

"Then I have my price."

His blue eyes glittered. "Name it."

"You must answer a question for me." I plastered on a grin. "It's clear that you think I'm not ready for court life. What's wrong, exactly? And don't fill my head with a pack of pleasant nonsense. I need your honesty."

Philippe frowned playfully. "Ah-ah-ah. You're asking me to insult a lady."

I rolled my eyes. "Come now. We both know I'm no lady." The bird flittered to another tree, and I started to follow it again. Philippe kept pace beside me.

"You've been following that creature for a while now. Is the bird enchanted?"

I arched my brows. "I don't recall *my* answering *your* questions as being part of this bargain."

Phillips chuckled. "All right, then. Here's where you fail. You're trying too hard, my dear."

I stopped. "Whatever does that mean?"

"When you force a smile, you drop your mask. I can see every hidden thought in your pretty amber eyes, and it's clear how much you loathe the courtly game. That's essentially admitting a weakness, and no one wants to be allied with the weak."

I slung my hair over my shoulder and began to absently braid it. This was a nervous habit that Mother Superior had discouraged in the Zelle Cloister, but Amelia told me it was appropriate for women to constantly preen. I was glad to have the ritual back. "Amelia encouraged me to smile."

"Because that works for her. I wouldn't suggest it for you, though. You're better off playing the cold beauty."

Ever since Amelia had begun her so-called lady lessons, I'd been carrying a burden of worry on my shoulders. For the first time in ages, that weight lessened a little. Cold beauty? That was essentially the emotionless way of acting that I'd been taught at the Cloister, only combined with a pretty gown. I could do that. "Thank you. That's most helpful." Philippe only stared at me in reply. I stepped closer and waved my hand in front of his face. "Hello?"

Again, no reaction.

My skin prickled into gooseflesh. The air had become heavy with magick. I reached out with my mage senses. Wild energy careened around me. I bit back a smile. I'd felt this power before.

Rowan was nearby.

Philippe remained perfectly frozen. The barest hint of red mist floated around him. No question about it. A stasis spell had been cast on Philippe.

I turned about, my pulse speeding faster than ever. "Rowan?"

A few seconds ticked by. Nothing happened. I was starting to wonder if I'd imagined it all. All of a sudden, Rowan stepped out from the shadows. He was still wearing his odd outfit—hunting leathers and a long cloak—but there was no mistaking the man's rugged face and intense green eyes. "Elea."

"How long have you been following us?"

"Since you left the mansion." He leaned against a tree and kicked his left ankle over his right. "This admirer of yours is a persistent fellow."

*Admirer.* Why did Rowan think that? For some reason, I wanted to make sure he knew that Philippe wasn't my sweetheart. Not that I cared what Rowan thought. This was merely for accuracy's sake, nothing more. "Philippe is no admirer. His sister Amelia is helping me. Philippe wants to aid in the effort. That's all."

"Glad to hear it." Rowan gave me the barest grin. Still, I felt the heat of it right through my stomach.

It took an effort to look away, but I needed to. If I wasn't careful, I'd be standing in the forest, ogling Rowan like a love-struck fool when I should be saving my friends.

*Only two days remained.*

I straightened my spine and refocused. "I have important news. There are two Royal estates that could be hiding Ada and my other Sisters. Philippe and Amelia are helping me inspect them."

Rowan stepped closer. He smelled of leather and musk. It made my insides squirm. "Excellent work."

My heart warmed under his praise. "There's more. Amelia Masson is *the* Lady Amelia. She's confirmed that the Vicomte is indeed charging a totem ring with Necromancer power." I pulled the witness watch from my pocket. "The ring itself is housed in a watch exactly like this one."

Rowan stared intently at the device. "That watch you're holding... Can it gather Necromancer energy too?"

"No, only the vortex watch can do that, and sadly, the Vicomte has that device." I tapped the machine in my palm. "This is a witness watch. Amelia built it to track what's happening with the vortex one." I quickly pointed to the different parts of the watch face. "See? This shows how much time is left until the ring is fully charged." I was proud of how I was able to keep my voice steady while I spoke.

"And how long until that comes to pass?"

"Two days." I fought hard to keep my features level. "That's poor news for me and my friends."

"It's bad for both of us."

"Why? You still don't know what the Vicomte plans to do. Once he has Necromancer power, he may not wish to destroy the Casters."

Rowan's gravelly voice became even deeper. "The Vicomte is already trying to hurt the Imperial family. We've gotten word that he's launching an assassination attempt against Genesis Rex."

"Your uncle?" My eyes widened. *This was news.* "How do you know?"

"The source we found in the Vicomte's court gave us irrefutable proof."

"Is Rex safe?"

"We're taking diplomatic steps. The King will be fine."

"But Rowan—"

"There's more, Elea. Things are worse than you know."

*That doesn't seem possible.* "How?"

"That's why I came to see you. I must show you something. Follow me."

I gestured to Philippe. "But what about him?"

"Oh, he's safe enough. My stasis spell will last for a few hours yet. And my people are close by, in case anything happens."

I squinted into the shadows. If Rowan's guards were lurking in the trees, I couldn't see them. "Is it anyone I know?" For a time, I'd stayed with the Casters in the Endlos desert. Until this moment, I hadn't realized how much I missed their bright spirits and quick laughter.

"No, sadly enough." Rowan moved off deeper into the shadows. I was about to call him back when his bird began diving before me while twittering excitedly.

"All right, I'm coming." I followed the bird through the forest until the roaring sound of water broke up the heavy silence. I hiked into a small clearing. Here a waterfall cascaded into a dark pool. Rowan stood by the water's edge.

"Amelia didn't mention anything like this on her land." Then again, she never left the house in anything but a ball gown, so I wouldn't have expected her to meander through the woods.

Rowan unclasped the cloak from his shoulders and tossed it onto a nearby rock. His loose hunter's tunic followed next. Now he was bare chested. I tried not to stare at how his muscles shifted as he moved. Not sure I succeeded.

"Elea? Is something wrong?"

I cleared my throat. *Traitorous mind.* It was always bringing me back to unwanted thoughts about Rowan. This was the definition of what Necromancers called zuchtlos. It was our word for impulsive behavior. It was also one of the greatest weaknesses a Necromancer could have. "No, I'm fine."

"What I discovered isn't easy to explain. Like I said, I must show you." Rowan flexed his hand. Creation Casters focused magick into their right arm, making the veins there glow red. Like so many things with Casters, it was the opposite of Necromancy. Our bones shone blue when we used our powers.

"Are you going to cast a spell?" I asked.

"Not here. There are too many wards on this waterfall."

"There are?" I stepped closer to the water's edge. Instantly, a wall of magick slammed into me. I knew this kind of spell. *A protective ward.* I tried pulling Necromancer power into my body. I couldn't summon so much as a drop. A chill of recognition crept up my neck. The solid strength behind this power was unique. I'd only felt it once before.

When I battled the Tsar.

*But what's the Tsar doing in the forest behind Amelia's mansion?*

Rowan gestured to the waterfall. "There's a small chamber on the other side of that wall. We need to swim into the pool to access it. Once we get there, you'll understand everything." He began loosening the ties on his leather pants.

I took a half step backward. "What are you doing?" I'd seen Rowan naked to the waist before. At the time, I'd been injured and Rowan was healing me. But that was a special circumstance. Plus, I'd been semiconscious and half dead. Now I was very much awake and alive.

"I'm getting ready to swim." Rowan frowned. "You can swim, right?"

It took all my Necromancer training to speak in a calm voice. "Not exactly."

Rowan finished loosening the ties at his waistline. A trail of dark hair ran down from his stomach. *By the Sire.* Another spike of heat ran through me. Suddenly, the tree bark in this part of the forest became utterly fascinating.

"Are you coming?" asked Rowan.

"You can go for a swim. I'll wait here."

"I need to show you firsthand what's in that cave. It's important."

"Well…" I risked another glance in his direction. A deep V of muscle arrowed down Rowan's lower belly. Who knew that kind of muscle was even a part of the male body? I liked it, and I hated that I liked it, all at the same time.

*Stay calm, Elea. Focus on your mission.*

I inhaled a firm breath. "I'll swim by myself. I can cast a spell to do it."

"No magick. The wards, remember?"

I twisted my fingers at my waistline. "But the wards here feel very old. I might be able to cast past them." I could feel the difference between old and new spells. The magick n this place must have been created years ago. It had a distinctive wobble to it.

"The wards here may be old, but they're still quite strong. You won't be able to break them without attracting attention."

*He's right. And at this moment, I really loathe that about him.*

I stared down at the water. It seemed everything black and foreboding. Was it my imagination, or did the current make a kind of whirlpool of death? I closed my eyes and forced myself to picture Ada's sweet face. That did it. I cleared my throat, inspected the water, and nodded sagely. "I can swim. It's just a shallow pool, right?"

Rowan stepped up to stand before me. His body radiated warmth, and I wanted nothing more than to lean into him. "Elea, that's a deep whirlpool. If you can't swim, you'll need my help." He raised his hands. A length of green rope now looped across his palms. "This will do it."

I fought hard to keep my voice level. "You want me *tied* to you?"

"Once you take off that gown, yes."

I folded my arms over my chest. "That plan makes no sense."

"My homeland is laced through with fierce waters. Not everyone can swim." He shook the rope in his hand. "We train for this from the time we're children. As long as you stay calm, we'll be fine." He tilted his head. "You're strong, Elea. You can do this."

His confidence made it impossible to back down. "Agreed. But the gown stays on."

"Really. That dress has how many layers?"

I could see his line of thinking, yet I didn't want it to give in. "Five."

"Once those get wet, they will weigh you down like a bag of stones. You'll sink straight to the bottom of the pool." He gentled his voice. "I know how Necromancers are about touch. I realize this is hard for you. Believe me, if I saw any other way to do this, I would. Trust me. You need to see what's beyond that wall. This is about far more than the Tsar setting magick wards."

*Meaning it's about my Sisters.*

Any concerns about bare skin and swimming disappeared. I turned around and offered Rowan my back. "Pull open these ties for me, will you?"

"Thank you, Elea." Rowan began loosening the ribbons that wove down my back. Every brush of his fingers sent waves of awareness through me. Soon the dress was loose enough.

I shimmied out of what ended up being a rather large pile of fabric. "Ready."

Rowan didn't say anything. He looked almost as frozen as Philippe had back in the forest. I was starting to wonder if he'd been placed under a spell too, when I noticed his heated gaze was moving up and down my body. I should feel embarrassed, yet I didn't. All those years of being taught that touch was a Necromancer's enemy seemed to vanish. I moved closer to Rowan. "I said, we should get ready."

Rowan nodded slowly, the heat still strong in his eyes. He wore only short cotton under-trousers. Ropes of muscle outlined his upper thighs. For my part, I had nothing on except for my pantalets and a thin cotton shirt. Suddenly, it became hard to breathe.

Bit by bit, Rowan looped the rope across my back, his fingers brushing over my bare skin. It made me shiver, and not from the cold. Rowan finished by knotting the cord around my chest. "Does that feel secure?"

"Yes." My voice came out low and husky. "How do we—" I gestured between us.

"We get into the water, and then I'll tie you against my back."

"Understood." The air between us became charged with its own kind of energy. Still, I needed to focus on stopping the Tsar and finding my people, not on whatever strange thing was happening between Rowan and me. I took the rest of the rope in my hand and stepped off into the water. A shock of cold liquid hit me. I gasped.

Rowan glided into the pool and stopped before me. With a few swift movements, he strapped me on. The cold water helped freeze out the sensation of my partly bare chest against his back. Not enough, though.

"Wrap your arms and legs around me." His voice was command-ing, and I liked that too. *Gods-damn it.*

I did as he asked. My calves rubbed against the firm planes of muscle on his stomach. I looped my arms tightly around his neck and fought the urge to nuzzle him. "How's this?"

"Good." If my closeness affected him, Rowan didn't show it anymore. "Three deep breaths and we go under, all right?"

My skin broke out in goose bumps. How exactly did I end up tied to a man I hardly knew and about to dive into a heavy current?

*Because of the Tsar, that's how.*

I tightened my hold. If I was going to die, it wouldn't be by drowning on Rowan's back. "I'm ready."

"One... Two... Three."

Together, Rowan and I plunged under the water. The current seemed to yank us in a dozen directions at once. Coils of rope dug into my skin. We began spiraling downward, caught in the pull of the whirlpool. Somehow, Rowan broke free from the current and swam into a side passageway carved into the rock. The rough walls scratched my skin and pulled at my hair. I couldn't have cared less. We were free.

The pressure in my ears lessened as we headed toward the surface again. Every inch of my body ached to breathe. I bit my lips together, forcing them to stay shut.

*Not much longer now.*

Finally, we broke through the surface of the water. I greedily sucked in breath after breath as Rowan untied me and set me onto the stony ground. Within a few seconds, he found a candle and flint and lit them up. The illumination seemed impossibly bright after such total darkness.

I found myself in a small cave with three archways that led off into the shadows. My home Cloister was built on caves, so I knew a bit about the first two passages. They were uneven and naturally made. The third one was something else entirely. I shucked off Rowan's ropes and walked up to the perfect arch. It was carved with runes of power and lined with gemstones.

*A gateway.*

I knew about these. Necromancers built them to connect allied Cloisters or Monasteries. They were hard to build, exhausting to maintain, and required a lot of magick to make them work. Still, few Necromancers developed enough skill for a transport spell. For those mages, this was the only alternative.

"We had a gateway in my old Cloister. Nothing as large as this

one. Where does it go?" Usually, a gateway had at least three desti-
nations.

"I was hoping you might know that." Rowan gestured across the
runes written into the stones. "That's Necromancer writing."

Moving closer, I carefully scanned the runes. "This says it's a
gateway to the Eternal Lands. It goes to the court of the Sire of Souls
or to the garden of the Lady of Creation."

"Do you think it's real?"

"If you'd asked me a year ago, I would have told you the Sire of
Souls and the Lady of Creation were nothing more than children's
stories." Since then, I'd met both of those deities in real life. In fact,
they were the ones who helped me defeat the Tsar and send him into
exile. "I've no doubt this gateway is precisely what it claims to be."

"And what can you tell me of these?" Rowan knelt before the
archway. His candlelight flickered over a pile of insect carcasses.

I crouched beside him for a better look. "These are bone crawlers.
It's one of the spells that only the Tsar can cast." The Tsar was unique
in that he could combine Creation Caster and Necromancer magick
at will. His hybrid magick gave bone crawlers like these their insect
side. His Necromancer power created their flexible bone shells.

Rowan frowned. "But why would he create bone crawlers here?"

"I don't think he created them here; I believe he brought them in.
Every one of the Tsar's followers is implanted with a bone crawler.
These creatures can drain our magick." I'd seen this happen firsthand
too. The thought made me shake with rage. "But bone crawlers can
also store magick, just like a totem ring."

"So he brought them here for extra power."

"Precisely."

"And what would he need more energy for?"

"My guess? Passing through a gateway can be hard work. He
might have left these here to help him return from his journey. I've
heard of regular Sisters doing something similar with gateways and
totem rings."

Rowan rubbed his chin. "Still, there may be other explanations.
Perhaps he was merely experimenting with casting bone crawlers.
He could have done the spells here to keep them secret."

"Not likely." I pointed at different dark marks on the shells. "See these burn marks? There's no mistaking the signs. Magick was placed into these creatures and then drained away. The marks are clear enough, but…" I shook my head "I just can't believe the Tsar wanted to visit the Eternal Lands."

Rowan chuckled. "It explains a few things to me."

"Like what?"

"In my opinion, the Sire and Lady always seemed overly concerned about the Tsar's welfare. In fact, they insisted you send him into exile instead of killing him, right?"

"I couldn't even raise a hand against the man." *Although I very much wanted to.*

"Precisely. I always suspected there was some history between them. This proves it. There was a time when Tsar visited the Sire and Lady."

I stared at the gateway. The Tsar and the god and goddess. It was possible. Still, what was he doing there? *Some divining spells would give me answers.* I tried to pull in magick, but the wards were still too strong.

*Well, there are ways to see things without magick.*

Reaching out, I set my palm against the gateway's smooth stones. Magick slammed into me. Fresh images began to appear in my mind.

"Elea, are you all right?" Rowan's voice echoed as if he were standing many leagues away.

"I'm seeing something. Gateways can hold the image where they lead to, assuming you've been there before."

"But you've never visited the Eternal Lands, have you?"

"Not that I know of." I gritted my teeth as an image appeared in my mind: the darkened tent where I'd first met the Sire and Lady. This was the place where I'd eventually sent the Tsar. *His eternal prison.* I'd assumed it existed on some nameless magickal plain. It didn't.

*I'd sent the Tsar to the Eternal Lands.*

I dropped my hand and stepped backward. "This is very bad."

"What did you see?"

"The Tsar is exiled in the Eternal Lands." A chill of realization crept up my neck. *And he could use a gateway just like this one in order to escape.* "The Tsar's a master schemer. He might have suspected that the Sire and Lady wanted to send him into exile. Even worse, he might have known they'd send him to the Eternal Lands."

Rowan frowned. "If that's true, then the Tsar might need extra magick for the return trip… Something to help him cross back."

I hugged my elbows as more pieces of the puzzle fell into place. "The Tsar built the original dungeons where the Necromancers were drained. I'll bet he chose a location with a gateway. It's just the kind of failsafe that he'd put in place." A shiver rolled across my shoulders. "The Tsar could be returning." I paced the floor and bit back a groan. "This is a catastrophe."

Rowan stepped into my path, forcing me to stop. "We can't worry about the Tsar just now."

"How can I not? This is the Tsar we're talking about. The man killed off thousands of my people. If he comes back, I'm his top target."

"No one is getting anywhere near you, Elea." Rowan's voice was a rough rasp. "You have my word. I know what you care about, and it's your Sisters. For now, simply think of this gateway as another clue for how to find them. A gateway like this one might be hidden in any of the places that you're inspecting with Amelia. Perhaps you'll find it under a tapestry or behind a wall. But if you see it, then you'll know your friends could be close by. That's all you need to think about. At least, for the next two days. Promise me?"

Rowan's words helped to center my thoughts. "You're right. Little time remains to save Ada and the others. I need to stay the course. Thank you, Rowan."

"I'll always be here for you." Rowan stared at me for a long moment. I thought he might have more to say. Instead, he shook his head, stepped across the cave floor, and picked up the loops of rope. "Any ideas on where your Sisters are imprisoned?"

"Amelia wants to check the Havilland mansion first."

"I can send in someone from my team. They're experts at subterfuge."

"No. These are my people. I have to go."

Once again, Rowan moved to stand so close our bodies were only inches apart. "Trust me on this. My people can handle the Royals." He brushed the backs of his fingertips up my cheek and I melted into the touch. "I want you safe, Elea." He leaned in until his mouth was only a breath away from mine.

This wasn't the time for emotion. I couldn't seem to stop my zuchtlos feelings, though. My heart thumped with such force I thought it might burst from my chest. Rowan's voice became low and gentle. "Return to Braddock Farm. Stay safe. I will end this. Once it's done, I'll find you there. I swear it."

My legs felt wobbly beneath me. In my mind's eye, it all appeared so easy and clear. Rowan could handle this. I'd return to my farm and help the faithful servants who'd kept it thriving. Then one day, Rowan would arrive and we'd be together. How wonderful would that be?

I closed my eyes and stepped away from his touch. This was impossible. My people were my responsibility. No one else's. And the idea that Rowan and I could be together? That was an illusion.

"It's a sweet dream. We both know it isn't the truth. You're part of the Caster Imperial family. Your uncle is none other than Genesis Rex. You can't have a life with me as a farmer, can you?"

Rowan's gaze intensified. "No." He stepped closer once again. "I'll still find you, though."

"And when you do, what will I be?" I wanted to touch him and to be with him. I knew that now. But not at any cost. "Your mistress? Your absentee wife?"

"You'll be mine." He pulled me into his arms. Every ridge of his hard body pressed against my soft curves. I'd never craved anything more in my life than I wanted to kiss Rowan right now. He leaned in closer than ever before. His warm breath cascaded over my lips. "Don't fight this. Please."

My control snapped, and I pressed my mouth to his. *Yes.* Our first few tastes were tentative. Gentle. Rowan was as delicious as I'd imagined, a flavor that was somewhere between musk and desire. Every touch of his lips sent spasms of want through my core.

Our kiss quickly turned rough. Rowan nipped my bottom lip, and I let out a rough groan. *This kiss could go on forever.* Still, some small part of my brain shouted for me to stop.

I didn't know how I found the strength, but I pushed Rowan away. "I want you too. That's not enough for me. We're from different worlds. Your place is with your people. I need to save mine. Once this is over, we'll never see each other again. I can't afford to feel more for you than I already do."

Rowan's eyes took on that intense look I knew so well. A muscle worked in his jaw for a long moment. "I understand. We both have work to do."

I exhaled. "I'm glad you can accept the truth."

"I didn't say that." He scooped up the ropes and offered them to me. "This isn't over."

I stared at the green cords coiled around his palm. I wanted real ties between us as well. Yet wanting a thing wasn't the same as having it. I pulled the rope from his hand and looped it around my shoulders. "We better get back."

The sooner I could return to my regular life and get away from this fantasy with Rowan, the better. We bound ourselves together again and plunged deep into the cold water.

In no time, we'd returned the forest. Tension was thick in the air. Rowan and I dressed in silence. We walked back toward Philippe without so much as looking at each other. The quiet between us turned deafening. At last, we reached the small clearing where Philippe still stood frozen. It felt like a year had passed since I last saw Amelia's brother.

"I'll wake him up," said Rowan.

"I'll do it." I stared at my hands, the ground, and the trees. Anything but Rowan.

"Elea."

"I know you said this isn't over. It is for me."

"Perhaps." Rowan nodded and slipped off into the darkening woods. I had no illusions that he would let what happened between us stop, yet there was nothing I could do about it right now. I cast a quick spell to awaken Philippe.

A few seconds later, Amelia's brother blinked up at me. "How did we get out here?" He scanned the sky. "And how did it get so late?"

"We went for a walk. Our conversation was so entertaining, we simply lost track of time." I lowered my voice. "That was rather strong wine we were drinking back at the cottage."

Philippe's eyes narrowed. Even so, he seemed to accept that

explanation. "Your dress is filthy." I didn't think it was all that bad, actually, what did I know about gowns? Philippe offered me his arm. "Shall we return to the mansion?"

I gave him a cool nod. "Sounds lovely."

"Now that was the perfect courtly reply," said Philippe. "Have I told you that you don't need to play the smiling fool?"

"You may have mentioned that."

"Well, I think you might have found your rhythm in your courtly dance, so to speak. Let's return and tell Amelia. After you practice a bit more, you could be ready for a visit to the Havilland family."

"Perfect." As I walked back toward the mansion with Philippe, I thought I saw Rowan watching us from the shadows. It was too brief a glimpse to be sure, though. And even if he was there, it wasn't anything I should worry about.

Soon I'd visit a place where my Sisters might be imprisoned. This time tomorrow, I might have Ada safely in my arms and have destroyed the Vicomte's vortex watch with its horrible totem. That was something to consider, indeed.

## 7

*J* spent the rest of the day at Amelia's table, practicing my new approach to Royal chitchat. Essentially, I kept my cool and learned how to assess the subtleties of small talk. Turns out, there was a lot hidden in the way one said hello or asked for the salt. Amelia was thrilled with the results. So was I, for that matter, especially because Amelia felt certain that we could visit the Havilland estate tomorrow.

Amelia had also been surprised to see me enter the cottage while sopping wet. I explained that Necromancers always went for a quick swim in the afternoon. Amelia accepted my words without question. That was one benefit of being the last of my kind, I supposed. No one to contradict any of our supposed habits.

It wasn't until late that night that I finally returned to my tavern room. By this point, I was bone-tired and yawning up a storm. Still, I needed to cast my seeing spell for the day. No way could I miss a chance for more information about Ada. Besides, there was an odd sense of anticipation in my soul. The reason was simple. When I cast, I pulled power into me. On a rare occasion, that energy called to me. And tonight? A spell was definitely tugging at my consciousness, waiting for me to bring it to life.

*A good sign.*

Surely, my next spell would show me a new vision of Ada.

I quickly prepared my room, jamming rags into all the appropriate spots. My focus should have been locked on my upcoming incantation, but other memories kept interrupting.

All right, it was one memory. Rowan's kiss.

I gently brushed my fingertips over my lips. Heat bloomed through my chest as I recalled how rough our kiss became. Closing my eyes, I could feel the way his firm hands pressed against the small of my back, how the hard planes of his chest pressed into mine, and the way our mouths devoured each other.

What a kiss.

It wasn't my first, but it was certainly my best. When I was sixteen, I'd kissed one of the local boys behind the barn for a minute or so. I only did it to prove that yes, a Necromancer could kiss someone without turning them into a toad. I suppose if I'd thought about it, I would have selected someone other than the fishmonger's son. It wasn't the most aromatic introduction to men.

Then I was a teenager when I met Tristan. He was handsome and charming, yet I never saw him as more than a brother.

I ran my tongue over my lower lip. From the moment I first saw Rowan, I'd wanted to touch him. Some part of me always wondered what his kisses would be like. Now that I knew the answer, I only wanted him all the more. His husky voice echoed through my thoughts.

*"You're mine. Don't fight it."*

I lay back on my bed. The lumpy mattress pressed into my spine, and I wished it was Rowan's body behind me instead. What if we had done more than kiss? I knew the mechanics of how sex worked, of course. Until Rowan, I'd never given the matter much thought. After all, Necromancers were trained against emotions. Lust was essentially forbidden. I brushed my hand over my breast. What would Rowan's touch feel like here?

*I sat bolt upright. Stop this nonsense. Focus on finding Ada.*

Rising, I shook all thoughts of Rowan from my mind. I had work to do, and that didn't involve contemplating kisses. Closing my eyes, I reached out with my mage awareness, searching for magick nearby. Instantly, power careened through my body, ready to be released as a spell. I focused energy into my left hand, making my bones glow bright blue. After that, I whispered the words to my spell and set my power free.

An azure-colored mist rolled out across the floor. The thick blue haze quickly wrapped around me, the tendrils of smoke turning thick as a blanket. Once the haze disappeared, my spell was complete. I expected to be standing in a dungeon hallway, just as I always had before.

Instead, I was brought into a large stone chamber lit by torches. Rusted chains hung along the walls. The musty scent of dust filled the air. A long wooden table sat against the opposite wall. Something or someone lay on the tabletop. It was hard to see for certain since a small group of Fantomes surrounded it.

What was on that table? The question pulled at my thoughts. I shifted about, anxious for a better look. The Fantomes always blocked my view though. All I could see was their black robes. Every so often, one of them would shift their arms, making their loose garments sway with the movement.

I frowned. Why would my spell have brought me here? My interest kept being drawn to the tabletop. I took a step forward, and all the mages paused. Moving in unison, they all shifted to stare in my direction. Their hoods were drawn low over their faces. I couldn't tell if they actually saw me or just sensed magick in the room.

I froze midstep, barely able to breathe. My heart hammered against my rib cage.

*Please don't let them see me.*

The seconds passed slowly. A murmur echoed through the air. I couldn't tell all that was said, but I heard the words "trick of the mind." At last, the mages all turned back to face whatever was on the tabletop. They couldn't see me. I heaved out a relieved breath.

*Thank the Sire.*

I stood on tiptoe, desperate for a better view of whatever the mages were doing. Part of me wanted to sprint across the room. However, the Fantomes had almost detected me when I'd been standing still. Moving closer—or even moving too much at all—was certain to expose my presence. Besides, this spell was getting trickier to cast by the second. It was taking almost all my focus to simply remain in this room.

A low moan echoed through the air. A jolt of fear moved down my spine. I'd have known that voice anywhere. It had been haunting me for weeks.

Ada.

The Fantomes erupted into a flurry of movement. Something sharp and shiny flashed in one of their hands. Was it a knife? Ada screamed in pain. The sound tore through my soul. Another mage raised his arm. His long pale fingertips dripped with blood.

Ada's blood.

Suddenly, my concentration fell apart. Magick poured out of my body like water through a sieve.

*No, no, no!*

I wanted to stay and see Ada. I tried to refocus my mind, but there was nothing I could do. The next thing I knew, I had returned to my room in the tavern. Alarm rushed through my limbs. I paced the floor.

*Focus, Elea.*

There was nothing more to be done now. Worrying wouldn't help me find Ada and the others. Searching the Havilland mansion would. There was a lot of work to complete before tomorrow. After taking in a few calming breaths, I began casting the protection spells I would need for the visit to the Havilland mansion. the same thoughts kept circling my mind like they were on a repeater spell.

Ada might be there.

In just a matter of hours, I might see her.

Whatever it took, no matter what the cost, I knew one thing.

*I would find that child or die trying.*

## 8

*I*t was early morning when I stepped up to Amelia's front gate. Clothilde was already waiting for me in the courtyard beyond. Once again, her blonde hair was pulled back into a tight bun. As I approached, her mouth thinned. Clearly, she was not happy to see me. "You're here to prepare for a visit to the Havilland estate, I suppose."

"I am."

She slowly swung the gate open, glaring at me the entire while. "I don't like you endangering my Lady."

I matched her glare with one of my own. "I don't like you questioning her decisions."

She slammed the gate shut with extra force. "I'll show you to her rooms." Without another word, she marched up to the front door of the so-called cottage. I followed.

Clothilde led me through the familiar labyrinth of furniture covered in dusty sheets. What was unfamiliar was the fact that, unlike yesterday, there were servants everywhere. Clothilde paused beside a coat of arms that had been painted onto one of the walls. It showed the tall sword wreathed in roses. Clothilde nodded toward the image. "Lady Amelia hails from the House of Theodora." Her voice took on a reverent tone. "Theodora snuck past the gateway to the Eternal Lands by devising an ingenious disguise. My Lady has such gifts too."

Everyone knew the story of Theodora. She was a poor girl without any magick or way to eat. After creating some kind of camouflage, she snuck through a gateway to the Eternal Lands and entreated the Sire of Souls and the Lady of Creation for help. She won their trust and a powerful sword. That was when the Royals were truly created, along with their love of learning and innovation.

I tried to feign interest and failed. "Is there a reason you're showing me this?"

"Lady Amelia comes from highborn family. She's the Vicomte's child, to boot." Clothilde folded her thin arms over her bony chest. "If you lead her into trouble, then you'll make serious enemies. I'm warning you."

"Warning received." I should chide her for such forward talk, but I couldn't find it in me. Clothilde was protective of her lady. "Now, her rooms?"

Clothilde grumbled something under her breath and led me deeper into the mansion. At last, we reached Amelia's chamber. The place was painted pink with tall windows and long silk curtains. Amelia sat before a small table covered with all sorts of brushes, puffs, and multicolored pastes. It reminded me of her workbench in the basement laboratory, only this time, the girl was engineering her own face instead of a watch's.

In fact, Amelia looked so perfect I thought she could be one of the portraits that must be hanging in the Havilland gallery. Her face appeared porcelain-smooth with big blue eyes and pursed pink lips. Her ginger hair hung in neat ringlets past her shoulders. Already, Amelia's pink gown was laced up tightly, making the skirt flounce out even more broadly at her waist. I pulled on the neckline of my own simple shift. Suddenly, I felt anxious about getting ready for today. I couldn't hope to compete with Amelia's beauty.

"You're early," said Amelia. "And you look ill."

"I had bad dreams last night." The vision of Ada screaming wouldn't leave my mind. I tried for hours to cast the spell again. For whatever reason, I couldn't get the incantation to work. That happened sometimes, especially when the previous casting had drained me of too much energy. I might have better luck tonight.

"What's wrong?" Her pretty face crumpled with worry.

"It's nothing worth retelling," I said.

At those words, Amelia seemed ready to cry, and I hadn't yet told her about Ada's torture. In any case, what help would that news afford? The best thing we could do now was focus on getting ready for the Havilland visit. "Why don't we prepare ourselves?"

"You have arrived as quite the mess. If we're to arrive on time for luncheon, then we must rush."

"Whatever you think is best."

"In that case, you can start by changing." She gestured to a massive gown of pale green. How exactly would I lever myself into that contraption?

*Remember, the faster you're strapped into one of those monstrosities, the quicker you can get answers about Ada and the other Necromancers.*

When I spoke again, I kept my face a mask of politeness. "Thank you, Amelia."

A crowd of servants suddenly descended into the room. I was scrubbed, perfumed, oiled, coiled, and loaded into the fancy green gown. I knew it was the latest fashion, but still. I felt as if I were masquerading as an artichoke.

Finally, we were ready to step out of the mansion and into the carriage that would take us to the Havilland estate. It took two men in formal jackets to load us into our wagon, which was a boxy affair with windows on either side. The men needed even more time to strap on all the gifts we were bringing along. All these delays were starting to wear on my nerves.

Plus, there was no sign of Philippe.

Amelia shot me a nervous glance. "We won't have formal guards to accompany us." Her cheeks reddened. "This was all I could afford. I figured you most needed help with preparing your ensemble."

"Quite right. Besides, if thieves do attack on the road, I'm rather an expert at getting rid of them." I sighed. Robbers were easy to dispose of. Fantomes though? They were a different matter entirely. Once we crossed onto the Havilland estate, I wouldn't be able to cast anything. Not without exposing myself, in any case.

*Damn those Fantomes.*

"Bother that brother of mine. I refuse to be late." Amelia slammed her palm on the carriage door. "Driver, let's not tarry."

Our wagon lurched forward. We were on our way. We hadn't gone far when Philippe rode into view. He pulled up alongside us on his black stallion. I had to admit he looked rather dapper with his golden hair and roguish smile. "Hello, ladies."

Amelia drummed her fingers on the wooden windowsill of the boxy carriage. "You're late, Philippe."

"No, you're perpetually early." He flashed me a white-toothed smile. "Isn't she, Elea?"

Amelia raised her gloved hand. "Don't call her Elea. For the purposes of this visit, her name is Fleur." She turned to face me. "Don't pay any attention to him, *Fleur*. We have far more important topics to discuss."

I leaned back in the carriage and eyed Amelia. She really was a marvel. For a girl who'd spent years hiding out in a mansion, she embraced her role as spy with gusto. She'd planned every last detail of this trip, from recruiting a small army of servants overnight to ensuring ribbons were woven into the horses' manes. I folded my hands neatly at my waist and gave her my full attention. "Whatever you wish to review, I'm ready and waiting."

"Now that we're all here..." Amelia glared over at Philippe. "We must discuss what to say to the Marchioness."

"Don't you include the Marquis as well?" I asked.

"Why bother?" Philippe rolled his eyes. "The Marchioness runs the place."

"Tell *Fleur* how you know that."

"No." Philippe winked. He really was a charming rogue.

"Oh yes, you will. This is key information." Amelia wagged her finger at her brother. "Tell, tell."

Philippe sighed dramatically. "No, I'll let my sister share that detail."

"Fine." Amelia rolled her eyes. "Philippe and the Marchioness have been lovers for months now. Secretly, of course."

My eyes widened. "Oh." I'd known Philippe was a scoundrel, but I'd no idea he went with married women. I tried not to look like a country bumpkin who was made speechless by such antics. Not sure I succeeded. "Oh. I suppose…"

"Yes?" Philippe pulled up right beside my window and leaned in closer. He was enjoying my discomfort far too much.

"I suppose you know her well, then."

He pursed his full lips. "In certain ways."

Now Philippe was getting on my nerves. I could see why Amelia found it a challenge to get him onto serious topics. "What is she like?"

"She'll play the courtier until she's ready to trade. Everything with her has a price. After that point, you might as well be bartering pigs at market."

I stifled the urge to grumble. "Then remind me, why am I playing the courtier? Wouldn't it be easier to simply get right to the trading? Simply ask the question. What do you want in exchange for allowing us to view the gallery?"

Philippe's blue eyes twinkled with mischief. "Please. The Royals adore their pomp and frippery. You'll get nowhere if you go right to bargaining. In fact, I had to stop by on formal visits for weeks before she let me into her bed. And then, when I got there—"

"That's quite enough, brother dear." Amelia made shoo fingers at him. "I'd rather not be sick on my gown." She turned to me. "Have you any other questions?"

I could only smile. She really did fuss over me. After a lifetime of being alone, it was nice to have someone my age who cared about my well-being. "I'm fine."

She narrowed her eyes. "And your *preparations*?" The way she said that word, it was clear she meant magick.

I counted off my spells on my fingertips. "I spoke a dozen incantations since last night. I've hidden my power well, I think. As for the rest…" I gestured to the skirts of my gown. "I should say you made some magick of your own. I scarcely recognize myself." Which was true. I'd never worn face paint before, let alone curled my hair. I looked like an entirely different person.

"You forgot all the work we did yesterday on your history, Fleur." Amelia tried to look stern, but there was no hiding the small smile rounding her mouth. "How are we related?"

Philippe rode up closer to the carriage again. "I need to remember this too." Amazing how he could keep perfect pace with us while moving. The man must flirt with women through carriage windows all the time.

I recited our story by heart. "We have the same father and different mothers. Your mum was of noble blood; mine wasn't. We discovered our shared father when he approached both of us, looking for money." That last part of the story was true. Amelia's father was a con man and gambler. To pay off a debt, he tried to kidnap her from the orphanage and sell her to a brothel. The nuns took him down with a kill spell. I'd say that was harsh, but if he'd tried something like that at my old Cloister, the Sisters would have tortured him for a week first. You don't want to mess with Necromancer nuns.

"Excellent." Amelia bobbed a little on her seat, she was so happy. "Now, I'm also wondering about the Marchioness—"

"Look," I said solemnly. "You've recited the minutiae of the Havilland family to me by the hour. If I don't remember it now, I never will." I gestured toward the window. "Besides, we're almost there."

Amelia's eyes got wide with fear. "You're right."

"We'll do swimmingly. No one could have done a better job preparing me. Veronique would be proud."

Amelia exhaled slowly. "Thank you, Elea. I mean, Fleur. I needed that."

"You're most welcome." I leaned out the window and waved to Philippe. "How much longer now?"

"Not far, my lovely Fleur."

I leaned back into the carriage and practiced looking serene. In my heart, I felt anything but. Tomorrow night, the time would run out on Amelia's watch. My friends would die, and the Vicomte would rise while wielding the power of a thousand Necromancers.

I gripped my hands together and twisted my fingers.

We simply had to find Ada and the others. Today.

It wasn't long in terms of time. Even so, it felt like years passed before we approached the Havilland estate. A tall iron fence surrounded what looked to be nothing but green and rolling hills. There was no view of the mansion yet, only a small guardhouse that stood by the gate. As we approached, a man in golden livery stepped out to greet us. His brown wig sat slightly askew atop his head. It was an effort not to frown.

*What? A wig?*

I stared at the thing for an overlong time. I'd heard that some Royals embraced odd fashions. The flouncy gown I now wore was proof of that. And to their minds, such dress was progressive, something akin to their love of machines and learning. Yet to me? Things like wigs were simply not necessary. I shook my head. Give me a simple frock and a Necromancer spell any day.

"Good afternoon. What's your business here?"

"Lady Amelia and guests are here to see the Marchioness and Marquis," said Philippe. "We're expected."

Upon closer inspection, it was clear that the guard was an older man with tawny skin and long jowls. "I saw the names of Lady Amelia and her brother, Philippe, on the register." He eyed me up and down. "It seems we have an unexpected guest along as well."

"She's our sister," said Philippe.

"I'll have to check if she's on the register." The guard meant the register of nobility, of course. Philippe and Amelia were included due to their mother.

"She's a half-relation. Not Royal." Philippe gave the man a sly wink. "Be a friend, Francois." Clearly, this wasn't the first time Philippe had snuck past the gate.

The guard awkwardly cleared his throat. "Strangers aren't always treated well in the mansion." Francois lowered his voice. "We've a Fantome on the grounds, you know. It's not safe for her here."

"But I assure you, the Marchioness is expecting all of us." Philippe lowered his voice as well. "You know how her, ah, *tastes* run to the extreme."

I rarely showed emotion, but that statement had my eyes widening. What kind of bedroom activities did Philippe engage in, exactly?

The guard looked unsure. "Well, if you say so."

Philippe raked his hand through his golden hair. I hadn't known him long, yet I knew that motion. It was his way of preening for his next encounter, all while saying the current one was over. "If you'll excuse us."

Francois frowned. Even so, he did open the gate that blocked our way forward. We passed on up the hill. I tried to ignore the nagging weight of foreboding on my shoulders. What did Francois mean about strangers and Fantomes?

It took ages for our carriage to navigate the winding road to the main estate. Every so often, a lone rider on horseback would pass us on the way down. All were handsome young men in simple trousers and tunics. I was starting to wonder how many lovers this Marchioness had.

One rider galloped toward us on a gray stallion. He had white-blond hair and a silver velvet jacket that reminded me of Philippe's. Amelia grabbed my hand. "Don't look now, but a handsome young man is coming our way. It's Louis Villeneuve. *The* Louis Villeneuve."

I kept my features carefully neutral. After all my issues with Rowan, the last thing I wanted was another attractive man on my mind. I shut my eyes. "I won't so much as peep."

She gave my wrist a friendly slap. "I was teasing. You must take a little look. He's breathtaking."

I reopened my eyes as Louis slowed his horse to a walk. As he moved past us, Louis gave polite hellos to Philippe and Amelia. I nodded in greeting. I must admit, I was a little surprised at Amelia's definition of handsome. The lad had a pimply face, thin frame, and too-large ears. Perhaps in a year or five he might be handsome. Now? Not a chance.

Once Louis passed, Amelia actually flushed. "I can't believe it." She fanned her face with her hands. "The Louis Villeneuve greeted me. Did you see that?"

"I did." I angled myself to get a better look at her. "Although, I must admit, I thought him a little young for you."

"Why would you think that? He's seventeen. I'm twenty. I like a sweet-faced lad. Don't you?"

*More like a burly giant with rugged features, rough hands, and a warm touch.* "I'm a Necromancer. We are trained to focus on logic instead of feelings."

"Sounds wise. Men are no end of trouble, I find."

Philippe brought his stallion closer to the window. "I heard that."

"You were meant to."

At last, the mansion appeared atop the crest of a hill. It was a sprawling estate that gleamed with golden paint. I supposed the scale was meant to intimidate. Based on how my stomach had begun to squirm, I was afraid it was working.

Amelia gripped my hands again. "Do you think we can really do this?"

"Absolutely." I was pleased that my voice didn't waver.

Amelia nodded slowly. "I believe you."

The carriage rolled to a stop. After all the hours of practice, the moment had arrived. Now I could only hope that we'd find answers in this den of social serpents. My fellow Necromancers were counting on it.

## 9

*I* stepped into the waiting chamber of the Marquis and Marchioness de Havilland. Once there, I stood stock-still. The place was empty, yet that wasn't what made me pause. There were magickal wards in here—spells of detection and security that had been cast by a Fantome. It all had an oily feeling to it, like my skin was being dipped in sludge. This was definitely the work of a single mage.

On reflex, I scanned the room. The guard had mentioned there was a mage in residence. Would this person be hiding here?

Everywhere I looked, there were images of lions tearing into their prey. The beasts were woven into the tapestries that hung along the walls, set into intricate mosaics on the floor, and painted onto the murals covering the vaulted ceiling. Even the chairs were carved with the faces of growling lions on the backrests.

The whole scene was meant to shock and impress visitors. After all, the lion was the animal on the Havilland coat of arms. I quickly caught myself and stopped staring. Philippe and Amelia stood beside me. A pair of servants in gold-colored livery stepped into the room.

"Wait here," said the first servant.

The second servant looked at me like I was week-old garbage. "Do not take a seat unless bidden to." News of my non-noble lineage must have passed quickly up from the guardhouse. The pair of servants stared at me expectantly.

I inclined my head slightly and turned away. If those servants were hoping to see me red-faced over being a supposed bastardess, they were both mistaken. In the world of Necromancy, lineage meant nothing. Magick was everything.

"Thank you," said Amelia smoothly. "You may take your leave now."

"As you wish, my lady." The servants turned away, closing the door quietly behind them.

Philippe folded his arms over his chest. "You could have called them out on their tone, Fleur. They don't know your lineage for certain. It would have been within your rights to chastise them."

"I've more important things to focus on." I paced around the room, my gown trailing behind me with each step. I'd only been wearing it for an hour or so, and already I wanted to tear the damned thing off. To pass the time, I scanned every scene of lion-led carnage. The number and variety of animals shown was amazing. There were lions killing gazelles, deer, bears, other lions... The list went on and on. Amelia told me how the Havilland family enjoyed hunting, but this was something else. What kind of bloodthirsty folks were they?

A golden door swung open on the opposite side of the room. Another servant stepped inside, this one a woman. She wore the same yellow livery with a small matching cap. She stopped and bowed in our direction. "The Marquis and Marchioness Havilland will now grace you with their presence."

Amelia and I curtsied as a willowy man and woman stepped into the chamber. Both had ebony skin, brown wigs, and elegant bone structure. The woman's yellow silk gown matched her husband's perfectly tailored longcoat as they crossed the room in lockstep. The Marquis was tall and broad-shouldered. Normally, I didn't like a man in a wig, but somehow the Marquis made it seem dignified. Meanwhile, the Marchioness was everything long limbed, slender, and elegant. Her wig towered on her head, and much as I hate to admit it, it suited her quite well. She looked nothing less than regal.

The noble pair first paused before Philippe. The Marchioness tilted her head as if trying to remember his name. "How nice of you to visit. Philippe, is it?"

Now, that was impressive. You wouldn't know the pair were lovers.

"Yes, Marchioness." Philippe took her hand in his and kissed the back of her knuckles. "How kind of you to remember me."

"My memory would improve if you visited more often." The Marchioness turned to her husband. "Don't you think Philippe should join our regular company?"

The Marquis lifted his brows. "You hunt?"

"Yes."

"Raise dogs?"

Philippe sniffed. "Only fools trust a breeder."

"Excellent. I must introduce you to my Master of the Hounds."

"It would be my honor."

I kept my features carefully calm, yet inside? I was wide-eyed with shock. The Marchioness had just manipulated her husband into agreeing to allow her lover to visit more often. And beyond that, to become his friend. Back on the farm, that kind of behavior got all parties involved nothing more than a fat lip. Here, no one seemed to bat an eyelash.

The Marchioness moved to stand before Amelia. "And how lovely to see you, my sweet."

Amelia dipped her chin. "I appreciate your granting me an audience."

"Nonsense, your visit was overdue and much anticipated." Next, the Marchioness turned to me. "And I see that you've brought a companion."

Amelia curtsied again. "Yes, my Lady. I'd like to present Fleur."

The Marchioness eyed me carefully. "And how are you two related, precisely?" The look of disdain in her chocolate-colored eyes said she already knew the answer.

"Amelia and I share the same father but have different mothers."

"I see." The Marchioness' nostrils flared. "How interesting." The way she said that last word, I could tell she thought me as engaging as a smear of dung.

Amelia took a protective step closer to my side. "I met Fleur in the orphanage when our father came to find us. You know how he was."

"How kind of you to take the girl in," said the Marchioness smoothly. "Few would do so much for full-blooded relation." She arched her thin brows. "In fact, some might have questions about allowing a stranger into their lives. After all, who can know their true intentions?"

It was an effort to keep looking lovely and aloof. In truth, all I wanted to do was cast a bone melter spell on the Marchioness. How dare she question my motives? It made me all the more angry because, deep down, I knew she was just a little bit right. By entering Amelia's life, I *had* placed her in danger.

Amelia lifted her chin. "I trust Fleur. Absolutely."

A warm sense of pride swelled in my chest. I hadn't known Amelia very long, but there was no question in my mind that she was an honest person. Her trust in me seemed genuine, and that was a great gift indeed.

"How fortunate for you." The Marchioness flicked her long fingers, and a servant stepped up from the doorway. "We'll enjoy some *refreshments.*" An odd look shone in her eyes as she spoke that last word. It was clearly some kind of signal. Suddenly, my dress seemed far too heavy and hot. I was certainly no favorite of the Marchioness. What exactly did the suspect about me?

The servant marched quickly from the room. A few seconds later, a Fantome walked into the reception chamber. It took everything I had not to gasp. She was a spritely thing that had the classic look of a Necromancer, with pale skin, dark features, and long black robes. My heart sank. She'd joined us based on the signal from the Marchioness.

That wasn't good.

All Fantomes wore loose robes with heavy hoods. It wasn't proper garb for a Necromancer. We had fitted robes that showed our different stations. Still, I didn't need a robe to know what level of mage now approached me. All Fantomes were Grand Masters or Mistresses, the same as me. The woman stepped closer, her face unreadable.

*Be careful, Elea.*

Amelia and Philippe shared a worried glance. The Marchioness waved off their fears. "Don't worry. She isn't here for either of you." She turned to me. "Fleur, meet Kamilla."

I curtsied and took a closer look at the mage before me. Kamilla was petite and elf-like with bone structure that was so sharp her cheeks looked hollowed out.

"Greetings, Kamilla." Philippe stepped directly between the Fantome and me. "I hope you realize how important my sisters are to me. Both of them."

In response, Kamilla only glared at him. For a tiny lady, I had no doubt she could level the room.

The Marchioness slowly seated herself in one of the larger throne-like chairs. "Don't be rude, Philippe. The Marquis and I are honored to have a Fantome present on our property." The way she spoke, the Marchioness seemed anything but honored. Angry beyond belief was more like it. "We defer to her will in all things."

"And in this, my will is clear." Kamilla glared in my direction. "You're to leave with me."

Philippe lifted his chin. "Not a chance." He struck a gallant figure with his blond hair and fitted longcoat. Defying a Fantome wasn't necessarily smart, although I admired his determination.

Sadly, he didn't stand a chance against a Grand Mistress Necromancer.

Kamilla raised her fist. Her fingers were decorated with totem rings. "Back."

With only that one word, one of Kamilla's totem rings lit up with a flare of magick blue flame. A ball of azure-colored energy pummeled Philippe's stomach, forcing him backward. The poor man's body whipped across the floor until he slammed into the wall. I gasped. What an outrage. Necromancers were schooled to save our powers for those who attacked. Philippe was just posturing. I rushed to his side, along with Amelia.

"Are you all right?" I asked.

Philippe took in a few shallow breaths before giving me a shaky grin. "Only if you kiss and make it better." He tapped his mouth. "It hurts here."

Amelia patted his shoulder. Relief was evident on her face. "He'll be fine."

Kamilla stalked toward Philippe. "No one tells a Fantome what to do."

A muscle twitched by the Marchioness' eye. When she spoke again, her voice overflowed with false calm. "You once asked to meet any strangers to my home." She pointed to me. "This one is strange."

*Strange? Oh, she doesn't know the half of it.*

Kamilla slowly turned to face me. My heart beat so hard I thought it might burst from my chest. "This girl has no magickal signature, which is very odd." She prowled closer to me. "Why is that, I wonder?"

I appeared perfectly calm. On the inside I wanted to scream. "Why would I have any magick?"

The Marchioness turned to her husband. "Love, why don't you take Philippe to see your hounds?" The pair exchanged a long look, and I had a feeling an entire conversation was hidden in that stare. I had the additional suspicion that whatever that talk was about, it didn't bode well for me.

"Excellent idea." The Marquis turned on his heel and walked out of the room. "Follow me quickly, lad, or you'll be left behind." The door slammed shut after him.

"Be right there." Philippe stepped up to the Marchioness and spoke in a low voice. "Are you certain you ladies will be fine on your own?"

The Marchioness narrowed her eyes. "Positive." She softened her tone to an intimate whisper. "And it wasn't a question, pet. Go play with the hounds. I won't harm your sister." I couldn't help but notice that I wasn't included on the list of those who would be safe. "Run along."

"Yes, love." Philippe took off at a quick pace.

The Marchioness waved at the handful of servants who puttered around the chamber. "You're all dismissed." After that, she shared a pointed look with Kamilla. Seconds passed before the Marchioness gave the mage the barest of nods. Kamilla left the room as well.

A knot of worry formed in my throat. Why didn't Kamilla fight being sent off? I didn't like how easily she gave in.

Still, the moment everyone left the room, my shoulders slumped with relief. Kamilla being gone made everything feel almost pleasant once more.

The Marchioness gestured to the chairs beside her. "Now, we can speak more comfortably." A predatory gleam shone in her eyes. There was something about this conversation I didn't like, at all.

Amelia slipped into the open seat to the Marchioness's right. "What would you like to discuss?" I stood halfway across the room, all the better to keep a good view of the conversation.

"What should we discuss?" The Marchioness patted her wig with her fingertips. "Please. Don't play coy. I had suspected that you might be visiting me."

"And why is that?" A little crease formed between Amelia's ginger brows. I was getting to know her faces. This one meant that she was genuinely confused.

"The rumors are rampant, my sweet. Everyone knows that your future is about to change. You're here to ally yourself to me." She shook her head. "Honestly, you used to be better at this."

"Rumors? My future? What are you talking about?"

The Marchioness leaned back in her chair. For a long minute, her gaze flickered between Amelia and me. "So you don't know." She tapped her chin.

"Know what?" asked Amelia.

The Marchioness kept speaking as if Amelia hadn't said a word. "Then you must have come here to help the bastardess. How very interesting."

A chilly feeling was creeping up the back of my skull. I appreciated Amelia wanting to focus on my quest. Still I didn't like the greedy look in the Marchioness's eyes. "What do you know about Amelia?"

The Marchioness glared at me. "You'll speak when you're spoken to." She returned refocused on Amelia. "Tell me. What do you wish for your half sister?"

Amelia opened her mouth, but I raised my hand, palm forward. "One moment." I stepped closer to the Marchioness. "Leave Amelia out of this. I'll be the one to tell you what I need, once you share your news about Amelia."

The Marchioness sniffed dismissively. "Spoken like a true Commoner. You people are always so crude. Fine." She turned her attention to Amelia. "I was referring to the rumors of your impending marriage, obviously."

Amelia's shoulders fell forward. "Oh, is that all? There are always whispers going around." She was speaking too quickly for my taste, though. Amelia only did that when she was worried or afraid.

I narrowed my eyes and considered this news. It would be no surprise if the Vicomte used Amelia as a marriage bargaining chip. She was his only legal offspring, after all. Still, Amelia told me that the Vicomte hadn't had anything to do with her in years. I turned to her. "When was the last time you heard one of these marriage rumors?"

"Oh, last week I think." Color rose in Amelia's cheeks. That only happened when my friend was lying. There was no question about it. Some time had passed since there had been wedding rumors for Amelia. So, what had changed recently? An idea appeared. Genesis Rex had been having diplomatic negotiations with the Vicomte. Perhaps the Caster King was behind all this. Marrying into the Vicomte's family would be a traditional way to protect the Casters. Not that it would work, in my opinion. The Vicomte was too much of a lying bastard.

"I've told you what I know." The Marchioness focused her attention on me. "Your turn."

I opened my mouth to speak, but Amelia replied first. "My sister and I wish to visit your galleries. Alone."

The Marchioness rubbed her temples and grew silent. My legs began to get wobbly beneath me.

*We're so close. Ada, Veronique, and the others could be seconds away.*

At last, the Marchioness addressed us once more. "That's a strange request. I rarely let anyone see the galleries alone. Still, I'll allow it this time."

Amelia's face brightened. "Thank you."

"Your half sister may go alone." The Marchioness patted Amelia's forearm. "You must stay and keep me company. We have so much to catch up on. Isn't that right?"

Amelia fidgeted in her chair. "Oh, yes."

The Marchioness rose and stepped up to my side. Resting her hand gently on my shoulder, she led me toward the door. Once we were far enough away from Amelia, she leaned in to whisper in my ear. "My Fantome is already waiting to accompany you to the gallery. It's her favorite place to take strangers. You see, she's cast wards to block all magick there."

"What?" The word tumbled from my lips before I could stop it. Magick-blocking wards were very complex and almost impossible to cast through. My chances of winning a battle in the gallery were slim.

"Of course" —the Marchioness shrugged— "if you're who you say you are, then you've nothing to fear, now do you? And if you're a lying Necromancer, then Kamilla will kill you on the spot." Her voice lowered with menace. "I have enough of your scum in my house as it is. I don't need more mages causing trouble. Do we understand each other?"

"We do."

She gestured to the door. "Then, the exit is that way."

I glanced over my shoulder. From across the room, Amelia was watching us. Her blue eyes were wide with worry. I gave her what I hoped was a carefree smile. My friend had placed herself in enough danger as it was. I didn't want her risking a trip to the gallery with a Fantome too.

Worry churned inside me as I walked toward the exit. Every step seemed to echo through the room, reminding me of the drumroll before an execution. Alone with a Grand Mistress Necromancer and unable to cast spells?

*Gods-damn it. I'm heading right into a trap.*

## 10

Kamilla waited for me in the outer hallway. Usually, Necromancers were careful to hide their emotions. There was no missing the hungry flare in Kamilla's brown eyes. In fact, she reminded me of my old cat Lucy. That same look appeared when there was a wriggling mouse trapped under her claws. My spine stiffened.

*I am no one's prey.*

My hand itched to cast an attack spell right now. After all, my Sisters could be hidden somewhere nearby. A scheme formed in my mind.

Kill Kamilla.

Invade the gallery.

Investigate.

With any luck, free Ada and the others.

I forced in a deep breath. Mother Superior would say that was my impulsive zuchtlos-side talking. Allowing my emotions to do my thinking for me wasn't an option today. A plan was already in motion, and it was to tour the gallery with Kamilla. If I found any sign of Ada or the others, then I'd consider matters from there.

*I still have until tomorrow night.*

Leaning on my Necromancer training, I slowly approached

Kamilla, my face a mask of calm. "The Marchioness says you're to give me a tour of the gallery."

"Try to keep up." Kamilla took off through the mansion's warren of golden passageways. I stayed close behind her. All the rooms looked the same—yellow walls, wooden furniture, and grisly hunting tapestries. From time to time, we'd pass a servant in golden livery. They always paused, shot me a pitying look, and hurried on.

Clearly, I wasn't the first to get a gallery tour from Kamilla. The guard's words about strangers made perfect sense now.

Soon Kamilla and I exited the mansion through a side door. A hillock opened up before us, all the grass gleaming emerald-bright in the afternoon sunshine. Kamilla pointed toward the horizon. A long and rectangular building stood atop a nearby hill. *The gallery.* Every inch seemed plated gold, so it hurt to stare at the place in direct sunlight.

I supposed that was the point.

Kamilla followed a thin footpath over the grass, leading me to one of the gallery's side doors. She pulled it open slowly. "After you, Fleur."

"Thank you."

I stepped inside. The galleries were a series of small rooms made of gleaming wood. Tall windows cast long beams of light across the floor. It wasn't much of a gallery, to be honest. Only a few pictures of the Havilland forebears covered the walls. Mostly, these depicted elder nobles who were withered and slumped.

This gallery was the pride of the Havilland family. It was supposed to be overflowing with portraits. Why had they cleaned out most of the paintings? The answer appeared in a flash.

Perhaps so Kamilla wouldn't coat them with blood.

With careful steps, I moved through the rooms, scanning for anything that might be unusual. Beyond the lack of actual paintings, nothing here seemed amiss. Kamilla followed close behind me. She hadn't done anything threatening yet, which I took as an encouraging sign. I decided to see if I could gather any useful information from her. Twisting my head from side to side, I made a great show of scanning the walls. "There are no pictures of the Vicomte here."

Kamilla took the bait. "The Marchioness is a fool. She doesn't want to show all her precious paintings here? Fine. But the Vicomte deserves a place of honor on these walls."

Clearly, Kamilla hadn't met the Vicomte. I doubt the man had done anything honorable in his entire life. Still, I was curious why she thought him worthy of admiration. "So true. Personally, I've been so impressed with his... What's the word?"

"Dedication. He has sworn to bring back the true Necromancer ways."

I bit back a smile. Kamilla was a zealot for Necromancer tradition. Excellent. I could work with this. "You're a Fantome. Can't you force the Marchioness to add his portrait?"

"The Vicomte has sworn to send me his portrait. Once it arrives, it shall become the centerpiece of this gallery." She turned to me. "You show interest in Necromancy then?"

"I admire it. Doesn't everyone?"

Kamilla eyed me from head to toe. It was as if she was seeing me for the first time. "I have a number of important duties for the Vicomte. One is to gather up those with Necromancer ability. My master wishes to bring them into his inner circle."

*Sure, he does. So he can drain their powers and become a Necromancer himself.*

I pushed that thought down and forced my mouth to fall open. "Is that true? How fascinating."

Kamilla stepped closer. "If you have Necromancer power, then I can take you to be trained."

*Or more accurately, drained.*

Still, my heart skipped a beat. This was the chance I'd been looking for. Kamilla may be ready to tell me about the other Necromancers. "That might be interesting, only..."

Kamilla's voice dripped with false kindness. "Only, what?"

"Would I have to go far? I mean, to be with the other Necromancers?" My palms turned slick with sweat. Would she say that the training area was here, in this gallery?

Kamilla stalked nearer. If I reached out, I could take her hand. "So you do have some power." Her eyes glittered. "The Tsar left us. He was weak. But the Vicomte remains and grows stronger. If you have any magick at all, you should tell me now. It's your duty as a citizen of the realm." Her voice lowered. "I have spells I can cast to find out, you know. It won't be pleasant."

I'd played the untrained Necromancer once before. I'd ended up imprisoned in the Midnight Cloister and almost killed. I wasn't about to make the same mistake twice. "No, I'm afraid I don't have any ability with magick."

All the light drained from Kamilla's eyes. "I feared as much. You're a Royal, through and through."

"Although, I would be honored to serve the Vicomte in other ways. Where are the other Necromancers being trained? Perhaps I can help." I clasped my hands together in supplication. "I truly wish to be of service to such a great man."

Kamilla pursed her thin lips. I held my breath. Was she really going to tell me where Ada was? "Perhaps."

"I'll do anything. Really." I was pleading. I didn't care.

"I shall ask the Vicomte. He may find something for you to do. If I took you to the others..." She tapped her chin again, thinking. "The ceremonial play for Theodora is a possibility."

Excitement sparked in my chest. This was my first real clue to Ada's whereabouts. Ceremonial play. Theodora. That sounded like a Royal event. "Where is this play?" Kamilla didn't answer. "What's wrong?"

Then I saw it. A shape moved under Kamilla's skin, right at her neckline. Every corner of my soul went on alert. I'd seen this before. It was a bone crawler. All the Tsar's servants had one of these creatures implanted under their flesh. I'd seen the process myself at the Midnight Cloister when my Sisters received their bone crawlers.

Kamilla lifted her hand to her neck. "Did you command this?"

I took a half step backward. "I didn't do anything."

Rage tightened her features. "Don't play the innocent with me. My bone crawler responded to you. I felt it. The insect only shifts on my command or the Tsar's." Kamilla stepped around me slowly. Her voice dripped with menace. "Some Fantomes have been testing new spells with their bone crawlers."

I hadn't thought of that, but if a Fantome was powerful enough, they could force their own bone crawler to do a few things. It wouldn't be wielding hybrid magick so much as manipulating a part of their body. Yet why would a Fantome do such a thing? Was there unrest about following the Tsar?

"I won't defile the old ways with such sacrilege." Kamilla's voice turned shrill. "Are you in league with them? Have you come here to spy on me?"

"I'm not allied with any Fantomes, I swear." My fingers itched to pull in magick. However doing so would expose me as the Necromancer I was. Just a few seconds ago, I had Kamilla convinced I was a Royal without magick. Maybe I could still make this work. "I'm a loyal subject to the realm. That's all."

Kamilla stopped her pacing. Her features softened with a new kind of calm. The sight was more alarming than her previous rage. "Hold now. I heard tell of a Caster girl. She was the one who sent the Tsar into exile. Whenever a bone crawler got near her, the insect would shift. And when she touched it, there was a flare of purple light."

*Gods-damn it. That was me, all right.*

I slapped on a look of Royal indignation. "You're insane. How could someone with no magick command the bone crawler inside you?"

Kamilla raised her left fist again. Her totem rings gleamed in the lantern light. "Guards!" One of her bands flashed with blue light. Smoke filled the room as two massive skeletons appeared, both wearing battle armor.

They headed straight for me.

I reached out with my mage senses, desperate to pull Necromancer power into my soul. The air was heavy with magick, but also with warding spells. I could sense the energy I needed. It hung in the air all around me. Sadly, the warding spells prevented me from pulling it in. I pressed against the energy block. Perhaps it was something I could break through.

Perhaps.

And even if I failed, it would still hurt like blazes. That was the least of my problems.

The skeletons grasped me from both sides, holding me firmly in place. I fought against their grip. The most I could do was rustle my dress.

Kamilla grinned. "Oh, you're a clever liar. I felt you just now. You were trying to pull in Necromancer magick." She eyed my gown. "Here you are, hiding as a fancy girl. All this time, we've been searching every filthy corner of the realm. I must admit, no one thought a Royal would take you in." She shook her head. "This won't end well for your friend."

"Leave Amelia out of this."

"You're in no position to demand anything!" Little bits of spittle flew from her mouth as she spoke. "I won't allow you to exile the Vicomte like you did the Tsar. I'll destroy you, right now and slowly. Then, just before you breathe your last, I'll make you watch the death of your friend."

My heart pounded so hard the whoosh in my ears became deafening. "I'm a Necromancer, yes. But I want the old ways returned, the same as you do. Whatever the Vicomte told you, it isn't true. If he gathers Necromancer magick into himself, then it will be for his glory alone. Not ours."

"More lies. And liars deserve pain." She raised her fist again.

*Here comes another spell from her totem rings.*

I couldn't give her another chance to cast. What happened next took only seconds, yet it felt as if time moved extra slowly. Closing my eyes, I reached out with my mage senses. A web of warding spells surrounded me. The tiny cords of energy worked together to create a magickal wall that blocked me from pulling in power.

That wall had to come down.

Every muscle in my body braced. Pain was coming.

Using all my focus, I punched through the warding spells and reached for the energy beyond. Agony shot through my body as if every bone I had was shattered. Still, I gritted my teeth and pulled Necromancer energy in to me. Magick careened through my limbs, making my veins feel like they were on fire. I held in a scream as more energy poured into me.

Once I held enough power, I expelled my Necromancer magick into the delicate strands of Kamilla's warding spell. The thin cords began to glow so brightly even Kamilla could see them. She froze in place.

That was when I made her warding spell implode.

A crash sounded, reminding me of glass breaking. The magickal web of blue light burst into pieces. The wards shattered. Thin strands of brilliance cascaded to the floor like dried leaves. The two skeletons that Kamilla created fell backward as well. Breaking the wards had severed their ties to Kamilla as well.

With the wards gone, the worst of the pain drained from my body. I swung around to face the skeletons and began drawing in more Necromancer energy. These warriors needed to answer to me.

Kamilla had the same notion. Unfortunately, she'd had time to summon additional power while I'd been breaking apart the wards. Now, she released her magick onto the skeletons. Blue mist surrounded the bony creatures. Within seconds, they hopped back up to standing. Turning in unison, they rushed toward me.

I quickly thought through my options. Since breaking the wards, I'd pulled in a little more energy. Not enough to command the skeletons.

But there were other ways to defeat them.

Raising my arm, I sent a fresh wave of magick out from my left hand. A blue haze filled the air around the skeletons. The mist solidified into a hailstorm of tiny teeth, each one sharp as a razor. The miniature bones sliced through the skeletons, shredding them into a pile of white shards.

I allowed myself a small smile. It was a good bit of spell casting. There was no time to gloat, though. Kamilla was still able to fight. I needed to draw in more energy for the next round of our battle. I pulled fresh power into me, but it came through as a thin trickle. The problem was obvious. After breaking the wards, my body felt as shredded at the defeated skeletons. Even as I summoned in more power, I knew I wasn't fast enough.

Kamilla raised her fist. The totem rings gleamed on her fingers. "Bone needles."

*By the Sire. Not bone needles.*

Another blue mist formed on the gallery floor. It twisted into a small vortex that pulled up all the bits of broken skeleton. My heart sank. As much as it hurt to break through a magick ward, bone needles would be far worse.

The haze settled into the floor. I made to run, yet my legs wouldn't go fast enough. Long needles of bone shot out from the floorboards, forming a makeshift cone around me. I felt every sharp tip as it pierced the top layer of my skin. I froze in place. Any more movements would only cause me pain.

Kamilla stalked up to me. A satisfied smile rounded her mouth. "Whatever shall I do now?" She tapped her chin. "I could skewer you through the brain which would mean a fast death. And where's the justice in that? You deserve to suffer for your crimes." She snapped her fingers, and a long needle of bone pierced through my thigh.

I kept my features calm. *Whatever happens, don't show any pain.* "Isn't it the Vicomte's right to choose how I die? Surely, he would want me brought to him."

"I'm a Grand Mistress. I keep my own counsel on how best to protect my master. Until he has enough Necromancer power, I'm going to keep him from the likes of you." She snapped her fingers again, and another sliver of bone jutted into my stomach.

It took everything I had not to moan. My insides felt on fire. Now I was a good mage, but I was also a practical one. I knew when I needed help. This was definitely one of those times. I reached inside my soul for whatever magick I had left. There wasn't much, yet I focused it all into one word. "Tamu."

"How dare you? That's a Creation Caster word." Kamilla bared her teeth. The bone crawler under her skin began to shift again. She set her hand on her throat. "This is what you did to the Tsar, isn't it? Creation Caster magick combined with Necromancer power. You want to destroy the Vicomte just like you did the Tsar." Her face turned wild with rage. "I won't allow it! Do you hear me?" She raised both arms high, and bone needles sliced through me. Arms, legs, belly, lungs… The needles pierced my body and burned with pain.

Kamilla stood only inches away from me. With a snap of her fingers, a bone needle began edging toward my face. It pierced my cheek, its angle leading it directly toward my brain.

This was it. I was good as dead.

I took in a deep breath, although the movement caused a riot of pain in my punctured lungs. If I was going to die, it wouldn't be while groveling and telling lies.

"So you know, Kamilla. I wanted to kill the Tsar. The Sire and Lady wouldn't allow me to. And if I had the chance right now, I'd kill the Vicomte."

"How I'll enjoy watching you die." Kamilla slowly raised her hand, her fingers poised for a final snap that would mean my doom.

She didn't notice the haze of red mist forming behind her. Although my body was pierced through with agony, I could only smile.

Rowan was coming.

The red haze solidified into his familiar shape. Tall, broad shoulders, wide chest, and a body that was solid as a mountain. His hair was wild and his features were drawn tight with rage. He took one look at the scene before him and pulled out both the short swords from his back. The blades didn't make a sound.

Rowan leaped forward, kicking Kamilla to the ground. She rolled over and stared up at him, her eyes glazed over with confusion.

"What?" She stammered. "How?"

Rowan raised his short swords high. "I don't like to kill women as a rule. But you know the saying. Destroy the mage; destroy the spell. And you've cast a bad spell."

Sweat beaded across her forehead. "I'll take it back." She snapped her fingers. The bone needles retracted into the floor. I fell forward onto my knees. Blood dripped from my mouth. My body was covered in tiny stab wounds. "See? She's free now."

Rowan looked over to me. All the rage in the realm shone in his eyes. "Sometimes, I break my own rules." He brought his swords down in a scissor-like motion and lopped off Kamilla's head. Her face was frozen in a scream as her skull rolled across the floor.

I couldn't say I felt bad about that.

The next thing I knew, Rowan scooped me into his arms. My eyes stung with tears. "Bone needles." Every word made my lungs gurgle with blood.

"Shh." Rowan kissed my brow and began a low incantation of healing. Warmth and strength spread through my body. My wounds closed over into unscarred skin. I could breathe again.

I wound my arms around his neck and pressed my cheek against his firm chest. "Thank you."

"I'll always come for you, Elea." He gently kissed my cheek.

I released my hold and leaned back. I was completely healed. Even my dress was cleaned from all the tiny bloodstains. Rowan really was the finest mage I knew. Our gazes locked.

"I know what you're about to say, Elea. I don't want you going back in that mansion. Go home and be safe. Please." He rubbed my back in slow circles. "I'll take care of everything."

Part of me wanted to believe him. I could walk away and all would be well, but even if Rowan could save Ada and the others, it was my mission to finish.

"I have to return. I found out something from Kamilla."

"Who?"

"The mage you just beheaded." After so much pain, I was feeling positively giddy with health and vigor. I couldn't resist smiling a little.

"Ah, her."

"You know the celebrations for Theodora?" These were held every year. Even my own shire had a little masquerade ball to mark the occasion. I wasn't sure if Rowan would know about them.

"I've been made aware of them recently."

"The celebrations are two days of festivities. It starts off with a play and ends with a masquerade ball. The festivities take place across the continent. Which one were you made aware of?"

"The ones held by the Montagne family. Their play will be held tonight in their gardens. Their masquerade ball takes place tomorrow."

*Montagne.* I knew that name. It was one of the ones that Amelia had listed as possibly hiding the Necromancers. Excitement sparked in my veins. A play tonight and a ball tomorrow. That meant two chances to find Ada and the others. "I need to go there."

"Those are rather exclusive events, I'm afraid."

I knew what that meant. A bastardess like me would never be allowed past the door. There was one person who could help me. The Marchioness. "I think I can get an invitation."

"I'd rather you didn't. Let me sneak you in as a Caster guard."

Caster women were small and pixie-like. I was tall and athletic. There was no way I'd blend in. Besides, Caster guards couldn't go off solo and snoop for passages to whatever was hidden underground. "No, I'll try to attend as a Royal." I had a few ideas about how to convince the Marchioness. She didn't like having Fantomes around. I might be able to help with that.

"Who do you think can get you invited?"

"The Marchioness." Much as I hated it, I rose from his hold and smoothed out the folds of my dress. "If I go and speak with her, can you take care of this place?"

Rowan's gaze turned intense. "You won't let me talk you out of this, will you?"

"Not a chance."

He looked around. "In that case, do you prefer a herd of wild animals tearing the place apart or that I burn it to the ground?"

"Burn it down. Once I'm well away, of course. I don't want any signs of what happened here."

"As my Lady wishes."

We stood toe to toe, staring at each other. Tendrils of feeling and connection wound between us. It disobeyed every tenant of Necromancer control. I wasn't sure how much I cared anymore.

"Do you wish me to go with you?" asked Rowan.

"No. The Marchioness will be more likely to help me without you there."

He blinked with mock-surprise. "I'm a member of the Caster Imperial family."

"Precisely. She had enough trouble adjusting to me as a bastard half sister to Amelia." I pictured the anger on the Marchioness's face when she spoke about having to endure a Fantome in her home. "Trust me. I know how to deal with her." *Maybe.*

"I'll still be nearby if you need me. Just say *Tamu*. He can appear and disappear in a heartbeat if you're in trouble, as you've already seen."

"I've seen. It's a strong spell." I stepped toward the door. "Thank you, Rowan."

Rowan leaned against the wall and folded his arms across his chest. "Stay safe."

A headache started biting into my temples. All the weeks of searching were beginning to drain me. I shook it off and walked away.

*There will be time enough to sleep when the Necromancers are safe.*

For now, it was time to have a discussion with the Marchioness.

*J* sped back to the Havilland mansion. Some of the servants give me odd stares as I walked along the rolling green. Nothing surprising there. They probably didn't expect to see me alive again. As a result, I took care to hold my head high and walk with purpose. Although the stares continued, no one actually stopped me.

Soon, I pulled open the heavy wooden door to the reception room. The Marchioness and Amelia were sitting on a pair of high-backed chairs in the far corner. They stopped speaking when I entered.

The Marchioness glanced over my shoulder. "Where's Kamilla?"

I closed the door behind me and scanned the room. No one here besides the Marchioness, Amelia, and me. *Perfect.*

In other words, there was no reason to hide the truth. "She's dead."

The Marchioness arched her brows. The look on her face ranked somewhere between fear and delight. "You killed her?"

"Essentially." I had called on Rowan to do the job, but I didn't think that nuance bore explaining right now.

Amelia slumped into her chair. "Fleur, no."

I sat down beside the Marchioness. "Don't pretend to mourn her."

The Marchioness patted her golden wig. "I won't." Her voice

seethed with rage. "I've been a prisoner in my own home since the Vicomte sent that witch here. Do you think I enjoy sending strangers to their deaths? My beloved gallery now hides too many bodies under the floorboards. I wish it was gone."

*You may get your wish.* "I have a friend waiting in the gallery. Once I leave, it will burn down in a controlled fire. Keep your servants away."

The Marchioness set her hand at her throat. "A fire? How awful. We'll have to rebuild. The Marquis won't be pleased." For a woman who'd just found out that a disaster was about to strike her property, she didn't seem too upset.

Amelia leaned forward. "You must understand. Fleur is doing this to protect you as well."

The Marchioness patted Amelia's hand. "I do, Amelia. Believe me. Otherwise, I'd be screaming bloody murder right now."

*And you'd be placed under a spell before you opened your mouth.* I decided not to share that part, however. Still, the Marchioness seemed to want to say more. "But?"

"It's not like a Necromancer to be anything but a thorn in my side. I can't help wondering." The Marchioness leaned in closer to me. "What do you want?"

*No question there.* "An ally."

"We both need one," added Amelia.

"I need an invitation to the celebrations for Theodora, both the play tonight and tomorrow's ball."

The Marchioness waved her hand. "You'll never get one of those. The Montagne family is ever so selective." She focused on Amelia. "Your half-sister is another matter. That I can do."

I lowered my voice to a menacing note. "You'll get invitations for Amelia, Philippe, and me."

"Or what?"

"Do I need to tell the story of the gallery again?"

"And why should I believe you about Kamilla?" The Marchioness folded her arms over her chest. "I should send a servant to inspect the gallery."

I stifled the urge to chuckle. "I really wouldn't do that. They won't come back alive. My friend who's waiting there is a powerful mage.

He has very explicit orders to kill any outsiders who set foot inside the gallery."

Which was a tiny lie. Rowan didn't have such orders, but I also knew the man well enough. He'd see anyone checking in on the gallery as a threat. And when it came to me, Rowan was very protective. The thought sent a wave of warm feelings through my chest.

*Rowan saved me.*

The Marchioness paused, considering. A long minute ticked by before she spoke again. "I don't believe you," she said simply. "Kamilla was a Grand Mistress Necromancer."

"So am I."

The Marchioness smiled. "Please. None still live who can best a Fantome. This is all some kind of ruse." She turned to Amelia. "Child, you must bring your bastardess sister back more often. She's ever so entertaining."

Anger heated my bloodstream. *Entertaining?* My powers were many things. A source of entertainment wasn't one of them. And after seeing the gallery, I knew Ada and the other Necromancers weren't here. There was no time to waste with these silly games.

Clearly, if the conversation was to move forward, the Marchioness needed more convincing.

I was happy to oblige.

Slowly rising to my feet, I lifted my arm and pulled in Necromancer energy. The bones in my left hand soon glowed blue. "My name is Elea. I'm the Grand Mistress Necromancer who sent the Tsar into exile." I released my power, sending a cloud of blue smoke across the chamber floor. For extra effect, I added small silver lightning bolts into the depths. "Kamilla is dead. I need you help. What is your answer?"

"I heard the stories, yet I never thought—" All the blood drained from the Marchioness's face. "The Vicomte said that he was the one who sent the Tsar into exile. He used one of his machines."

"That's a lie," said Amelia. "Elea did it."

The Marchioness nodded slowly. "Elea."

At last, we were getting somewhere. "You asked me before what I wanted. Your gallery is going to burn to the ground. You will allow it to do so. You will say only lovely things about the visit today from

Amelia, Philippe, and me." I made the smoke billow higher about the chamber. "And you will get me an invitation to the Montagne play and ball."

The Marchioness frowned. "This is blackmail."

"You haven't heard my full terms yet. As a gesture of my gratitude, I'll cast spells across your entire property against future Necromancers. They won't be able to hurt you and yours."

The Marchioness pursed her lips. "And?"

"What do you mean?" asked Amelia. "Isn't that enough?"

"No," said the Marchioness. "There's always a catch."

"True," I said. "The spells will protect me against you as well. If you betray me to the Vicomte, I'll know. I'll find you, and it won't be pleasant."

The Marchioness rubbed her delicate fingers across her temples. She suddenly looked much older. "Believe me, I'd love to have some security against these awful mages. Even if you cast these wards, what good will it do? The Vicomte is sure to send another Fantome. Our family is too powerful to ignore."

"I can't stop them from arriving, but with the proper spells, they won't be able to harm you, your servants, or your property. I'll add in spells of forgetfulness so they never contact the Vicomte about the wards."

"Interesting." The Marchioness tapped her chin. "We've had a plague of fires this summer. It would be a believable way for Kamilla to die. And I would love a measure of protection from your kind. No offense."

"None taken."

The Marchioness lifted her chin. "I agree to your terms."

A weight of worry dropped from my shoulders. "Excellent."

"How soon can you ward our property?"

"I'll come by tomorrow morning." An acrid smell filled the air, and I knew exactly where it came from. "It would be best if we left now. I do believe your gallery is on fire." I snapped my fingers, and the haze filling the room disappeared. "Be sure to act surprised when the servants arrive."

Across the chamber, the door whipped open. "Marchioness! There's a fire!"

The Marchioness did an admirable job of widening her eyes and gasping. "I'd better go." She turned to me. "You can see yourselves out, I hope?"

I curtsied. "Don't worry about us."

As the Marchioness rushed from the room, Philippe rushed in. "Have you heard? There's a fire!"

"We know all about it." Amelia stepped up and wrapped her arm protectively through mine. "I'll explain everything at home." She beamed at me. "But Elea has it all under control, just as she always does."

Philippe quirked his brows at me. "Is *that* how it works?"

I opened my mouth, ready to say that Philippe was right—my emotions got the better of me all the time. But seeing the trusting look in Amelia's big blue eyes, I couldn't say any of that. She needed to think I was always in control.

"I say it's time for us to leave."

As I stepped out the door, I realized that Amelia wasn't the only one who should question my skills. I got through today by the skin of my teeth. What would tomorrow bring? Too many people were relying on me, and my control was clearly at a breaking point. A leaden feeling settled into my bones.

*Perhaps it's just a matter of time before I got us all killed.*

*L*ate morning light sifted through the trees. Everything seemed cast in an emerald glow as I strode through the woods behind the Havilland estate. I'd been at it for hours, searching for the perfect places to set up my protection spells.

I paused beside one of the larger trees—a massive fir—and reached out with my mage senses. My last spell was now so far enough away. The magick was barely detectable. It was time to cast again.

Frustration tightened up my neck and shoulders. I'd wanted to be done by now. Unfortunately, the lands here were so vast, it was all taking longer than I'd like. I needed to return to Amelia's and get ready for tonight's ball.

A red mist appeared on the ground. Excitement twisted through my stomach.

*Creation Caster magick.*

The mist swirled upward, solidifying into the familiar outline of Rowan. I wanted to run over and embrace him. Instead, I stayed stock-still and calm looking.

Even so, I greedily soaked in the sight of him. Rowan stood tall and broad-shouldered in his fitted brown leathers. A pair of short swords was strapped to his back. All this was the classic garb for a Creation Caster, but the loose brown hair, piercing green eyes, and rugged features were all Rowan. His mouth tilted into a crooked smile. My body suddenly felt overheated even though I stood in the shade.

"Elea."

"Rowan."

"I needed to see you. Are you well? Fully recovered?" He stepped closer. My pulse sped faster.

"I'm fine." There were a dozen things I wanted to say in this moment. How I felt about him. The danger my emotions embodied. The way I desperately wanted to kiss him again.

"You look perfect."

"Thank you." A blush colored my cheeks. I stepped back under the cool shade of the fire tree, leaned against the huge trunk, and forced my features into the classic show of Necromancer calm. *Don't lose your head. Keep control.* I cleared my throat. "Since you're here, I wanted to ask you something."

"Anything."

"Amelia's been helping me search for my lost Sisters. Yesterday, she got some strange news."

Suddenly, there stood six-plus feet of Rowan right before me, his body giving off waves of heat. He rested his palms on the massive trunk so his arms framed my head. At least a foot of space still separated us. His green eyes turned so intense. "What did you hear?"

"Someone's asking for Amelia's hand in marriage."

Rowan's features didn't so much as twitch. "That's happened before."

I lifted my chin. "You seem to know a lot about it. Something come up in your political work with Genesis Rex?"

"I know what you're suspecting, but don't go near this, Elea. It isn't safe. Keep looking for your Necromancers and stay out of Caster politics."

My brows lifted. "So, Genesis Rex is negotiating for her hand in marriage, isn't he?"

"And if he is?" Rowan moved closer until our bodies were inches apart. I couldn't tell if he wanted to hold me or was getting ready to press off and run. Maybe he didn't know either.

"You should tell me, Rowan."

"When it comes to Genesis Rex, there are some things I can't discuss, Elea. Even with you."

"If there's some marriage being planned between Rex and Amelia, then it's my business. She's my friend, Rowan. Everyone around her is trying to pull her puppet strings, and it's all because I stepped into her life."

"And if a wedding was in the works, what objections would you have?"

I'd met Genesis Rex before. "The obvious one. Rex is simply too old for her."

Rowan narrowed his eyes. It didn't seem fair that the man should have thick lashes on top of all his other gifts. "What about Rex? Not worried about his side of things?" There was an edge to his tone that I couldn't quite place or understand.

"Your uncle seemed nice enough. Even so, he's lived a long life. Amelia's young in a lot of ways. She's sweet and trusting. Your uncle seemed very—" I looked around the forest, trying to find the right words. "Worldly."

"You care about her, don't you?"

I nodded. It was a weakness to have gotten attached to another person so quickly, but I had. "I don't want to see her used as a pawn."

Rowan sighed. "She's the Vicomte's only heir. There's no way to prevent that. If it isn't Rex, it could be someone else." He lifted his hand and gently rubbed my cheek with the backs of his fingers. Every brush of his skin sent pleasant shivers through my core. Rowan leaned in until his breath brushed my ear. "Not all of us are lucky enough to be Commoners like you."

I frowned as his words sunk in. I leaned my head against the trunk, despair weighing down my bones. "This is why we're impossible. I'm a Commoner and you're a member of the Imperial family. You shouldn't be anywhere near me."

"I told you that I'd find a way for us. If you don't believe me, you can walk away at any time." He shifted his head until his mouth hovered just above mine. "But I think you believe me."

I meant to march off, I really did. Somehow, I couldn't move a muscle. Instead, I slowly licked my lips. "So, what's this 'way' you're talking about?"

"I'm working on it."

"I won't be some secret, Rowan."

"And I don't want that either. We belong together, Elea. Openly." His voice deepened, and every word seemed to resonate through my soul. "When you left me in the desert, it was the hardest night of my life. I thought the pain of losing you would fade, but it only grew worse. I want you with me, and I think you want me too." He brushed his nose up and down mine. My legs shook. "I will make things happen between us, Elea. And in whatever way you want. No secrets. Count on it."

With those words, something inside me snapped. I leaned in, pressing my mouth to his. All of a sudden, I couldn't touch him enough. Our kiss turned fierce. I brushed my fingertips against the scruff of his chin, then ran my palms over the firm planes of his chest and even slid my hand down his thigh, feeling the steel of his muscles under the soft leather.

Rowan's mouth devoured mine. Still, his hands stayed firmly in place, set against the tree trunk while mine explored. Every so often, he'd let out a low growl of pleasure to show what he liked. It was a rush of power to know how I could affect him.

Finally, Rowan broke our kiss and stepped away. I kept leaning against the tree trunk, panting for breath. "What's wrong?"

"Transport spell." Rowan nodded to a small red cloud that had appeared on the forest floor. Red meant it was a Creation Caster. Someone was looking for him.

My shoulders slumped. *A man like Rowan can't forget his responsibilities and run off.* He may want to, but his people would never let him.

Rowan hitched his thumbs into the waistband of his leathers. "I can see what you're thinking." He gestured to the solidifying mist. "My responsibilities won't always interfere between us. I give you my word."

"And I believe you." The words tumbled from my mouth, unbidden. What really shocked me was how fiercely I meant them. Beyond all reason, I trusted Rowan over anyone else in my life. Not that I should. My judgment wasn't the finest. The last man I trusted, Tristan, had lied to me and tricked me into taking on a curse.

Linden materialized in the clearing beside us. He appeared just as I remembered him—a lanky man with light brown hair and a missing arm. He'd changed since Rowan and I had freed him from the Midnight Cloister. After his release, Linden had looked positively skeletal. He'd been the victim of one of the Tsar's experiments. It made my heart glad to see him looking so fit. He smiled. "Elea! It's good to see you."

"And you, Linden."

He turned to Rowan. "You're needed back at camp. Your uncle has new ideas for tonight."

My eyes widened. "Tonight? As in, the Montagne celebrations for Theodora?" There were two events for the celebration. The play took place tonight while the ball would be held tomorrow.

Linden frowned. There was no real anger in it though. "I can't speak about that."

"You and your secrets." The Casters were forever hiding where they were going and what they were doing. When it came to Genesis Rex, their secrets turned extreme. Rex had a series of body doubles. All the guards wore leather helms over their faces to hide which man was their king. Rex was constantly under death threats, but still. "There's no point in playing coy. Both of you are too easy to read. I'm going to attend tonight as well. I'll see you there."

Rowan's brows drew together. "It's impossible for you to attend."

I shrugged. "I can be very persuasive."

Linden shook his head. "I've seen the aftermath of your magickal handiwork. I don't even want to know how you plan to get an invitation. I've no doubt that you will succeed."

"Does that mean you'll both be there?" I tried to ignore the way the thought of Rowan made my heart thud faster.

Rowan gave me another one of his crooked grins. "Yes, I'll be present." He stepped up and pressed his palm against my cheek. I leaned into his touch. "Remember what I said." His voice was so low, only I could hear him. "We'll be together." He moved in close enough to whisper in my ear. "Look for me at the ball tonight. I'll be guarding Rex."

"I will."

He brushed a gentle kiss on my forehead and walked back to

Linden. Soon, a red haze formed around both of them, and they vanished.

For a long minute, I stared at the spot where Rowan had last stood. Bit by bit, my Necromancer training came back to me. Finally, I scrubbed my hands over my face and got back to work. I needed to ward this property, prepare for the ball at the Montagne estate, and forget about Rowan for a while. Too many lives were depending on me to do anything else.

There was no doubt about it. Casting these gods-damned protection spells was taking far too long. Still, I couldn't stop now without risking everything I had cast before.

As much as I wanted to leave, there was no other option. I simply had to finish my spellwork.

I followed a trail deeper into the forest. Stout trees towered around me, their heavy branches blotting out any sign of the late afternoon sun. Hours had passed since I'd last spied another soul. No question why, either. This part of the forest was a muddy mess. With every step, my boots took on fresh streams of chilly sludge. Swarms of angry gnats buzzed around my head. The stale smell of rotting leaves filled the air. And my wards weren't done yet.

*How I wish this was over.*

I trudged onto some high ground under an oak tree. At least, the earth here only oozed up to my ankles. There were no gnats either. Some tension left my shoulders. This spot was a definite improvement. I paused, ready to cast again.

Closing my eyes, I reached out with my mage senses, searching for the cords of energy that I'd placed across this property. Every strand of power represented a different spell to protect the Havillands.

The spells were all there, strong and solid. My heart lightened. My work was almost done.

Raising my left hand, I spoke an incantation for giving my magick a visual form. Suddenly, my spells materialized as a glowing spider's web of blue power that stretched off in every direction—a sight only I could see. Dainty lines of energy linked every rotting leaf, ridged tree trunk, and blade of grass. The ties appeared bright, solid, and strong. I lowered my hand and sighed.

*My casting's complete.*

Satisfaction warmed my chest. The entire Havilland estate was now fully protected from virtually any mage. I glanced down at my mud-stained frock. The land might be fixed, but when it came to my appearance? What a mess. Normally, this wouldn't bother me. I grew up on a farm, after all. The Montagne passion play started in a matter of hours. My pulse sped as I thought about what Kamilla had said in the Havilland's gallery. Ada and the others might be hidden at Montage estate.

*I could rescue them all tonight. The thought made my head swim.*

I patted my pocket. Today, I'd headed out with my witness watch. I pulled out the device and glanced at the face. I still had until midnight tomorrow night. After that, the totem ring would be fully charged and my friends were good as dead. Determination made my hands ball into fists.

Time to find out if Ada, Veronique, and the others were at the Montagne estate. My heart warmed at the thought. Perhaps I might even find some other trained Necromancers as well.

I was tired of being the last of my kind.

No matter what happened, I needed to get ready for tonight. Unfortunately, I'd wasted too much time casting spells today. I'd have to transport to Amelia's mansion. I bit back a groan. Transport spells were the worst. They hurt like blazes and drained me of magick for hours.

I sighed. There was no avoiding it. I'd never get a carriage in time.

Raising my left arm, I gathered fresh Necromancer power to me. An azure mist swirled around my feet as the bones in my left palm glowed blue. I spoke the incantation for a transport spell to Amelia's chamber.

*Strong as stone and fast as wind*
*Magick moving without end*
*Take me to my heart's desire*
*Travel racing fast as fire*

Darkness enveloped me. My muscles tensed, preparing for the pain that would surely follow. Transportation magick always hurt. It only got worse when my energy was low from casting, like it was today. The transport hit me like a boulder. Every bone felt crushed under enormous weight. Agony streamed through my limbs. All air left my body. I couldn't even scream.

The pain vanished. The spell was complete, but I couldn't focus on my new surroundings. Air was my first priority. I leaned forward, bracing my arms on my knees as I gasped in breath after breath. Seconds passed before I noticed the familiar lines of Amelia's chamber, from her elegantly carved furniture to her many tapestries of unicorns. Then, I noticed something that wasn't familiar at all.

Philippe stood half naked over Amelia's washbasin.

My mouth fell open. It wasn't that Philippe was unattractive. I just saw him as more of a brother. Maybe.

I quickly covered my eyes. "What are you doing here?"

"My chamber is occupied and I needed to wash off."

"Occupied?" I peeped through my fingers. "You have more guests?"

Philippe tossed his washcloth into the basin, picked up a white towel, and wrapped it loosely around his shoulders. Why didn't the man put on a shirt? "Who said it was a guest? One of the new chambermaids is a dirty little vixen. She wanted me to—"

I raised my hand. "I'd rather not know the specifics."

"In any case, she's now asleep in my bed, and I needed to clean up." He looked me over from head to toe. "But I'd say you're in far worse shape than I am."

I couldn't stop my smile. "That's true. Could you send in a servant to help me, assuming that there are some you haven't ravished into oblivion?"

A mischievous light danced in his eyes. "There are, in fact, one or two who are still conscious."

As a good Necromancer, I should act appalled. Philippe seemed to make everything a grand adventure. I didn't bother to keep the slyness out of my voice. "Glad to hear it."

Philippe rubbed his neck in a slow rhythm. "That was very impressive, by the by."

"What was?"

"Your transport spell. I'd never seen one before. Amelia has some magick, but not enough to—" He grinned. "You know."

My heart warmed under his compliment. Only Grand Mistress Necromancers could manage transport spells, and even then, it was a rare skill. "Thank you."

The door flew open, and Amelia stepped into the room. She was wearing a silk dressing gown with her hair tied into loops using long strips of white cloth. "Elea! When did you arrive?"

"Not long ago. I cast a transport spell from the Havilland estate after I'd finished their warding."

Amelia turned to her brother and gasped. "Philippe! Have you no shame?"

He shrugged. "Not in particular."

Amelia gripped his forearm and dragged him toward the door. "You have to leave." She paused. "No, you have to stay and put some clothes on first. What if the servants saw you this way?"

At that comment, Philippe shot me a sly look. I could guess his meaning. Most of the servants here were young, female, and had already seen him naked. I fought down a laugh.

Amelia scooped up a white shirt from the floor and handed it to her brother. "Now, put this on and leave. Summon Clothilde. We must get Elea ready."

Philippe slipped on the garment and turned to Amelia with a mock flourish. "Better?"

"Presentable." Her voice lowered to a hush. "And what were you doing in here with Elea, anyway?"

Philippe just kept on smiling. "Why are we whispering?"

"Because I don't want the servants—" Amelia rushed over to the door and pulled it open. "Just get out of here."

"I can't," said Philippe.

Amelia set her fist on her hip. "Now, you're just being contrary."

"No, he isn't." I pointed past Philippe's shoulder. A servant stood in the hallway beyond. I'd seen that kind of multicolored livery before. It was what servants of the Vicomte wore. My hands curled into fists. The last thing we needed was interference from that man.

Amelia swung around and took in the new figure. All the blood drained from her pretty face. "What are you doing here, Giles?"

"What I always do when I reach your door." Giles bowed, but the disdain in his eyes said that he thought Amelia unworthy of such a gesture. "The Vicomte would like to see you in the reception room. Now."

Amelia's eyes widened. "Daddy Dearest is here?"

Giles sniffed, a motion that showed off the thin nostrils of his overlong nose. "Obviously."

"Yes, I'll be right down." Amelia closed the door and began pacing the floor. My heart went out to her. "I haven't seen the Vicomte in years. What could he want?" She kept her voice so quiet I could hardly hear her. "Do you think he knows what we're looking for?"

"I don't think so, Amelia," I whispered. "If he knew, then the Vicomte would have sent guards, not come himself. Most likely, he's here for another purpose."

Amelia and I shared a glance. I thought back to our conversation with the Marchioness.

*The Vicomte wants to sell Amelia off in marriage.*

Philippe's charming face turned stony. "Whatever your Daddy Dearest has planned, it won't be good. And I won't let him get away with it."

"Don't be rash, Philippe. You know how he hates you already." Amelia turned to me. "Can you do anything to help?" Her gaze landed pointedly on my left hand. "Make him forget why he came here?"

I shook my head. "He's sure to have Fantomes nearby." I stepped closer and spoke in a whisper. "And if I'm to reveal myself, it must be for a higher purpose. Don't forget what we're working toward." It was on the tip of my tongue to describe my vision of Ada and Veronique. Amelia needed to understand how horrible things really were for our friends. I'd held off before because she had such a sensitive nature. But now?

Amelia stared at the tapestry for a long minute before speaking again. "You're right. I can't forget Veronique."

"Veronique." Philippe folded his arms over his chest. "What a waste to try to help *that one*."

Amelia raised her chin. "We're not having this discussion again, Philippe."

I stepped closer to Philippe and spoke in a gentle voice. "It's more than Veronique, you know."

Philippe rubbed his neck in a nervous rhythm. "I know." His carefree face became lined with worry. "I don't like the idea of you risking yourself, Amelia."

"Thank you. I'll be fine. Elea will be with me."

I took a half step backward. "I'm not at all sure I should accompany you."

Amelia grasped my arm. "He won't recognize you, I swear." Her fingers trembled against my skin. "And you're so powerful. I'd feel better with you at my side."

"He'll recognize me. I sent the Tsar into exile."

She rolled her eyes. "You saw him for a day. I've known the man all my life. If we dress you as a Royal, he won't look at you twice."

I shot Philippe a questioning look. Amelia had said this before, but I still wasn't sure. "Is this true?"

"Certainly," said Philippe. "Women rank about the same level as furniture in the Vicomte's world. Royal women even less so. If you're perfumed and dressed up like a little doll, he'll never recognize you."

"See?" Amelia gripped my arm even tighter. "You have to join me."

I didn't like this. However, if my presence calmed Amelia, it was probably for the best. A worried Amelia could say or do anything. "I will."

She sighed. "Thank you."

"I'll be there as well, of course." Philippe forced a grin. The motion had none of his normal enthusiasm. "Until we meet in the reception room." He trudged out the door.

Once we were alone once more, Amelia rounded on me. "I'm more concerned about rumors. You don't think the Vicomte heard about everything that's happened?"

I knew what she meant, and it wasn't a short list of happenings, either. A dead Fantome. Gallery burned to the ground. Spells cast all over the Montagne estate. I straightened my shoulders and fixed Amelia with a determined gaze. "Honestly? I do think he's here about your marriage." *Perhaps.*

"Marriage I can handle." Amelia gave me a sad smile. "The idea is foul, but there have been whispers for years. Yet if he suspects something larger, then he'll send a Fantome to live with me, like he did with the Marchioness." She shivered. "Are they really as terrible as they say?"

*Worse.*

"I can take care of them. That's all that matters." I took her hands in mine. "Whatever takes place, we'll find a way. Believe it."

"Yes, Elea. We can do this." As Amelia bustled off in search of Clothilde and my evening gown, her words echoed through my mind.

*We can do this.*

It was two of us against the Vicomte and all his Fantomes. We could certainly do this. However, I feared we had a better chance to find a single grain of sand on a beach than to locate our Necromancer friends in time.

𝒶melia, Philippe, and I stepped into her small reception room. The place looked hastily set up. Although all the tarps had been pulled off all the chairs, the floor was covered in dust, cobwebs hung from the ceiling, and the plaster walls were bare. Not that the Vicomte seemed to notice. His lanky form paced along the back wall, an angular figure in a garish pink coat with tall black boots. Multiple watches hung from his pockets. The bright colors of his clothes made for an odd contrast to the man himself. The Vicomte's hair, eyes, and skin were all a dull shade of gray.

He hadn't changed a bit.

I worked hard to keep my face level. The last time I'd seen the Vicomte, we were at the Midnight Cloister. That was when I'd sent his old master, the Tsar, into exile. At the time, I was bloodied and wearing fitted Caster leathers. Amelia said the Vicomte wouldn't notice me in the Royal garb. And in truth, it was amazing how quickly she and her servants had transformed my appearance. I now wore an elaborate blue gown with my hair piled high atop my head.

*Please let this disguise be enough.*

The Vicomte stopped his manic pacing. His gaze locked on Amelia. *So far, so good.* "Where have you been, daughter?"

Amelia curtsied. "Hello, Daddy Dearest."

Philippe bowed slightly at the waist. "Your Eminence."

Amelia gently nudged me in the ribs with her elbow, breaking me out of my memories of the Midnight Cloister and fighting there with Rowan.

*Oh, yes. I'm supposed to greet the Vicomte as well.*

I curtsied low. "It's an honor to meet you, Your—"

"You made me wait far too long, daughter." The Vicomte didn't so much as glance in my direction before he marched directly over to Amelia. My shoulders slumped with relief. Amelia was right. Gaspard didn't pay much attention to anyone.

The Vicomte paused before Amelia, his gray eyes narrowing into slits. "I suspect that you've been up to no good."

Amelia met his gaze straight on. *Brave girl.* "I don't know what you mean."

"Don't I? We'll see." The Vicomte's glare shifted between Philippe and me. My heart sank.

*This is it. He knows everything.*

Philippe lifted his chin. "You have something to say?"

"You'll speak when I tell you to." The Vicomte rounded on Amelia, looking her over from head to toe. It reminded me of the inspection one might give a horse before deciding whether it was suitable for sale. "And you, daughter, will do as you're told for once."

"Depends on what you wish." Amelia's voice came out strong. Even so, I couldn't miss the slight wobble of her chin.

"I have plans for your future," said the Vicomte slowly.

Some of the tension left my body. He didn't know that we were rescuing the lost Necromancers.

*This is about the marriage.*

"Excuse me." Philippe stepped protectively between the Vicomte and his sister. "If you have a situation in mind for my sister, then it should first be discussed with me. I am her elder brother, after all."

"And to me, you're nothing. I adopted your sister and kept you along as her pet. So, when I want to hear your voice, boy, I'll ask for it." The Vicomte pulled out one of the many watches from his pockets and examined the face. "And I don't have time for this nonsense."

I leaned forward, trying for a better glimpse of the watch. Was this the one with the totem ring inside it? How lovely would that be? I could simply grab the vortex watch and run.

My desire became overwhelming. Without even realizing it, I stepped closer to the Vicomte.

*By the Sire. How could I be so foolish? My body froze with fear.*

Amelia crossed the floor to stand between the Vicomte and me. In one smooth movement, she took over the Vicomte's attention while gently ushering me out of view. *Clever girl.*

"What plans do you have for me, Father?"

"You're to marry Genesis Rex, the ruler of the Creation Casters. He's a brute and a thug, so don't plan for an easy life."

"Am I to meet him before the wedding?" asked Amelia coolly.

"Yes, as a matter of fact. You'll meet him tonight at the play and be grateful for it." The Vicomte fiddled with some dials on his watch. "Barbarian fools. Tiptoeing through the shadows with their body doubles and long helms."

Philippe wrapped his arm around his sister's shoulder. "I'm afraid none of us knows what you mean."

"I mean that Rex will find my wayward daughter when he's good and ready." The Vicomte glared at Amelia. "It's a garden party, so I expect he'll pull you into a promising shrubbery and have his way with you."

"I see." Amelia's calm broke as a flush crawled up her neck. Suddenly, I wished I'd killed the Vicomte back at the Midnight Cloister.

"Thank you for that elegant description." Philippe bowed again. "Now, if you'll excuse us."

"Not until you're dismissed." The Vicomte snapped his watch face shut and jammed the device back into his overlarge pocket. "I have something else to say to you two."

Two? I stepped back farther into the shadows. Indeed, the Vicomte wasn't even counting me as a person in the room. *Perfect.*

The Vicomte eyed at Philippe and Amelia in turn. "I said before that I suspect you've been up to no good, and I intend to get to the truth of the matter."

Philippe put on his most suave smile. "Whatever do you mean?"

"The gallery at the Havilland estate just burned down. Know anything about it?" the Vicomte's beady eyes narrowed. "No?"

None of us said a word. My legs felt boneless beneath me.

*Here it is. We're caught.*

"I thought as much," said the Vicomte. "My spies tell me that my useless daughter and her rogue brother were in visiting the Havilland mansion. After that, a fire broke out. Damned odd coincidence, I'd say."

With her red ringlets, wide blue eyes, and bow-shaped mouth, Amelia's face became a doll-like image of innocence. "You can't possibly think—"

"Quiet, you." The Vicomte's gray complexion seemed to darken with anger. "The Montagne estate is guarded by a troop of Fantomes. They'll attend every celebration. If any of you are guilty of sneaking around behind my back, then they'll find it out. If I find you've betrayed me, then I've given orders for them to peel Philippe like a pear." He pointed at Amelia. "And as for you, my dear daughter, they have instructions to turn your brain into mush. Since your womb would still function, I'm sure a brute like Rex will never notice."

"You can't hurt me." Amelia's voice was almost a whisper. "Mother Superior at the orphanage cast spells. Philippe and I are protected from you."

"My Fantomes tell me they can break those spells. Don't test me, daughter. I will destroy you both."

My jaw locked. How dare he threaten Amelia? I wanted to crush this man while I had the chance. But I couldn't risk it. Not until I found Ada and the other Necromancers. Until my Sisters were safe, murdering the Vicomte could mean their death as well. It was a risk I simply couldn't take. With a great force of will, I stayed quiet in the shadows.

Amelia's mouth fell open. "Father, please."

"I'm far from finished. Listen to me closely, daughter. If you do anything to foil this marriage treaty, I will kill you so slowly and painfully, the gods themselves will weep for you." His voice lowered to a hiss. "Do we understand each other?"

"We do, Father."

My friend's shoulders slumped with defeat. Clearly, the Vicomte had been haranguing her for years. I made a silent vow.

*I understand you too. And you will pay for what you've done to her.*

The Vicomte stared at Amelia for a long moment. "Excellent. Now, I have more intelligent people to visit." He strode out the door, slammed it behind him, and was gone.

The moment we were alone again, Amelia crumpled into her brother's embrace. She was everything sweet, gentle, and bright. How could the Vicomte be so cruel?

Philippe patted her back. "You did well, sister."

She stepped away from his embrace and patted away the tears from her cheeks. "I always vow that I won't let him bother me, but he always does. And Fantomes will be testing us. How can we protect ourselves from them?"

"It won't be easy," I said. "But it's possible. I need you both to stay focused on why we're really attending this silly play. We must find our friends."

"Yes." Amelia straightened her shoulders. "And that we will do."

"I take it all back," said Philippe. "This plan has merit."

I frowned. "What made you change your mind? You weren't excited before in Amelia's chamber."

Philippe flashed me a roguish smile. "One reason." He lowered his voice to the barest whisper. "After your handiwork at the Havilland estate, tonight promises to be quite entertaining."

Philippe never took anything seriously. In this moment, I could have kissed him for it. I allowed myself a small grin in return. "Let's get ready. We've a big night ahead of us."

*A*melia and I sat inside a boxy carriage, waiting our turn to be received at the Montagne mansion. I fidgeted in my fluffy gown and glared out the window. All I could see was the long line of bright-colored carriages before us.

Leaning forward, I peeped out the window again. The cobblestone road led up to a low wall made of white rock. After that there towered a pristine castle made of pearl-colored marble. The square structure stood three stories high and was decorated with far too many turrets for my taste. Then again, the Royals did everything to excess. I huffed out a breath.

Amelia gave me a sympathetic grin. "This is the worst part, you know. Waiting." She looked perfect in her pink gown. This edition was adorned with dainty lace and tiny pearls. I didn't know how many versions she had of the same dress, but they were all unique and gorgeous on her. I yanked on the collar of my gray dress. It was far too large in the skirts for my liking. Even so, I was pleased with the color. Perhaps I could blend into the background.

Philippe pulled his steed up to the window. The setting sun cast a golden halo behind his blond head. His gaze immediately fell on his sister. "It's all right to be worried."

Amelia sighed. "It feels silly with so much more at stake." She gave me another sweet smile. "You're the one with the most to risk here."

I stared at her for a moment. What were they talking about? Then it hit me. Genesis Rex and her engagement. In all my obsessing about Ada and the others, I'd forgotten that Amelia was about to meet her future betrothed.

Philippe kept his steed at a perfect pace with the window. "I'm sure you'll find him a good man. When you meet him, that is."

"Oh, I have met Rex," I said quickly. "Didn't I tell you?" Suddenly, I felt like the worst friend in the realm.

Amelia brightened a little. "No, you didn't."

"He's a very fine man, Amelia." In truth, he was older and a bit flighty. I didn't share that part. "I spoke with him a number of times."

There, that was putting it nicely. Still, Amelia and Philippe kept staring at me. Clearly, they wanted more detail on the positive side of Genesis Rex. It took a few moments, but I finally came up with something. "He was very well respected by his people."

"What were the Casters like? Would I be allowed any freedom?"

"Caster women are given a lot of leeway. Many are warriors and healers."

"But what about the Imperial family?"

"Oh, that." I worried my lower lip with my teeth. I'd promised Rowan never to reveal his true purpose here. Surely I could give Amelia a little information to ease her mind. "I'm close with someone who knows the Imperial family. If I see him tonight, I'll find out all I can."

Amelia's eyes widened. "Is your friend another mage like you?"

"He is." The less said on that account, the better.

Philippe pulled his mount closer to the carriage window. "Only a few minutes more. Are my ladies presentable?"

Amelia forced on a smile. "We're ready."

"Excellent." He guided his horse farther away from our carriage.

Although night was falling, the temperature inside the wagon seemed to increase with every inch we moved closer to the castle. I leaned out the window, eager for a breath of fresh air and a better look at the estate.

The cobblestone road ended at the castle's outer wall. The heavy wooden doors had been flung open. We rode on to the castle's front entrance. Our carriage paused before a flight of brilliant white steps that ended in a small landing. There, the Baron and Baroness de Montagne greeted visitors. Both of them were petite, pale, and slender. They had white-blonde hair and ice-blue eyes. Not like the kind of people you'd suspect would be imprisoning Necromancers under their home. Then again, I didn't suspect my best friend of tricking me into a curse, so how well could I judge?

I leaned back inside the carriage. "Not long now."

Amelia sat up and gripped my hands. "You don't think they're suffering, do you?"

No question which *"they"* she was referring to. The Necromancers. Memories of my vision appeared. Little Ada being held down... The flash of blood and steel... And her pitiful cries for help. I still didn't want to tell Amelia about it. What would that accomplish anyway?

It was an effort to keep my features calm and even. "I think we need to focus on finding a way into the dungeons under the Montagne mansion. Tell me about them again."

Amelia frowned. "I already did." We'd discussed them for a long time on the ride over. Amelia knew there were old dungeons under the castle. Most likely, those had been refurbished to make a magickal prison.

"One last time." Talking always calmed Amelia, and my friend seemed to be unraveling as we neared the front door.

"Philippe and I came here as children. We'd always end up playing in the garden. There's a huge stretch of land behind the castle. The older boys would threaten to throw the girls into the old dungeon. There were these wells in the gardens, you see. If you pulled out the copper basins, then you'd find out that they are actually old air-shafts for the dungeon below. One of the Montagne girls even fell in once by mistake. Broke her leg and everything."

I nodded slowly as if this was the first time Amelia told the story. We'd discussed the plan on the ride over. Even so, it felt good to say it one last time. "Once it becomes dark, we'll split up and look for the different wells."

Amelia twisted the folds of her skirt with her fingers. "I still worry about the Fantomes."

"They're holding the play in the gardens, right?" I didn't wait for

Amelia to answer. We both knew this to be true. "They'll be hundreds of Royals walking about the garden paths and looking into the wells. All we need do tonight is find which well leads to the dungeons." I planned to do more, if possible, but Amelia didn't need to know that. "We still have until tomorrow at midnight to save everyone."

"You're right. It's just a quiet walk through the gardens. What could go wrong?" The wagon rolled to a stop. Amelia gave my hands a shaky squeeze. "We're here."

The carriage's half door swung open, and my heart leaped into my throat. *This was it. Ada could be here.*

I steeled my features and peeped outside. Philippe stood at the base of the staircase, looking dapper in his purple velvet overcoat. He offered me his hand to help me down from the carriage. I didn't need any assistance, but I also didn't need to attract any attention. "Thank you."

I took Philippe's hand and stepped down. Amelia followed along behind me, and together we all walked up the golden staircase to our hosts. The willowy Baroness and Baron greeted Amelia and Philippe with barely-there kisses on either cheek. When it came time for my greeting, they scrunched up their noses as if a small turd had been placed before them.

*I stifled the urge to roll my eyes. Point taken. I'm not Royal and don't belong here.*

Amelia and I curtsied low. Philippe bowed gallantly. The ritual of greeting was over. The tension in my chest loosened up a little.

That had been quite easy. Now all that remained was a walk in the gardens.

I wanted to cheer. Things would go smoothly. I knew it.

I slipped past the Baron and Baroness into the castle proper. From tapestries to rugs and tables, the mansion was a monotone of white and gray. Servants scurried about everywhere. Royals huddled in small circles of conversation. There was no sign of the Vicomte. *Good.* I scanned the crowd more closely. No traces of the Fantomes, either. *Even better.*

Amelia began to follow me inside. The Baroness moved to block her. "One moment, Amelia."

I was so close now. It would be easy to slip off into the crowd. But I couldn't leave Amelia alone. My friend was already trembling.

Even so, Amelia bravely forced on a large smile. Her doll-like face was the picture of innocence. "Yes, Baroness?"

"The Baron and I have heard of your impending—how do I say it —boost in status?"

Amelia blinked. "I'm sure I don't know what you mean."

I stifled the urge to roll my eyes. If news of Amelia's engagement was already circulating, then there would be far more scrutiny on us.

*Stay positive. Things are going easily for once. Believe that, and it will come true.*

Our hosts exchanged knowing looks. The Baron was the first to speak. "We have a great honor we'd like to bestow on you." He straightened the lapels of his white silk longcoat. "We'd like you to play Theodora in the play tonight."

Worry tightened around my throat. Giving Amelia a part in the play? That would be a disaster. We'd be forced to prepare for the performance instead of look around. "Perhaps next year," I offered. "Amelia hasn't practiced."

"But we insist," said Baroness. "And there is no speaking to this play. All our dear girl needs to do is fall down, step through a gate, and come back carrying a sword. What could be simpler?"

Amelia hugged her elbows. "It's too much of an honor for me. Wouldn't one of the other Ladies be offended?"

"Nonsense. You're from the House of Theodora. Who else should play the role?" The Baroness tossed her head, making her white-blonde hair move in a single perfect wave. "And besides, it's about time your family participated again."

The Baron sniffed, an action that highlighted his very long and pale nose. "Your relatives have all but disappeared from good society."

"Michel, please." The Baroness shot her husband an angry look.

"What about the Fantomes?" asked Philippe. "You've so many here. Everyone says how they keep order in your castle. I'm sure they wouldn't appreciate a change in plans at this late hour."

The Baroness's pale pink lips rounded into a small smile. "The

Fantomes are all such dear people. There's no need to worry about them."

*A lead weight seemed to fall into my stomach. The Baroness thinks Fantomes are dear people? What kind of place is this?*

"Now, Amelia." The Baroness spoke as if addressing a small child. "You must see how important this is, considering your new, uh, role in society." She waved her dainty hand toward Philippe. "We'll give your brother a little part as well. Remember, this is a sacred play to honor the patroness of all Royals. Being selected to play any part in this ceremony is a great honor. And your family line traces directly to Theodora."

Amelia worried her lower lip with her teeth. "Which is why I must refuse. I couldn't possibly learn the ritual part so quickly."

"Fiddle-faddle," said the Baron. "Everyone knows the story of Theodora. You especially. The Fantomes will be thrilled." He seemed especially pleased with that last statement.

I eyed the Baron and Baroness carefully. When I'd met the Marchioness, it was clear how much she hated having a Fantome around. I liked that in a person. On the other hand, the Baron and Baroness spoke fondly of Fantomes. How could I trust someone who liked the Vicomte's mages? I'd have to stay on alert for a hidden motive.

Amelia stayed thunderstruck, so I decided to step in. I gave the Baroness another curtsey. "What Lady Amelia means to say is that she's honored to be selected." I turned to Amelia, who nodded woodenly. "For my part, I shall watch your performance with pride. I'm sure you'll do well."

Philippe gave everyone a white-toothed grin. "And I'd love to play one of the poor starving beggars who's saved by Theodora's fire. I look exceptional in rags."

The Baroness winked and tapped Philippe on the shoulder with her fan. A strange look passed between them and was quickly gone. Could Philippe and the Baroness be having an affair as well? I wouldn't rule it out.

"I'll show you where to prepare yourselves," said Baroness as she hustled Amelia and Philippe off into the mansion.

We all passed the threshold. The Baroness guided Amelia and

Philippe into the crowd. I held back. Once they were gone, then I could start to explore on my own.

The Baroness paused, spun on her heel, and faced me. "Come along now. The Vicomte warned me about you." The way she said the word *"you,"* it was clear that I ranked somewhere between pond scum and pig slop.

"He did?" It didn't bode well that the Vicomte remembered me at all.

"Stay close now," ordered the Baroness. "I won't have you causing any trouble."

I curtsied and hurried to join their group. "I don't know where the Vicomte would have gotten such an idea."

Baroness stepped through the crowd, which parted for her without a word. "I don't either. You seem like such a harmless little creature."

"Well, I won't give you any trouble."

*Yet.*

*T*he castle's corridors were packed. As I inspected the mass of colorfully dressed Royals, every inch of me itched to cast a transport spell. Without magick, it could take forever to get out of here and reach the gardens.

*I need to search those wells and find the entrance to the dungeons below.*

The Baroness snapped her fingers, interrupting my worries. "Follow quickly now." She took off into the crowd. All the Royals shifted out of her path. It appeared to be an unspoken rule: unless the Baroness acknowledged you, you didn't get in her way. The deference was extended to Amelia and Philippe as well.

Not to me, though.

Everywhere I went there was an intricate dance of shoving elbows and stomping toes, followed by a chorus of false apologies and leading questions.

"Did I step on your gown, sweetling? How silly of me, uh, what's your name?"

"You shouldn't sneak up on people. Where *did* you learn manners?"

"Are you lost? The ball is tomorrow night. The play is a far more exclusive event."

It was the most restrained show of outright hatred I'd ever encountered.

At last, we reached the gardens behind the castle. My shoulders slumped as I scanned the scene. A labyrinth of tall saplings and thick hedgerows seemed to stretch off into infinity. I stood on tiptoe, straining to look past the tall shrubbery.

Not a single well in sight.

I worried my lower lip with my teeth. These gardens were massive. If I ever wanted to find the well that led down to the dungeons, then I needed a true chance to explore.

The Baroness focused on Amelia and Philippe. "All the upper nobility congregate here. Never in the castle. I'll introduce you to some of the more important families." She glared at me. "You stay quiet."

I nodded. *Not a problem.* I'd no desire to chitchat with Royals. I tried to appear calm despite the nervous energy in my limbs. When would I be able to sneak away? My hand rested on the inner pocket where Amelia's witness watch was hidden.

*Tomorrow night, little Ada ran out of time.*

I had to find one of those wells and soon.

The Baroness led us up to a small group of short Royal ladies with wide waistlines and billowing purple gowns. She approached the gray-haired crone of the group. "Duchess," she cooed.

The elder woman stepped forward. "Don't stand on ceremony with me, Bertie. Call me Irena like everyone else."

I fought back a smile. Irena was a woman after my own heart.

The Baroness pressed Amelia toward the clutch of ladies. Philippe stayed glued to his sister's side, his suave smile firmly in place. "I'm sure you know the Lady Amelia Masson and her brother Philippe," said the Baroness. "Amelia's the sole heir to the Vicomte."

Irena set her plump hands on her ample belly. "The one in all rumors?"

"Rumors?" The Baroness blinked innocently. "I hadn't heard anything. However—" She allowed a significant pause to follow. "The Lady Amelia *will* play Theodora tonight."

"Aren't you the clever one, Bertie?" If she'd been a cat, Irena would have hissed and arched her back.

"Always." The Baroness appeared overly pleased with herself. Amelia was about to become the Caster Queen. Rowan's lands hadn't been ravaged by war like ours had been with the Tsar. The Caster continent remained a rich and powerful place. Clearly, the Baroness planned to make the most of Amelia's upcoming fortune.

Irena sighed. "Such a shame, though. No one *important* from the House of Theodora is here tonight, are they?"

"They'll attend my next party. Mark my words." The Baroness kissed Irena on both cheeks. It was a simple enough gesture, but it was done with icy intent. There was no love lost between these two.

The Baroness led us out of earshot of Irena before turning to Amelia and Philippe once more. "Stay close now." She glared at me again. "Especially you."

After that, we slowly made our way across the garden. Every few feet, the Baroness would pause and engage another Royal family. It was always the same conversation, which was essentially what we'd discussed with Irena. I wanted to pull my hair out. All the while, the sun dipped lower in the sky. Shadows lengthened around us. Time was running out.

A few Fantomes walked by. I did my best not to stare. They stayed to the garden's outer paths as they scurried into the growing darkness. There was a short list of reasons why the Fantomes would be so busy tonight. The most likely? With this many visitors, prisoners like Ada would need extra guards, and no one could guard like a Fantome. I gritted my teeth.

*I must steal away.*

Philippe took my hand and gave it a gentle squeeze. "Patience, *Fleur*."

I gave him a forced smile. Patience was never my strong suit.

At last, we stepped into a clearing lined with wooden benches. A stage stood at the far end of the space. White tents flanked either side. The Baroness focused on Philippe. "You're expected in the far right tent. I've arranged for you to play one of the starving peasants."

"Thank you, Baroness."

In a flash, I pictured the perfect means of escape. In fact, my idea was so good I had to work hard not to grin. There was only one catch. I had to rely on Amelia's quick mind to catch on or my plan would end before it began.

I eyed Amelia from head to toe and made a tut-tut noise. "You're looking pale, my friend. We can't have you passing out on stage, now can we?"

"What are you talking about?" The Baroness's thin nostrils flared. "My family has hosted the Passion Play of Theodora for a hundred years. No one has ever passed out on our stage."

"And they won't tonight." I edged away. "I'll simply get Amelia her tonic."

The Baroness pursed her lips. "One of the servants can do it."

"Oh, no." Amelia's face became the image of wide-eyed innocence. "They never get it right. Last time I asked a stranger to prepare the concoction, I became unwell." She puffed out her cheeks.

I could have cheered with joy. Of course, Amelia knew exactly what I planned.

The Baroness gasped. If she thought fainting was outrageous, then the idea of Amelia vomiting sent her into a panic. She whirled on me. "And you know how to prepare this tonic?"

"I've done it a hundred times." I took another half step backward. "I'll return as soon as I can."

The Baroness pointed to the castle. "The kitchens are that way. You'll find whatever you need there."

"Of course."

"Fine. Only be quick about it. The play starts in few minutes." The Baroness grabbed Amelia's arm and led her off to a nearby tent. The moment the canvas flap closed, it was as if I could finally breathe again.

*At last, I'm free to search.*

Hiking up my heavy skirts, I stole off along one of the garden's outer pathways. On the carriage ride over here, Amelia had told me the precise location of every well that she could remember from her childhood visits. There was one that sounded particularly promising. It was large and located in the far corner of the gardens.

I navigated my way along the winding paths. It was slow going in my heavy gown, but eventually I happened upon a small clearing lined with tall hedges. A massive well stood in the far corner.

Unfortunately, it was in use at the moment.

A Royal woman in a bright yellow and green gown was seated atop the well's edge. A gentleman stood between her thighs. *Ugh.* His blue longcoat hid the status of his pants, yet there was no question about what was happening. My face burned with embarrassment. I debated trying another well, but this really was the best location.

I began searching for a stone to toss in their direction. Just then, a servant stepped onto the garden path behind me. "All hail! Your presence is requested at the main pavilion!"

The couple immediately stepped apart and began tidying up their wigs and garments. I exhaled with relief.

*Yes. Finally.*

The servant kept on his rounds while the couple rushed off along the main path. With any luck, Amelia would convince the Baroness that she didn't need the tonic after all. I didn't want any servants coming after me.

My heart thumped harder against my rib cage. I couldn't count on Amelia's powers of persuasion, though. I needed to search that well and do it quickly. Once the clearing was truly deserted, I stepped closer. The well was a low stone circle with a huge copper basin sitting in its center. The bowl was shallow enough to serve as a birdbath, nothing more. I hooked my fingers in around the edges and hauled the basin out. Water slopped as I tossed it onto the nearby grass.

I leaned over the opening, feeling a rush of stale air against my face. A sense of triumph charged through my veins. It was just as Amelia said.

This was no well.

I picked up a few small stones and dropped them in. They clattered against a distant stone floor.

*Some kind of chamber is down there, definitely.*

I listened hard, hoping to hear voices. Everything stayed silent. I patted the inner edge of the well. The stones were wide apart. Excellent for climbing down.

There was only one problem, however. My dress. The well was large enough for a man. My gown was positively massive, however. I had worried about getting it dirty, which was why my top layer was an overdress. It was easy enough to remove. But everything underneath? That was a different story.

I patted my thigh. At least, I'd brought along a small dagger, just in case. There was no other option—I'd simply have to remove my overgown, cut myself out of my underdress, and worry about the rest later. My fingers trembled as I unlaced my overgown and set it carefully onto a nearby bench. I scanned the darkness. No one was about. Moving quickly, I hiked up my skirts and pulled my dagger from its sheath. After that, I stopped. The small hairs on the back of my neck stood on end.

Someone was watching.

I flipped the dagger so the point of the blade pointed downward —all the better for an attack. I slowly swung around. "Who's there?"

The barest rustling sounded from the nearby trees. It could be nothing. Even so, I felt it better to be wary.

Suddenly, a hand grabbed my wrist from behind. I gasped. How could anyone sneak up on me so quickly? No matter. They wouldn't live long enough to do it again. I spun around and raised my weapon, ready to strike. That was when I saw a familiar face in the shadows. Rowan. I exhaled and lowered my arm. "You gave me quite a fright."

"I didn't mean to." His thumb rubbed a soothing arc along my wrist. Tonight, Rowan wore his traditional brown fitted leathers. *My favorite.* An intense look gleamed in his green eyes.

My desire to smile became almost overwhelming. Somehow, I kept my features calm and pointed at Rowan with my dagger. "Don't you know it's rude to creep through the bushes?"

He gave me one of his crooked grins that warmed me to my toes. "It's far worse to watch someone cut off their clothes without announcing yourself."

"Oh." My blush came back, even more fiercely this time. Thank goodness it was getting dark out. "This isn't as odd as it looks."

He raised his brows. "Tell me."

"I have it on good authority that this well leads to the dungeons below. I'm afraid I underestimated the dimensions, however." I gestured across the massive folds of my skirt. "This is far too unwieldy."

"Allow me." He set his hands on my shoulders, spun me about, and began to quickly open the elaborate sets of hooks and eyes that trailed their way down my back.

I tried my best to think of the impending rescue mission,

however the situation was infinitely distracting. To begin with, Rowan's bare fingers kept brushing my shoulders and spine. Also, I kept wondering how the man knew to undo these hooks so well. Most servants had trouble with them.

Rowan leaned in closer. His lips almost touched my ear. "I thought you'd never leave the Baroness."

I couldn't stop my smile. He'd been watching me. "The Vicomte told the Baroness to keep me close."

"That's unfortunate."

"It could have been worse. The Baroness is making Amelia play Theodora."

Rowan stopped undoing my corset for a moment. "Indeed."

I glanced at him over my shoulder. His features were unreadable. "What was that? What do you know about my friend?"

His face stayed still as stone. How I hated it when he did that. "It's nothing I can discuss."

The muscles along my shoulders tightened to painful levels. I didn't like the idea of Rowan keeping things from me. "You don't have to be secretive. The Vicomte already told us about Amelia and Rex."

"Ah. I see." Rowan slowly pulled me against him. My almost bare back pressed against the firm planes of his chest. Bit by bit, his heavy arms looped around my waist.

I frowned. Rowan was never spontaneously cuddly or sentimental. The other times he'd held me, it was because I was in danger or obviously upset. "What's wrong?"

"Not a thing." Rowan leaned his cheek against my hair. "What you say is the truth. Both Rex and Amelia are creatures of state. They always knew they'd have a marriage of convenience, just not to each other. And Rex is a good man. You don't need to worry about your friend."

It still didn't explain his odd behavior. "And what about you? Are you a good man?"

"I try to be." His arms tightened. "I have a plan for us, Elea. Believe it."

His reply wasn't very comforting. *I try to be?* "What is this plan, exactly?"

"Nothing I can discuss now, sadly enough." Rowan released me and undid the last of the hooks along my back. My layered skirts fell from my body. I stepped outside the pile of fabric. Now, I stood only in my undershift and pantalets. Rowan stepped around to face me. The lines of his rugged face were tight. Our moment of intimacy was over. We were warrior mages again.

I stepped up to the well and hoisted myself up to sit along the edge. My legs dangled into the growing darkness. I looked into inky black below me.

*My people could be down there. Ada. Veronique. I need to save them.*

Rowan looked down the throat of the well. "The surface here looks uneven." Reaching forward, he brushed his palms across the inner stone. "There are good handholds, though. I can climb it. How about you?"

"Not to worry." My old Cloister was set into the side of a mountain. In the summer months, I'd often scale up to the peak. Mother Superior said it was good exercise. I think she just wanted me to see the sun once in a while. I did nothing but study in those days.

Rowan inspected me carefully. "How long since you last climbed?"

"Months." Actually, it was more than a year. Still, I didn't like the worried look in Rowan's eyes. I was going down this well, whether he liked it or not.

"I'll go first, then," he said.

"And why's that?"

"Landing on an unknown floor in the dark? That can tricky in slippers and pantalets, unless you have help. Or do you want to use magick?"

"The spells I'd have to use would be too powerful. Any Fantome within a league of here would sense that kind of casting. I accept you offer of help." And, if I were being honest with myself, I liked the idea of Rowan grabbing me in the dark.

"Agreed." Rowan slipped into the well. For such a large man, his movements were smooth and graceful. He quickly disappeared into the darkness below.

I sat on the well's edge, my legs swinging below me in a nervous rhythm. It seemed like hours ticked by as I waited for some word from Rowan. At last, his voice echoed up from the well. "Ready."

I checked to ensure that Amelia's watch was safely stowed in the pocket of my pantalets. *Still there.* There was nothing else to wait for. Taking a deep breath, I gripped the lip of the well and began the long climb down. One thought occupied my mind.

*Please, let Ada be here.*

*T*he stones felt slimy under my fingertips as I slowly made my way down the darkened well. Fortunately, some of the mortar between the rocks had rotted away, so there were good holds for my hands and feet, even if I couldn't see them clearly. The moonlight grew dimmer as I relaxed into a downward rhythm.

Left hand.

Right hand.

Left foot, right.

Stale air filled my lungs. Heavy shadows enveloped me. I gripped the wet stones more tightly. How far had I gone? Was the end of the well near?

"Rowan?" I whispered. "Where are you?"

"I've got you." Rowan's deep voice sounded right below me. Warm hands cupped my waist as he gently lowered me to the floor. For a long moment, we waited there, my back pressed against Rowan's firm chest once again. His heart thudded with such force I could feel the beat against my skin.

Rowan leaned forward to whisper in my ear. "We're at the end of a dead-end hallway." His breath cascaded down my bare neck, making me shiver. "I think—"

A light appeared at the far side of a long stone passage. It was the barest flicker of a torch, and it was growing brighter. My eyes widened.

*Someone is down here.*

All of a sudden, the Vicomte appeared at the end of the hallway. Even in the dim light, it was clear how he dressed in a garish pink coat over yellow pants and tall black boots. He paused for a moment, pulled out a watch, and checked the time. Rowan's grip on my waist tightened. I held my breath.

*Please don't let him detect us.*

A Fantome stepped up beside the Vicomte. A jolt of worry tightened my chest. The Vicomte and a Fantome? Things were becoming dangerous, indeed.

"You're late," snapped the Vicomte.

"I came as soon as I could." The mage was a woman. In the dim light, I could see that she wore the long robes and had a slight frame. Even from a distance, there was no mistaking the way her shoulders trembled. What could be bad enough to frighten a Fantome?

"You dawdled, Gretel. Don't bother to deny it. You've been having dream visits from the Tsar again. When I summoned you here to meet me, you became worried as to what I'd do."

"Visits in my dreams? I don't know what you're talking about." The tremor in Gretel's voice told a different story, though. Memories flickered through my mind. For years, I'd had nightmares of my friend Tristan as he suffered in his afterlife. In that case, it was all because we shared a curse. Gretel must have gotten connected to the Tsar through their magick, most likely whatever spells were on the bone crawler inside her. I shivered. It couldn't be pleasant, having a magickal connection to the most evil Necromancer in history.

The Vicomte's voice lowered to a menacing whisper. "Are you still my loyal servant, Gretel?"

"I pledged my fealty wholly to you, my master."

"Then follow me."

"Whatever you command."

The Vicomte took off down another hallway with Gretel close behind. The flicker of torchlight faded as they went on. I exhaled slowly.

Rowan let go of my waist and I spun around. The reflection from the Vicomte's torch gave us just enough light. As our gazes locked, I knew Rowan was thinking the same thing that I was.

*Let's follow.*

Rowan gestured for me to go first, and I stole down the stone passageway, careful to keep a safe distance between us and the Vicomte. The flickering shadows from the Vicomte's torch shifted across the rough rock walls. Our path wound steadily downward. Rowan stayed close behind me, a calming presence in the darkness.

At last, the Vicomte and Gretel entered a large stone space. Here, the walls were mottled and reddish-gray. Long cones of white sediment dripped down from the ceiling, filling the room with natural columns. My eyes widened with recognition. I'd lived in a mountain for years, so I knew what a cave looked like. That said, the far wall in this place was far more than just rock.

*It's a gateway.*

A series of smooth black stones had been set into the uneven wall, creating an arch that was slightly taller than me. What was once an opening beneath the arch had been bricked up with thin stones. I quickly scanned the runes etched into gateway itself. This one led to the Eternal Lands.

My pulse sped. This was just as Rowan and I discussed in the underwater cave. I fought the urge to gasp.

My people could be nearer than ever.

The Vicomte marched over to the far wall and set his torch into an obliging crevice. Gretel kept a close step behind him. At the same time, Rowan and I crept to hide behind a thick column of white stone. The air around me crackled with anticipation.

I'd never been so close to rescuing my friends.

The Vicomte turned to Gretel. "Summon the Tsar."

"You can't be serious." Gretel pulled back her hood, revealing a childlike face. Her cheeks were quite rounded for a Necromancer, and her small nose turned up at the end. "You can't expect me to face him."

"But I do, and as you said, I am your master. Summon him." The Vicomte stepped closer to Gretel and lowered his voice to a menacing whisper. "I know he's visited your dreams. I'm not here to punish you for that, only to ask him to stop invading your mind."

"You are?"

"What else would you think?"

I fought the urge to roll my eyes. If the Vicomte thought the Tsar was in contact with one of his Fantomes, that mage was as good as dead. The man had serious problems trusting anyone. Most likely, he believed this was the easiest way to discover what they had been discussing. And once the Vicomte had gotten all the information that he could? I shuddered. Gretel was doomed.

Still, Gretel seemed to believe the Vicomte's words. Her posture visibly slumped with relief. "As you command, my master." Gretel raised her left arm. My skin prickled as the magick in the room shifted toward her. Soon, the bones in Gretel's left hand glowed bright blue. Meanwhile, an azure-colored mist crawled up the rock wall under the gateway. When the magickal haze disappeared, the bricks that had blocked the gate were gone.

Vanished.

Instead, the Tsar now stood under the gateway. He was little more than a silhouette against the perfect darkness behind him.

The Vicomte rocked on his heels. "Greetings, my Tsar."

"Gaspard." I'd have known that voice anywhere. The Tsar was here for certain.

The Vicomte opened his arms wide. "Come closer, why don't you, and greet me as a brother?"

"And why would I do that?" asked the Tsar. "We both know very well that I can't cross the gateway yet. Well, not without pain." He sighed. "If you wish to hurt me, you'll need to do better."

"I had no idea that would happen," said the Vicomte. He wasn't a very good liar.

"Still, I can move a little closer without crossing the gateway. After all, I'd like a better look at my one-time loyal follower." The Tsar stepped forward into the torchlight. He looked the same as when I last saw him at the Midnight Cloister—tall and broad-shouldered in long black robes with the elegant bone structure and pale skin of a Necromancer. He glared at Gretel. "How are you, traitor?"

Gretel lifted her chin. "I'm fine. Much better now that I follow the Vicomte." Her voice trembled with every word. A pang of sympathy twisted through me.

The Vicomte rubbed his palms together. "Now, I'm sure you're wondering. Why have I summoned you?"

"Not in particular." The Tsar's features stayed perfectly still as he spoke. "No doubt you've tried hoarding up Necromancer power into one of my totem rings. Now you want information. How far have you gotten?"

My mouth fell open. The Tsar always seemed three steps ahead.

The Vicomte frowned. "Who told you this?"

A small smile rounded the Tsar's mouth. "Please. I don't need spies to predict what you'll do next. Have you tried to drain one of the Fantomes of their magick yet?"

The lines of the Vicomte's face deepened. "Perhaps."

"In that case, you know it's a waste of time," said the Tsar smoothly. "At one time, the Fantomes were all members of my entourage. I'd have been a great fool to allow my most powerful mages to drain one another. That could create someone strong enough to challenge my power. Give me more credit than that."

"I said *perhaps*," snapped the Vicomte. His voice was as petulant as a child's. "I didn't say that I did it."

"But you did try something," said the Tsar leadingly.

I shook my head. I'd spent years in training, learning how to control my emotions and manipulate others into revealing their own. The Tsar was using classic Necromancer interrogation methods, and the Vicomte was falling for every trick.

The Vicomte jammed his hands into his pockets. "Of course, I looked into the possibilities. I'm a scientist. Besides, Fantomes aren't the only ones with Necromancer power."

"True. And you knew about my bone crawlers, too. Those creatures are custom-made to drain Necromancer power. I'll bet you explored what those insects can do."

"Yes, that's precisely what I did. I tested having bone crawlers drain those with Necromancer power but not Fantomes." The Vicomte sighed dramatically. "Alas. The bone crawlers answer only to you. It was a dead end, all of it. No one can carry on your work in gathering up all Necromancer power. It was a bold goal. It's over now, though."

The Tsar's features stayed chillingly calm. "So you've no alternate way to transfer Necromancer power into a totem ring."

"None at all." I had to give the Vicomte credit. He told that lie rather believably. If I hadn't spoken with Amelia, I'd never have thought there was an alternative to the bone crawlers.

"My focus is now on machines," said the Vicomte. "All kinds of useful, scientific devices. I called you here today because I demand that you to stop taunting my loyal Fantomes."

A wisp of a smile rounded Gretel's mouth. For a Necromancer, that was a positive avalanche of emotion. I wished I could share her faith in the Vicomte. I didn't believe for an instant that he'd given up on taking in Necromancer magick. Or that he would waste time calling the Tsar just to protect his people.

"Your mages are mine," said the Tsar. "They bear my bone crawlers, and I'll talk to them when I wish it. And don't pretend you aren't using them to help you gather Necromancer power into a totem ring."

"But I told you already—"

"Enough! For years, I've known about the little laboratories that are run by your so-called children. One made watches to hold my totem rings inside. Those devices could even transfer Necromancer power into a non-mage, if the totem ring had enough energy within."

The Vicomte rolled his eyes. "Where do you get such dribble? Those watches never worked, I assure you. It was a misplaced experiment by a rogue machinist. All prototypes of that sad idea were destroyed."

My brows rose. Destroyed? I patted the witness watch in my pocket. *Good thing the Vicomte wasn't too thorough.*

Gretel straightened her shoulders. "You're avoiding the Vicomte's demand. I have your bone crawler in me, that's true. But I don't want to endure your nightly visits anymore."

The Vicomte rested his hand on her shoulder. "Gretel's right. Leave her and the others alone." He turned to her, his face gentle. "There are others, aren't there?"

Gretel's eyes widened. For a Necromancer, that was a good as a rousing cry of *yes.* "I don't know, my master."

"No matter," said the Vicomte.

I was sure it mattered a great deal to the other Fantomes.

"Now." The Vicomte pointed right at the Tsar's nose. "I demand that you make the girl's nightmares go away."

A long silence followed. A flicker of a smile appeared on the Tsar's mouth. It was gone too quickly to be certain, though. "In that case, I will do as you ask."

"You will?" asked Gretel and the Vicomte. There was no mistaking the shock in their voices. I agreed with them.

The Tsar gestured to the gateway. "It's a reasonable request, after all. Gretel was kind enough to open this gateway. And since she stands so close, I have all sorts of options open to me." The Tsar waved his hand.

Gretel began to die.

The bone crawler beneath her skin glowed bright purple. The thing whipped under her flesh and wrapped itself tightly around her throat. On reflex, I grabbed Rowan's hand.

*No, no, no.*

The Vicomte stared at Gretel. His mouth curled into a look of disgust. The scene was something was beyond belief. At last, he spoke. "Release Gretel this instant." There was no heat behind the Vicomte's words, though. I doubted he cared if Gretel lived. Bastard.

The Tsar watched Gretel gasp for air. While the Vicomte seemed repulsed, the Tsar appeared empty of all feeling. The sight sent chills down my spine. "Let's finish our real discussion, shall we?" asked the Tsar. "For months now, you've known that I've been visiting my old mages in their dreams. Now, this fact suddenly concerns you."

"No, it doesn't. My people are loyal to me." This time, the Vicomte seemed less confident in his declaration, though. I couldn't help noticing how he'd quickly dropped the charade of asking the Tsar to release Gretel.

The poor girl still clawed at the bone crawler under her skin. It made me ill.

"You have a vortex watch," began the Tsar.

"Now, see here. How can you possibly—"

"And I said enough!" The Tsar raised his hand. "You must have the watch, or you wouldn't be here. And the thing must also be nearly fully charged, or you wouldn't have brought her." He nodded to

Gretel. "Once that device reaches midnight, you can become the most powerful Necromancer in the land. Yet so can the Fantomes, can't they? I cast spells to stop them from draining one other, but not you. So suddenly, you're wondering what we've been discussing in their dreams." His voice lowered. "Once you have enough power, you wonder if you should kill them all."

Gretel collapsed onto her knees, her hands clasping at the bone crawler around her throat. On reflex, I started to move toward her.

Rowan gripped my upper arm, holding me back. I could have fought him. I didn't. It was better to stay hidden in the shadows. If I sided with Gretel, I could end up dead.

"Kill them," said the Tsar. "That's what I'd do. Doesn't matter what they've said to me. Power is the ultimate lure." He lifted his chin. "This conversation is over." The Tsar snapped his fingers. A sickening crunch sounded as Gretel's neck snapped. Bile crept up my throat. Once Gretel was dead, her spell would die with her.

The gateway was about to close.

A second later, the Tsar disappeared. The gateway became brick and mortar once more. Gretel lay unmoving on the stone floor.

I clutched my stomach. I'd seen some cold and cruel things in my lifetime. This was one of the worst. A loyal mage was murdered before my eyes, and for what? A power play between two rivals. The temperature seemed to drop to icy levels. Gretel thought she'd left the cruelties of the Tsar for the safety of the Vicomte. As much as I dreaded the Fantomes, I could only pity her.

Gretel's body shifted as the bone crawler under her skin glowed a brighter shade than ever before. Flames erupted where the insect lay hidden. Smoke poured off Gretel's flesh as she burned up from the inside out. Within seconds, she was nothing but a pile of ash on the stone. What a waste.

Without so much as a glance at her body, the Vicomte scooped up the torch from the wall and strode out of the cave.

I stood and watched him go. For a long minute, I stared at the darkening shadows he left behind. "We must find Ada before the Vicomte charges up that vortex watch. We've less than a day left."

"Your Sisters are close by. I'm certain of it."

Excitement sped through my bloodstream. "As am I."

"These dungeons are massive. To find them quickly, we should cast a searcher sphere. As long as we keep the power levels low, it shouldn't attract attention." Rowan lowered his voice. "I can cast the spell, if you like."

"No, I'll do it." Closing my eyes, I pulled Necromancer power to me. I only allowed a small trickle to ease into my fingertips. My bones soon glowed dimly with power. Blue mist appeared around my hand as I whispered the incantation.

*Search the night*
*Brothers and Sisters of death*
*Find where they gather*
*Show me their breath*

The mist solidified into the form of a glowing orb made of blue light. *A searcher sphere.* It hovered weightlessly before me. Raising my left hand again, I turned to the shining orb. "Your Grand Mistress commands you. Find my people."

The sphere bobbed in the air and then sped toward the exit. I followed it at a run.

*R*owan and I raced after the shimmering orb as it sped through the maze of passageways. Around us, everything was quiet and deserted. The pale blue light from the sphere gave us our only illumination. As I rushed along, I swung my head from side to side, searching for any sign of guards or Fantomes. We were definitely alone.

At least, we were so far.

The small sphere whipped down another passage and through an open doorway. After that, it paused.

We were here, wherever *here* was. My forehead sheened over with sweat.

Rowan and I stepped into a massive and empty laboratory. Long wooden tables filled the space. The sphere now hovered by the far wall.

I stopped by the nearest table. "I've seen a laboratory like this one before. It's where the Vicomte's so-called children conducted experiments."

Rowan picked up a small blade from the tabletop. "These are thick with dust." His forehead creased. "The coating is far too heavy to be natural."

He handed me the tiny knife. There was no mistaking the thick, flaky substance covering the metal. The hairs on my neck stood on end. "This isn't dust. It's ashes."

"What kind of ashes?"

"The kind that Gretel left behind." I forced my voice to stay calm. Inside, I felt anything but.

Rowan gently rested his hand on my shoulder. "The Vicomte tried using bone crawlers to drain those with Necromancer power."

I nodded. "And those bone crawlers would only answer to the Tsar." A chill of worry wound down my spine. "That wouldn't have stopped the Vicomte from trying to manipulate them anyway. And if the Necromancers didn't live through the experiments, then...' I didn't need to finish the thought. We'd seen firsthand what happened when the bone crawler inside Gretel died.

Rowan strode toward the door. "We should leave, Elea. There are no live Necromancers here."

Part of me knew I should listen to Rowan. After all, moving on was the most logical thing to do. I was after living Necromancers, not the dead.

But I couldn't go.

Instead, I walked deeper into the old laboratory. With every step, the tables changed. They became heavier. One had broken parts of a crank attached. I'd seen these before. Torturers called it the rack. I picked up a heavy length of leather from the floor.

*A restraining belt.*

Bile crawled up my throat. "What happened here?"

"Nothing we should concern ourselves with now. Let's ask my contacts for more information. Perhaps your Sisters are held in an estate nearby."

That logical part of me spoke louder in my soul.

*Leave, Elea.*

I tossed the belt to the floor. Rage and disgust wheeled inside me. My people had been brought here and tortured, all to gather up their Necromancer power. "I'm not going anywhere until I know what happened." I moved closer to the far wall.

Only this wasn't a wall.

It was a massive pile of blackened ash that filled the back of the laboratory from floor to ceiling.

My mouth fell open. "This can't be."

Rowan stepped to my side. "By the gods."

"So much ash. It can't be mages." My voice was steady, yet my limbs trembled with fear. "I have to cast a spell to find out. If there are the remains of someone who can help me here, then my casting will detect it."

Rowan's voice was gentle. "Whatever you need." Still, he unsheathed the short swords from his back, ready for a fight.

I called Necromancer power to me. The air became thick with memory and energy. I pulled it into my body, focused it on my left arm, and spoke the incantation.

*Ghost and shadow*
*Flesh and bone*
*Necromancer souls*
*I summon you home*

Blue mist materialized by my feet. I lowered my left hand, releasing the spell. The azure-colored haze crawled up the pile of ashes. Finding a spot it liked, the spell slipped its way inside.

Long seconds passed. Tension bit into my temples.

*Please, let the spell find me someone trustworthy. Or no one at all.* Perhaps this was all ash from dead animals or bone crawlers. That was unlikely, but I'd learned how the impossible happened all the time.

A low hiss sounded. My breath caught. The spell has found a mage who could assist. Mist began oozing back out of the wall of ash.

My mage would soon appear.

The blue haze lengthened and solidified into the shape of a tall man in Necromancer robes. He had a bald head and scarred face. I'd have known that visage anywhere.

It was Quinn, the blood brother of Tristan, my one-time best friend.

Once his spirit took shape, Quinn's transparent form glared at me. "Whoever you are, send me back. Run for your life." As he spoke, one side of his mouth ticked up in a strange rhythm. The man looked seconds away from going berserk.

I shook my head. The change in Quinn was almost too much to process. How could this happen? The last time I'd seen him, it was the night that Tristan died. At the time, Quinn had been a Brother in one of the monasteries. He'd acted and spoken without any emotion, just like a proper Necromancer. Now, Quinn positively radiated terror and feeling. It took a lot to break a trained Necromancer. What had happened to Quinn before he died?

"I said send me back!"

"Listen, Quinn." I tapped my chest with my fingertips. "It's me. Elea. Tristan's friend."

Quinn's eye began to twitch as well. "Elea? What are you doing here?"

"I'm a Grand Mistress Necromancer. I summoned you." *Poor Quinn.* I'd seen this before. His memory was trapped in knowing only what had happened right before he died. As far as Quinn was aware, there was some kind of threat nearby. The man was only trying to protect me.

"Didn't you hear me? Run!" Quinn's voice boomed around the chamber. "They're killing us!"

Bands of worry tightened around my throat. *They're killing us.* This was my worst fear confirmed.

When I next spoke, I took care to put the weight of magick into my voice. "Listen to me. You must explain exactly what happened here."

Quinn glared at Rowan. "Who's he?"

"My ally."

"I'll tell you nothing." Quinn narrowed his eyes. "You've poor skills in choosing your friends." *Meaning Tristan.*

I balled my hands into fists. Ghosts could be unruly when summoned against their will. A Necromancer had to be firm. "Talk to me or I'll cast a truth spell." My voice lowered to a menacing tone. "And believe me, that will hurt."

Quinn frowned, and the motion twisted the slashes of battle scars across his face. "As you command, Grand Mistress." The last two words were spoken with deepest sarcasm. "You know I pledged fealty to the Tsar. One of his agents placed a bone crawler in me. So long as I followed the Tsar's rules, it wasn't too awful."

I gritted my teeth as rage flowed through me. I'd seen the Tsar's so-called rules in action back at the Midnight Cloister. You were either someone who brought him Necromancers to drain... Or you got drained yourself. "You betrayed your own people and joined the Tsar's entourage. Glad it worked out for you."

Quinn lifted his chin. "I did what I had to in order to survive. It's what anyone would have done."

"Elea didn't join," said Rowan.

Quinn rounded on the Caster. "Then she's more of a fool than I thought."

Rowan whispered a quick incantation. The blade in his right hand shone with crimson light. "Watch how you speak of Elea. She's under my protection."

My chest warmed with pride and confidence. I wasn't accustomed to having anyone help me in my battles. I returned my attention to Quinn. "Following the Tsar's orders didn't get you dead, though. What happened?"

"You did, it would seem." Quinn's misshapen mouth thinned to an angry line. "When you sent the Tsar away, the Vicomte asked for members of the entourage to pledge fealty to him. I refused."

"How shocking," I said coolly. "You were always so open to changing alliances."

"It didn't seem possible for the Tsar to be well and truly gone. I was certain that he'd return any moment." Quinn hugged his elbows. "When he didn't, I was taken here. There were already thousands of people with Necromancer power locked up in these dungeons. I'd never seen so many in one place."

I remembered how the Midnight Cloister was rounding people up. "How did they keep so many hidden?" The compulsion for truth burned like a fire within my soul. I had to know what happened.

"Stasis spells, mostly. You only woke up when they..." He swallowed. "When the Vicomte tried to take your power."

My heart thudded more quickly. "And then what did the Vicomte do?"

"He did little. He had experimenters do most of the work. They tried to pull out bone crawlers and place them in new subjects, thinking that the insects would then respond to the Vicomte."

Quinn's shoulder's slumped. "It didn't work, but that didn't stop them from trying. Over and over. Thousands of us passed through here, Elea. Once the Vicomte's people pulled those insects out of us, we'd crumble to ash within minutes."

*Just like Gretel.*

All the breath left my body. It took a force of will to inhale again. "How many of you are left?"

"When I died? Only a few hundred." He gestured behind him. "Look behind you. This is all that's left of our people."

I straightened my back. "There are still the Fantomes."

Quinn sniffed. "They're not true Necromancers. Our way of life is dead, Elea. Face it."

I took a half step backward. "No, that's not true. Some of my Sisters and Brothers survived. I'm going to find them."

A malevolent gleam appeared in Quinn's ghostly eyes. "You should have done what I said to, right after Tristan died. Do you remember my words, Elea? I told you to go home to your farm and enjoy your life while you could. And now, you've put on airs to become a Grand Mistress Necromancer, sent our Tsar off into exile, and what's become of all your hard work? You've changed nothing. We're still all as good as dead. Only some of us might have lived. Unlike you."

My bottom lip wobbled. *By the gods, Quinn is right.* I'd spent so long trying to save my people from the Tsar, and what had I done? Raised up the Vicomte instead. Avoided enjoying the gift of my life. Tears stung my eyes.

Still, I couldn't give up.

"What about my Sisters? They might be hidden here while being drained. Do you sense any of them?" A ghost could search within the present if he wished. Unlike any spell that I would cast, Quinn could search without raising alarms among the Fantomes.

Quinn's eye twitched once again. "Haven't you been listening?" His voice took on a hysterical tone. "Everyone here is dead. Dead, dead, dead, and you're next!"

Rowan stepped forward and raised his glowing sword. "That's enough out of you." He swung the bright blade through Quinn's transparent body, and the ghost disappeared. Quinn's soul wasn't destroyed, but the way he'd left wouldn't feel too good, either. I couldn't find it in me to pity him right now.

A weight of grief settled into my bones. I hunched forward under the burden. *Everyone here is dead.* "This can't be happening."

Rowan quickly encased me in his arms. "Don't give up hope. Quinn didn't seem in his right mind. Perhaps every Necromancer here is dead. That doesn't mean your friends aren't alive somewhere else. You might still save them. I bet Amelia will know where else to look."

My entire body felt leaden with sadness. "I hope so." Even so, I knew the words were lies before they even left my mouth. The Montagne and Havilland estates were the only two places that seemed likely to hide my Sisters. Other than that? There were too many Royal estates and not enough time to search them.

I leaned into the warmth of Rowan's embrace and tried to process what had happened. My great quest was likely over. I had indeed found the lost Necromancers, and they were a pile of dust. My friends were likely lost as well.

Still, it wasn't in me to give up. A day remained to find Ada and the others.

Rowan rubbed my back in gentle circles. "What do you plan to do?"

"Get a list of nearby estates from Amelia's library. After that, I'll start searching again." I forced myself to step away from his embrace. "I can't give up, Rowan. I will save them."

"I believe you, Elea."

It was good that one of us had faith in me. Because one thought kept echoing through my heart.

*Ada, Veronique, and the others are gone.*

or a long moment, I could only stare at the ash pile. One thought kept echoing through my mind.

*Here are all that remains of a thousand Necromancers.*

Rowan held me close, yet the heat of his skin gave me no warmth. The icy truth only pressed more deeply into my bones.

*My way of life had almost vanished.*

The elderly Sisters at my Cloister might still be clever, but they couldn't cast major spells anymore. Once, I'd hoped they could train new recruits or perhaps rehabilitate some Fantomes. With every passing moment, those dreams seemed farther out of reach.

My eyes stung with held-in tears. When I'd lived with the Casters, they'd always called me the Last Necromancer. Since I was the only Grand Mistress they'd ever seen, I thought the term was sweet.

Now the name seemed to be coming true.

Rowan gently kissed the top of my head. "We need to return to the play."

"I know." My words sounded as hollow as my heart.

Suddenly, the blue sphere of magick moved. Instead of hovering by the back wall of ashes, it sped toward the open entranceway. All my senses went on alert. I stepped away from Rowan's embrace, my mind reeling. The orb was moving. That could only mean one thing.

My spell had detected new Necromancers.

The Fantomes were coming.

I pictured the complex route it took for Rowan and me to reach this room. If the mages could have transported to this spot, they would have already. Which meant that they weren't sure where to find us and were using tracking spells. We had some time to prepare.

I raised my left hand, careful to lace my voice with magick as I called to the sphere. "Halt!"

The glowing orb paused by the archway door. I exhaled. If a troop of expert Necromancers was coming to kill me, at least they wouldn't have a glowing guide to help them find my location.

Rowan gestured toward the sphere. "Does that mean what I think it means?"

I nodded. "Fantomes."

"All of them?"

I closed my eyes and felt in my soul for magick. A small amount remained, and I pushed it into the sphere, asking it how many mages approached. The answer instantly appeared in my mind's eye. "Six of them are coming." I opened my eyes and squashed the desire to kick something. "Summoning Quinn must have drawn their attention."

"If it had been me, I'd have done the same."

A sickly feeling crept into my stomach. Six mages might very well be coming here to kill Rowan and me. That was a goodly amount of all the Necromancers left alive. What would I do when they attacked? In order to survive, I'd have to destroy them.

My mind raced through the implications. I would murder more my people when so many had already died. It was an impossible situation.

*There had to be another way.*

Rowan eyed me carefully. "What're you thinking about?"

"Spells."

"Don't worry. They won't expect Caster magick. I can kill them easily enough with a sneak attack." Rowan raised his right arm and pulled magick into him. The veins in his right hand glowed red.

A pang of worry tightened my heart. Rowan was the most powerful mage I'd ever met. He was right that they wouldn't expect his kind of power. Together, we might very well destroy all the Fantomes who were heading this way.

*But I couldn't let them die without giving them a chance.*

I stepped in front of Rowan, gripped his right hand, and forced it down. "Don't hurt them." The light disappeared from his bones.

Rowan narrowed his eyes. "What do you mean? They're evil."

"We don't know that. I was alive when the Tsar first came to power. All the Fantomes were true Necromancers back then. You saw Quinn. Many were terrorized into joining the Tsar. Plus, after seeing Gretel, I've no doubt that some were conned into following the Vicomte. Now, with so few Necromancers left, I can't just kill trained Necromancers out of hand. I must give them a chance to embrace our true ways again."

"Perhaps." A muscle twitched along Rowan's jawline. It was a sure sign he was worried. "But they're coming here to kill you." His gravelly voice became even lower. "I will *never* let that happen." He raised his hand once more.

Part of me felt honored that Rowan was so determined to protect my life. More of me wanted to ensure the Necromancers didn't vanish.

I gripped Rowan's wrist again. "Suppose you were about to face some of the last of your Casters. Could *you* kill them?"

Rowan's gaze locked with mine. Intensity burned in his emerald eyes. A long moment passed before he spoke again. "No, I couldn't." He lowered his arm.

I exhaled. "Good." The beginnings of an idea were forming in the back of my mind.

*It was so insane it might even work.*

Rowan moved closer, interrupting my thoughts. "We'll have a short time to prepare before they find us."

"I don't want to fight in a hallway. The passages down here are too cramped. That limits what spells I can cast."

"Agreed. If we make a stand, it should be in this room. There are tables to act as barriers, and the door seems stout." He cracked the knuckles on his right hand. "I could create some animals that will slow them down as well."

I turned to face the wall of ashes. For my plan to work, I needed to break my ban against summoning ghosts. "And I'll summon some ghosts. It's easier to do when you have their remains nearby."

"What do you want ghosts for? Not to fight, surely."

Rowan's question made perfect sense. When it came to spirits, their transparent bodies made them pretty useless in battles. Besides, ghosts had a lot of opinions about what they would or wouldn't do. It wasn't like summoning up a bunch of bones and animating them, which was my favorite kind of fighting spell. Ghosts needed convincing, especially to do what I was about to ask.

"I don't want them to fight. I need them to possess the living."

Rowan let out a low whistle. "That's not too easy. They don't like doing that, do they?"

"It's hard work to control a living mind, not to mention incredibly painful. But there are so many spirits here, some of them should agree. I only need six."

Rowan shot a worried glance at the door. "It won't take the Fantomes long to arrive. How much time do you need for your spellwork?"

"A quarter-hour, perhaps less."

"In that case, I know just the spell."

Rowan raised his right arm and began a new incantation. Within seconds, a whirl of red mist materialized around his boots. The crimson haze rose up and began to spin in a cone-shaped vortex. Soon, the mist solidified into hundreds of red bats with tiny glowing eyes and dagger-sharp teeth. The animals screeched as they flew faster and faster. Within seconds, Rowan was surrounded by a single blur of red-winged creatures. He lowered his arm. "Fly!"

Moving as a single unit, the bats sped out the door. It wasn't until they were gone that I realized I'd been holding my breath. I knew Casters could create an animal or two, but what Rowan could accomplish was extraordinary. Once the creatures left, the door slammed shut behind them. The wood glistened with red light.

*A sealing spell.*

We stood alone in the room once more. The air felt heavy with meaning. Was I really about to attempt to possess a half-dozen powerful Necromancers? Behind me, there stood the ashes of those who'd been betrayed by Fantomes. What were my chances of convincing any of these ghosts to save Fantome lives?

I shook my head. *This is something I simply must try.* I looked over to Rowan. "I'll start my spell to summon the spirits."

Rowan gave me a crooked smile. "I love to watch you work."

His compliment had my chest swelling with pride. I focused on the wall of ashes, pulled Necromancer power into my limbs, and spoke another incantation.

*Awaken, arise, take thought and form*
*Dust and spirit, master and thrall*
*Your Sister summons you*
*Answer my call*

The screeches of bats sounded from deep inside the dungeons, followed by raised voices. There was no mistaking the lilt of their speech. Someone was casting spells.

The Fantomes were coming.

I released my power. Blue mist materialized around my feet I pumped more energy into the spell. A sapphire-colored haze drifted up the ash wall. Like a thousand tiny fingers, tendrils of blue smoke burrowed their way into the cinders.

A moment later, the entire wall of ashes seemed to disappear. In its place, there stood thousands of Necromancer spirits stretching off into the darkness. My mouth fell open. I'd cast this spell on a few graves, and the result had been a handful of blue ghosts.

I'd never seen anything like this, though.

Before me, there stood men and women, old and young, wizened and smooth-faced. All of them wore various levels of Necromancer robes. In the distance, their bodies merged into a shifting sea of transparent blue light.

I folded my arms across my chest, careful to keep my left hand glowing blue. This was the traditional way to welcome a ghost. "Greetings."

All of them turned to focus on me. Thousands of eyes flared a brighter shade of blue as they glared in my direction. The rage pouring off these spirits was almost a palpable thing. The air felt thick with it. These ghosts had been torn from their lives and loved ones. Now, I'd yanked them from their afterlife with the Sire of Souls as well.

Rowan stepped up to my side. "Remember what I did before?"

"That spell with your sword?"

"Yes." His voice lowered. "If they make one false move, I'm doing it again."

I felt the thousands of angry stares burn into my soul. "Thank you."

Quinn stepped in front of the group. "You." His scarred face twisted with rage. "We all died in pain. The Eternal Lands of the Sire of Souls are now our haven of peace. How dare you call us away?"

"I wouldn't summon you if I didn't need your help." The silence that met my words was absolute. My heart pounded harder.

Quinn's frown deepened. "We're done with the living."

"I understand that. But you all dedicated your lives to your Monastery or Cloister." I pulled at the neckline of my shift. "This isn't my proper clothing. If I could, I'd greet you as a Grand Mistress Necromancer and show you the respect you deserve."

The room stayed silent. Even so, the weight of anger faded a little. It felt easier to breathe. I glanced over at Rowan, who gave me the barest of nods. We'd been guessing each other's thoughts for a while now. I could almost hear his words in my mind.

*You're doing well. Keep going.*

I pressed my palms together in the Necromancer gesture for supplication. "You've already given so much, yet I need your help once again. Six Grand Master and Mistress Necromancers are coming this way."

As if emphasizing the point, heavy booms echoed through the chamber. The door rattled on its hinges. The Fantomes were getting closer.

Quinn bared his teeth in a snarl. "They don't deserve the honor of that name."

"I realize that. However, we don't know why they betrayed their own and…" I took in a long breath. This fact wasn't easy to think about, let alone say out loud. "They're some of the last of our kind alive. If they enter this room, they'll attack me and Rowan. We may have to kill them. I simply can't destroy so many without giving them a chance."

"At what?" asked Quinn. "Delivering you into a quicker death?"

"I need you to possess them."

Quinn lifted his chin. There was no mistaking the interest in his ghostly eyes. "I can wipe out their souls?"

"No, I'm asking for a partial possession only. I need you to stop them from doing anything to harm us or others. Once Rowan and I defeat the Vicomte, then we can see how many of them wish to return to the true Necromancer life."

Quinn's mouth thinned to an angry line. "Do you have any idea how much power that takes for us to do?"

"I'm aware." My voice was pleading. It wasn't the Necromancer way, but I couldn't help it.

Quinn stepped closer. I'd forgotten how tall and lanky he was in real life. "Never!"

Here was where my Necromancer training could have kept me calm and organized. I should be able to control my emotions and convince Quinn to help. Instead, his response set my soul burning with white-hot rage. "How dare you!" I poked him in his transparent chest. "I was there when the Tsar took power. You betrayed everyone you knew in order to join his entourage. By the gods, you even betrayed me! You and Tristan left me to bear the brunt of a curse that should have been yours alone."

Quinn looked away. His skin was too transparent to be sure, yet I thought I saw the twinge of color in his cheeks. *Serves him right.* "That was Tristan's idea. I had a hard choice ahead of me."

"Precisely. Now, who's to say that the mages coming here didn't have their own hard choices? When someone like the Tsar comes to power, it's easy to make mistakes." I scanned the faces of as many ghosts as I could. "We're all still Necromancers, aren't we? Controlling our emotions makes us who we are. I'm asking you to control your anger and resentment. I know possession is hard for you, but wouldn't it be worth it if you could help save our way of life?"

Some of the ghosts shifted uneasily. I could tell I was wearing them down.

Quinn stared guiltily at the floor. "What do you want, precisely?"

"Six volunteers to partially possess these Fantomes. They can't remember finding me on this property. They must have their memories erased and then return to their service to the Vicomte."

"And then?" Quinn kicked at the floor with his ghostly boot.

"I need you to poke around in their minds. See which of them may be open to returning to our true Necromancer ways. Once I defeat the Vicomte, I'll need to send those with a chance at redemption to visit the Zelle Cloister. The Sisters there will rehabilitate anyone, so long as they undergo a compulsion spell against causing others harm."

Rowan stepped forward. "And if any are deemed unwilling to change, then I will take care of them."

"Partial possession." Quinn shook his head. "That's a massive amount of effort."

Rowan shot me a sideways look. He didn't say a word. Even so, I knew what he was thinking. He agreed with Quinn.

"There are thousands of you. I only need six volunteers."

Quinn sniffed. "Well, I won't do it." He turned to face the crowd. "Anyone else want more pain than they've ever felt before? And all just to spare the useless lives of these murderers?"

Frustration tightened up my neck and shoulders. Ghosts were hard enough to convince. But after a speech like Quinn's? It wasn't looking good. I slowly scanned the crowd of ghosts. None came forward.

Quinn swung around to face me. "Looks like you'll have to kill them after all." He looked down his scarred nose at me. "Our way of life is over. Accept this. The sooner you join us in the Eternal Lands of the Sire of Souls, the better. That's the only place where true Necromancy will survive." Turning on his heel, he strode off into the wall of ashes.

For a moment, the ghostly crowd kept up their steady stare. Rage was written into the lines of all their glowing faces. I sighed. Why did I think I could talk them into helping? A second later, all the ghosts disappeared. The room felt emptier than ever. My hope was gone as well.

The pounding at the door turned to an ear-shattering level. It wouldn't be long now.

Rowan stepped up behind me. When he spoke, his voice was both deep and gentle. "They're almost here. What's your plan?" He didn't need to say the words. I knew what he was asking.

*Are we killing your fellow mages?*

I pressed the tips of my fingers into my temples. If I could wipe this thought out of my mind, I would. But I'd done my best. There was nothing else for it.

"Let's try paralytic spells. If that doesn't work, then yes, we kill them."

The last two words were like a knife that cut into my soul. I closed my eyes and began to prepare my next spells.

*The Last Necromancer, indeed.*

## 20

*F*rom just outside the door, the bats let out a chorus of high-pitched screeches. I winced. No question what those sounds were. *Death cries.* I'd put down enough farm animals to know that noise firsthand. I shook my head in disbelief.

The Fantomes were killing the bats that Rowan had summoned.

I gritted my teeth in frustration. *What a foolish thing to do.* Casters were incredibly protective of their creations. Killing magickal animals almost always led to a bloodbath. Most mages were wise enough to only incapacitate any opposing beasties made by a Creation Caster, maybe with a sleeping spell or freezing charm.

Not the Fantomes, though.

I worried my lower lip with my teeth. If the last of my people had to die, I wanted it to be as painless as possible. Goading Rowan wasn't helping. He was strong enough to cast a parasite that would kill a Fantome painfully over a hundred years.

Rowan glared at the opened archway. "That was unwise of your fellow mages."

"Be merciful." My voice took on a pleading edge.

"I'll keep my word. Paralytic spells. And if I must kill, I won't draw out their pain." Rowan raised his right hand. A plume of crimson smoke quickly wound up his arm. "I might enjoy the battle, though."

I couldn't deny him that. "Fair enough."

Rowan and I slowly turned to face the entranceway. A patchwork of wooden tables separated us from the closed door. My blue orb now hovered at the center of the ceiling. Had I only cast that a few minutes ago? It felt like a lifetime had passed since then.

The battle would start any second now.

Rowan's Caster power lit up the veins in his right hand. His rumbling voice spoke the classic incantations to prepare for battle. I heard the words for protection from harm and the strength of hundreds. We Necromancers had our own versions of all these spells.

Time for me to cast them.

I lifted my left arm, pulling Necromancer power into my soul. The air here was rich with memory. It would help the Fantomes' spells, but it aided mine, too. Power flowed into my limbs. I cast my own set of protection spells, leaving plenty of energy behind for my first volley in battle. Normally, manipulating magick gave me a welcome jolt of excitement. Not this casting, however. My bones felt heavy with foreboding. I had just finished my preparations when it happened.

The door imploded.

Wooden shards scattered across the floor. The Necromancers stepped into view. Three men, three women. They all appeared young with pale skin, long black hair, and dark brown eyes Something hungry and evil lurked in their elegant features. I remembered Marlene, the Mother Superior of the Midnight Cloister. She'd happily tortured and killed Necromancers for the Tsar. My insides twisted with dread.

I'd worried so much about saving the last of my people. Maybe Quinn and Rowan had been right—there was nothing left to save.

The Fantomes raced into the room, their dark robes billowing with each step. Behind them, there followed a dozen battle skeletons. These were silver-boned creatures with wide shoulders and sharp battleaxes grasped tightly in each hand. Blue light shone out from their eye sockets.

Rowan released his power. A half-dozen red scorpions appeared before us, each one as large as me. They snapped their claws and went after the battle skeletons.

After that, six red spheres of light hovered in the air. Rowan spoke another incantation. I knew the words.

These orbs were paralytic spells.

Rowan lowered his arm, and the spheres shot out across the room, striking each of the Fantomes squarely in the chest. I'd seen paralytic spells at work before. Normally, they were a few glimmers of light no larger than fireflies. These ones were massive. I couldn't imagine anyone having enough magickal protection to fight those off. Still, I released some blue orbs of my own into the mix. More paralytics, more power. I took in a calming breath.

*If anything could freeze them, that volley of spells ought to do it.*

Dust settled into my eyes, making me blink. I looked up and gasped. Even more battle skeletons were crawling along the ceiling. It appeared that the Fantomes hadn't wasted their time in the hallway.

*Gods-damn it.*

I spoke a fast incantation and released more power. Instantly a blue haze appeared around me. The mist quickly rose up to the ceiling, where it solidified into a dozen battle skeletons of my own. While the Fantome warriors were silver, mine had ebony-dark bones with bright sapphire eyes. Long razor-sharp claws jutted out from their hands and feet. Perfect for crawling around upside-down while shredding everything in sight.

More power rushed out of me as the skeletons engaged the enemy. My limbs turned boneless as my power flowed out. Hunching over, I braced my arms on my knees and gasped for breath. From the corner of my eye, I scanned the ceiling, seeing my ebony skeletons take on the silver warriors. My fighters sliced through the opposition, turning them into a cascade of small bones and white dust that fell to the floor.

I grinned. Perhaps these Fantomes weren't so strong after all.

All around us, the skeletons and scorpions kept up a chaos of battle. Rowan's giant creatures chittered as their huge claws bit through bone. My ebony skeletons laughed as they sliced into their opponents. The Fantome's silver skeletons gave as good as they got.

Soon, all the skeletons had been pummeled into shards of bone that lay strewn across the laboratory floor. Rowan's scorpions lay in pieces around us, dead. I tried to see through the cloud of dust and bone.

We'd survived, but what about the Fantomes? Had the paralytic spells worked?

It took a few seconds for the air to clear. When I could see again, there were six Fantomes standing by the smashed-in doorway. Moving in unison, they raised their left arms. All of their hands glowed blue with power. Not good.

Our paralytic spells had failed. The Tsar must have cast some serious protections on these mages. There was no question about it. I needed to launch a counterstrike.

I searched my soul for more magick. Casting the battle skeletons and paralytic orbs had drained me. Now, it would take a little bit to recharge. I looked over to Rowan. "Tell me you're ready to cast."

He shook his head and kept mumbling an incantation. *Gods-damn it.*

The Fantomes lowered their arms and set loose another spell. A crackling sound filled the air as hundreds of skeletal hands burst through the stone floor. Bits of gray rock shot out in every direction. These hands weren't attached to any bodies. That didn't make them any less dangerous than a full skeleton. I knew this spell, and it was bad news.

Skitter lancets.

A skitter was a skeletal hand that could crawl across a room in the blink of an eye. Every bone in this casting was razor-sharp. One skitter lancet could slice through virtually anything in its path, and hundreds were coming at me. Even worse, my protection spells were useless against these things. My heart sank to my toes.

The skitters crawled toward me at incredible speed. Their fingertips clicked against the rock floor. I pulled in magick, but it wasn't enough. *Gods-damn.* I looked to Rowan. "I can't cast yet."

*Please tell me you're ready.*

"I got you." Rowan knelt down, set his hands on the floor, and whispered the end of an incantation. A thick coating of red scales spread out from his fingertips. The movement reminded me of ripples in a pond.

*A protective skin. Yes.*

The scales spread out over the mages and lancets, covering them all in a layer of red alligator-thick skin. Everything became frozen in place, both the Fantomes and the lancets. I had thought that impossible to do both, yet somehow, Rowan had managed it.

*Or not.*

The skitters wiggled under the alligator skin before bursting free. They tore through their scaled coverings and came after us once again, only faster this time.

At last, enough magick inhabited my soul once more. I was ready to cast. I spoke a new battle incantation at double-speed. Power glowed in my left hand. I set it loose. Blue mist shot across the floor, covering the biting hands.

After that, my bone melter spell went to work. The skitters twisted as they were reduced to small puddles of white goo. It was a beautiful sight.

My spell had worked.

Agony erupted in my ribs. I looked down at my right side. A lancet had burrowed into my rib cage. I hissed in a pained breath. Blood oozed across my torn dress. I gripped the skitter, tore it out of me, and tossed the skeletal hand onto the floor. Fresh waves of hurt burned through my chest and up my arm.

Rowan marched over to the skitter, stomped on the thing with his boot, and called out a single word. "Die!" His voice was laced with magick as the skitter got smashed into bits.

I fell forward onto my knees. *What a relief.*

Rowan knelt beside me, his eyes wide with concern. "Let me see your wound."

"What about them?" I spoke the last word through gritted teeth. There was no need to say more. No question what *"them"* I meant here.

"I have the Fantomes encased in a Caster shell. They aren't going anywhere for a while." His voice gentled. "Show me your side."

I lifted my arm and Rowan leaned in closer. My breath came in rough gasps. "How bad is it?"

Rowan gripped my wrist and turned it up. The skin there was sliced to ribbons from the skitter. Rowan met my gaze. Rage glimmered in his emerald eyes. "You're too good for these people. I'm killing them. Now."

"But there are paralytic spells…"

"And we both cast them already. They didn't work. Right now, you need me to get you somewhere safe so I can heal this. Enough, Elea." His eyes glistened. "Please."

Blood dripped from my palm onto the ash-covered floor. *Some of the last of my people.* "Do it."

"Good. It won't take me a minute to finish them off." Rowan rose and turned to face the Fantomes. The mages resembled six crimson-colored statues on the stone floor. Small puffs of ash drifted around them.

Rowan raised his right arm. The veins there glowed with red light.

"No!" A man's voice sounded from behind us. Both Rowan and I turned to see the ghost of Quinn standing by the back wall. "We'll do it."

My brows lifted. "You'll accept a partial possession?"

"Yes." He gestured behind him, and five more spirits stepped out of the ashes. "I can't stand by and watch some the last of our people die. You were right, Elea. We all deserve one last chance." He focused on me, his transparent eyes still bright. "We'll see what we can find out and report back."

"Thank you." Speaking only sent a fresh spike of agony into my side. "Be sure to—" I hissed in a pained breath.

Rowan held me closer. "Don't speak. I know what you would order them." He turned to Quinn. "Remember, erase all memory of us and this battle. They never saw Elea or me. And keep it to a partial possession. Do you understand?"

Quinn nodded, straightened his shoulders, and stepped into the first Fantome. The strangled sound of a scream rang through the air, followed by absolute quiet. My body became boneless with relief as I leaned into Rowan's hold.

Quinn had done it. He'd possessed the first Fantome.

One by one, the other spirits stepped into the mages. More

muffled cries sounded, followed by silence. When it was all done, Rowan raised his hand once more. "Release!"

The red scales that had covered the Fantomes vanished. The mages all blinked and looked around, like sleepwalkers awakening from a dream. None of them appeared to notice Rowan and me. Without another word, the Fantomes marched from the room.

I wanted to thank Quinn and Rowan, but the words stayed trapped in my throat. Pain burned through my body until it was all I could think about. My mind clouded over with agony, and the world faded into darkness.

n my dreams, I returned to the Zelle Cloister, the place where I'd trained to become a Grand Mistress Necromancer. It was nighttime, and I lay curled on my small cot in the far corner of the Sisters' dorm. My thin blanket had frozen solid around me. Every inch of my body shivered from the cold.

I peeped over the edge of my bed. The long stone room lay empty. Where were all my Sisters? One by one, their beloved and wrinkled faces seemed to smile at me from the shadows. How I longed to see them again. Sadly, every time I thought I caught their eye, they'd completely disappear. My heart cracked with grief. The silence turned so absolute my ears began to ring.

I'd never felt more alone.

A dream version of Rowan materialized at my bedside. Despite the dim light, I could clearly make out his tall frame, loose brown hair, and bare chest. He wore his leather pants and nothing else. I reached out and grabbed his hand.

"Cold," I whispered.

"I don't understand." His voice was a gentle rumble. "I cast a spell to keep you warm." He sat down beside me and pulled up my thin blanket. "Your wound doesn't look infected, either."

My teeth chattered harder as I pulled him toward me. "Cold!"

Rowan's rugged features turned unreadable. "You want me to sleep with you?"

I moved back and made room for him. In some corner of my mind, I thought I should worry about the other Sisters. What if they showed up to see a stranger here? Then, I thought better of it.

*Let them find their own man to warm their bed.*

I patted the open stretch of bed beside me. There was a long speech I wanted to say—something about mages protecting each other—but my dream wouldn't let me get it out. Instead, I could only repeat one word. "Cold."

Rowan gave me one of his crooked smiles, and I knew I'd won. He slipped into the cot and pulled me against his side. Cuddling against him, I discovered something very important. Rowan's body was the most comfortable place ever. My entire being filled with warmth and contentment.

What a lovely dream.

I opened my eyes to find the familiar lines of my tavern room. My sleepy thoughts slowly adjusted to my surroundings. Everything was as it should be.

Threadbare rug.

Shabby wooden door.

Small table with a pitcher and washbasin.

And an unclothed man in my bed.

*Wait. What?*

I raised my head for a better view. Indeed, it was true. My cheek was resting on a wide, bare, and very male chest. Shock vibrated down my spine. This wasn't just any naked man, either.

It was Rowan.

In my tavern room.

Wearing naught but his leather pants.

I sat bolt upright. "What are you doing here?"

"She speaks." Rowan grinned, stretched, and laced his fingers behind his head. The movement highlighted the heavy ropes of muscle that wound along his arms. My stomach fell to my toes. This was bad. Had I gone on some kind of drinking bender and forgotten? No, I never took spirits. Perhaps I was still asleep.

A dream. That was all this was. I simply needed to wake up.

Easy enough.

I pinched my forearm, hard. Pain shot across my skin. Rowan didn't disappear. I pinched myself again. "Ouch."

Rowan frowned, yet there was plenty of humor in his expression. "Why are you doing that, exactly?"

"Because I'm really asleep." So I pinched myself again. And it hurt again.

This was worse than bad. It was a disaster.

Rowan chuckled. "No, Elea. You're definitely awake. What's more, you're now speaking in full sentences. I consider that great progress." He shifted his gaze to the window above my bed. A full moon shone through the mottled glass. "And it isn't even morning yet. You slept for about ten hours."

"What are you doing here?" I bit my lower lip softly. That hurt, too.

*Still awake.*

"What's the last thing that you remember?" Rowan shifted position, and the play of muscles across his chest was nothing less than mouthwatering. I hated to admit this, even to myself, but I'd spent a lot of time thinking about this very situation. Only, in my fantasies I actually knew how Rowan had ended up in my bed. Rowan cleared his throat. "Did you hear me?"

*Focus, Elea.*

*No more ogling handsome mages that you're somewhat obsessed with. There are far more important things to contemplate. A weight settled onto my shoulders as I remembered what those things were.*

*Veronique. Ada. Thousands of other Necromancers. All dead.*

A knot of grief tightened around my throat. "The last thing I remember, we found a wall of ashes. Most of my people are—" I blinked hard as more memories appeared. "Not all of them are dead. Ada and Veronique may still be somewhere on Royal lands. A few dozen Fantomes remain." I hunched forward and hugged my elbows. "We fought some of them."

"That's right. What else do you remember?" Rowan sat up and

began rubbing my back in a gentle rhythm. It helped.

"There were lancets. One touched me." *More than touched, actually.*

Harsh memories appeared. I pictured the skeletal hand inside my rib cage. Blood was everywhere. Twisting, I hitched up the fabric of my nightshirt until it came just above my waistline.

My eyes widened as I realized what I'd done. Without so much as a second thought, I'd lifted my shirt before Rowan. Surely, I was still exhausted from my battle with the Fantomes. It wasn't that I was getting more comfortable around Rowan.

An angry red mark colored my skin where the lancet had attacked. Other than that, I appeared to be perfectly fine. There was only one mage who could do something like that. I looked to Rowan. "Thank you for healing me."

He exhaled a slow breath. "You passed out after the battle. I had my people sneak you off the mansion grounds and bring you here."

My eyes widened. "I dreamed that I had returned to the Cloister dormitory. It was so cold. You walked in and—" I winced. "That wasn't a dream, was it? I basically dragged you into bed, didn't I?"

"I'm not complaining." A mischievous gleam settled into his emerald eyes. "I didn't mind helping you be comfortable." He leaned in closer until our foreheads touched. "There was so much blood." His deep voice rattled with fear. "Scared me half to death."

"You?" I always thought of Rowan as the one person who was impossible to frighten. Even when I was dying in the cave after escaping the Midnight Cloister, he never showed any fear.

"Yes, me." Rowan leaned back and cupped my face in his hands. His skin was so warm against mine. "The thought of losing you terrifies me, Elea. You're so strong, in every way. My soul is so much more grounded when I'm around you. For once, I can see something in the future that's mine and beautiful."

"So everything you do is for others. Has it always been like that?" I didn't add the words *to be a member of the Imperial family.* We'd been finishing each other's thoughts for a while now.

"My life isn't my own." Rowan dropped his hands and leaned back against the headboard. "I live for my people. Always have. You can't imagine how much I want something that's mine." His gaze intensified. "My existence isn't complete without you."

My chest warmed at his words. Rowan was sharing a part of his soul with me, and I wanted to give him something in return. "From the first time I saw you, I felt drawn to your strength."

Rowan raised his brows. "You mean, when I yelled at you in the desert?"

"No, before that. I saw you in a vision. You were calling to the Sire of Souls for help."

"Ah." His eyes narrowed. "Do you think the Sire and Lady have something to do with us?"

I chuckled. "I think they have far better things to worry about."

Rowan shook his head. "You have no idea how exceptional you are, do you?"

A blush bloomed along my neck. How I hated this kind of attention. My old Mother Superior always said I was a strong mage. But with so many of my Brothers and Sisters gone, who was to say what was truly exceptional? I fiddled with the neckline of my nightshirt, anxious for a change of subject. "How did I get changed into this?"

"I gave the job to one of the female guards."

My blush deepened. "Not you?"

A hungry look shone in his eyes. "Would you have wanted me to?"

For a moment, panic shot through my body. Yes, I'd wanted to change the subject, but did I really mean to veer it into the territory of Rowan seeing me naked?

The answer rang through every corner of my consciousness.

*Yes, yes I did.*

Some small part of me screamed that I was giving in to my impulsive nature. This was a classic act of a Necromancer who was zuchtlos and out of control.

Most of me didn't care.

"Yes, I would have wanted you to." I swallowed hard. "I still do."

Rowan sat back up, closing the distance between us. "Show me."

His voice had a rough edge, and it made my mind unhinge. My zuchtlos nature grew stronger. In one swift movement, I gripped the edge of my nightshirt, pulled it over my head, and tossed it aside. The coverlet lay loose around my waist, and my long black hair hung over my breasts. My cotton pantalets were the only thing I wore now. My Necromancer side made one last attempt to bring me under control. The words of my training mantra rang through my mind.

*You should ashamed of your weakness.*

*You should always be modest.*

*You should never be attracted to a man.*

And maybe the training was right, yet I didn't care anymore. All I wanted was Rowan. Now, he knew that without question.

Desire burned in Rowan's green eyes. Slowly, he reached forward. His fingertips softly brushed against my cheek. After that, his gentle touch ran down my neck. Everywhere he touched, he left behind a line of heat. My core tightened. I might be a virgin, yet ever since I'd met Rowan, thoughts of his body had haunted me. Making love with him had always seemed like the most natural thing in the world.

"You're so beautiful." Rowan slowly ran his hand across my shoulder. He guided my hair so it hung down my back and exposed my right breast. My nipple puckered with cold. Rowan watched the change; his gaze darkened with want. I loved it. "By the Gods, Elea." Suddenly, Rowan's mouth was on mine. His lips were everything soft and delicious. Our tongues slid across each other in a luscious dance that set my heart pounding.

Our kiss turned fierce. Instinct took over. I didn't know who shifted, but soon I was on my back with Rowan braced above me. Our mouths tangled in a deepening kiss while his hard length pressed against me. Only a thin layer of leather and cotton separated us. I reached down his chest, greedily soaking in the feel of his velvet-soft skin over firm muscle. My fingertips played along the waistband of his leathers.

Rowan stilled. "What are we doing?"

"I want this. I want you."

He slowly shook his head. "I can't. Not here. Not yet." He slipped off me and rose to stand. "I still have duties, Elea."

I sat up and clutched the sheet against my naked torso. The haze of lust left my mind. What just happened? I threw myself at Rowan, and now he was walking away.

*I'm not only zuchtlos, I'm terrible at it.*

"I don't know what you mean, Rowan." My voice cracked as I spoke.

Rowan moved so quickly he was a blur. One moment he was standing by the door. The next, Rowan scooped me onto his lap and began kissing my hair. "It means we belong together. I'm going to fight for that. Believe me when I say that it will happen, just not right now." He set his knuckle under my chin, guiding me closer. Our gazes met. Everything open, honest, and good in this world shone through his eyes. "Do you believe me?"

Here, in his arms, there was no question in my mind. "I do."

"I have to go. What will you do?"

"Find Amelia. Ask her where Ada and the others might be hidden." I exhaled a long breath. "There's nothing else for it. We can only begin the search anew. I have a day left. I'll simply make the most of it."

"I wish I could help you, but I've duties of my own today." He squeezed me a little tighter. I decided that the lands of Sire of Souls could disappear—being held against Rowan's bare chest was heaven.

I shifted in his arms. "I should start now."

"As your healer, I'd say you're in no shape to do that. Give yourself a little time, Elea. Only an hour or so, and you can leave."

"If you're sure."

"Certain."

Everything was so warm and cozy. My eyes drifted shut. "Perhaps I'll nap a bit, then."

"Good." Rowan set me under the covers and tucked the blanket gently under my chin. "And don't forget. No matter where you go, I will find you. Believe that."

I meant to say that I believed him, yet the words didn't come. Instead, my body felt heavy as I drifted off into what promised to be my deepest sleep in years.

## 22

*W*hen I closed my eyes, my dreams took me back to the Midnight Cloister once again. Ada and Veronique were running through the stone hallways and laughing. Veronique looked the way I'd imagined she'd been when she first met Amelia—a bright-eyed and willowy girl with long blonde hair. Her buttercup-yellow gown had an empire waist and billowed around her as she ran.

And Ava was the sweet moppet I'd first met at the Midnight Cloister. Dark, straight hair, exotic eyes, and a smile that dared you not to return it. She wore her gray Novice's robes as Veronique chased her through the halls.

I tried my best to keep pace with them both. Every fiber of my soul wanted one last embrace. It wasn't fair that I'd only seen a pile of ashes. That couldn't be goodbye.

No matter how fast I ran, though, I couldn't keep up with them. Soon, they raced on ahead of me. I could hear their laughter but couldn't find them at all. Somehow, I ended up at the door of Petra, my old Mother Superior. Blue light flared through the keyhole. Smoke wafted out from under her door. My eyes widened as I realized what this meant.

A spell. Petra was summoning me through my dream.

For days, I'd been meaning to send another message to Petra.

Things kept getting in the way, though. And now? After so much excitement, what I needed was rest, not to confront my old Mother Superior. I'd hoped the few scraps of information I sent before would be enough to satisfy her. Obviously not.

And I especially didn't want to see her not face-to-face. I'd changed so much since I left the Zelle. Petra would not approve. Necromancers were supposed to control their emotions, especially when it came to sexuality.

She'd never understand Rowan.

The door swung open. Blue light poured into the hallway around me.

"Come in, Elea." Petra's reedy voice echoed from the room beyond. I took in a deep breath, straightened my shoulders, and crossed the threshold.

Petra's room was small and spare, with a tiny cot, writing desk, and wooden trunk. She lay under a thin coverlet, her long gray hair spreading across the pillow like a halo. Her body looked as frail as a child's.

My breath caught. Petra didn't look well. Dark circles hung under her eyes, and her skin was so pale it was almost colorless. I rushed over to kneel at her side.

"Mother, what's wrong?"

"I'm getting older, Elea."

I ached to comfort her with a hug, but good Necromancers weren't weak in that way. "What can I do?"

"Nothing. It's the way of things." Petra let out a rattling breath. "It's been a rough winter at the Zelle Cloister. Only eight of us left."

I fought hard not to show emotion. However, there was no avoiding the quiver in my voice. "Who went on to the Sire of Souls?"

"The Zaft sisters. Olga, Klara, Gita, and Frieda."

Images of their faces appeared in my mind. The Zaft sisters were elflike ladies who loved to clean the chapel while finishing one another's sentences. Olga was over ninety, but still seemed strong enough to lift an oxcart. Klara, Gita, and Frieda worked in the kitchens and always brought me fresh bread when I'd forgotten to eat while studying.

Now, they were gone too. My eyes stung with held-in tears.

"Don't abandon your training. They go to a better place, as will I. This is no time for mourning or shows of frivolous emotion. You must find trained Necromancers who can keep our ways alive."

A bitter taste crept up my throat. "There's no chance of that, I'm afraid."

"What do you mean? Last I knew, there were thousands of Necromancers under the Vicomte's control. He couldn't have killed them all so quickly."

I set my hand over my mouth. It was better than sobbing. "He did. They're all gone."

There was a flicker of rage in Petra's eyes before her features settled into a mask of calm once more. "And what did he do with their power?"

*Leave it to Mother to ask the right question.*

"It's stored inside a totem ring."

"Like the one in the witness watch that Amelia gave to you?"

"Almost the same. Only the totem ring in the vortex watch can actually transfer the magick."

Petra wheezed out a slow breath. "To anyone?"

"Once there's enough power, yes. The vortex watch will be fully charged tonight. After that, anyone can be infused with its power."

Petra half-closed her eyes. Her lids looked thin as the most delicate lace. "That's why he's using your Sisters from the Midnight Cloister. He needs to drain the last of their power and activate the ring."

"Ada and the others are still alive, Mother." I leaned closer. "Time remains to save them. I have almost a full day before the Vicomte completely drains my Sisters. I know they're at a Royal estate. Once I awaken, I'll start combing through different sites as quickly as possible."

Petra's eyes opened wide. "You'll do no such thing."

I leaned back. A chill crept across my skin. What Petra was saying made no sense. "What do you mean, Mother?"

"Think with your head and not your heart, child. There are hundreds of Royal estates. You'll never find your Sisters in time. But that totem ring inside the Vicomte's vortex watch?" She pursed her papery lips. "Now that, you can find. You know where the Vicomte will be tonight, don't you?"

"At the Montagne's masquerade ball." My words came out dreamy.

*By the Sire. She's right.* To save the realms, I may have to sacrifice my friends. Bands of grief constricted around my windpipe. After all this work, I couldn't leave them to die, could I?

"Listen to me carefully, Elea." Petra's voice took on the ring of authority. "You must get that vortex watch. That's our people's power. Our legacy."

I hugged my elbows. This wasn't what I wanted. My whole goal had been to find Ada, Veronique, and my other Sisters. Still, I couldn't avoid Petra's logic. Preventing the Vicomte from becoming the Tsar was more important.

*My shoulders slumped. I just sentenced my Sisters to death.*

Petra hauled herself up on her pillows. "Did you hear me, Elea? I want your word that you'll get that totem ring."

"You don't want me to take in the power, do you?"

"Absolutely not. Who knows what that much magick would do to you? Your spells will be wild at best. No, just get the watch and return to the Zelle. We'll figure something out." She exhaled and leaned back into her pillow. "Perhaps we can find some way to redistribute the power. I refuse to believe that the Sire of Souls would allow his people to disappear."

"I'll do my best. And thank you for the advice." My voice sounded anything but thankful, though.

"My plan doesn't please you?"

"It's not that. It's just… I'd so wanted to return to the Zelle with my Sisters from the Midnight Cloister. We had plans, remember? You would train them as you had me. And I'd hoped to find other expert Necromancers as well. If you opened up the deep caves, there would be room for thousands here. The Cloister would be alive again."

"It's a fine dream, Elea."

"I'd even thought that perhaps some of the Fantomes would come along for rehabilitation."

"This hope of yours isn't dead. Your Sisters weren't the only ones with some Necromancer ability, you know. Any young mages you send to me will always be welcome." A flicker of a smile crossed her mouth. "And if the Fantomes will subject themselves to enough compulsion spells to keep us safe, then they may join us as well. Are any interested?"

"Some might be." I scrubbed my hands over my face. "It's nothing I can worry about until I get the totem ring, though. If the Vicomte rises to power, he plans to kill them all. If he doesn't?" I shook my head. "I have no idea what will happen."

Petra's face stayed still as stone. "Focus on what you can control. Get that totem ring. Leave the rest to the Sire of Souls. He watches us, even now."

"Perhaps." I'd never told her that I met the Sire of Souls as well as the Lady of Creation. They only seemed concerned about the Tsar. "The gods may have interests, but I'm not sure we're one of them." There was no mistaking the bitterness in my voice. I didn't care.

"Elea." Petra's withered voice took on some of its old bite. "Control yourself. Where is the girl I trained?"

I sighed. "A lot has happened since then."

"You're still friends with those Casters, aren't you?" The way she said the word *Casters* it might as well have been *plague*.

I couldn't lie to her. "Yes."

"Mark my words. There's a reason Casters and Necromancers exist on separate continents. Our ways of life do not mix." She shook her head with disappointment, and it felt as if the marrow had seeped out of my bones. "You've been sending me bits of written messages and hiding the truth. You can't do that anymore." Fierce determination shone through every line in her face. "If you want to claim the totem ring, then you must forget the Casters. Lean into what I taught you. No more acting in a zuchtlos manner."

Rowan's words came back to me. He'd once told me that zuchtlos was nothing to be ashamed of. I lifted my chin. "I am my own person, Petra. My friendship with the Casters gives me strength. I wouldn't have gotten this far without them." I straightened my spine. "And without one Caster mage in particular. Rowan."

Petra looked at me as if I were a Novice again, trying for the umpteenth time to do a basic spell and failing miserably. "Be careful, Elea. That's all I ask. Everything rests on you now."

I could almost feel the weight of her words settle onto my bones. It took everything I had not to crumple forward and swear never to talk to a Caster again. I couldn't do that, though. My feelings for Rowan made that impossible.

Instead, I met her gaze straight on and spoke in an unwavering voice. "I know what is expected of me. I won't fail you."

Blue smoke instantly filled the room. The spell was over, and I was alone in my dreams once again. I took to wandering through the halls of the Zelle once more, trying to find Ada and Veronique for one last goodbye. They were always just out of reach.

## 23

*M*y dream ended when a great pounding sounded on my bedroom door. I jammed my pillow over my head. My mind screamed for more sleep.

The pounding only grew louder.

I kept a tight hold on my pillow as I debated whether or not to answer the door. Every muscle in my body ached with fatigue. I needed to rest up if I was to face down the Vicomte tonight. Plus, my head still felt hazy and unsettled after the spell that took me to Petra, too. All the more reason to sleep.

An explosion of cracking wood shattered my thoughts. I sat bolt upright. My broken door lay in pieces on the threadbare carpet. A very red-faced Amelia stood on the threshold, wearing yet another frilly pink gown. Her left hand still glowed blue with power. "Oops. I didn't know I could do that."

I blinked hard, trying to focus my sleepy mind. What was she doing here? I glanced at the window. The daylight was brighter now. How long had I been asleep?

"Oh, my," said Amelia. "We thought you were dead." She fidgeted with the lacy sleeves of her silk dress, her red hair hanging in perfect ringlets to her shoulders. I swear, I didn't think it ever occurred to Amelia to leave her mansion in anything less than proper attire for a formal ball.

I rubbed my temples, trying to squeeze some sense into my mind. Amelia couldn't really be here. It still felt like the middle of the night. Perhaps this was all a lifelike dream. Or could another spell be at work?

"See, Amelia?" Philippe's voice echoed in from the outer hallway. "I told you that Elea was alive. Those Casters can heal anything." He popped his head into the opened doorway and his gaze locked onto my chest.

*My very bare chest.*

Philippe's mouth stretched into a wide grin. "Elea looks very well, in fact."

The words snapped me out of my sleepy haze. "Philippe!" I gripped the sheet and quickly covered myself. How could I have forgotten I was half naked?

Amelia shoved her brother into the hallway. "Step back, you dog."

He complied with a "woof." Philippe really was a rogue.

Amelia stared at the shattered remains of the door. She shifted her weight from foot to foot. "Apologies for breaking in while you were, uh…"

"Disrobed? Exposed?" A chuckle came from the hallway.

"Quiet, Philippe!" Amelia stared at me, her large eyes pleading. "I'm so sorry. When you left the estate last night, we'd heard that you were ill. Some Caster guards found us. They said you were unwell and that they'd care for you, so we tried not to worry. But then, you didn't come by the mansion this morning. Both Philippe and I became gravely concerned."

"I'm no longer concerned!" called Philippe from the hallway. He sounded exceptionally satisfied with himself.

*Cheeky bastard.*

"Don't worry, Amelia. You and Philippe are like brother and sister to me. There's nothing to apologize for." I motioned to a trunk by the wall. "Would you mind pulling me out something to wear, though?"

"Of course." Amelia bustled into the room, opened the trunk, and pulled out a simple green shift. "How about this?"

"Perfect." I quickly pulled on my dress as well as some fresh underthings. I couldn't help but compare last night with Rowan to this morning with Philippe. When Rowan had seen me naked, my entire body felt on fire. And this morning with Philippe? It was as if my little brother had walked in on me using the privy. Not that I'd ever had a little brother. Even so, now I could imagine the situation with ease. I toed on a pair of slippers and sat down on the bed. "All set."

Amelia rushed over and situated her ruffled self beside me. Her blue eyes widened with concern. "Are you certain that you're all right?"

"Perfectly well." I tried to meet Amelia's gaze. I couldn't. My heart tightened in my chest. Amelia's next question was sure to be about the lost Necromancers. I didn't look forward to explaining the truth.

*I'd just decided to let our friends die.*

"Did you find out anything?" Amelia's face looked so hopeful. "Any news of Veronique?"

And there it was.

I remembered when I'd first met Amelia. Veronique was her only true friend in the world. In fact, Veronique was the main reason Amelia decided to help me in the first place. And now, I'd uncovered news that would break poor Amelia's heart. "You'd better come in, Philippe."

Amelia set her hand on her throat. "Is it bad, then?"

"I'm afraid so."

Philippe walked in slowly. Any air of playfulness had vanished. He set his hands into the pockets of his breeches, setting back the long lapels of his gray velvet coat. I'd noticed that he often did that when he was worried. "What happened?" He glanced toward the doorway. "Should we go somewhere else to chat?"

"No, we're fine here. I've cast wards against eavesdropping ages ago." *But not against breaking down the door.* I'd have to fix that.

Amelia gripped her hands at her waist. "Please tell me what's happened."

Tension tightened up my neck and shoulders. *Best to make this simple and quick.* "There's nothing we can do to save our friends."

A heavy silence filled the room. The air suddenly felt too thick to breathe. If there was anything worse than leaving the Necromancers for dead, it was telling Amelia. My Sisters could be alive somewhere with hours left to live. Even so, there was no point in raising

Amelia's hopes in the matter. My responsibilities lay elsewhere now. "It's time to mourn them, Amelia. We've done all we can do." Every word felt like a knife wound in my chest. How could I abandon them?

*Rein in your emotions, Elea. You can't allow the Vicomte to take your people's power.*

Amelia crumpled to her knees. Her hands covered her mouth as if to hold in a scream. Philippe knelt beside his sister. "I'm so sorry." With his golden hair, he looked like a visiting angel. "I know how much Veronique meant to you."

Amelia's lower lip trembled. A long moment passed before she spoke again. "Everyone I care about leaves me."

Philippe gently wrapped his arm around his sister's shoulder. "Not me."

Amelia sniffled. "No, not you. Veronique is gone, though." She turned to me, her pretty blue eyes rimmed with red. "And you're leaving soon, aren't you?"

Bands of sadness tightened around my throat. Amelia was right. Once my work here was done, I'd vowed to return to Braddock Farm. "I'll remain for a while yet."

"You're leaving me. And Rex will leave me too. I can feel it."

A small jolt of surprise moved through me. "What do you mean?"

"Yes, we've spent time together." Her shoulders trembled. "Alone."

*They did?* The urge to protect Amelia welled up inside me. How could they leave her alone with Genesis Rex so soon? Amelia knew about manners, but not the intricacies of statecraft. An experienced politician like Genesis Rex could manipulate her in a dozen different ways, none of them good. "When did this happen?"

"After the play." Amelia gripped the folds of her gown so tightly I thought she might tear it open. I'd never seen her act like this before.

"Do you like him?" To me, Rex seemed like a father figure. He was all gray hair and cavalier attitude. I couldn't imagine falling for him.

Amelia stared at her lap. "I know it must sound silly, yet I do."

"Yet you hardly know him." The hairs on the back of my neck stood on end. Something about all this didn't seem right. "And he's so old."

"Elea has a point, you know." Philippe pulled a kerchief from his pocket and began patting the tears on Amelia's cheeks. "In fact, the boys you normally like are so young, they have faces full of acne."

Amelia frowned. "Not all of them had acne, Philippe."

"True. Some had voices that hadn't deepened."

At last, Amelia broke out into a small smile. "Even so, Rex is different. He may be older than the boys I usually admire, yet his age suits him perfectly." She huffed out a slow breath. "Still, I don't think he'll ever be attracted to me. I'm simply another alliance to him." She looked up at the ceiling, trying to hold back more tears. "What a fool I'm being. I lose a few friends, meet one new man, and what do I do? Turn into some kind of blubbering idiot."

My protective urges for Amelia came back a hundredfold. "Don't apologize for how to feel. It's not like you've had a horde of people in your life to rely on. And the gods know the Vicomte hasn't been kind, to put it mildly."

"That *is* putting it mildly," said Philippe.

I shot Philippe a frustrated look. Sometimes, his commentary simply didn't help things. I refocused on Amelia. "It's true that Veronique and I can't be close to you physically. We'll always be with you in spirit, though. And you know why? Because you're a valuable and lovely person, Amelia. Your friendship is precious to all who know you."

Amelia stopped sniffling, and I took that as a good sign and kept on talking. "And don't forget—Rex only just met you. 'Love at first sight' may be a pretty tale for bards, however it rarely happens in real life." I glanced at Philippe, as he was much more of an expert in the amorous arts than I was. "Wouldn't you say so, Philippe?"

"Of course. I've never been in love personally, but I've seen it grow." He leaned back and tapped his square chin. "Elea's right. Give Rex some time. If he's half the man you say he is, he'll come around."

I turned to Philippe. "You haven't met Rex?"

Amelia shook her head. "I'm the only one."

"You know the Casters." Philippe rolls his eyes. "Obsessed with secrecy."

Amelia lifted her chin. "Rex has good reasons for that, you know. The last three Caster Kings were all murdered. And someone tried to assassinate Rex, too."

Philippe chuckled. "And the solution is for everyone to wear face masks?"

Amelia sniffed. "They're helms, Philippe. And it's one of many security measures that they've employed for generations."

"It's security against intimacy, if you ask me." Philippe folded his arms over his chest. "How can you get to know each other with all this sneaking about? And don't get me started on all this Royal frippery that the Vicomte is strong-arming you into. Tell me, when you met Rex, were you acting like Amelia, or were you playing the Royal like the Vicomte had ordered you to?"

Philippe had a point. If Amelia wanted a real relationship, then she needed to act like her true self.

"I had to follow Royal protocol," said Amelia.

Philippe's mouth thinned. "The Vicomte's version of protocol has you tottering about like a pretty toy. I won't have it."

My hands balled into fists. I hated how the Vicomte treated Amelia.

"But I have to," said Amelia. "The Vicomte talked to me right before I saw Rex. He said that if I did anything embarrassing, I was as good as dead."

"The Vicomte won't always be around," said Philippe. "All I'm saying is that it's better to act as a real human being than a Royal sleepwalker. Every real man prefers an honest show of womanly affection."

Amelia paused, her small brows drawing together. After a few seconds, she turned to me. "What do you say, Elea? You stayed with the Casters for a time."

I rubbed my neck as I thought things through. "Philippe may be right."

"Of course, I am."

"The Casters were a very affectionate group," I went on. "I couldn't believe how often they embraced one another. I'm sure they'd rather openness and honesty to playing a part."

Amelia twisted her skirts around her fingers so tightly I thought she might do herself harm. "You're both correct. I can see that now."

Philippe grinned and leaned against the wall, kicking his right ankle over his left. "I always am, especially when it comes to matters of the opposite sex."

"I just lost Veronique. I'm about to lose Elea." Amelia's bow-shaped mouth thinned to a determined line. "I won't lose Rex, too."

I didn't like how all Amelia's thoughts kept centering on Rex. "You'll always have my friendship, Amelia. Even if I move away." I sighed. "Which isn't happening any time soon. I need to get that vortex watch away from the Vicomte. Tonight."

Amelia stared out the window. I wasn't sure she heard me at all.

Philippe gave his sister's hand a friendly squeeze. "Did you hear Elea? She wants to prevent the Vicomte from becoming a Necromancer tyrant. Personally, I think that's a far better use of your time than…"

Amelia's big blue eyes flashed with an icy gleam. "Than what? Than caring for my friends and my heart? What good is having a realm in safety when there is no one I love in it?"

"Let's keep focused on the facts, dear sister." Philippe gave me a dry look. Evidently, this kind of show of emotion wasn't unusual for Amelia. "First, I am here and that counts for something. Second, what kind of future would you and Rex have if the Vicomte comes into power?"

"Same as we have now." Amelia lifted her chin. "None."

At this point, the conversation was rubbing on my nerves. I needed to plan for tonight's ball, not cajole Amelia any longer. I took care to lower my voice to my most gentle tone. "Focusing on Rex won't make up for losing Veronique. You need to grieve her on your own."

Amelia kept staring at the far wall and not saying a word. I leaned in closer to her. "Don't you agree?" I asked. She still said nothing in reply. I cleared my throat. "Did you hear me?"

Amelia gave me her best baby-doll face, the one she normally reserved for servants and the Vicomte. "I heard every word."

*But paid no attention.*

Philippe's eyes narrowed. "Elea spoke the truth. I hope you listened. This is a time to grieve, not chase after a new relationship. And we've plenty of work to do in the meantime."

"Absolutely." Amelia smoothed down her bodice. "Whatever you say."

*That settled it. She is paying no attention at all.*

"Anything I say?" I shot Philippe a sly look. "Because I plan to strip naked again."

"That's fine." Amelia clapped her hands. "Let's talk about more important things." Her voice took on a pleading tone. "You are going to the ball tonight, aren't you? They're announcing my engagement and everything."

"Amelia. This is what I warned you about. You're obsessing about Rex and the ball. You haven't listened to Philippe and me."

"Don't be silly. Now, are you witnessing my engagement or aren't you?"

I turned to Philippe. "Is there any point trying to convince her?"

"She gets this way sometimes. Just move on."

And indeed, I'd seen Amelia in one of these moods before. The girl was impossible to sway once she'd set her mind on something. So far, her goals had always aligned with mine, so her stubbornness hadn't been an issue.

"Evidently, it is I who needs to convince you." Amelia looked up at me from under her long lashes. "Please join the ceremony?"

She was so sweet in her manipulations. I couldn't help but smile. Whatever happened between Amelia and Rex, tonight was my friend's engagement announcement. I'd do my best to help her enjoy it. All while I stole the Vicomte's watch, of course.

"I'll be there. I may have to run off here and there on a little errand. Even so, I'll do my best to be there for the big announcement."

Philippe lowered his voice. "And I'll help where I can, too." He gave me a surreptitious wink. I appreciated the sentiment. At least I had one focused ally tonight.

Amelia clapped. "Perfect. Then, you'll go with me to the mansion and get ready? Clothilde has all sorts of ideas for your gown."

"I'll go to the mansion. First I must discuss my broken door with the innkeeper." I could cast a spell to fix it, but I was still feeling winded from last night.

"We'll see you soon, then." Amelia kissed me lightly on the cheek and sauntered out into the hallway.

Philippe kissed my hand and spoke in a low voice. "I'll see what I can do with her. Don't hold your breath."

"Thank you."

Once Philippe and Amelia were gone, I sat back down on my bed. I needed a quiet moment to process everything that had happened. I leaned back on the mattress and stared up at the cracked plaster ceiling. Who was I to tell Amelia that she needed to find time for her grief? I'd been avoiding doing the same myself.

*Thousands of Necromancers. Gone.*

Virtually all of my people were dead. Soon, that number would include Ada and Veronique.

I rolled over onto my side, feeling darkness and grief seep into my pores. Tears blurred my vision. The loss in my soul felt so vast, it was as if nothing could ever fill the emptiness again. Not even Rowan. Not even home.

## 24

*A*melia, Philippe, and I stepped down from our carriage and strolled up to the Montagne mansion, ready to be received for tonight's ball. My friend positively bubbled over with a forced kind of excitement.

"The Vicomte didn't say when they'd announce my engagement. Do you think it will be later in the evening? I think it won't happen until well after everyone's arrived." Amelia kept speaking without seeming to draw breath between sentences.

No question what all this false joy was about. Amelia didn't want to feel the pain of losing Veronique. I knew this for a fact because I wore a forced smile of my own. Only I wasn't so focused on the engagement.

*I need that vortex watch.*

A shiver rolled across my shoulders. That much power in the hands of any one person? They could raze the realm with a single spell. It was more magick than a good mage would want... Or an evil mage should have.

A line of well-dressed dignitaries and socialites filled the stone walkway behind us. The ladies all wore full-skirted ball gowns; the men had donned long coats. Everyone had on a formal mask. Tonight's ball was the last event in the Festival of Theodora. In the legend, Theodora snuck past the gods' gateway by wearing a disguise. All the final celebrations in her honor were masquerades.

Soon it was our turn to mount the staircase that led to the mansion's main doors. The Baroness de Montagne stood at the top of the golden staircase. Her white gown, silk mask, and pearly wig all accented her pale skin and willowy form to perfection. She stared through Philippe and me as if we weren't there. Her focus quickly locked on Amelia.

"My dear, you're here!" The Baroness kissed Amelia lightly on both cheeks. "You did such a wonderful job at the play last night. I'm simply dying to discuss it with you."

Amelia curtsied. "Thank you, Baroness."

"Only, there were a few things you could have done better. I should like to review them with you now before I forget. After all, you'll be playing Theodora next year, too. We can't have those same mistakes again."

Philippe and I shared a meaningful look. The Baroness seemed ready to give a long lecture. *I was not in the mood.*

Time to end this.

I set my hand on my belly and forced on a glum face. "Pardon me. I'm afraid I'm still not fully recovered from last night."

"Recovered?" The Baroness's nostrils flared. "You ran off to get a tincture for Amelia and never returned."

"That's because I became ill myself. Didn't anyone tell you? They found me in a pool of my own vomit." After yesterday, I suspected the Baroness de Montagne wouldn't keep chatting once I'd tossed out the word *vomit*. "Didn't they tell you? It was quite grisly." I inhaled a long breath as if ready to describe everything.

"Come inside." The Baroness shooed us into the mansion. "Don't be vulgar."

I couldn't stop my smile. What a perfect ruse. I'd just sidestepped a ten-minute lecture about nothing. All I needed to do now was find the Vicomte and get that watch.

We all stepped into the reception room, which was a large square space made of white granite. The place was crammed with Royals in their fancy gowns and longcoats. The Baroness snapped her fingers, and a servant in white livery stepped to our side. He was young and fit with an elaborate white mask made of feathers. "Excuse me," he said. "The Vicomte wishes to see his daughter."

All the blood drained from Amelia's face. "He does?"

"By all means." The Baroness waved her hand casually. "Georges, please take these three to the Vicomte."

Amelia took a half step backward. The room was so filled with people, someone almost tripped on the train of her pretty pink gown. "I don't need to see him."

On the other hand, I wanted to see him. Very much.

"Don't be ridiculous. If he calls you, you must go." The Baroness returned to the front door and greeted another guest with air kisses on both cheeks. I supposed that meant the conversation was over.

Amelia's gaze shifted between Philippe and me. Her blue eyes widened with worry. I could understand her concern. The Vicomte was a callous bastard, and that was on a good day. Amelia gripped the wide cuffs of her brother's longcoat. "Why don't we go into the ball for a moment?"

Philippe gently patted his sister's shoulder. "You know we have to visit him now."

"Both Philippe and I will be with you." I lowered my voice to a whisper. "Besides, if the Vicomte gets out of line, I'll fillet him with magick." *Right after I steal the vortex watch.*

Amelia brightened a little. "Can you really do that?"

"All the fun is in trying." I added extra menace to the phrase. That seemed to help even more.

"Let's go, then."

"Follow me." Georges quickly navigated through the crowded hallways. From what I could see, this part of the mansion was made of polished gray stone with vaulted ceilings. It has hard to see much since there were so many bodies in the way.

At last, we reached a quiet corner with an unassuming door. Georges pulled it open and leaned inside. "Your Eminence, your daughter and her guests are here."

"Send them in already." The Vicomte's dismissive tone set my teeth on edge. I wished he'd treat others with more respect. Or any respect, really.

Georges moved aside, gesturing for us to enter the room. Amelia stepped in first, followed by me and Philippe. The chamber was a small and simple space with wooden walls that were inlaid with white stone. The Vicomte paced by the window, wearing his garish orange pants, tall black boots, and a frilly pink shirt.

No longcoat. My heart sank. The longcoat was where the man kept all this watches. I quickly scanned the room.

No coat there, either.

And no sign of any watches.

The servant turned toward the door. Without meaning to, I gripped his shoulder. "Georges, wait!"

Everyone in the room froze. If I'd screamed *fire*, I couldn't have drawn more attention to myself.

"Yes, my Lady?"

I forced my face back into a semblance of calm. "This room is frightfully cold. I should think the Vicomte would like his longcoat." I turned to the Vicomte. "Or do you have it close at hand?"

*Please, have it close at hand.*

"Looking for my watches, eh?"

It took every ounce of my Necromancer training not to gasp. "I don't know what you mean."

"What a silly little animal you are. My devices are precious. Everyone wants to see them. Which is why I don't leave them laying about for addlebrained nitwits to waste my time." He pointed to the door. "Georges. Out."

The servant quickly left the room while the Vicomte glared at me like I was a mangy dog begging for leftover views of his lovely toys. The words for a half-dozen attack spells flickered through my mind.

*What I wouldn't give to kill the man right now.*

I forced my face into some semblance of calm. *Time enough to kill the Vicomte later.* Namely, once the vortex watch was in my possession.

The moment Georges closed the door, the Vicomte rounded on Amelia. "Back to the matter at hand. I brought you here, daughter, for one reason only. And that wasn't to entertain your useless friends." He stepped closer and bared his yellowed teeth at her. "Don't you dare foul this engagement up for me."

Amelia set her hand on her bare neck. "I would never."

"Please. Some of my Fantomes gave me trouble today."

I rubbed my chin. Could they be the same mages that I'd possessed last night? I certainly hoped not. If I was going to find the vortex watch, I needed every ally I could get.

Amelia blinked innocently. "So your servants are giving you trouble. What could that possibly have to do with me?"

"When it comes to Fantomes, things like this simply don't happen. That is, unless you're around for some reason. In fact, this is the second time such odd goings-on have occurred. First, you visit the de Havilland mansion. That time, one of my mages ended up dead in flames."

Philippe stepped up to his sister's side. "There was no sign of foul play."

"Even worse. These mages are far too powerful to be killed by a random fire."

"We all have our off days," said Amelia. "Even Fantomes." I was so proud of her calm tone of voice.

"I don't believe in coincidences. Yet I do believe in warnings. And I gave you one, didn't I?" The Vicomte set his fists on his hips. "So imagine my surprise when I awoke this morning to learn that one of my mages hesitated before killing a servant. I had them all looked into, and there's something wrong with six of them. Know anything about it?"

"No," said Amelia.

The Vicomte stepped up closer to his so-called daughter. He stared at Amelia for a long moment before speaking. "No, I don't think you do. Genesis Rex is open to your marriage, and you seem smitten with him for some fool reason, so I don't think you're the one behind this."

"Excellent," said Amelia. "Now, if you don't mind we need to —"

"Silence!" The Vicomte stepped up to Philippe next. Nervous energy zinged through my limbs. In all the excitement, I hadn't considered that the possessed Fantomes would expose themselves so quickly. *Who asks people to murder innocent servants anyway?*

My stomach fell to my toes. *The Vicomte, that's who.* I should have guessed that this would happen.

The Vicomte looked Philippe over from head to toe. "I don't

think you had anything to do with it, either. Meddling with my mages wouldn't get you into anyone's bed."

Philippe pressed his lips together hard. I knew he was dying to say something. By the gods, I was dying to say something too. Philippe may be a rogue, but there was more to him than that. He'd actually been helping us all along, and for no other reason than Amelia wished it.

After that, the Vicomte stepped up to stand before me. He moved so slowly I felt like a rabbit being hunted by a fox. He stared down his thin nose at me. "Which leaves you, the one who wanted a peep at my watches."

My heart beat so hard I thought it might break out of my rib cage. *Remember your training. Don't reveal any emotion.*

The Vicomte gripped my chin. "You look familiar, too." He leaned in closer, and the scent of stale smoke and whiskey wafted from his breath. "Where have I seen you before?"

*When I dressed in Caster leathers and sent the Tsar into exile?*

"I didn't realize you dallied in ladies," I said coolly.

The Vicomte's thin mouth stretched into an evil smile. "Trying to goad me, eh? It won't work." He dropped my chin. "Besides, I don't have the time for this nonsense. I need all my powers of persuasion in order to ensure Genesis Rex engages himself to my wayward daughter today." His features turned dreamy. "Imagine. I'd be in the line of succession for the Caster throne. My scouts have been all over their continent, you know. The Casters have gold mines galore. Rooms filled with diamonds. Yet they toss those riches aside to fornicate in the trees like animals. Mark my words. That place is a ripe fruit waiting to be plucked." He glared at Amelia. "Once you're Queen, we'll have to take very good care of you. Wouldn't want anything to befall you or Rex, now would we?"

Amelia's face fell. The Vicomte basically admitted to planning to murder her and Rex so he could take over their continent. The man was insane.

The Vicomte tapped his chin. "Rex hasn't said anything about my plans, has he?"

"He knows nothing, Father."

"Not that you'd tell me anyway," the Vicomte sighed. "You're always loyal to the dullest knife in the drawer. Well, if Rex does say anything, you can tell him to stop snooping around the dungeons here. I don't know what his people did, but I have Fantomes missing and signs of Caster magick everywhere."

It took a force of will for my eyes not to bulge out of my head. The Vicomte knew about the signs of our battle from yesterday.

Amelia kept up her innocent face. She could make a master spy herself, one day. "I don't know what you mean. Rex and I spoke of nothing like that."

The Vicomte sniffed. "I suppose not. Sharing secrets wouldn't help him put a baby in your belly. I'm sure that's all he wants."

*Disgusting pig.* If I didn't need that vortex watch, I'd crush the man right now.

The Vicomte sauntered over to the door and pounded on it with his bony fist. "Jonas! Hannah!"

The door slowly swung open. Two Fantomes stepped inside, a man and a woman in black robes. They had the classic look of Necromancers. Both were tall and lithe with aristocratic features, pale skin, dark hair, and brown eyes. The woman spoke first. "What do you wish, Your Eminence?"

"This one." He shoved me forward. "Torture her until she confesses to something." He snapped his fingers, an idea appearing. "We had to lock up those six Fantomes. None of them would follow the rules today. Make her take the blame for that."

It took everything I had not to gasp. If Jonas and Hannah got their spells into me, I could confess to more than they bargained for.

And I still wouldn't have the vortex watch.

The Vicomte waved his hand dismissively "However you kill her, just do it quietly and out of sight. I don't want to upset Genesis Rex."

The man bowed slightly at the waist. "As you command, Your Eminence."

Amelia stepped forward. "No!"

The Vicomte rounded on her. His gray face suddenly turned pale with rage. "I've half a mind to end you as well. Think I can't take another heir? I can and easily." His voice lowered to menacing whisper. "Do I make myself clear?"

Amelia nodded.

I gave her my most serene gaze. "I'll be fine, Amelia."

The Vicomte's eyes locked with mine. Every line of his gray face darkened with pure hatred. "No, you won't. You'll be dead in an hour." He paused, waiting for someone else to speak.

Frustration and rage careened through me. My hands balled into fists. I wanted to take down these two Fantomes now, but I needed to be smart. It would be much easier to fight them if we were somewhere secluded.

I didn't want anyone to hear the screams, either.

## 25

The Fantomes guided me through a series of deserted garden pathways. Behind us, the windows of the Montagne mansion flickered with candlelight—a hundred tiny beacons against a darkening sky. The sickly-sweet smell of withering flowers hung heavily in the air. With every step, my silk gown rustled gently.

I shook my head in disbelief. In some ways, this evening resembled another fairy tale. I was wearing a lovely red ball gown. In a few hours, I might watch my friend become engaged to a powerful king.

Trouble was, in my version of the tale, I had to fight a few mages first.

In my silk gown.

With a party mask on.

My pulse beat so hard I could feel it in my throat. I wanted nothing more than to cast some spells and defeat these Necromancers, right now. I clenched my casting hand, repeating the same two words over and over.

*Not yet.*

Casting this close to the mansion would only attract more Fantomes, and I'd have enough trouble with these two. Plus, I must conserve my energy. Not only would I need to stay alive, but I also had to find the Vicomte's watch. My throat tightened.

*I don't want to kill other Necromancers. I may have to, though.*

The mages led me to a small clearing in the far corner of the gardens. Despite the growing shadows, I could tell the place was large enough for a lover's bench and little else. I gritted my teeth in frustration.

No way could I conjure battle skeletons here.

The spot was simply too small. Which meant that I'd have to do my own fighting. I took in a deep breath.

*Fine. I'll take this hand to hand.*

The mages stopped at the opposite side of the clearing. Moving in unison, they slowly turned around to face me. Hannah was the first to speak. "The Vicomte seems to think you had something to do with our fellow Fantomes acting strangely. What do you know of this?"

I gave her a look of doe-eyed innocence. "And what do you think?"

Jonas lifted his chin. The movement meant he looked down his elegant nose at me. "I think anyone who could cast that well is long dead."

"Agreed," said Hannah. "I doubt she even has any power worth draining."

I clasped my hands under my chin and widened my eyes further. It was a pitiful attempt at begging, but I was a mage, not an actress. "You can drain Necromancer power?" I forced out a gasp. "I may, uh, know someone who wants to get rid of hers."

In my mind, this was an obvious ploy. However, the mages didn't doubt my intent in the slightest.

"Why?" asked Jonas. "Do you have power to speak of?"

I kicked at the grass with my slipper. "I might."

Hannah stepped closer. "The Vicomte asked us to interrogate you, but he thought you were only a troublemaker. Why, if he knew you had power, he'd…"

*Kill me? Drain me?*

"If he knew, then he'd want to help me?" I glanced between them, doing my best to appear wide-eyed and helpless. It didn't seem possible that they'd keep believing my act, yet they did.

"Precisely," said Jonas. "The Vicomte runs a charity where he helps those like you to rid yourself of cumbersome magick."

*What a bastard.* Jonas spoke the lie so smoothly it was obvious that he'd done so before.

"Why don't you tell us?" asked Hannah. "How much power do you have?"

I shifted my weight from foot to foot. "Well, I've nothing like you two." I scrunched up my eyes as if concentrating with all my strength. Magick flowed into me, but I kept most of it in reserve. I released the smallest amount. A spark of blue light flew across my palm. I slumped my shoulders, pretending to be winded. "See? It's only a little power. Even so, it's dangerous to have it."

A ghost of a smile rounded Hannah's mouth. "We can help you."

"Really? When?"

"Right now," answered Jonas. "The Vicomte has need of mages like you."

*Sure, so he can power his totem ring and take over the realm.*

I worried my lower lip with my teeth. Pretending to be frightened was a surprisingly fatiguing activity. "Is it far? I wouldn't want to leave Amelia for too long."

"Why, it's right below our feet." Jonas pointed to the ground. "The Vicomte has a special infirmary set up for people like you."

*People like me.*

The words sent a jolt of awareness straight up my spine. Could he be talking about Ada and Veronique? That couldn't be possible. Quinn said they were all dead. My logical side jumped on that thought.

*At the time, Quinn also seemed somewhat barking mad.*

When I spoke again, my voice took on a hollow sound. "There are others? Here? Now?"

"Of course, there are." Hannah reached for me. "Just come along and we'll show you."

The jangle of metal stopped me cold. Jonas had pulled enchanted manacles from the folds of his robes. I'd encountered those before. They could block the power of even the most advanced mage. Even worse, they hurt like hell to get off.

I still had plenty of magick left, so I put it to good use. I sent a blast of blue smoke from my left palm. It shot over to Hannah and Jonas, wrapping around them in a swirl of blue. When the haze disappeared, Jonas's enchanted manacles had dissolved into sapphire-colored dust. The trick was to cast the dissolver spell before they got those irons on.

The elegant lines of Jonas's face fell slack with shock. "How is this possible? The only Grand Mistresses left are Fantomes."

Hannah sniffed. "It's a low-level mage trick. The Vicomte warned us about her." She reached into the folds of her robes, ready to pull out her own set of enchanted manacles. When she removed her hand again, her palm held a small pile of blue dust. She stared at it, open-mouthed. "What?"

"It's a Grand Mistress level spell," I said simply. "You didn't think it would only effect Jonas, did you?"

I fought the urge to smile. People believed what they wanted to believe. I stood before these two mages, having just completed a rather complex spell. Still, this reality threatened their status as the greatest Necromancers around, so the two didn't even think to start a counter-spell.

*All the better for me.*

Raising my arm, I released more of my magick. A glowing blue mist appeared by my feet. The haze quickly swirled up my body, solidifying into a suit of enchanted bone armor. Giant femurs protected my shoulders, the ball sockets covering my upper arms. Layers of heavy ribs shielded my torso. Carved fibulas encased the rest of me. Satisfaction warmed my chest. *A perfect casting.* This armor was impervious to most weapons. Even better, it would give me extra strength when fighting hand to hand.

Unfortunately, the casting itself took a toll. My head felt woozy and my legs were unsure. Still, I couldn't pause to catch my breath. I marched toward Hannah, who had finally snapped out of her disbelief. Her shoulders straightened and malice lit up her brown eyes.

*Excellent. I enjoy a good fight.*

Hannah lifted her left hand, showing off the totem rings on her fingers. "Kill, destroy, burn."

Hannah's rings flared blue as her totem rings came to life. An array of tiny weapons sped toward me through the night. There were bone darts and small daggers. Fireballs and throwing stars. Hammers and arrows.

And all of them bounced off my armor harmlessly.

This really was one of my favorite spells.

Raising my arm high, I slammed my fist into the side of Hannah's head. She dropped to the ground, unconscious.

Jonas whirled around to face me. "I don't know who you are or how you escaped us for so long, but your power belongs to the Vicomte now." I could tell that Jonas had been pulling magick into himself. Now, he quickly released his own mist and spell. I expected another volley of weapons. Instead, the glowing mist opened a small incision on the man's neck. A chill of fear rolled across my shoulders. There was only one reason he'd open up his flesh like that.

Jonas was about to release his bone crawler. Why?

A memory appeared. Back at the Havilland's gallery, Kamilla had said that some Fantomes were experimenting with their bone crawlers. Was Jonas one of them?

An ugly smile rounded Jonas's mouth. A heartbeat later, his bone crawler skittered out of the incision and onto his shoulder.

My stomach heaved with disgust. I'd seen these creatures before, back at the Midnight Cloister. Like all the others, this bone crawler had a centipede's body and long twitching antennae. The outer segments of its exoskeleton were covered with a thin, indestructible layer of bone.

The creature soaked in more magick from Jonas's spell. Blue mist seeped into its segmented body. After that, the bone crawler completely transformed. I'd never seen anything like it. The creature's many segments stretched and multiplied. Soon, Jonas was covered in bone crawler armor.

I blinked hard, not believing my own eyes. I knew the Fantomes all had bone crawlers inside them. Back in the gallery, I'd seen one move inside Kamilla, but nothing like this. My breath caught as the realization struck.

The Tsar was gone now. The Fantomes really were working on ways to use the bone crawlers to their advantage.

And to my defeat.

Alarm rattled through me. This wasn't good. Bone crawlers were indestructible. My armor wouldn't last long.

Neither would I, for that matter.

Jonas lunged at me, pinning me to the ground with his heavier weight. His right hand wrapped around my throat, shattering the armored plate around my neck. The insect gauntlets he wore twitched against my skin. I couldn't breathe.

With his left hand, Jonas tore through my breastplate as if it were made of paper. His grip tightened on my throat. Pain shot through my neck. My lungs ached. All my thoughts about spellwork disappeared. My enchanted armor fell to dust around me. I could only think about one thing.

*Air. I need to breathe.*

I wrapped my bare hands around the Jonas's. For the first time since I fought the Tsar, my palms touched a bone crawler made with hybrid magick.

Suddenly, a different kind of power shot through me. Purple light flared around my hands and neck.

My body went on alert. This level of power was something I'd only felt once before—when I was fighting the Tsar. That had been the one time I used hybrid magick. Afterward, I'd never been able to repeat the casting. Now I knew why. When I fought the Tsar, I'd been holding a bone crawler. Somehow, that had helped use with both Necromancer and Caster power. Excitement flared through my bloodstream.

I could counterattack.

On reflex, I pushed against the mage. He flew off me like a rag doll.

I stared down at my hands. The purple light still danced across my skin.

*This was hybrid magick. Again. And it was mine to command.*

Jonas slowly rose to his feet. "How did you do that? The bone crawler answers only to its host and the Tsar. And they never transfer power."

In truth, I had no idea why the bone crawler would give its hybrid magick to me. Jonas didn't know that, though.

"Come closer, Jonas. I'll show you."

"I've a better idea." Jonas tilted his head and spoke a quick incantation. The incision along his neck glowed blue once more. His bone crawler armor shrank to its regular size and then wiggled back inside his neck. "I'll keep my bone crawler of reach for now. Once we have you in our control, we'll find out what you're really up to."

"I've got different plans for the evening." I released more of my hybrid power. Purple mist flew off my left hand and wrapped around Jonas's body. The haze solidified into a winding sheet that tightened around him, secure as a mummy. He stared at me for a moment, dumbfounded, and then toppled backward.

I stepped up to loom over him. This kind of angle worked the best during interrogations. "Where are the other Necromancers being held?"

Jonas writhed beneath me. "What Necromancers?"

"The ones you've been draining." I snapped my fingers, and the winding sheet tightened around Jonas' body. He wheezed.

I leaned closer. "Not being able to breathe is unpleasant, isn't it?"

It took him a few gasps to reply. "Bitch."

"What kind of attitude is that?" I rolled my eyes. "Don't make me cast something more painful. I've already had a tiring day."

The purple light was fading from my hands. I didn't have much longer to use my stolen hybrid power. I loosened the winding sheet ever so slightly, just enough to allow him to speak more easily. "Talk."

"You'll see for yourself where they are, considering that you'll soon be drained too. We haven't had a mage of your quality in ages. The Vicomte will be so pleased."

The last wisps of purple light faded from my hands. My hybrid magick was gone. A chilly sense of awareness crawled up my skull.

*Someone is watching me.*

Bit by bit, I angled my head to look behind me. A pack of Fantomes stood at the other side of the small clearing, their hooded forms barely visible in the moonlight.

*Gods-damn it.* I didn't know if I had enough power to fight one mage, let alone eight. All my Necromancer magick was gone, and my hybrid power had been expended as well.

*I still have to try.*

Reaching out with my mage awareness, I pulled fresh magick into my limbs. Energy trickled into my body. I began the words to an incantation for attack.

The clearing brightened as all the mages summoned power into themselves. Their blue smoke soon covered the grassy earth, congealing into the shape of a skeletal snake with long bright fangs. Although the creature was an empty hulk of bone, it was powered by magick. The snake slithered quickly toward me, jaws opened wide. My heart sank. I knew what was coming.

A sleeper spell.

I tried to release some of my power, but I'd barely gotten halfway through the incantation when sharp fangs bit into my shoulder. I hissed in pain as my consciousness drifted into darkness.

he next thing I knew, I was awake once more. Sleeper spells were like that. For the victim, the blackout came and went in a heartbeat. For everyone else, the spell could last for hours.

*How long have I been asleep exactly?*

Dull pain burned up my arms. I opened my eyelids the barest amount. Jonas and Hannah stood on either side of me. Each Fantome had draped one of my arms over their shoulders, making it easier to drag me along. That explained the pain. It didn't answer how much time had passed, though.

Still trying to look asleep, I stole a few more careful glances at my surroundings. It helped that my mask was gone and some of my hair had fallen over my face. The mages were lugging me down a darkened passageway. I exhaled. This was familiar territory. We were in the dungeons just underneath the Montagne mansion. Which meant there was no question where they were taking me.

Straight to Ada and Veronique.

And to a place that the Fantomes thought would mean my death.

*At last.*

Footsteps and muffled music echoed in from the ceiling. I let out another relieved sigh. The ball continued upstairs. At most, I'd been passed out for an hour.

I carefully reached out with my mage senses. When it was clear that Hannah and Jonas didn't notice what I was doing, I tested the magick around me. There was hardly any power in the air. Still, I pulled in what I could. Another force crept across my skin. It was some kind of ward. Not against Necromancer power, though.

*That's right.* The Vicomte blocked Caster magick down here after our battle yesterday with the Fantomes.

A hollow sensation spread through my chest. Since they'd blocked Caster magick in the dungeons, I couldn't call Tamu.

I would have to fight alone this time. No help from Rowan.

Fine. I could do that.

Hannah and Jonas dragged me deeper into the dungeons. With every step, the ache in my arms grew worse. I wanted nothing more than to walk on my own power. It wasn't something I could risk, though. As long as Jonas and Hannah thought I was passed out, I had the chance for a surprise attack.

That was an opportunity I wouldn't waste.

Instead, I focused on drawing in a steady stream of magick. After the battle in the gardens, I was empty and tired. I needed to prepare for another fight and fast.

Finally, Jonas and Hannah stopped before a heavy wooden door. My skin prickled with gooseflesh.

This was it; I could feel it in my bones.

All I needed to do was keep up the appearance of being passed out. As long as the Fantomes thought I was helpless, I could launch into a surprise attack, free my Sisters, and get us all to safety. In the journey here, I'd gathered enough magick for a decent spell or two. But escape alone wasn't enough.

*I must get that vortex watch.*

A hazy plan began to take shape in my mind. The Fantomes would need the vortex watch in order to drain me. And the moment they brought out that device? There was my opportunity to strike. The witness watch still sat safely tucked away in my pocket. Even better, it looked identical to the vortex watch. Perhaps I could use the witness device as a decoy, cause a diversion, and then grab the vortex watch for my own. A spark of hope lit in my heart.

*The plan might work.*

Hannah knocked on the door in an odd rhythm. "We brought her."

The portal swung open, sending a beam of torchlight across my face. The Vicomte stood on the threshold, wearing a garish yellow longcoat. His gray features were tight with rage. "This better be worth my time. I left the ball for your nonsense."

I risked a quick look. The chamber was huge and made of gray rock. Apart from our small pool of torchlight, most of the place was cast in darkness. A dozen more Fantomes stood in a neat line behind the Vicomte. There was no mistaking the glimmer of totem rings on all their fingers.

*Gods-damn it. That man came prepared.*

Jonas jostled me, sending a shooting pain up my arm. "This one's got magick, I tell you."

"Her? How much?" asked the Vicomte.

"She cast a winding sheet spell on me," said Jonas. "I escaped easily, of course."

The Vicomte's gray eyes narrowed. "But that's Mistress level." His voice dripped with doubt. Like the mages back in the garden, he couldn't imagine a real Necromancer would survive the Tsar's purges.

*Wait until I unleash my power.*

"No, Your Eminence." Hannah helped Jonas drag me inside. "She's a *Grand* Mistress."

The Vicomte chuckled. "Did I hear you correctly? I sent you off to deal with a troublemaker. Now you say she's a Grand Mistress Necromancer. Why I trust you Fantomes is beyond me."

"We are sorry to disappoint," said Jonas earnestly.

The Vicomte waved his arm. "We'll see. Hopefully, there's a little power in this wench. I've been killing myself trying to eke out magick from the sad specimens that are currently in my collection."

A jolt of anger rushed up my spine. Specimens? These were my people.

"She will complete your vortex watch," said Hannah. "You can rely on it."

"Perhaps. If this bitch has had any kind of training, then it's a distinct possibility." His gray eyes flared with hunger. "Genesis Rex has given me nothing but trouble tonight. How I'd love to have that vortex watch charged up and ready before I return to the ball."

*So you can kill him, you mean.*

Worry churned inside me. The Vicomte was out to murder Genesis Rex. Down here in the dungeons, there were still wards against Caster magick. I couldn't get a message to Rowan through Tamu. Even worse, I couldn't afford to use the little magick I had for anything outside of grabbing vortex watch and escaping. Rowan would have a far worse problems if the Vicomte got his hands on a fully charged totem ring.

Some rustling sounded in the distant corners of the darkened room. Were Ada and Veronique out there somewhere? With the size of this chamber, it could easily be a trick of the ears.

The Vicomte eyed me carefully. "Don't you think you need to restrain her more properly?"

I worked hard to stay limp in Hannah and Jonas's arms. A surprise move was my best chance here. I must save it for the perfect moment.

Jonas sniffed. "No, she's under a sleeper spell. Eight of us cast it. This one won't awaken for hours yet."

It was an effort to keep from smiling. *That's what you think.* That hybrid magick must have protected me from the full effects of the sleeper spell. Something to remember for the future.

*If I have one, that is.*

"So you say." The Vicomte did not sound convinced. "I'll have a look myself."

Sharp footsteps sounded across the stone floor. My heart beat so fast, I felt sure everyone could see the pulse in my throat. The Vicomte's chilly hand gripped my chin and forced my head upright. It took every scrap of my Necromancer training to appear asleep when what I really wanted to do was cast an attack spell.

*Wait, Elea. You need that vortex watch first.*

Foul breath cascaded down my cheek as the Vicomte moved in closer. "Are you really asleep, I wonder?" The Vicomte then slammed his fist into the side of my head. Pain ricocheted down my skull. I didn't show any reaction. After years of controlling the painful deluge of magick, that punch felt like nothing. The Vicomte leaned in once again. "She doesn't look like much. Still, I'd rather have my vortex watch working sooner rather than later. Set her onto the machine."

Hannah and Jonas dragged me deeper into the chamber. We hadn't gotten more than a few steps inside when I felt it.

*A total void of magick in the air.*

Every last wisp of Necromancer energy was gone. It made sense since this was the place where they drained Necromancer power. It didn't help me any, though. If I was going to get the vortex watch and escape, I couldn't rely on being able to quickly pull in fresh power.

Oh well. The little magick I had gathered would have to do.

"Elea! Elea!"

*That was Ada. She's here, right now, in this very room.*

I pushed away Hannah and Jonas. Standing on my own, I scanned the darkened recesses of the chamber. I couldn't see a thing.

"She awakens," said the Vicomte. There was a calculating note to this voice. My training told me to consider that before anything else, but my heart wouldn't have it. Ada was somewhere nearby. All I wanted to do was find her.

"I'm here, Elea. Here!"

I took off into the darkness, following the direction of Ada's voice. Rushed footsteps sounded behind me. I was pretty sure Hannah and Jonas were trailing me. Even so, I couldn't be bothered with them right now. Ada needed me.

"Jonas. Hannah. Cease your pursuit," commanded the Vicomte. "I want to see what she'll do."

"But she's strong," said Hannah.

"And there are fourteen of you in this room. Call it an experiment."

I didn't care what the Vicomte called it so long as I found Ada. I stumbled around as my eyes adjusted to the lack of light. Other than the mages, the place seemed empty.

*Did I imagine that voice?*

"Elea!"

Finally, my vision cleared. I found Ada sitting in a far corner. Her bony limbs jutted out from her loose robes. A tangle of dark hair sat matted against her head, and her brown eyes seemed sunken into her skull. A large table stood beside her.

I ran over to Ada, knelt at her side, and scooped her tiny frame into my arms. Heavy chains rattled with the movement. Someone had manacled her hands and feet. Rage coursed through me. How dare anyone touch her?

"You came for me," Ada said between sobs. Her tiny body felt so frail against mine.

"I never forgot you." I rocked her gently.

"There aren't many of us left."

My breath caught. If Ada was alive, then there was still hope for others, too. Amelia would be thrilled. "Is Veronique here?"

"Yes, she's—"

"Now I understand." The Vicomte's voice boomed around the stone room. Ada immediately fell silent. I pulled her more closely to me. "You're here to rescue this little thing. My fool of a daughter wants to save Veronique's useless hide. How brainless of you both." He paused before me and Ada, his boots gleaming in the low light. "You sent the Tsar into exile, didn't you?"

I glared up at him. "You're next, only it won't be exile."

The Vicomte smiled. "I should thank you for that. Saved me the trouble of killing him. Perhaps I could even offer you a place with me as a Fantome. However, I can't. Your kind is worse than useless. Need to save everyone, don't you?"

"Not everyone." I carefully reset Ada into her corner. The motion exposed new stretches of her skin to the torchlight. Tiny sores covered her everywhere. Many of them oozed blood. Rage burned through me. "Some people I'd rather kill."

I rose, faced the Vicomte, and tapped into the little bit of magick inside my soul. No, I didn't yet have the vortex watch, but I couldn't get myself to care any longer.

The Vicomte was going to die, right now.

*H*annah and Jonas tackled me before the incantation had left my lips. Cold metal pressed onto my wrists. Damn, they'd gotten another pair of enchanted manacles. I couldn't cast a thing while these were on.

"Well done," said the Vicomte.

"Thank you, Your Eminence," said Jonas. He and Hannah stood behind me, holding me in place.

The Vicomte rubbed his papery hands together. "You've been nothing but trouble to me, girl. I know exactly how to repay you."

"You want to drain me."

"Eventually." The Vicomte motioned to one of his other Fantomes. "Bring me a torch." I didn't like the smug look on his wrinkled face. "Set it right by the wall over there."

The mage stalked closer, illuminating the back wall. That was when I saw her. Veronique. Her broken body was strapped to the high table that stood beside Ada. I blinked hard, hoping that what I saw was a trick of the firelight.

It wasn't.

Veronique lay with her arms stretched far above her. Her ankles were braced apart. *She's on the rack.* The Vicomte moved to stand at the foot of the table, his hand resting on the crank that would pull the structure apart. The rack was known to snap a person's spine. It was a horrible way to die.

An angry gleam shone in the Vicomte's charcoal-gray eyes. There was no doubt in my mind. He intended to kill her while I watched.

Options and ideas flew through my head.

*Lunge for the Vicomte.*

*Run for my life.*

*Scream for help.*

None of them seemed a viable choice. Amelia's witness watch weighed heavily in my pocket. When I'd last checked, the time was a few minutes before midnight. My insides trembled with worry. By tapping into my power, the Vicomte would quickly load up this vortex watch.

There had to be some way to stop him.

I still had my small cache of Necromancer energy. The enchanted manacles blocked me from using my magick, but not for long. Hannah and Jonas would have to take them off in order to strap me down to the table. When that happened, I'd need to cast and quickly.

It was my only chance.

The Vicomte gave the wheel of the rack a spin. Veronique moaned and shook. The Vicomte grinned. "Good evening, Veronique. I brought you a visitor."

Veronique slowly angled her head in my direction. Pity and anger tightened my throat. Veronique's Necromancer robes were little more than bloody rags now. Her face was white as death. Small red welts dotted her skin. Blood and puss oozed from the holes. The sight made me ill and enraged all at once.

"Elea, you're here." Veronique's large blue eyes, once so full of fight, stared blankly at me. "Kill me. Please."

A moan caught in my throat. What horrors had they exposed her to? I pulled against the enchanted manacles that held me. The metal chaffed my skin, and I welcomed the pain. From behind, Jonas and Hannah tightened their hold on me.

I glared at the Vicomte. "Set her free. I'll put magick into your damned watch."

The Vicomte shook his head. "Hurting Veronique bothers you, eh? Now, you just made sure that your friend would spend even more time on the rack." He bared his yellow teeth. "You made a fool of me, Elea. Don't think you're getting an easy death. She certainly won't."

I opened my mouth and then closed it again. There was nothing I could say that would speed things along. My best chance was to wait my turn.

*And watch him kill Veronique. The thought made me queasy.*

The Vicomte gripped the wooden crank. "Since that we're all set and paying attention, I'll begin my demonstration."

Veronique's chest barely rose and fell. Her lips and fingertips took on a blue tinge. "You don't need to do this, Gaspard."

"Ah, but I do. It's all your friend's fault." He gestured toward me, blaming me for Veronique's pain. I hated him even more for that. "Elea cares for you, my sweet, and so she needs to watch you perish."

A tear rolled down Veronique's dirty cheek. Rage blazed through my soul. *This isn't how anyone deserves to die.*

The Vicomte turned to me. "Now, be a good girl and watch silently, or I'll be forced to bring on another subject for my demonstration." He stared pointedly at Ada, who cowered more deeply into the corner. "Do we understand each other?"

How I hated answering him. "Yes."

*Lean on your Necromancer training. Don't show emotion.*

"Excellent. I knew you'd see reason." The Vicomte nodded toward Veronique. "This pathetic creature was a machinist for me once. Not as talented as Amelia, mind you. Even so, I thought she could develop skills over time." His thin lips curled with distaste. "She didn't."

Rage had me seeing red. The Vicomte was about to kill Veronique, and yet, he talked about her as if she were nothing more than a defective gear in one of his machines. Every corner of my soul wanted to take him down.

*Not yet, Elea.*

I forced myself to focus on my breathing, something that Mother Superior taught me long ago. My control hung on by a thread.

"She does have some useful skills, as it turns out," continued the Vicomte. "Veronique can't pull Necromancer power into herself. She does naturally attract it, however. Every few days I can bring her here and harvest more energy from her." He smiled down at Veronique. There was nothing gentle in his grin. "Just like a cow, you see? Only she gives out a different kind of milk."

Ada began weeping in the corner. This was what the Vicomte had done to her. To all of them. Broken their spirits like animals. My hands balled into fists. I simply had to make him pay.

"First, I shall place the device on her." The Vicomte pulled the vortex watch from his pocket and pressed the sides. Long, sharp prongs jutted out from the base.

I scanned Veronique's body and fought the urge to gasp. Like Ada, she was covered in small, oozing sores. It was clear where those wounds were coming from: the prongs on the vortex watch.

The Vicomte stepped up to the head of the table. He was so close now I could strangle him if my hands were free. I struggled to lunge forward, but Hannah and Jonas held me firmly.

In one swift movement, the Vicomte jammed the watch face onto the base of Veronique's throat. Thin trickles of blood ran out from where the prongs dug into her skin. She whimpered with pain. It was an effort to focus on the mission instead of screaming.

*Get that vortex watch. Forget everything else.*

"There, you see?" The Vicomte tapped the watch face in Veronique's neck. "She's ready to be milked, as it were." He chuckled softly at his own joke. I wanted to gouge out his eyeballs with my bare fingernails.

The Vicomte stepped back to the base of the table and reset his hands onto the crank. "As you can see, the watch face isn't lighting up. No power yet. Veronique doesn't know how to access magick or refuses to. Either way, it doesn't matter. We just need a little more pain, don't we?"

Veronique moaned, and I never wanted to kill the Vicomte more than I did right now.

The Vicomte spun the wheel. Veronique's hands and feet were wrenched in opposite directions. She writhed on the table, her pale lips widening with a pathetic scream. The Vicomte didn't seem affected in the least. "Normally, we'd put a silencer spell on her, but for your benefit? Not today." His eyes narrowed as he stared at the watch face at the base of Veronique's throat. "Nothing yet. Let's try a little more pain."

"No." The word left my lips before I could stop myself. Foolish move. Seeing my anguish only made the Vicomte more vicious.

"Yes." The Vicomte gave the wheel a vigorous twist. The planes of the table drew farther apart than ever. Veronique howled in agony. Snapping noises sounded as something terrible happened to her joints and tendons.

The watch face flickered with the barest level of brightness.

"There, now." The Vicomte glared at me, as if daring me to say *no* again. "We got a little bit more." He leaned in and scanned the watch face. "We're so close now."

I couldn't take this much longer. "Put me on the machine. You don't need to torture her."

"You're right. I'll give Veronique here a breather. You can see her die later." He nodded toward Ada. "And we'll bring the child in for a turn."

"Ada?" My voice came out a hoarse whisper. No, he couldn't do that. Watching Veronique get tortured to death was one thing. But not Ada. Not a child. He wouldn't.

My heart sank. *He would.*

All of a sudden, a column of blue smoke appeared by the doorway. When the haze lifted, another Fantome stood in the room. Fresh totem rings gleamed on his fingers. He must have just used one to transport here. "Your Eminence."

The Vicomte gripped the bars of the crank so tightly the wood creaked under his grasp. "How dare you bother me?"

"It's Genesis Rex. He's moving forward with his announcement. Says he doesn't wish to prolong the ceremony."

Excitement fluttered inside my rib cage. They hadn't announced the engagement at the ball yet. Genesis Rex was here with his guards. Rowan would be with him as well. The thought helped to center me. I pictured the firm lines of Rowan's face. He always said I was a far stronger mage than I knew. I couldn't be sure if that was true. However, I did know one thing for certain.

I wasn't the kind of girl who gave up.

"What an arrogant bastard," said the Vicomte. "Hannah. Jonas. You stay here. The rest of you I want in the ballroom, now. Find some way to stall Rex, but don't upset the guests or the party. I won't have this treaty ruined with your simpleminded attempts at diplomacy."

"Yes, Your Eminence." More totem rings flashed on the hands of the Fantomes. Fresh columns of blue smoke appeared and vanished.

I was left alone with two Fantomes, the Vicomte, and my plan.

Things were looking better by the second.

The Vicomte sighed. "It appears we've run out of time thanks to that ingrate Genesis Rex." He patted Veronique's matted hair. "You're too weak to be really useful, as usual."

"No. Kill me." Veronique's face was the definition of despair.

"You don't get to decide such things." The Vicomte snapped his fingers. "Hannah. Jonas. Keep the bitch still. I'll clear the table. I'd like to charge up my totem ring before Genesis Rex causes me a diplomatic headache."

Veronique whimpered in pain. The Vicomte stalked up to her head, grabbed the watch face, and tore it from her neck. He set the device into his left pocket.

Without thinking, I took a half step toward the Vicomte. Hannah and Jonas yanked me back.

With practiced movements, the Vicomte undid the ties that bound Veronique to the table and pushed her onto the floor. She landed on the stone with a low moan. My heart ached to comfort her.

The Vicomte rounded on me. "Your turn."

Jonas held me tightly in place while Hannah unlocked the manacle on my left hand. My casting hand. They really had no idea how powerful I was, did they?

*Time for them to find out.*

Acting quickly, I released some of the magick I'd stored up. A wall of blue energy hurtled behind me. Hannah and Jonas went flying backward. I leapt forward and tackled the Vicomte. His head hit the stone floor with a thwack.

*Gods-damn. That felt good.*

Using my manacled hand, I punched the Vicomte smack in the temple. He yelped and it was a beautiful sound. The Vicomte clawed and shoved at me while I fumbled between the vortex and witness watches. For a scrawny old man, there was a lot of fight in him.

One of the watches tumbled away and flew across the floor. But was it the vortex watch or the witness watch?

Hannah and Jonas grabbed me from behind, pulling me off the Vicomte. I didn't use up all my magick on them, so it came as no surprise that they'd recovered quickly. Hannah snapped another set of enchanted manacles on my left hand. Now, I had a pair of irons dangling from each wrist. Still, I could only think about the watch in my pocket. In all the fighting, I'd lost track of things.

I still had a watch in my possession. But which one was it?

Hannah and Jonas shoved me onto the table and strapped me down roughly. My red dress flowed over the sides of the tabletop, like blood from a sacrificial altar.

The Vicomte brushed off his yellow longcoat, his eyes bright with rage. "I've had enough of all these tricks." He jammed the watch face onto my throat. The prongs dug into my skin and pain exploded along my neck. A trickle of red oozed down my chest. The Vicomte stalked over to the crank and gave it two full revolutions. My arms and legs felt ripped from their sockets. I screamed in pain.

But no power left my soul.

I exhaled. The Vicomte had the witness watch after all.

"What a damned waste of time!" The Vicomte glared at Hannah and Jonas. "You said she had power."

"You saw it," said Hannah.

"She cast a spell that threw us backward," added Jonas.

"I know power when I see it." The Vicomte's eyes blazed. "You think you're fooling me with your dreams and games?"

Hannah and Jonas froze. Their faces paled. The truth was obvious. The Tsar had been contacting them in their dreams, as well.

"Don't bother to deny it," said the Vicomte. "You've been in contact with the Tsar. Speaking with him in your sleep, right? You're plotting to overthrow me once I have the vortex watch fully loaded with power. And you're scheming with this little bitch on some elaborate trick to make me look the fool. Well, whatever you're up to, it won't work."

Hannah fell to her knees. "We're loyal to you, Your Eminence."

"You must believe us," added Jonas.

I saw my chance and I took it. "There's no point in pretending anymore." I pitched my voice to a tone of utter despair. In reality, my heart was filling with hope. The Vicomte was so paranoid that everyone was betraying him. I could use that to my advantage. "You heard the Vicomte. He's smart. He knows how we've all been working together."

Hannah leapt to her feet. "Liar!"

I focused on the Vicomte and gave him my most innocent face. "Release me and I'll tell you everything."

"Someone being reasonable," snarled the Vicomte. "At last."

Jonas staggered backward. "What are you doing? You can't believe her."

The Vicomte stalked over to Hannah. "I knew this was all nothing but a trick. Some girl from the backside of nowhere is a Grand Mistress Necromancer? Please." He paused before her. "Give me the keys to her manacles."

Hannah gaped. "But you can't believe—"

"Hand them over!"

Trembling, Hannah pulled a small silver key from her pocket and gave it to the Vicomte. "She's a powerful necromancer. Mark my words."

"Marked." The Vicomte marched back over to me and unlocked the manacles from both my wrists. "I did as you asked. Now do as you promised. Give me everything you've got."

*Happy to.*

I pulled the watch from my pocket, released the prongs, and jammed it into my wrist. Instantly, I felt the totem ring call to my magick. I focused my power straight at the device.

*Take it.*

The watch face instantly lit up. The hands hit midnight. The vortex watch became fully charged. I allowed myself a small smile.

The Vicomte stared at me in disbelief. "You stole the vortex watch and gave me a decoy."

"What can I say? It seems that I am rather tricky."

The Vicomte wheeled toward Hannah and Jonas. They were

already racing for me at full-speed. The bones in their left arms glowed blue as they prepared to cast major spells.

I knew I needed a counter-spell. The power of the totem ring seemed one step ahead of me, though. I didn't even need to pull in magick for the casting to begin. The moment I thought of the incantation that I wanted, the vortex watch illuminated more brightly than ever before. Brilliant blue light flooded the chamber. Power thrummed inside my soul.

I had barely thought of the spell and then it came into being

Raw energy poured out of my hands. Tendrils of blue smoke wound around Hannah and Jonas. I tried to retake control of the casting by speaking an incantation to transform the mist into bone rope, but the push of power was too strong. Energy careened through me, making me wince. The lines of blue haze solidified right where they were.

I couldn't believe the result. My twisting lines of mist had instantly hardened into razor-sharp bone. I'd pumped in too much energy, too soon, so the rope froze in place wherever the mist was headed. Hannah and Jonas got skewered in a hundred spots at once. They were dead.

I blinked hard, not sure if what I saw was real. The spell was supposed to hold them, not kill them. Normally, I only used the precise amount of energy a spell required. This time, I lost control. In fact, the residual effects of the spell were still overwhelming. Every inch of me felt numb. And I'd killed two of my own kind.

Looking down at my wrist, I prepared to tear the device from my flesh.

But the vortex watch was already gone.

*Oh, no.*

The Vicomte stood nearby, the vortex watch gripped in his right hand and an evil smile on his face. "Thank you, Elea. I've been meaning to murder them for ages."

*Gods-damn it.* I had become so overwhelmed with power, I didn't notice the Vicomte stealing the vortex watch. This was terrible. With that realization, my mind shut down. I could only stare in shock as the very thing I'd fought so hard against now came to pass.

The Vicomte jammed the vortex watch into his left wrist.

"Finally." The round dial glowed blue once more. The Vicomte gasped. "I feel the energy." His rolled his eyes into his head. "It's Power. Magick. Beauty."

My mind began to function once more. I had to move. Unfortunately, my feet were still tied to the rack. Leaning forward, I began undoing the leather knots around my ankles. It took ages for my left foot to become free. Then my right. I leapt to the floor.

The Vicomte rounded on me. "You're staying right here. I've wanted to test out Necromancer magick for ages. I know all your spells."

I nodded slowly. "Right."

*Because it's so easy being a Necromancer.*

The Vicomte raised his left arm and summoned in power to him. Instantly, blue light poured through his body. All his bones lit up at once. The Vicomte groaned in pain as he struggled to control the flow. "Blasted magick."

I fought back the urge to roll my eyes. *Please.* I spent years honing my craft, learning how to focus the flow of magick from a torrent of power into a pinprick of energy. How arrogant of the Vicomte to think he could master the craft without any practice.

And how typical.

I searched inside me for residual energy. I still had some magick left behind. It wasn't enough for a major spell, yet with what I had planned for the Vicomte? A serious incantation wasn't necessary.

All I wanted to do was give the Vicomte his ultimate wish. Keep that Necromancer power inside him.

Lifting my left arm, I sent out another puff of blue smoke. The haze sped across the room and wreathed around the Vicomte. The cloud around him was so light you might not even know it was there. But this was a holder spell. Although it appeared almost transparent, it could contain any kind of magick within itself. And holding that much uncontrolled power into the Vicomte? That would hurt like hell.

The Vicomte collapsed onto his knees, curling his arms over his stomach. His skin began to bubble with blue light. "Fire and... Bone..."

I moved to stand beside him. The Vicomte had started a fireball incantation. There were about a hundred things wrong with his casting, and he'd only said three words. With the holder spell on him, he wasn't going to live long, and that suited me fine.

*I sighed. Still, I had my rules. Always give the villain a way out.*

"That's my holder spell giving you pain," I said. "Promise you'll go into a dungeon cell quietly, I'll consider releasing you from it."

He spoke through gritted teeth. "Power... Of..."

"I'll assume that means no."

*Some day, a villain might actually take me up on my offer.*

The Vicomte's mouth twisted into a snarl. "Bitch." The light in his bones grew brighter. His skin turned blue and began to peel away. The Vicomte screeched in pain and fell over onto his side. He didn't stop his incantation, though. "Stone... Fulfill my... Need..."

With that much power inside him and no way to control it, he wouldn't last long. "Do your best, Necromancer. I'm waiting."

His next words came out as a hoarse whisper. "Kill... With... Speed." The Vicomte slumped onto the floor, dead. I released my holder spell, leaned over, and checked the Vicomte's pulse for good measure. The villain was gone, all right.

*Good.*

I pulled out the vortex watch from his arm and set it safely into my pocket. I couldn't wait to get this thing into Petra's hands.

Whimpers sounded from the corner of the room. I raced over to Ada and Veronique. They were huddled against the far wall. Veronique looked half dead, but Ada's eyes were bright. "You killed him," she said between sniffles. "Didn't you?"

"Oh, yes." I set my palm against her thin cheek. "Are you well?"

"Very well, now that you're here. I knew you'd come."

*That made one of us.*

"Are there any more of you?"

"Dozens. Only they're in lots worse shape than Veronique and me. Will you take us home?" She lowered her voice. "I saw your spell go after Hannah and Jonas. You can do anything."

"That last casting didn't exactly go as planned. I need practice with the vortex watch or I could kill you as easily as save you."

"So how will we get out of here?"

I thought of Rowan and the other Casters. "I'll need some help for that. Can you wait here for a few minutes?"

"What if the Fantomes come back?"

"If they do, then I'll take care of them." I wanted to cast a dozen ward spells to protect this place. However, I wasn't strong enough to do it on my own, and I couldn't risk using the vortex watch again. "I won't be long."

"I believe you, Elea. I'll be here when you come back."

My heart lightened. Dozens of Necromancers were imprisoned in these dungeons. *I can still save some of my people.* I gripped the vortex watch in my pocket. It was tempting to use the power inside in order to cast a transport spell, but that was precise magick. I could easily end up dead if I lost control.

No, if I needed to find Rowan, I'd have to do it the nonmagick way.

I turned toward the door and took off at a run.

A massive boom sounded. The floor rocked beneath my feet. "What's that?" I asked.

"It's coming from below us," said Ada. "There's some kind of secret chamber down there. The Fantomes talk about it all the time."

Veronique fluttered her eyes half open. "No one knows... What's in there."

A pang of worry shot up my torso. I knew what lay beneath us. A secret room in the deepest cave of the dungeons?

It was the gateway.

By the Sire. The vortex watch gets charged and the gateway starts to shake. That can't be a coincidence. The Tsar must have built some kind of back door to the totem ring inside the watch. Now that his totem ring was fully charged, the Tsar must be able to access its power somehow. Just like the bone crawlers in the cave with Rowan —he could be using that power to escape. I pulled out the vortex watch. It still showed the time as midnight. None of the power appeared to have gone anywhere. Perhaps it was just a coincidence, after all.

*Or maybe the Tsar is coming.*

"I'll be back as soon as I'm able." I took off for the door at a run.

## 28

*I* paused at the end of another dungeon passageway. This time, the hall branched off into three different directions. *Gods-damn it. Which way do I choose?* Tension tightened up my neck and shoulders. How long had I been searching for the way back to the gardens? *Too long.*

Closing my eyes, I tried to pull in magick to me. Perhaps I could cast another seeing sphere. Power loomed in the air, but I was too worn-out from my fight with the Vicomte. I touched the vortex watch in my pocket. *Should I use this?*

I shook my head. *Too risky.*

A low rumble shook the floor. My heart lurched in my chest.

That could be the Tsar.

I had to get help for Ada, Veronique, and the other Necromancers. The way out of these dungeons must be close. Trouble was, all these stone corridors looked identical.

Everywhere I went, I found drifting cobwebs, burned-down torches, heavy shadows, and little vermin that scritch-scratched away. So far, my plan had been simple: choose any path that seemed to slope upward and have some kind of light.

*Please let it work this time.*

Kneeling down, I rested my palm against the dusty rock floor of each passageway. Of the three directions before me, the first seemed to slope up slightly.

*That's the one.*

I rushed forward into the semidarkness. With every step, my dress felt heavier. Sweat trickled down my spine.

Finally, the passageway ended in a thin metal door. With trembling hands, I yanked it open. A stone staircase rose up before me. Fresh air drifted across my cheeks. *Yes.* I jogged up the steps and into the gardens beyond. Night air never tasted so sweet.

I sped through the hedges and trees until I saw the mansion's windows blazing with candlelight. The warmth of hope spread through my chest. *At last.* I rushed through the deserted garden paths and toward the castle's side entrances. Pulling open the heavy wooden door, I stepped into one of the lesser reception chambers. The place looked empty. I'd barely gotten past the threshold when Philippe stepped toward me. "Elea, are you all right?" Although he wore a black mask, there was no mistaking the tight lines of worry on his mouth and chin. "You've been gone for ages."

"I'm fine. Where are the Casters?"

"You're *not* fine. You lost your mask."

I patted my cheeks. The red silk mask was indeed gone. "That's the least of my concerns."

"And you have blood on your throat." He pulled out a handkerchief from his pocket and dabbed gently at my neck. "You want to see the Casters? No one will let you anywhere near Rex or his people looking like this."

It took everything I had not to push him over and run. "It's only a little blood."

"And dirt. And cobwebs in your hair. We're at a ball for *Royals,* remember? Do you really want to attract the attention of the guards and Fantomes?"

I pressed my palms against my eyes. Guards, I could handle. Fantomes were another matter entirely. *By the Sire.* In all the excitement, I forgot that the Vicomte sent the other mages back to the ball. They'd seen me in the dungeons. As far as they knew, the Vicomte was alive and wanted me dead. If any of them saw me up here, they'd attack on the spot. The least I could do was not walk in a frightful mess and attract undue attention.

"You're right, Philippe."

He gave me a toothy grin. "I'm always right."

"Can you fix me? Amelia did all this." I gestured awkwardly across my hair and torso. "I've no idea how it works."

Philippe winked. "Fortunately for you, making disheveled women look presentable is one of my finest skills. Seems to come up all the time." He began dusting me off with his handkerchief, smoothing back my curls, and rearranging the folds of my gown. It took forever. Eventually, he stepped back and admired his work. "There you go. Presentable."

"What about my mask?" Even the servants were wearing them.

"Once again, I came prepared." He pulled another red silk mask from the pocket of his longcoat. I could have kissed him. He winked again. "I figured yours would have a short lifespan. Fancy things always seem to fall apart when you're around. In fact, I'm shocked that you still have shoes."

"Amelia made me enchant them onto my feet." That woman already knew me too well.

"Clever girl, my sister. She'll be thrilled that you've returned in time for the engagement ceremony."

An engagement? The idea of a celebrating an upcoming wedding seemed silly compared with the possibility of the Tsar about to break free. His escape could bring the entire network of caves down. Ada and the others would be buried alive. And that was just for starters. Who knew what would happen if the gateway blew open?

*Stay calm. You don't know for certain if the Tsar is about to escape.*

The ground rattled beneath my feet. I focused on Philippe. "Did you feel that?"

"The tiny rumble?" He shrugged. "It happens out here from time to time. These lands have more caves than solid ground, I'm afraid. Don't tell me you're using that as an excuse to avoid Amelia's engagement? She's counting on you."

I forced my breathing to slow. The tremors could be something natural, couldn't they? I gripped Philippe's arm. "Believe me, I do want to see the ceremony, but it's safer if I find the Casters first." The mansion became oddly quiet. A prickle of awareness crept over my skin. "What's that?"

"That, my dear Elea, would be the beginning of the engagement ceremony. Now before you get any ideas, think of this. If you rush off and interrupt the Creation Casters right now, it will undo all my hard work to make you blend into the crowd. Whatever you're so worried about, you'll simply have to wait a few minutes. The ritual won't take long." He plucked my clenched fingers from the cuff of his longcoat and pointedly set my arm on his sleeve. "Besides, Amelia will be heartbroken if you don't see her engagement. She has some master plan for impressing her husband-to-be. I swore we both would see it."

I stared blankly at Philippe. My friends were near death under this horrible mansion, and I had to watch some insane ceremony?

"Oh, look," said Philippe blandly. "Fantomes."

I took a half step backward. "Where?"

"Ah, my mistake."

I yanked my arm away from him. "That wasn't funny."

"It wasn't meant to be. I was trying to make a point. The Fantomes are somewhere nearby. The bottom line is this, dear Elea. You simply can't do anything impetuous for two whole minutes." He jiggled his elbow at me. "Now, be a good girl and take my arm like a lady. You know, without shutting off the blood flow."

Much as I hated to admit this, he was making sense. I really didn't have a choice. I gently wrapped my fingers around his forearm and lowered my voice. "I have to tell you what happened in the dungeons."

We started walking toward the ballroom. "I'd love to hear, but whispering about death and destruction is another sure way to attract attention."

"Who says I killed anything?"

"Didn't you?"

I opened my mouth, wishing I had a witty retort on the tip of my tongue. Truth was, I was already accumulating quite the body count tonight. "Perhaps."

"Thought so. Don't take this the wrong way, sweet lady. I have only one sister, and she's getting engaged tonight. I'd like to enjoy the next few minutes before our lives are once again dragged into the whirlwind of whatever you're up to."

I frowned. "I'm not always a whirlwind."

He shot me a sly look. "Of course, you are. Death, destruction, and Elea. Wouldn't have it any other way. Things were blasted boring until you came along. Nothing but pretty ladies to seduce. Ah, here we are."

We stepped inside the massive ballroom. The huge place was made of white marble, just like everything else in the Montagne mansion. Royals were everywhere. All their bright gowns and long-coats seemed to blend into a single swath of shifting color.

Philippe led us to a secluded spot in the corner behind a large stone column. He chose well. The view here was excellent, and I had an easy hiding spot if needed. I hadn't spied any Fantomes yet. I had no doubt they were close by, though.

The Baron and Baroness de Montagne stepped into the center of the dance floor. All the guests backed away, clearing a large circle of space for them. The Baroness looked pristine in her white gown and tall wig. She clapped her hands and the room fell silent. "It is my great pleasure to announce the highlight of tonight's ball," she said. "We're here to witness an engagement ceremony for none other than our very own Lady Amelia Masson!"

Amelia stepped forward from the crowd, her pink gown swishing with the movement. Her doll-like face was framed by perfect ringlets of red hair. Every inch of her seemed to radiate excitement. I allowed myself a small smile. When I'd first met Amelia, she'd been a bitter recluse. Now, a true lady and leader was starting to blossom.

The crowd broke out into carefully polite applause. They wouldn't show any real emotion. After all, Amelia's father was a common criminal, and her Royal family didn't acknowledge her existence. Sure, the Vicomte had adopted her, but that didn't change her tainted blood. Besides, she was marrying a mage. No Royal trusted anyone with magick.

The Baron moved to stand beside his wife. He cut a different figure from what I remembered just a few hours ago. The man now wobbled as he stood. He rubbed his red eyes and tried to straighten his longcoat. There was no doubt about it.

The man was piss drunk.

The Baron hiccupped. "We had hoped that our great leader, the Vicomte Gaspard, would be here to officiate, but he has been delayed. Therefore, it's with deep disappointment that the Baroness and I must step in to play the Vicomte's part." The Baron didn't look the least bit disappointed. "Luckily for you all, I know the Vicomte as well as my own brother. This is what he'd want to say. He's simply thrilled to have brokered this union. This occasion represents the first alliance between our continents and people. It's sure to usher in new era of peace and trade."

The Baroness nodded in agreement. "As we all know, Royal ceremonies tend to be rather long and formal affairs. However, Genesis Rex has asked that we follow his traditions, which call for a short exchange of engagement vows. Not marriage, mind you. We speak of the promise of one to come."

"The ritual involves a little more than that." The Baron gave us a lopsided smile. "When Casters do this ceremony, there's barely any clothing involved. And afterward, the couple kiss and even—"

The Baroness jammed her dainty elbow into her husband's ribs. He immediately silenced his ramblings. "As I was saying," she went on. "In a nod to both of our cultures, we will have a short ceremony followed by a dance. That will be more than sufficient and proper."

Beside me, Philippe wagged his brows. He lowered his voice to a whisper. "Wait until you see what Amelia has planned. She'll follow the Caster ritual."

My mouth fell open. "She's not going to strip down, is she?"

"Don't be crude. She has a minor act of rebellion planned. I thought she might not get up the nerve, but now that the Vicomte isn't here? I'm certain she'll follow through."

I kept my features level. "I see."

Philippe flashed me his palm. "Don't say it. I know. She's gotten unusually attached to Genesis Rex because she lost Veronique. Well, all the more reason to enjoy the now. Soon enough, I'm sure she'll be miserable for years to come." He rubbed his palms together. "Aren't you excited?"

I pinched the bridge of my nose. *No, I'm not excited.* All I could think about was the fact that I had friends to rescue and a Tsar that might escape at any moment. Even so, there was nothing I could do about any of that at the moment. In only a few more minutes, I could get my friends some help.

I forced my features into some semblance of calm. "I'm happy for her, certainly."

The Baron's voice bellowed across the ballroom. "Now, I present to you the King of the Creation Casters, Genesis Rex."

A tall man stepped up to stand beside Amelia. As I looked him over from head to toe, a chill crept up my limbs. The man wore red fitted leathers. There was no mistaking the outline of his form. Broad chest. Stout legs. Arms roped with muscle. A half-helm covered most of his face. Still, it didn't conceal the strong ines of his chin.

*Was that Rowan?*

I shook my head. It couldn't be Rowan. The man never went anywhere with a clean-shaven face, not to mention enough weapons to kill a small horde. Besides, I'd met Genesis Rex in the desert. He was Rowan's uncle. From this distance, I was certain the two could be mistaken for each other. The Casters played a game of "body doubles" all the time.

I forced out a slow breath. *That has to be it.* After so much excitement, my mind was simply playing tricks on me. I needed to focus on finding Rowan, not imagining things. I scanned the crowd None of the other Casters were visible yet.

I glared at the Baron and Baroness, willing them to speak faster.

The barest rumble shook the floor. A few Royals noticed, but except for some guarded whispers, they seemed as unconcerned as Philippe. My hands balled into fists. I needed to get Ada and the others out of here.

The Baron spoke once more. "If you'll both put out your right hands."

Amelia and Rex raised their arms. Her small hand rested atop his much larger one.

The Baroness stepped forward and wrapped their wrists with a golden ribbon. "By taking this troth, you are now bound to marry each another." She tied the ribbon into a loose knot and smiled "The engagement is official."

The Baron grinned from ear to ear. "Aren't you going to kiss your fiancée? It's your tradition, isn't it?" He wagged his eyebrows up and down.

"Francois!" The Baroness swatted him on the shoulder.

Rex turned to face Amelia. Their bodies were only a few inches apart. My heart thudded so hard I thought it might burst. I kept repeating two thoughts over and over.

*This isn't Rowan. I'm imagining things.*

Rex leaned forward and brushed his lips on Amelia's cheek. The kiss was stiff and formal. I suppose it was in respect of Royal culture. That was when Amelia made her move. Grinning from ear to ear, my friend tore off her own mask as well as Rex's leather helm. My breath caught. I couldn't believe my eyes.

It was Rowan.

My mind raced. Was he really Genesis Rex? Or was this another case of body doubles? Every inch of my body froze with the thought. The ballroom took on a dreamlike haze. It didn't seem possible.

Amelia went up on tiptoe and wove her fingers through Rowan's brown hair and planted another longer kiss on his lips. Rowan didn't react, but that didn't stop my stomach from turning queasy. I remembered what his kisses were like.

"There," said Amelia, her eyes glistening with joy. "That's more how a Caster would do it, isn't it?"

Rowan's face was still as stone. "Yes, it is."

Amelia bounced a bit on the balls of her feet. "I knew you'd be pleased."

I took a half step backward. Rowan's gaze locked with mine. Guilt and rage sparked in his brown eyes. We'd been able to read each other's thoughts for ages. Now I wished I didn't have the ability, because there was no question what that look meant.

Rowan was Genesis Rex.

He looked away again and my heart cracked.

*Rowan lied to me.*

All this time.

So many sweet words.

All lies.

The music started for the couple's first dance. There was no way I could stand by and watch that happen. I turned on my heel and marched out of the ballroom.

Philippe was close on my heels. "Elea, what's wrong? Where are you going?"

"Back into the dungeons."

"I thought you needed help from the Casters."

"Turns out, I was wrong." Using the vortex watch was sounding better by the second. I might turn everything into dust for many leagues in every direction. At this moment, that didn't seem like such a horrible idea.

In no time, I'd found my way back to the deserted reception room. I'd barely set my foot inside the door when Philippe gripped my shoulder. "Elea, what are you doing?"

I pointed toward the ballroom. "Did you know that particular man was Genesis Rex?"

"No, but I know his type of so-called noble. You know him, don't you?"

I nodded.

Philippe exhaled a long breath. "Tell me you didn't give him your heart." Candlelight glimmered through his blond hair, making it seem like a halo. "I warned you about Royals, Elea."

My heart felt like it was crumbling inside my chest. *He did warn me.* "I didn't think he was King."

"And *I* didn't think anyone from the nobility could be worthy of your trust." Philippe stepped closer. "Move on from this nonsense. Whatever happened back there? It was merely a political alliance. Don't lose your friendship with Amelia on top of everything else."

"I don't blame Amelia." I hated the bitter tone in my voice, though.

"Good. Blame the overgrown liar."

"Mother Superior warned me against emotion. I should have listened to her too."

"Stop blaming yourself. This is how noble families are, Elea. His kind doesn't feel the way other people do. You and me? We're pawns on a chessboard."

I scrubbed my hands over my face. Our swim together. Those kisses. The way Rowan eyed me in the tavern bedroom. Those weren't the acts of someone who was playing games. Still, it didn't make the situation any less impossible. "Whatever he was doing, it's all over now."

"That's the spirit." Philippe offered me his arm. "Now, come dance with me."

A familiar voice reverberated through the marble room. "Give us a moment, Philippe." I'd know that deep tone anywhere. I could hear him speaking other words. Asking me to trust him. To believe in him.

It was Rowan.

Philippe set my hand on his arm. "I'm sorry, your Highness. Elea and I are due to dance."

Rowan's voice lowered. "I've asked them to hold off on dances for a time. Please excuse us. I must speak with Elea alone."

Philippe turned to me. "Is this all right?"

I didn't trust my voice, so I merely nodded again. Philippe released my hand and bowed to Rowan—or Rex—whoever he was. Soon, the two of us were alone.

Bit by bit, I forced myself to meet Rowan's gaze. His eyes were dark and his mouth grim. Again, I wasn't happy that I could read his emotions so well. I still knew exactly what this face meant. Guilt.

This was no misunderstanding. Anger heated my blood. "You lied to me."

"I had reasons. I can't speak of them now. Where is the Vicomte?"

"What?" I couldn't understand what I was hearing. "You asked me to trust you. You said we'd be together. Now, I see you get engaged to another woman and all you have to say to me is 'where's the Vicomte?'"

He stepped closer. "I have reasons, Elea. It's important."

*And I'm not.*

"He's dead. I killed him."

Rowan rubbed his neck. "You didn't."

"Would you have preferred that I die? There wasn't a lot of choice at the time."

He gripped my shoulders. "Tell me what happened."

"Go to hell."

"Trust me, I'm there. But I'm still responsible for the lives of millions of people." His eyes were wild with worry. "Tell me what happened. Please."

"The vortex watch got charged with my Necromancer power. The Vicomte tried to steal it. He failed. The man's worm fodder now."

"So, you have the vortex watch? May I see it?"

The vortex watch. Yet another thing that was more important to Rowan than the topic of getting engaged to someone else. *Millions of lives better be at stake, or I know one lying Caster who'll be losing his own.* I gritted my teeth, lifted the device from my pocket, and placed it on his palm. A tiny jolt of connection erupted as our skin brushed. How I hated my body for still craving him.

Rowan flipped over the small device. "There are no markings. Nothing about the sword."

"The Sword of Theodora? Is that what you're looking for?"

Rowan didn't answer, and my understanding for his plight faded. He'd lied to me about so many things already. At this point, I was betting the only thing at risk was Rowan's sword collection. "Answer me."

"Yes, that's what the treaty was all about. A wedding with Amelia in exchange for the sword. The Vicomte knows where it is."

My hands balled into fists. "You and your damned weapons." *I hope they keep you warm at night, because the gods know, I won't.* I turned toward the door.

"Where are you off to?"

I stared at him for a long moment. He was a liar, but he had a small army of guards at his call, and I needed to get those Necromancers out of the dungeon. "I found the lost Necromancers. They're weak and injured." I forced the next words past my lips. "I came here to ask your help in evacuating them."

"Of course. How many are down there?"

"A few dozen."

Rowan stalked toward the open archway that led back to the ballroom and let out a low whistle. When Rowan returned, he had Jakob alongside him. I'd met the man before; he was one of Rowan's guards. We'd had our differences in the past, however we'd moved past that.

Jakob eyed me with open contempt. "Elea. I should have known you'd be delaying Rowan in doing his duties."

Then again, he could still hate me.

"Depends on how you define *duty*, Jakob."

"Enough." Rowan focused on Jakob. "There are two dozen Necromancers in the dungeons under this mansion. I need them taken to safety as quickly as possible. Find the Caster guards on perimeter patrol. Round them up, cast a low-level tracking spell, and rescue the mages. They may have cast some wards. Break them. I'll catch up with you shortly. Elea and I still have things to discuss."

"No, we don't." Still, I didn't walk out the door.

Jakob bowed slightly at the waist. "As you command." He slipped out the side exit and off into the night.

Rowan focused his attention on me. "We need to talk."

"First, I need that watch." I held out my hand, and he reset the device onto my palm. I was proud that I managed the transfer without touching him at all. Something to get used to, I supposed.

The floor shook with another tremor. This was the worst one yet. Rowan frowned. "These have been happening all night. I'm told it's normal for this area."

"I'm not so sure." I knelt down and set my palm against the floor. The stone was cool to the touch. The tremor was still there. An assessor spell would tell me if the threat was real. Closing my eyes, I reached out with my mage senses, searching for fresh magick. A thin trickle of power moved through me.

"What are you trying to cast?"

"Assessor spell." I shot him a cold look. "When I fought the Vicomte, I tired myself out. It's taking a while to pull in enough energy."

Rowan knelt at my side. "Let me try."

I glanced toward the open archway. "We don't want to attract Fantomes."

"I'll keep my levels low. They won't sense a thing." He set his palm against the floor. The veins in his right hand glowed red with magick. Rowan whispered a low incantation. He was increasing the power of the spell. It wasn't a good sign.

"What do you see?"

"The gateway. Someone's trying to break through."

"It's the Tsar."

"Why now?"

*That's right.* I'd forgotten that Casters didn't use totem rings. I raised the device I still held in my palm. "The gateway starts to open when the totem ring is fully charged? It's not a coincidence. I think the Tsar set this all up as a back door to leave the Eternal Lands. It's not an easy kind of magick to manage, but—" My insides twisted with worry.

"The Tsar has done all sorts of things that aren't easy." Rowan scrubbed his hands over his face. "My spell showed immense underground damage. If he breaks through that gateway, the entire foundation of this place could collapse. Not to mention whatever he plans to do when he breaks free."

"Ada." I rose and strode toward the exit. No way was I leaving them to die underground.

Rowan grabbed my upper arm. "You still can't cast well, Elea. Let me go after your Sisters."

"No."

The floor rocked again, only more violently this time. My head felt stuffed with cotton and my body hollow. I really was in no condition to go scouring dungeons. *Perhaps Rowan had a point.* "I'll evacuate the castle."

At this point, more words were useless, so I turned on my heel and headed back to the ballroom. Amelia was there, standing alongside the Baron and Baroness. Just the people I needed to talk to in order to get everyone to safety. I could only hope that Ada, Veronique, and the others would get out as well. Much as I hated this fact, keeping them alive meant trusting the man who'd just broken my heart.

## 29

*I*'d barely set foot inside the ballroom when the stone floor buckled beneath my feet. Long cracks formed in the pristine white walls. Plaster tumbled from the ceiling. Screams erupted all around.

That was when I noticed it. The ceiling beams had broken through the plaster. Now, a handful of them hung at an odd angle. The heavy wooden timbers shook, ready to drop at any second. My breath caught.

Amelia was standing right under them.

I pulled magick into me. The room was heavy with memory, but none of it would flow into my limbs. I was still too weak from the battle with the Vicomte.

The beams teetered above Amelia's head. Her gaze flicked from side to side as she watched the crowd erupt into chaos around her. She had no idea of the danger.

I ran forward without thinking. The ballroom around me became a blur of movement. All I saw was Amelia as I closed in on her. A great crack sounded above me. The beams broke free. My friend seemed impossibly far away. Panic tightened every muscle in my body.

*No, not Amelia.*

I lunged forward with my arms outstretched. At the last possible second, I pushed Amelia to safety.

A loud crunch sounded as one of the beams fell on my leg instead. Pain shot through my limb. Amelia and Philippe rushed to my side.

"You shouldn't have done that." Amelia fanned herself with her hands. "Now, what are we going to do? The castle is falling apart. We can't leave you here to die!"

Philippe straightened his shoulders. "We'll get help."

"Don't. Now that the support beams are coming down, the whole building isn't far behind. I'm a Necromancer. I can heal myself and escape." Or I could, once I had time to recover from my battle with the Vicomte. I grabbed Amelia's hand. "You need to go."

Amelia gripped my hand more tightly. "We won't leave you."

Fresh chunks of plaster fell from the ceiling. "I'll be better able to cast if I know you're safe." The floor buckled and rolled again. More screams sounded. "Go. I'm begging you."

"No. I can't lose you, Elea. Not after Veronique."

"You will lose me if I can't focus and cast."

Philippe gently wrapped his arm around his sister's shoulder. "Come along, Amelia." With careful movements, he rushed his sister through the fleeing throng. I watched them leave and exhaled. *They'll be safe.* Now, all I needed to do was cast a transport spell and this nightmare would be over. Wetness crawled up my thigh as blood pooled in my gown. The massive beam lay over my leg. My head felt woozy on my shoulders. I didn't have much time.

Closing my eyes, I called on every bit of my training to focus past the pain. This spell had to be my greatest yet. Gritting my teeth, I reached out with my mage senses. Once again, the air felt heavy with memory and power. I tried to drag some of it into me.

Nothing came.

I pressed my hands against the heavy beam. It didn't budge. The room was all but empty now. The Fantomes were still nowhere to be seen. For the first time, I wished they'd show themselves. Being captive would at least get me out of here.

I closed my eyes and pulled at the magick once more. Every part of me felt empty and weak. This was hopeless. The thought appeared in my mind. I was really about to die. The walls trembled more violently than ever.

My pulse sped. I cupped my hand by my mouth. "Help!"

Across the room, Rowan burst through the last of the Royals pressing their way out the door. "Elea!"

Some small part of me was thrilled that he'd returned. Most of me was still angry as hell. I'd rather bleed to death under this beam than be rescued by Rowan. "What are you doing here? I asked you to help the Necromancers." I pointed to the exit door.

"The Casters are gathering them up. They're fine." With his heavy stride, he tore across the ballroom floor. "You're the one in need of aid." He knelt by my side. The ballroom wobbled. Long cracks formed in the stone floor. Some of the Royals screamed as they shoved one another aside in the rush to escape. Rowan's gaze met mine. The intensity in his green eyes was unlike anything I'd ever seen before. "I know you've every reason to turn me away. Let me help you."

The rest of the chaos faded away until there was just Rowan and me. Yes, he was a lying bastard. Even so, he'd returned to ensure I was safe, and I believed he felt something for me. Maybe I still did for him, too? Mother Superior always said that people think anger is the opposite of caring. That's not the case. Indifference, not hate, is the opposite of love. And I did not feel indifferent to Rowan. Talk about a confusing relationship.

"Please, Elea."

Suddenly, my plan to bleed out in defiance of Rowan seemed a little ill conceived. "All right."

Rowan heaved the wooden beam off my leg. Agony ripped up my thigh. I hissed in a breath through clenched teeth. Rowan reached for my leg, and I shifted away as another kind of pain tore through me.

It wasn't my smartest plan, but I didn't want his warm hands anywhere near me. "Don't touch me."

"Your leg is crushed, Elea. You know how Caster magick works. I have to touch you to heal you."

The ground rumbled beneath us. Plaster dust swirled through in the air.

*The Tsar.*

I balled my hands into fists. "All right."

"This won't take long. I saved up some power from my last spell." Rowan knelt at my side and glanced pointedly at my thigh. "You remember how this works?"

I nodded. *How can I forget?* For the healing to work, Rowan had to touch my bare skin.

Rowan quickly pulled up my skirts and set his hands on my naked thigh. His palms were warm and rough all at once. *Gods-damn him.* His touch felt wonderful. His low voice rumbled an incantation. "Touch, help, heal."

More warmth radiated out from his palms, setting every inch of my skin on fire. Only this time, the heat wasn't painful. I pressed my lips together, stifling the urge to moan. When Rowan began lifting his hands, it took everything I had not to ask him to stop.

Our gazes met once again. This was, without question, one of the strangest moments in my already-odd life. I was in a ballroom dressed in a bloody gown. The Tsar could break through to our realm any second. The other partygoers had rushed out toward safety while I sat here with Rowan. He ran his hand up my bare leg. "Good as new."

I made a great show of looking at my leg. The skin was red and swollen. Still, it wasn't the mass of broken bone and blood that I'd seen before. "Looks better." I tried to stand and pain shot down my side. "Doesn't feel perfect, though."

"Give it a few minutes." Rowan scooped me into his arms and held me against his chest. "I'll help you reach the gardens. By the time we get there, the spell will have finished its work. You should be strong enough to both walk and cast spells again." He pressed me closer.

A dozen emotions streamed through my heart at once. Love. Loathing. Betrayal. Gratitude. In the end, I said the only thing a girl could in this situation. "I really hate you right now."

"You've every right to. Whatever you may think, I love you, Elea. I have from the first time I saw you. You need to—"

"Elea! You're free from that horrible beam!" Amelia rushed across the ballroom floor to pause at our side. Her face glowed with joy as she rushed up to Rowan's side. Philippe followed behind. His blue eyes were dark with anger.

Amelia grabbed Rowan's arm. "Look, Philippe! Rex saved Elea." She stared up at Rowan adoringly. "I told you all about her. That's why you returned, isn't it? To make sure my dear friend was safe?" She eyed Rowan's hold on me. "That's why you're carrying her... And everything. Right?"

Philippe folded his arms over his chest. "I can't wait to hear this."

Rowan's face became unreadable. For once, I didn't mind that one bit. Right now was no time to reveal the true nature of my relationship with Rowan. I gestured toward the exit. "We need to get out of here. The Tsar might break free any minute. If that happens, this place could very well implode."

"Now that my dear sister is certain that Elea is safe, we do need to go." Philippe stepped closer to me and lowered his voice. "No need to discuss things that are best left in the past."

Philippe's meaning was clear. I should move on from Rowan and leave Amelia to her illusions.

Rowan glared at Philippe. "Some things are always in the future."

The floor rumbled once more. Great cracks ran up the walls. A jolt of worry went up my neck. "Can we have this discussion another time?"

"Agreed," said Philippe. A sheen of sweat had broken out along his forehead. "Come along, sister."

Amelia gripped Rowan's arm even harder. "My fiancée and I should go together."

"And you'll be sick of him soon enough," said Philippe. "But there's a very good reason we need to leave separately now." He looked at me pleadingly. "Isn't there, Elea?"

The answer appeared in a flash. "Yes, I have great news! We found Veronique. She's out in the gardens with Rowan—I mean, Rex's—people. She only wants to see you, though."

Amelia clasped her hands under her chin. "She's alive?"

Philippe frowned. "She is?" I'd forgotten how Philippe wasn't exactly Veronique's greatest supporter.

"She is absolutely alive." My eyes prickled with tears. After so long, it felt wonderful to say those words. "Go find her."

"Oh, I will!" Amelia sped toward the main doorway with Philippe following close behind. As I watched them leave, an odd sense of foreboding settled into my bones. I couldn't help feeling like it was the last time I'd see either of them.

## 30

The moment Philippe and Amelia stepped away I squirmed in Rowan's arms. "I'm feeling better. I can walk by myself."

Suddenly, the ballroom began to shake worse than ever before. Before us, the floor tiles erupted as a huge stone shape broke through. I gasped as I realized what was coming.

The gateway.

The Tsar was lifting the archway up. It burst forth from the lower dungeons to rest on a cloud of purple magick. This was hybrid power, yet again. My mouth fell open. I'd never heard of a spell that could do anything like this. What else was the Tsar's hybrid magick capable of?

I pulled the vortex watch from my pocket. The dials on the watch face were spinning fast.

6 p.m.

Noon.

11 a.m.

3 a.m.

It was happening. The Tsar was draining the power of my people.

The purple mist cleared to show the Tsar standing in the center of the archway. His body appeared so still, it looked like he was caught in a stasis spell. After that, he began speaking the words to an incantation. All the blood drained from my face. I knew what that spell was.

*An imploder spell.* The Tsar was going to destroy part of the castle.

I gripped Rowan's arm. "Get down!"

Rowan pulled me to him as he crouched on the floor. Angling himself away from the Tsar, Rowan held my back against his chest, his body shielding me from the upcoming spell.

Purple-colored smoke filled the air. *More hybrid magick.* The haze was so thick I could hardly breathe, let alone see anything. A series of deafening booms sounded. The ground shook beneath us. I couldn't see anything past the purple smoke, but I could hear plenty. Wood snapping. Stone cracking. A heavy wind swept past us. A red dome of power surrounded both Rowan and me.

*I let out a relieved breath. Rowan had cast a shield spell.*

Even so, the magickal protection didn't stop the wind from howling around us. It was like a tornado. How could that happen inside the castle? The gales roared louder than ever before. Then everything fell quiet. Rowan's shield spell vanished. A heavy purple fog covered everything. The very air seemed to press in around me.

Little by little, the mist cleared.

The castle was gone. Only the flooring remained. I scanned father afield. As the clouds shifted, I could see more. Moonlight fell across what had once been the garden.

Every last tree and shrub had been leveled.

My breathing came in shallow gasps. *That should have been impossible.* At their worst, imploder spells might tear up the ballroom. I'd never heard of one taking out a whole league of territory. I yanked the vortex watch from my pocket. The time was back to the first hour. It was empty.

The Tsar had drained all the power thousands of Necromancers.

And I had failed.

Despite the solid feel of Rowan behind me, I began to tremble.

My mind turned into a blank slate of shock. Moving away from the comfort of Rowan's arms, I forced myself to stand despite my wobbly legs. My right knee still shot through with a pain whenever I put any weight on it. Rowan stayed at my side, his arm wrapped protectively around my waist. Some small part of me wanted to tell him to stop touching me. Most of me was glad he was still here, even if it did put him in danger.

I scanned the settling debris, looking for a safe path to escape. We needed to get out of here.

The clouds shifted again, allowing more moonlight to fall on what was once the Montagne castle. The place was nothing more than rubble.

And the Fantomes were here.

About twenty of them stood at the far end of what was once the ballroom. They looked tall and elegant in their dark robes, pale faces gleaming in the moonlight. They all stared at Rowan and me. None made a move to speak or attack.

They were waiting, same as we were.

The Tsar stepped out from under the gateway and walked straight toward us. Not good. The man looked just how I remembered from our last battle: tall and broad-shouldered with a whip-strong body and long black hair tied back with a leather strap. He scanned the grounds, his amber-colored eyes seething with hatred.

"I remember both of you." The Tsar glared at me. "Especially you. Now, thanks to our good friend the Vicomte, I have the power to deal with the pair of you properly." He raised his hands to chest level. A shifting purple sphere appeared between his palms. I'd never seen anything like it—sharp cords of bone were laced through with writhing red serpents.

The Tsar lowered his hands, and the violet ball sped straight for Rowan. I quickly cast a bone shield and tossed it to Rowan, who knelt behind its protection.

The sphere slammed into the shield, splitting it in two before smashing into Rowan. He fell flat on his back. After a second or two, I expected him to stand up again. After all, it was only one volley and Rowan was a strong warrior.

But Rowan didn't move. I raced to his side. Something was wrong. Rowan looked deathly pale. I inspected his skin, seeing a crimson snake latched onto his throat. *Poison.* I ripped the serpent away and tossed it aside.

I needed to cast a spell of healing before the poison took too great a hold. I lifted my left hand, trying to pull fresh power into me.

Rowan had saved my life. Whatever else happened between us, I couldn't allow him to die.

A rush of power sped into me just as rough hands grabbed me from behind. My flow of Necromancer energy stopped. I looked at the hands restraining me. Blue mist danced across the man's skin.

This was a Fantome, and he'd cast some spell to block my magick. *Bastard*. I tried to pull power into myself, but I couldn't. I wasn't even possible to set loose the power I'd been able to gather.

An idea appeared. The bone crawlers. All of the Tsar's followers had one of those creatures inside them. If I could get my hands on one, then I'd have access to hybrid power, too.

And I'd kill the Tsar once and for all.

As the Fantome held me from behind, the Tsar strode toward me, the lines of his face still tight with fury. "You were the ones who sent me to exile. You'll pay."

I lifted my chin. "Your kind of evil doesn't belong here."

The Tsar's eyes narrowed with cool rage. Something in what I'd said hit a sore spot. His hands balled into fists. "You think me evil?"

"You're killing all my Brothers and Sisters. That's the definition of evil."

"You have it all wrong." The Tsar stalked closer, and I could see the thin spider web of scars over his elegant features. "In truth, we're a lot alike." His voice lowered. "I know that you've killed Fantomes, little girl."

"That was different."

"We both think we know what's best for the magick of our kind. I happen to believe that a small number of Necromancers must wield all the power in order for us to survive. You think it's best strewn out across the masses. But what happens when a plague strikes or a civilization falls? The weak die. Those who survive are the strongest. I am doing the same. Sacrificing the weak so those who remain will be strong as the gods themselves." He raised his fist. "That is true power and security. That is actual goodness." A sneer twisted his mouth. "You save lesser creatures and call it a boon to the realm. Meanwhile, I perfect us for the ultimate battle."

I couldn't believe what I was hearing. This was all some kind of blood purge to create an ultimate mage. "Who do you think you're battling? The realm was peaceful before you arrived."

The Tsar chuckled. "You have no idea what is coming, little girl. This is the only way we will survive."

My mouth fell open with shock. He was clearly insane. That meant I needed a bone crawler and fast.

I scanned my surroundings, searching for any way to escape. In every direction, stacks of rubble stretched off into the night. Plus, the Fantome behind me still held me firmly in place. All the other Fantomes stood unmoving, their dark robes shifting in the soft breeze.

A face in the crowd slowly came into clearer focus. It was familiar. A spark of hope lit inside me. This was the mage that Quinn had possessed for me. The Tsar must have set them all free without knowing what I'd done. I locked gazes with him across the darkness and tilted my head slightly. *Are you still in control, Quinn?*

He gave me the slightest nod. *Yes.*

My heart beat with such force I thought it might burst. A plan quickly formed in my mind.

*Please, let this work.*

I tilted my head back, exposing my bare shoulder. I hoped that was enough to convey what I needed. *Bone crawler.*

Quinn frowned. Using his pointer finger, he outlined the shape of a V on his shoulder. After that, he shook his fingers slightly, like the legs of a bone crawler.

I gave him the barest of nods. *Yes, that's what I want.* All the bone crawlers made a V shape on the mage's shoulder.

Quinn made no more signs but hiked over the rubble as he approached the Tsar. "I know this girl, my master. Allow me to show you her weakness."

"Go on."

Quinn stepped toward me while whispering an incantation. I'd heard ones like these before. *A spell of release.* It could be used to free my tongue so I'd share all my secrets.

Or it could be used to free a bone crawler. *Clever Quinn.*

I anxiously scanned the other Fantomes. The ones who knew I

could use a bone crawler for power were already dead. Would the others figure out what was happening?

All the Fantomes stayed still in the moonlight. If they knew what was about to take place, none of them informed their Tsar.

*Yes, yes, yes.*

Quinn paused to stand between the Tsar and me. *More cleverness.* With the Tsar behind him, Quinn's movements would be hidden in shadow. When this was all over, I vowed to hate Quinn a little less.

Quinn set his hand against his neck, drawing a dark line that was still hidden in the shadows. All the muscles in my body tensed, ready to act. I'd seen a Fantome take out his bone crawler before. Only a few more seconds, and I'd have Quinn's creature and its hybrid magick at my call. My breaths came in short gasps.

The bone crawler began to wiggle out. My stomach churned with disgust, yet my head felt light with joy.

So close.

The Tsar stepped forward. His brows lifted as he saw Quinn's bone crawler wriggling free. Quick as lightning, the Tsar pulled a dagger from the folds of his black cloak and jammed the blade through Quinn's neck.

"No!" I cried.

Quinn crumpled forward onto the ground, moaning. For a moment, I saw a glowing, spectral face appear above the mortal one. Quinn mouthed two words. *I'm sorry.*

*Here it is.* Another failure.

I knew my plan to get a bone crawler was tricky at best, but at least it was something. Now, what were my options? How could I fight a mage who was this powerful… Especially when he had access to hybrid magick and I did not?

The Tsar stepped up to Quinn's dead body, yanked out the dagger, and wiped off his bloody blade on his robes. "I'd suggest no more attempts at murder or escape. It's tiresome. I had a lot of time to contemplate how things went wrong before. There was only one way you could have activated your hybrid magick. My bone crawlers. Well, with the power of all the Necromancers now concentrated in my soul, I don't need those insects to control my people anymore. And the need to round up mages for draining is over as well. So let's get rid of that little temptation, shall we?"

I wanted to threaten to pound elegant face into dust. Somehow, I managed to keep quiet, however.

The Tsar raised his hands again. A ball of purple fire appeared between his palms. He looked down into the sphere of flame. "Destroy all the bone crawlers in my entourage." The fire shot out from his grasp, bouncing from Fantome to Fantome. Each time it reached someone, some of the flames burrowed inside their shoulders.

The result of the spell was nothing less than disgusting. My stomach heaved as the bone crawlers crept out of their hosts. The Fantomes watched in on in shocked silence as the bone crawlers tumbled to the ground, their exoskeletons glowing as they burned up from the inside out. None of the Fantomes moved. Within seconds, the bone crawlers had all turned to dust.

The Tsar turned to the Fantomes. "My beautiful entourage. I can see worried looks on some of your faces. I'm a gracious man. Rest assured, my magick will keep you alive and bound to me. I've no plans to kill you."

Somehow, I didn't believe him.

As the Fantomes murmured their thanks, hopelessness pressed in around me. The bone crawlers were my plan to activate hybrid power. That wasn't possible, so I tried once more to pull regular Necromancer energy into me. The Fantome who held me still had me blocked. *Gods-damn it.*

The Tsar rounded on me again. "You told me once that you were trained by Petra. If so, then she did a horrible job of it. I can read your emotions easier than a child's."

My gaze fell on Rowan's unmoving body. A shudder rolled across my shoulders. I'd never seen the man so pale and lifeless.

Still, I swallowed past the knot of grief in my throat. I had to focus on the success that had already come from my mission. Yes, the Tsar had me. He could kill me. And it was likely that he'd already murdered Rowan. But Ada and the others were safe. Rowan said his people had taken care of them. I'd saved the last of the free Necromancers.

I forced my face into a mask of calm once more. As long as the Tsar was wasting time with me, he wouldn't be going after my friends.

The Tsar rubbed his square chin. "You think your little Necromancer friends are safe, don't you?"

His words struck me like knives. "I don't know what you're talking about."

"They're done for, you know."

I worked hard to keep my features calm. He was lying. Had to be.

The Tsar snapped his fingers. "Bring forth our audience. It's time Elea saw her admirers."

More Fantomes stepped out of the darkness. My knees turned rubbery as I saw who they brought with them. The Fantomes had bound and gagged all the freed Necromancers. They shuffled along in a lopsided line, most of them barely conscious. It seemed even more cruel for them to be bound and gagged, when they struggled to stand upright.

My eyes burned with held-in tears. Ada and Veronique were there, too. They both looked pale. Fresh cuts dripped blood from their arms and legs. Angry bruises covered their faces. Grief weighed down my soul.

*No, not Ada and Veronique.*

More figures stepped forward. This time, the Fantomes led the Creation Casters. Rowan's guard. They were bloodied, gagged, and chained in a long row.

*Gods-damn it. There's no way we can survive this.*

The Tsar gestured around him. "Now, this if what I call true beauty. A Royal house smashed to rubble. My enemies chained and near death." He rounded on me. "And my greatest foe about to die."

I lifted my chin. "If you're going to do it, do it. I'm right here."

"Ah, now that's the tricky part, isn't it? Didn't you ever wonder why the Sire and Lady had you put me into exile instead of murder me outright?" The Tsar lifted his dagger and rested it again my cheek. I tried to fight my way free. The Fantome behind me still held me tightly, though.

*So this is it. Torture. Just like the Vicomte. I won't let him see me weep*

I forced my features into a semblance of calm as the Tsar slowly cut a line down my cheek. Pain burned down my skin… Until I saw what was happening to the Tsar. A line of blood appeared on his face as well. Shock rolled through me. I couldn't focus on anything outside of the red mark on the Tsar's skin.

"That's a trick."

"No, that's a fact. Our magick is too similar. Whenever I try to hurt you, I hurt myself. Which is why I can't destroy you, but I could send you into exile." He tapped his chin as if seriously considering this option. "But I won't." He raised his dagger again. "Instead, I'll ask one of your own to do the honors." He pointed at Veronique. "Bring her here."

Veronique barely stood upright in her rags, with her head lolling from side to side. I flashed an angry look at the Tsar. "Leave her be."

"Oh, I can't do that. Someone besides myself must be your executioner."

A pair of Fantomes dragged Veronique over to stand before me. One of them roughly pulled the gag from her mouth. Up close, Veronique looked deathly pale and bleary-eyed, a faint shell of the fierce girl she'd once been.

The Tsar stalked over to her. "Do you understand what I want you to do, girl?"

Her voice was a harsh rasp. "Yes."

The Tsar cut loose Veronique's hands and set the dagger onto her palm. "Then slit her throat while the others watch."

Across the darkened rubble, Ada fell onto her knees, her face streaked with tears.

So much time. All my work. And now, Ada would watch me die, right before the Tsar killed her, too.

I locked gazes with Veronique. If I was about to die with an audience, at least I could do it with dignity. "Go on."

"I can't." Veronique looked to the Tsar, her heads wide and pleading. "You forgot something."

The Tsar sniffed in disgust. "What could I have possibly have missed?"

Veronique's gaze turned sly. Her stance straightened despite her battered body. She mouthed six words so I only I could see them.

*I still have a bone crawler.*

My eyes widened as I realized the truth. Mother Superior had put a bone crawler in all my new Sisters right before they left the Midnight Cloisters, Veronique included. The Tsar was so concerned with his all-powerful Fantomes he must have forgotten.

Voices rose among the Fantomes. I recognized more of the ones I'd possessed starting toward us at a run. They were trying to help by causing a distraction. The Tsar swung around to face them. 'What's all this?"

Acting with a speed I hadn't thought possible, Veronique lifted the knife to her shoulder, sliced a line in her skin, and tore out the creature. She dropped the wriggling bone crawler into my hands.

Instantly, fresh power slammed into me, stronger than ever before. Hybrid magick lit up my body with more strength and energy than I ever thought possible. I merely shrugged my shoulders, but the motion was so laden with magick the Fantome behind me was thrown across the rubble into the darkness.

The Tsar looked back at me and roared with rage. He raised his arm. The bones there glowed so brightly it was almost blinding. "I hold all the Necromancer power! It is mine! You are nothing." A great column of purple smoke stretched across the ground. When the haze cleared, the earth was covered in skeleton warriors. Only, they were unlike any fighters I'd ever seen before.

The bones of the Tsar's army were twisted into odd shapes. Spines bristled with spikes. Bone swords and clubs replaced their hands. Many had overlarge heads filled with jagged teeth. Thick hides of violet alligator skin acted as armor. A chill of fear ran up my neck. These were a mixture of skeleton and animal, bone and skin. Hybrid magick.

The Tsar pointed directly at me. "Kill her!"

The Tsar's skeleton army started marching forward. He'd conjured thousands of them. Their twisted outlines stretched off into the devastated landscape. I'd never seen an army this large.

The twisted figures clawed their way across the rubble. Moonlight reflected off their spikes and swords. Meanwhile, the Fantomes all raised their arms. The bones in their left hands glowed blue in the night as they began speaking an incantation in unison. I couldn't make out the words, yet the meaning was clear.

The Fantomes were about to cast, and I was their target, too.

I looked down at the bone crawler in my hand. Its power wouldn't be enough. A memory appeared. Back in the gardens, the Fantomes had changed their bone crawlers into something else. I could do that, too, if I had enough power.

A thrill of realization energized my soul. Every follower of the Tsar received a bone crawler. The Tsar only destroyed the bone crawlers in the Fantomes. All the prisoners still had their bone crawlers, though. At least a dozen of them stood nearby.

An idea appeared in my mind. It was insane. It was all I had.

There was no time to lose. I reached out through the bone crawler in my hands, just as I reached out to find Necromancer power in the air.

Instantly, I felt it. The connection from this bone crawler to all the others that still lived. I yanked their power into my own body. My veins felt as if they were on fire. Every inch of me vibrated with energy. My stance loosened as I teetered from side to side.

*Stay focused, Elea. You have to do this.*

The power inside me became stronger and stronger. All my bones and veins lit up with purple flame. I remembered how the Tsar did his spells. No incantations this time. I pictured what I wanted. Another army of skeletons appeared. *Mine.*

I set the energy loose.

Purple light flashed all around me. When the brightness faded, thousands of skeletons now stood nearby. They were of all different sizes and shapes.

That was the Necromancer side of my hybrid power, summoning the skeletons. But I needed more than that. Caster energy must be part of this spell as well. It was the only way to generate a hybrid army that could fight and beat the Tsar.

Besides, I wanted my gods-damned Brothers and Sisters back.

Using all my focus, I pumped more magick into the skeletons. The skeletal bones became covered in muscle, flesh, and leather robes. Dark purple markings of bone covered their skin.

Flesh and bone, with faces painted as skeletons.

They were my army.

They were perfect.

Next, I used my power to contact the souls I'd connected with in the dungeons. I opened the channel of communication with the dead. It looked like I was speaking aloud to myself, but the message went to Quinn and his people. *"I offer you a chance at life again. Even more importantly, I give you the hope of revenge. Come back and destroy the Tsar and his army. Take mortal form once more."*

There wasn't time for me to explain my full plan, yet that didn't seem to matter. Ghostly voices echoed through my mind.

*Give us life and revenge.*

"Thank you, my Brothers and Sisters." Pulling in fresh power, I summoned their souls back from the dead. Thousands of ghosts rose up from the ground, an army of blue spirits from the ashes below. Each ghost found the flesh and bone body that I'd prepared for them and slipped inside. With a burst of purple light, the two sides merged. Heights changed. Faces altered. The flesh and bone creations became matched the spirit they now housed. My spell was complete.

My army began to move.

What a sight. They were pale bodies with the images of skeletons painted on their skin in deep purple. They were alive and ready to fight.

And the Tsar's skeleton horde ran to meet them.

The field of rubble became a blur of battle. Blue flashes of light filled the air as the Fantomes cast against my Necromancers. The Tsar's skeletons leapt into the fray, their bone-white weapons gleaming in the starlight.

I stumbled across the rubble until I saw them. The captured Creation Casters, along with Ada, Veronique, and the others. My hand still glowed with purple light. Good. I had some hybrid power left. Using my new magick, I pictured the spells I wanted. Again, the spells worked. Ada, Veronique, and the others became invisible to all but me. Meanwhile, the Creation Casters broke free of their chains and began to fight. I scanned the battlefield, looking for Rowan.

He lay nearby, his body still immobile. Acting on instinct, I rushed to his side and set my hands on his chest.

I hated him.

I loved him.

I didn't want him to die.

My hands glowed with a pale purple light. My hybrid magick was waning. I had perhaps one casting left in me. There was no question in my mind. I knew exactly how I would use the last of this hybrid power. I focused my magick into Rowan. The venom in his bloodstream pushed back with supernatural force. Too much time had gone by. His organs were failing. His soul was almost gone.

The Tsar's skeletons fought the Casters and Necromancers around me. Flashes of blue light exploded in the skies. I barely saw any of it. All I knew was that Rowan was dying. I wouldn't let that happen. I pumped the last of my hybrid power into his body.

He still didn't move.

A voice sounded behind my shoulder. "Are we done toying with hybrid magick?" It was the Tsar. "You'd best leave that work to those of us who understand our powers."

I slowly rose to face him. "My army is winning."

"But you're about to die. There are no more bone crawlers here. No more lovers in the wings. An army at war, but too busy to fight for you. There are no more second chances. You're all alone. And you're mine."

A warm hand wrapped around my wrist. I looked down to see Rowan propped up on his elbow, his right hand grasping my left. The veins in his entire arm glowed red as he pumped Caster power into me. My body felt on fire. Pain like I'd never known ripped me from the inside out.

But the hybrid magick came back.

I reached out with my mage senses. The gateway was still nearby. Agony shot through me as I released a cloud of purple magick. When the haze vanished, the gate had moved. This time, it had formed right behind the Tsar.

*So close. One small push and he's back through the gateway.*

I crumpled forward onto my knees. Hurt ripped through my brain. Every inch of my being felt like it was tearing apart. I moaned in agony.

Rowan gripped my hand more tightly. "You can do it, Elea. Send that bastard back."

With one last rush of pain and power, I hurled our hybrid magick at the Tsar. He flew backward through the gate. Another flash of violet light tore through the night sky, and the gateway was gone. I exhaled. At last. The Tsar was gone, too.

The final thing I saw was all the Tsar's skeletons fall lifeless to the ground as my body collapsed. After that, my mind faded into oblivion. All the while, I still felt Rowan's hand in mine.

## 31

*J* awoke in my tavern bed and rolled onto my side, every muscle in my body aching with the effort. When I saw who was seated beside my mattress, I thought perhaps I was still asleep.

I blinked hard. Then, I did it again.

Rowan was still sitting beside me. He wore his brown leathers and an intense look on his rugged face. Heavy scruff covered his chin. It looked like he hadn't slept in days.

*Not sure how I feel about that.*

One part of me was glad to see him alive. He'd saved my life in the battle with the Tsar. Another part of me knew that had changed nothing. We still couldn't be together. And he was engaged to Amelia.

I always knew Rowan was a member of the Imperial family. They always married for political advantage. So, I shouldn't be upset that Rowan had gotten engaged.

I was furious.

Fortunately, I was now alert enough to school my emotions. True, I might be angry, but I wouldn't let him see it. I forced myself to sit up. The movement revealed that I was now wearing a cotton nightshift. I'd been here for some time, then. "How long have I been asleep?"

Rowan leaned forward, resting his elbows on his knees. "A fortnight."

My brows lifted. *Fourteen nights?* For me to stay asleep that long, that meant magick. "Did you put me in stasis?" That involved slowing a body down until it was almost frozen solid. It was complex and draining magick.

Rowan nodded. "My Caster power wouldn't leave your body. You were burning up with it. Once you were in stasis, I could heal you in phases."

In other words, Rowan had been casting healing spells at my bedside. It wasn't that he hadn't slept in a few days. It had been more like a few weeks. The realization should have blunted my anger.

It didn't though. The bastard was engaged to someone else. It was an effort to keep my tone heavy and formal. "Thank you for watching over me."

Rowan eyed me carefully. I had the upsetting impression that he was guessing my thoughts. Again. "The engagement means nothing. It's a means to get the Sword of Theodora. That weapon is the only way my people can survive." His voice turned pleading. "If you'll only allow me to explain."

"No." Low chanting echoed into the room. I welcomed the distraction. "What's that noise?"

Rowan scrubbed his palms over his face. "I'd rather finish our discussion."

"I'd rather not." I rose from the bed. The voices grew louder. Unease twisted through my stomach. With shaky steps, I walked over to the window. Anxiety prickled my skin into gooseflesh.

*Please don't let this be what I think it is.*

I braced my arms on the wooden sill. Outside, a harvest moon hung low in the night sky. In the moonlight, I could see the entire town was crammed with people. The thin, winding streets, the rickety wooden buildings, even the pushcarts... Every free patch of ground was inhabited by mages in purple robes, all of them holding candles. I shielded my eyes against the glass, trying for a better look. The mages all had the images of the skeletons on their skin.

*These were the ghosts I'd raised and placed into bodies on the battlefield.*

The scene was almost beyond belief. I shook my head. "They're still alive and waiting for me."

"They've been here for the last two weeks," said Rowan. "It's all a vigil for your health and survival."

"A vigil for me." I rubbed my eyes. This must be a dream. *Somehow, I'm still asleep and recovering from my battle with the Tsar.* No matter how I rubbed my eyes, the vision from my window didn't change. Bit by bit, the crowd's chant grew more clear.

"Tsarina. Tsarina. Tsarina."

With a gasp, I stepped away from the windowsill. *Tsarina.* They thought I could rule the Necromancers? I was a farm girl. "I'm not their leader. That should be Petra."

Rowan moved to stand beside me. Moonlight outlined his profile as he gazed out the window. "They seem to disagree. I've been where you are now. They won't let you go." His gaze intensified. Once again, I could imagine his thoughts as clearly as if they were my own.

*I won't let you go, either.*

My insides twisted into knots. "And we—" I gestured between Rowan and me. "Any kind of relationship simply isn't possible. Not after what happened."

"I understand." Rowan's body heat radiated against me. I was torn between wanting to push him away and needing to lean in closer. He slowly raised his hand and ran his fingertip along my jawline. Everywhere he touched I felt a rush of warmth.

*By the Sire.* I wanted him, but I could never have him. Which was why I needed to walk away.

Yet I stayed rooted to the spot.

"You need time to heal." Rowan trailed his hand around to the back of my neck, his fingers brushing up and down the base of my skull. "And I can be patient." His rough voice lowered an octave. "But make no mistake, Elea. This isn't over." He started to lean forward.

*Don't let him kiss you, Elea. He's a liar. You're a strong Necromancer. Push him away.*

I couldn't. One last kiss didn't seem like a terrible idea.

A knock sounded on the door, breaking the moment. Coming back to my senses, I took a huge step away from Rowan. His gaze never wavered from mine. His last words seemed to hang in the air between us.

*"This isn't over."*

Quinn stepped into the room. Sure, I knew from looking out the window that the Necromancers I'd raised were still nearby, yet seeing one in the flesh? My mouth fell open. Quinn looked just as he had when I'd first conjured him on the battlefield. The image of the skeleton inside him was still painted on his face in purple. His shaved head and scarred face were just as they'd been in life.

When he saw me standing, Quinn immediately fell to his knees. "Tsarina."

All the blood drained from my face. "You're still alive."

"We all are." He kept his gaze locked to the floor.

"Quinn." I tugged on the shoulder of his robes. "Please, get off your knees."

Quinn rose, a large smile brightening his scarred face. "You look fit and well. Genesis Rex said he'd heal you, and he did."

"Yes, well, I'm healed now." This was all beyond overwhelming. I'd raised thousands of Necromancers from the dead, and now one of them was in my bedroom. "You can take your leave."

Quinn straightened his stance. "Where would you have us all go, Tsarina?"

My eyes widened. *He thinks I'm giving him orders to head out.* "That wasn't what meant. Those weren't orders to go anywhere. I'm not your Tsarina."

Quinn frowned. "Of course, you're not."

I sighed. "Thank you."

Quinn's face took on a dreamy look. "No, you're far more than a Tsarina. Perhaps you would like us to address you as something else? A deity perhaps?"

"No, that won't be necessary," I said quickly. "*Tsarina* will be fine for now."

*Until I can get you under Petra's rule.*

Rowan leaned against the wall and hitched his left leg across the right. His gaze met mine, and a look of sympathy flashed across his face. His words echoed through my mind.

*"I've been where you are now. They won't let you go."*

My eyes narrowed as I considered my options. All in all, there was really only one thing to do. If they wanted me to be their Tsarina, I'd simply command them to march on off. "I wish you all to travel to the Zelle Cloister. My old Mother Superior, Petra, is waiting for you. She'll assess your skills and train each of you into achieving your full potential as a Necromancer."

"Quite wise," said Quinn. "You'll want to train us as your army."

"No, no armies." My voice came out harsher than I thought. "All of you going to the Zelle Cloister to learn. That's my only wish."

Quinn tilted his head, confused. "You're not going with us?"

"Not now. I'll come and visit as soon as possible."

Quinn's jaw fell slack. "So, who is to lead us?"

I said the first thing that came into my head. "I appoint you, Quinn."

It was an impetuous decision. However, the more I turned the thought over the more it appealed to me. Quinn was the one I trusted the most. He tried to save me on the battlefield when everyone else gave up. Plus, he'd been a Master Necromancer in life. You didn't reach that level without understanding how to lead your fellow mages.

*Quinn would be fine.*

A long moment passed in silence. "Did you hear what I said?" I asked.

"Yes, thank you for this honor." The way Quinn said the words he seemed anything but appreciative. In fact, the man appeared downright confused by the fact that I wasn't waving my Tsarina flag high. Why could no one understand that power wasn't attractive to everyone?

"You're most welcome," I said.

Quinn shifted his weight from foot to foot. "What do you want to do with the Fantomes? Many wish to see them executed."

"Don't kill them." I didn't work this hard to save our people only to execute them without any thought. "No one murders the Fantomes. Just get them safely to Petra, and she'll decide from there." Quinn frowned, so I went on. "I want to try to rehabilitate them. I believe that some of the mages do want redemption."

"So Petra will decide."

"Yes." This seemed safe. Petra hated bloodshed more than I did. Quinn opened his mouth, ready to ask another question. The longer this conversation went on, the more I'd be tempted to act as Tsarina.

*Our chat needed to end.*

I quickly stepped to the door, pulled it open, and gestured to the outer hall. "That's all for now, Quinn. If you'll excuse me, I need my rest."

"As you wish, Tsarina." Quinn bowed slightly and shuffled out into the hallway. With Quinn gone, I refocused my attention on Rowan. He hadn't moved from his spot by the wall. "I am rather tired, Rowan, so…"

He kicked off the wall and turned to face me. The rugged lines of his face were set with determination. "And you wish me to leave?"

It took a force of will to say the next word. "Yes."

Rowan stepped up until only an inch separated our bodies. A slow smile rounded his lips. "Now, who's lying?"

*And gods-damn it, he was right.*

Still, I watched him saunter through the door, down the outer hallway, and out of my life. As he disappeared down the steps, I gripped the handle of my door so tightly my knuckles flared white.

*Goodbye, Rowan. You may not agree, but what was between us has to be over.*

Suddenly, every inch of my body felt empty. My eyelids had never felt heavier. I returned to bed, huddled under the sheets, and fell into a deep sleep.

In my dreams, I stepped along the road to Braddock Farm. Every footfall took a life's age. No matter how quickly I tried to move, I never seemed to move forward. My old life seemed forever out of reach. Still, I wouldn't give up.

Home was waiting.

I'd be back soon.

## 32

*W*hen I opened my eyes again, pale beams of morning light shifted across my bedroom wall. I pulled back my thin coverlet, padded across the floor, and peeped out the tavern window. The quiet town stretched out below me, a labyrinth of dirt roads flanked by rickety wooden buildings. I let out a relieved breath.

All the Necromancers were gone. They'd followed my orders.

A knock sounded on the bedroom door. "Who is it?" I asked.

"Tsarina, it's Quinn."

I gritted my teeth together. *He's still here and calling me Tsarina. That has to stop.* I scooped up a small blanket from the bed and wrapped it around my shoulders. "Come in, please."

The door swung open, and Quinn stepped inside the room. In the morning light, it was even clearer how the markings on his face were actually a part of his skin. What kind of spell had I cast, anyway? I'd been out of my head when it came to me. *I won't be able to access hybrid magick again.* All the bone crawlers were gone, so that option was closed. And working to access the hybrid power through Rowan? I wasn't going near him again if I could ever avoid it. Plus, I didn't know how to control that power without burning up. I was lucky that Quinn and the others seemed well and healthy.

Quinn spoke, jarring me from my thoughts. "Good morning, Tsarina."

"Why are you here, Quinn? I asked you to go."

"I have need of your wisdom. It will only take a minute, Tsarina."

"Please. Call me by my first name. Elea."

"As you command, Elea."

I opened my mouth, ready to argue the fact that I wasn't commanding anything. But I shut it just as quickly. *Let him think whatever he likes. Soon enough, they'll all be taking orders from Petra and forget all about me.* Even as I tried to rationalize this thought, some small part of me screamed that was impossible. My old life was gone. They'd always see me as their maker. Meanwhile, the Necromancers I'd freed saw me as their savior, Ada and Veronique included. I wasn't sure how I felt about any of that, to be honest.

*No point worrying about it now.*

"Was there something you needed, Quinn?"

"Yes. There's been a magickal message. Petra would like you to transport to the Zelle Cloister. She'd like to speak with you."

"Is there some problem getting everyone to the Zelle?"

"Not to worry. The Fantomes gave us totem rings to transport. They had quite a hoard of them saved up over the years." His scarred mouth tipped up into a smile. "It seemed you were right that some of them might be worth saving."

A shiver of worry rolled up my spine. Then why did Petra want me? "The Zelle hasn't turned my Necromancers away, have they?"

I winced as I realized what I'd said. *My Necromancers. By the Sire.* I was getting attached to them already.

"Petra is taking everyone in, not to worry."

Quinn rubbed his chin slowly. I half expected the purple image of a skull and teeth to brush off on his fingertips. "But she'd still like to talk. She asks that you transport directly into her office."

A request to talk... That was never a good sign from Petra. I pulled my blanket more tightly around my shoulders. "Do you think she's angry?"

Quinn shrugged. "She's a Grand Mistress Necromancer. Who can tell how she feels?"

"Of course." I scrubbed my hand over my face. "I'll get ready and transport myself there."

"Are you certain you're healthy enough?"

"I'll be fine."

Quinn stared at me, wide-eyed. "Are you going to use hybrid magick?"

"I drained the last bone crawlers with my spell to raise the dead." I tilted my head. "Unless you've found some?"

It was meant in jest. Quinn's mouth thinned with worry all the same. "We've searched for more of those without success. My deepest apologies, Tsarina."

I raised my pointer finger, ready to correct Quinn for calling me Tsarina yet again. But I noticed how his shoulders were shaking with worry. When did I become such a frightening character? "Please, don't fret. That was simply an attempt at humor, Quinn. I don't know how to use hybrid magick without the bone crawlers."

"What about teaming with Genesis Rex?"

*You mean the liar who's marrying someone else?*

I cleared my throat. "Genesis Rex and I won't share magick again." I meant to sound serene, but my words had an edge of anger to them. This conversation wasn't helping, so I gestured to the door. "I need to get ready for Petra now."

"As you command." Quinn left in a blur of movement and purple robes.

Once he was gone, I walked over to my traveling trunk, pulled open the lid, and began searching inside for my Grand Mistress Necromancer robes.

*Time to see my Mother Superior.*

An hour later, I was leaning against the stone wall of Petra's study in the Zelle Cloister. My old Mother Superior sat behind her desk, carefully setting quill to paper. With every brushstroke, small poufs of blue dust flew up from her work. Petra didn't need to ask me to wait quietly. I knew what it was like to get partially done with a casting, only to have it ruined by an interruption.

At last, Petra set down her quill. She looked as she had before, only the lines on her face had deepened, and her hair was now a purer shade of white. Her gaze was sharp as ever, though. Her eyes locked onto mine. "Elea."

"Mother."

"You've dropped a great many people on my doorstep." She spoke the words in the classic monotone of a proper Necromancer.

"We discussed this before. You were going to take them all in."

"And so I have." She leaned forward, bracing her elbows on her desktop. "But that was before you raised two thousand Necromancers from the dead. They don't wish my leadership. They crave yours."

"It's over for me, Petra. We talked about this before I left to find Ada and the others. Once this quest was done, I'd go back to my old life." I'd had it with magick. It had brought me nothing but pain and heartache. The more I'd thought about it, the more I wanted my old life back. That meant Braddock Farm.

Petra's gaze pinned me to the spot. "Amelia is here, you know. She's watching over Veronique. She suspects some kind of bond between you and Rex."

The words hurt me more than I thought they would. "I'd like to see her."

"She's asked to be kept in seclusion with Veronique."

"Why?"

"On my suggestion." Petra's face stayed emotionless. The woman was a true Necromancer. "I don't want either of you doing anything rash. You both need time."

"A wise suggestion, Mother."

"I cast a seeing spell. I know everything about you and Genesis Rex."

My back stiffened. "That's my personal business."

Petra's voice took on a hard edge. "Not when thousands of Necromancers see you as their Tsarina, it isn't. Especially when you asked me to lead them for you."

I bowed my head. "You've taken on a huge burden for me and our people. Of course, you need to do what you think is best to lead us."

Petra rose. "I had warned you about emotion, Elea."

My shoulders slumped. I hated disappointing Petra. "I did my best, Mother."

"I summoned you here to see if you were ready to lead our people." Petra slowly stepped closer. "Obviously, that is not the case."

I sighed. "On that, we agree."

Petra eyed me slowly from head to toe. "Return to your farm. Take some time. Practice meditation and the routines of the Sire of Souls. I'll summon you when I've need of you." She shuffle-walked back to her desk and slowly eased herself back into her seat. Her whole body shook with the movement.

My spine straightened. It felt good to be under Petra's guidance again. The Necromancers would be safe under her care. All I needed was to get back to my farm, and everything could return to normal. "Thank you, Mother."

Petra picked up her quill and dipped it into her inkwell. "I have only one request before you leave."

"What is it, Mother?"

"Someone's waiting for you in the hallway outside. They'd like a word before you go."

I frowned, picturing the long list of people I'd rather not face right now. "I'm not sure that's a good idea."

"That may be true." A wry smile might have curled her lips, but the expression was gone too quickly to be sure. "But if you don't, Ada will never give me a moment's peace."

My heart lightened. That sounded like the old Ada. I couldn't wait to see her. "You can count on it, Mother." I sped toward the door and pulled it open.

Ada stood in the outer hallway, flanked by two of the elder Zelle Sisters. The change in her was unbelievable. In just a matter of weeks, her bony frame had begun to fill out, all her welts had healed over to small scars, and a light now shone in her brown eyes.

"Elea!" Ada rushed up and hugged my waistline.

I patted her head and grinned from ear to ear. "It's so good to see you."

Ada stepped back and pulled up the sleeve on her Novice robes. A thin rope of muscle popped from her upper arm. "Look how strong I am."

I set my hand on my throat in an overblown show of amazement. "Oh, my."

"The Sisters let me climb up the mountain face all day long. And look at this." She raised her left hand. A pulse of blue light moved across her palm. "I have magick, Elea! Just like you." She frowned. "Only not exactly like you. You made all those people with their skeleton faces. I can't do that yet. But I can pull in enough power to be a Novice." She twirled, showing the fullness of her skirt. "Look, I have new robes now and everything!"

"So you do." I knelt before her and felt my eyes prickle with tears. *This moment. Right now. That's what I've worked for. And it's all worth it.* "I'm very proud of you, Ada."

She swished her torso from side to side and smiled. "Wulf's been climbing, too. Even though he's a boy, they're letting him sleep by my bed in the Sisters' dormitory."

More warmth spread through my chest. I'd forgotten about Ada's imaginary friend. "Is that so?" I looked over to the pair of Sisters who were glancing with small smiles down at Ada. For traditional Necromancers, that was an overwhelming show of emotion. I was surprised Petra allowed it. "Does other Mother Superior know about this?"

The taller Sister, Mina, spoke first. As she turned to me, a mask of calm settled over her face. "We act on Mother's orders. She says that Ada needs time to be a child."

"We're to spoil her rotten," added Sister Lorelei.

Ada bounced on the balls of her feet. "The Sisters let me eat whatever I want, climb the mountainside, and if I ask to learn magick, then they teach me!"

"I'm so glad, Ada."

"Now that you're the Tsarina, will you stay and teach me, too? I want to be a great mage just like you."

The Sisters eyed me carefully. No doubt, they knew that Mother Superior had summoned me here to find out if I was ready to stay and lead. I sighed. "I'm going back to my old farm, Ada."

"But you're the Tsarina."

"Mother Superior will lead the Necromancers."

Ada frowned and bit her thumbnail. "You'll come back and visit me, right?"

My throat tightened with grief. Ada had been so happy just a moment ago. Now, her bottom lip wobbled. "I'll try, Ada."

"But I waited for you. It was awful!"

"I know it was." My voice cracked. "I worked hard to find you."

"Now you're leaving again. It's because of that man, isn't it? The one Veronique and Amelia are talking about."

I hugged my elbows. "I've always wanted to return to my farm." Even as the words left my mouth, they felt hollow. Why did I want to run away from here? That wasn't me.

"Amelia didn't leave Veronique once she was found." Ada's little hands balled into fists. "She stayed with her because she loves her."

The implication was clear. I was leaving, so I didn't care for Ada. "Wherever I am, I'll always have you in my heart, Ada."

"You're mean." Huge tears lined Ada's big brown eyes. I felt like a villain for putting them there. "Veronique and Amelia never want to see you again. I don't either." She grabbed Mina's hand and dragged her away. I watched the pair of them go. Part of me wanted to rush after Ada and promise to stay.

*I can't.*

Sister Lorelei stood quietly. A long pause followed before she spoke. "You've done amazing things, Elea. You shouldn't feel guilt for wanting some peace."

I heard her words, yet the meaning couldn't break through my guilt. All I could focus on was what Ada had told me. "Is it true? Amelia and Veronique are here, only they don't want to see me?"

"They need time, as well."

"I understand." After everything that had happened, it was to return to Braddock. Alone. I'd thought my life was solitary before. Back then, I'd always had Tristan. Now, I'd gained friends, only to lose them all. Despair wrapped around me, tight as a winding sheet.

"I'd better go," said Lorelei. Walking away, she followed the path that Ada and Mina had taken a moment ago.

The hallway felt cold and empty without Ada. The small hairs prickled on my neck. I hadn't heard her approach. Even so, Petra now stood by my side. "You're still rather stealthy in your old age, Mother."

"Oh, I have a quite a few surprises left in me." She gave me the smallest of smiles. "You always have a place here, if you should wish it."

I wanted to soak up this moment, write it in parchment and save it forever. Mostly because it wasn't true. I looked around the familiar stone hallways with their murals of laughing skeletons. For years, I'd wandered this Cloister. At one time, I'd been the young girl that all the elder Sisters adopted as their favorite. Now, I didn't belong here.

"Thank you, Petra."

"Be well, Elea."

My eyes began to sting with held-in tears. I couldn't cry in front of Petra. With a quick wave, I took off in search of a good spot to transport. I needed to return to Braddock Farm. That was the place for me. Some small part of my heart said a prayer to the Sire of Souls.

*This time, let that be the truth.*

## 33

*I* hiked up the road leading to Braddock Farm. With every step, my heart beat faster. The trees lining the side of the road were tall and lush. I couldn't believe how much they'd grown in the last five and a half years.

My steps froze. Five and a half years? Had I really been away that long?

Why, yes I had.

I paused at the top of the hill. Here was my favorite view of the farm, right before dawn was about to break. Once the sun rose, everything in Braddock would be cast in a golden glow. I scanned the sky and frowned.

Gray clouds hung overhead. Not a good sign.

A rumble sounded behind me. I swung around to see my neighbor, Wyatt, driving toward me. His wagon was the same as I remembered—an open bed that had been painted white, large yellow wheels, and a small bench for the driver. At one time, I thought this transportation was quite fancy. Since then, I'd ridden in Royal covered carriages. Wyatt's wagon looked very small and plain now. For some reason, that realization made my chest hurt a little.

As Wyatt drove closer, I noticed the other passengers in his cart. Beside him, there sat a slender woman in a simple blue frock. Her long golden hair cascaded over her shoulders. An infant lay swaddled in her arms. The back of the truck held a small child, a boy of no more than three years old. He had yellow curls and large bright eyes. A chilly realization crept through me.

This must be Wyatt's family. He'd proposed to me shortly before I left for the Cloister. Well, *proposed* wasn't exactly the word. Wyatt essentially demanded that I marry him, being that I was a lowly Necromancer and our lands abutted each other. He swore to marry a local girl. I suppose he did.

The sight hurt. Not that I wanted to marry Wyatt—he was too much of a bully for that—but because if I had stayed here, that might have been my life, too. Perhaps I'd have fallen in love with some kind farmer. I might have children now. I could have a life with someone who was actually available to share it with me.

Not like Rowan.

I held back the urge to groan. Why couldn't I stop thinking about him? Rowan was engaged to someone else.

Wyatt's gaze met mine. Like every bully, the man could sense when he'd caused pain, and he thrived on it. After stopping his wagon, he swung off the front bench and sauntered over toward me. I wanted to order him to leave, but this was my home now. Wyatt's land ran beside mine. Things would be easier if I could control my temper and be as pleasant as possible.

Trouble was, my temper was already running hot.

Wyatt came closer, and I could see that he hadn't changed. The man was still wearing his too-tight pants and an open shirt to expose his chest. I suppose some girls must find that overall look appealing. I glanced at the woman seated on the front bench of the wagon. She must have found it attractive. That or Wyatt blackmailed her. I frowned. I wouldn't put it past the man.

Wyatt stopped before me and set his hands on his hips. He now wore yellow calfskin gloves to match his wagon wheels. I suppose that was one change, at least. "Can this be?" he asked. "Is this my long-lost neighbor Elea?"

I schooled my features into a look of calm. "Yes, I've returned."

"You look quite the lady now." Wyatt stared me down from head to toe. His thin tongue flickered across his lips, a movement that was both unnecessary and disgusting.

My eyes widened. All thoughts of avoiding my temper evaporated. "Isn't that your wife and two children back in your wagon? I can't believe you're disrespecting them in this way. They're almost within earshot, and you're eyeing me like I'm a slab of fresh meat."

Wyatt glanced over his shoulder. A small smile rounded his pink lips. "Some women know their place, you know." He raked his hand through his white-blond hair. "If only you'd learned that, Elea, then you wouldn't be alone. No man has put a ring on your finger, I see."

On reflex, my hand went to my throat. Under my gown, I still wore my mating ring from Rowan on a chain around my neck. I told myself that I'd throw it away. Tomorrow, perhaps.

Wyatt's smile widened. "Well?"

"My personal life is no business of yours."

Wyatt took a step closer. His grin disappeared, and a sick kind of menace oozed off him. "It will be my business, all right. My wife lets me do whatever I like. Some night, I'll walk by that little cottage of yours. A lonely woman like you can't afford to pass up some company." His eyes narrowed. "You *will* open the door for me."

I'd never had a lot of control when I was around Wyatt. What little I had today snapped. Raising my left arm, I started to pull Necromancer energy into my body. It was beyond time I cast a serious spell to shut this man's mouth, once and for all.

Wyatt pointed at my hand. "You're still practicing that death magick? Knew it! No one wants people like you around."

I gritted my teeth. *By the Sire.* I was playing right into his plan yet again. The local farmers were Forgotten Ones, Commoners without magick. They'd almost had me kicked off my own land when Wyatt told them I was a rogue Necromancer. What had I opened myself up to?

The gallop of horses' hooves echoed through the air. Wyatt and I both turned to see someone riding toward us on a black steed. Even from a distance, there was no mistaking the man's halo of golden hair.

Philippe.

I couldn't help but smile. I hadn't been able to say goodbye to Philippe after the battle at the Montagne estate. My chest warmed. He'd tracked me down. Philippe pulled his horse up to my side, dismounted, and took stock of the situation. I could almost hear the clockwork gears of his mind spinning.

Wyatt frowned. "Is this your man? I thought you were alone." His voice deepened. "We had an understanding, Elea."

I pinched the bridge of my nose. "You demanded that I open my door to you. I never agreed to it, which is what makes you a menace to all women." I gestured to the cart. "I pity your poor wife."

Philippe strode to my side and wrapped his arm possessively around my waist. "Hello, darling. Sorry I'm late." Before I could think, he planted a gentle kiss on my lips. "Do I need to kill this fool for you?"

In that moment, I couldn't remember being happier to see anyone in my life.

Wyatt gulped. "Kill me? In front of my wife and children?"

Philippe chuckled. "That's someone's family, but not yours. Your brother's perhaps?"

"But... I..."

"Don't bother to deny it. As I approached, the little boy was pointing in the opposite direction and asking for his da. Clearly, it's not you." Philippe pursed his lips. "Or should I ask *them* if they belong to you? The lady seems like the type who won't tolerate liars."

I glanced over to the woman. Indeed, she was glaring at Wyatt. Clearly, she knew his ways as much as I did. All of a sudden, the morning was looking up. I leaned my head against Philippe's chest. "Darling, how I've missed you."

Philippe set his hand on the pommel of his sword and focused on Wyatt. "Here's what happens next. You walk away and never speak to my woman again. In return, I won't run you through with my blade. Do we have an agreement?"

Wyatt mumbled something unintelligible and rushed back to his cart. Within a matter of seconds, he was rolling away. What a beautiful sight.

I watched the wagon grow smaller down the road and wanted to cheer. "You handled that well."

Philippe shrugged. "All in a day's work of protecting my lady."

I stepped away from Philippe's embrace. "About that."

"Please." Philippe rolled his eyes. "Don't give me some speech about how we don't belong together. All I ask is the chance to prove something to you." A mischievous light danced in his deep blue eyes.

"And what would that *something* be?"

"You've been spending months with the King of Gloom. I've been carefully waiting for my chance, and at last, it's here. This is my opportunity to keep you company as you settle into your new life, and if possible, have a torrid love affair at the same time."

I couldn't help but smile. "This is your plan, eh?"

"Brilliant, isn't it? You need a break from all the overblown seriousness with Genesis Rex. Mindless enjoyment… That's what I recommend. I'm the perfect man for the job."

The offer was tempting. The gods knew I could use the company. I worried my lower lip with my teeth, debating if this was a good idea.

Philippe stepped closer again. I was weakening and he knew it. "Besides," he said smoothly. "I've already been you naked. We're halfway there." He offered me his arm.

"This is a farm, Philippe. Not a Royal mansion."

"Oh, I might even do physical labor if required."

"You? Actual work?"

"I'm quite strong. Although my best muscles don't show in this outfit." I knew he was referring to more than his velvet longcoat. Cheeky.

"That was terrible." I still couldn't help smiling, though. "Tell me, do your charms work on other women?"

"Inevitably. Still, why not find out for yourself?" He wagged his elbow in my direction.

I shifted my weight from foot to foot. "I'm not sure that's a good idea."

Philippe lowered his voice. "In all seriousness, Elea. You need a friend. Let me make you smile."

Those words made my decision clear. I did need a good smile from time to time. "All right." I wrapped my hand around his forearm and together, we walked up the hill toward Braddock Farm. I gave Philippe's arm a gentle squeeze. "Thank you for finding me, by the way."

"I could say the same to you, you know."

"You could?" Philippe seemed to be getting awfully serious, all of a sudden.

"That's a conversation for another day. Come, let's enjoy a pleasant stroll in the sunshine."

I glanced about. Philippe was right. The sun had fully risen and burned off the last of the clouds. I'd been so concerned with Wyatt, I hadn't even noticed. Now, the forest's leaves gleamed like emeralds under a sapphire-blue sky. This was the life I remembered: my farm, a lovely landscape, and the chance to make something grow.

I was coming home. At last.

—*The End*—

～

*The adventure continues with CHERISHED, Book 3 in the Beholder series. Read on for a sample chapter!*

# APPENDIX I - BONUS CONTENT

# WHAT BEHOLDER TEACHES ME

*N*ow that I've finished book two of the Beholder series, it's time for a little self-reflection. Looking back, I think Beholder shows some (hopefully interesting!) insights about yours truly as an author.

## I have some serious issues with deities

I don't think of myself as grappling with the concept of god all the time, but in looking at my writing? I'm like:

*Sheesh, what is UP with YOU and the divine?*

In my Angelbound series, I have an afterlife where all the angels and demons are as clueless about the Almighty as we are. In Beholder, the gods—well, let's just say it gets really complicated. I don't know why that inspires me, but it does!

## For some reason, I like to play around with identity

Here's what I mean. I tend to have characters confront their kid-self or spirit-self. In fact, I do this so much so that I actually need to name a character Spirit-Rowan or whatever. Go figure.

### Colors are big too

I often end up color-coding things and yeah, that makes me happy for some reason. In Beholder, the Creation Caster magic is red while Necromancer is blue.

### I loves me some monsters

This is somewhat of an obsession. I don't 'do' monsters that have been done before. For instance, when I read a book with a retread monster (Wow, another hydra! Pinch me!) I want to throw my kindle through a wall. I'll sometimes use a classic category, like dragon or chimera, but I always try to put in a twist.

### Battle scenes float my boat

Another thing that gets my inner writer going is devising new ways for partners to fight side by side, as in 1) no one cowers in a corner while someone else fights and 2) it doesn't count if they are fighting halfway across the room from each other. Side by side. BOOM. That's life.

### Snark, snark and, oh that's right, SNARK

My heroines all have snarky voices, and Elea is no exception. Go sass!

### I can't do antiheroes

I know bad boys are a great draw, but I just can't write them. Believe me, I've tried!!! Turns out, I like a good man with a strong moral compass and lots of powers and-or muscles. In that order.

### I appreciate my readers

It's been said before but that doesn't make it any less true: what inspires me to write stories are the people who dig my work.

So THANK YOU for reading.

# WRITING TIPS

*B*eholder marks my second major series as an author. At this point, I can look back at the ten-plus novels I've written and pull together some tips for new writers. Hope some of these are useful!

### It's okay to suck as a writer

Every author is positively rotten when they start out. Why do you think we begin with the alphabet? Everyone starts with nothing and needs to work their way up. The trick is ...

### Stick with it

Writing is an endurance sport. Be prepared. I find that greasy snack foods help a lot.

### Play with words

A fun part of writing (for me anyway) is figuring out how to use language to simulate experience. Whether you alternate consonants or vowels, play with the length of words, or love alliteration ... there are a ton of tools at your disposal to create a vivid world for your readers.

## Have a business plan

Most writers can create a number of different stories for a wide variety of audiences. Why not research which of those options can also make you some money? If it's all the same, there's no shame in pursuing the ideas that can financially support you through your next book.

## Welcome criticism

As an author, there can be a lot of boo-hooing about bad reviews. Here's my advice: ask for people to pick your stuff apart, both in terms of your writing and your business plan. Feedback is a gift.

## Appreciate your support system

It's a romantic idea … *the lone writer*. In reality however, successful writers rely on reviewers, editors, proofreaders, other readers and loved ones. Know who yours are and thank them a lot.

## Be patient

I didn't really get into my groove with writing until book eight. There's a lot of focus in the industry on new writers and manuscripts. Ignore it. Work your craft.

## Read a ton

What you put *in* your mind is what comes *out* on the page. Be super careful of any and all storytelling you consume, especially if you want to create something unique. If you're reading the same stories as everyone else, that's what you'll produce.

## Enjoy your tribe

As you publish more books, you'll get the chance to gain wonderful readers who enjoy your writing. This is THE BEST.

Enjoy!

# MY RULES FOR ELEA

*W*henever I write, I keep a list of *to don'ts* handy. In creating CONCEALED, I updated those for our heroine. Here's the latest.

### Heroines don't run away from trouble.

Well, sometimes they have to, but that's only when there is no other choice. This is especially true in CONCEALED. Elea has power. She's safe from her curse. Our girl could go hang out on her farm and tell everyone to stick it. But she doesn't.

### Remember Bugs Bunny

Warrior heroines always give people a chance to back off before killing them. This is what I call the Bugs Bunny rule. Bugs always gave his antagonists at least one opportunity before declaring, *"Of course you realize this means war."*

### Value life

Heroines have a reaction to the taking of any life. It's just creepy to kill and walk away without having any feels about it.

### Plan, plan, plan

Elea always has a scheme going. When there are setbacks, she regroups, thinks it over, and comes up with another strategy.

NOTE: This one is really hard for me. In my first drafts, I tend to have a very passive heroine. Then I go back and give her action.

### Don't forget goals

This ties in with the planning rule. You can't scheme without a serious goal, but you'd be surprised how easy it is to write hundreds of pages without one. It happens. Plus, it's important to have a life goal *outside* of finding your significant other. Romance is important, but it's not the only thing going on. That said...

### We all deserve love

Heroines who have goals outside of love still deserve rich and satisfying romantic arcs, period. In other words, no one gets stripped of their femininity just because they have an atypical life goal for a romance novel.

### Work, work, work

Elea makes a conscious choice to develop her skills. In CURSED, she works for years to develop her magick. In CONCEALED, she takes herself to the next level by developing social abilities outside her supernatural powers. Namely, our heroine learns how to hide within a new type of society.

Hence the name CONCEALED :)

∽

## FIVE PARANORMAL BIG BADS

When I created Elea, I listed out other characters (from life that's both real and not-so-real) in order to inspire her personality. I follow this same process when creating my villains as well. In that spirit, here are some so-called *big bads* that inspire me.

### Grendel

Grendel is the main antagonist of BEOWULF, a Nordic saga where there's a shit-ton of mead and smiting. What I like about Grendel is that although he's definitely a big bad monster, the REALLY BIG big bad is none other than Grendel's mother. I'd like to read a reimagining of that story where Grendel's mother kicks Beowulf's ass, but I'm a romantic like that.

### The headless horseman

This is a personal childhood memory for me. As a kid, I was freaking terrified of the headless horseman. Specifically, I was convinced that he'd chop off my head at night unless I slept with my hair in curlers, because no self-respecting headless horseman wanted a head full of curls. What can I say? I was six.

### Jenny Greenteeth

No one can scare the ever-loving crap out of me better than an evil Irish fairy. Jenny Greenteeth is a dark fae who lurks by the edges of ponds and pulls kids in to their deaths. I first read about her when I was thirteen and have been avoiding ponds ever since.

### Stupid Peter

If the Irish are great for sheer fright, then the Germans are proficient in a good mind fuck. In fact, there's a series of children's stories called Stupid Peter in which said boy doesn't eat his dinner and so he dies of starvation, doesn't clip his nails so he turns into a wild man, and so on. Great inspiration in here, believe it or not.

### Krampus

And what list of paranormal nonsense would be complete without Krampus, the evil version of Santa who takes kids away in sacks because, again, this is a Germanic story and Santa Claus kidnapping you is yet another mind fuck.

So there you have it. Paranormal nightmares that inspire my literary villains to this day. The badassness never ceases.

## SECRETS OF ELEA

*N*ow that you've known Elea through two books, I thought you might appreciate some secrets about our favorite Necromancer.

### Elea is short for Eleanor

I'm a big history fan and there are a lot of cool Eleanors in the past, such as Eleanor Roosevelt and Eleanor of Aquitaine. Unfortunately, growing up we also had a cleaning woman named Eleanor who was a figure of—how shall I put it?—*not some small angst*. My mother was bi-polar (truth) and when she'd get in a mood, she and Eleanor would hang in the kitchen, drink tea, and talk about how I and my siblings sucked (more truth).

I'm not sure Eleanor really hated us kids so much as liked the big tip my mother gave after any of these sessions, but I still had some torn feelings about the name Eleanor. So, I shortened the name to Elea (ah-LAY-ahh). Extra geek bonus that the pronunciation has Princess Leia's name in it!

### Elea was originally trapped in a dungeon-well at the opening of CURSED

I tried to make it work, but it was just too SILENCE OF THE LAMBS. It was also dark as hell. Eventually, I put Elea on her farm and that was much better for everyone.

### I feel really bad for what I did to Elea and Rowan in CONCEALED

So much so in fact, that I couldn't start writing the next book in the series for ages. Which is crazy because these are fake people in my head.

Good news: The next book, CHERISHED, is already here, so you don't have to wait for some resolution. Huzzah!

ALSO BY CHRISTINA BAUER

CHERISHED

Elea's adventure continues with CHERISHED ... more at
Bauersbooks.com!

ANGELBOUND

The kick-ass paranormal romance with more than 1 million copies sold ... more at Bauersbooks.com!

# FAIRY TALES OF THE MAGICORUM

Modern fairy tales that *USA Today* calls a 'must-read!' More at Bauersbooks.com!

DIMENSION DRIFT

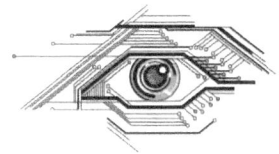

DIVERGENT meets OCEAN'S EIGHT in this dystopian adventure … more at Bauersbooks.com!

CHERISHED SAMPLE CHAPTER

*I*n the last three months, I hadn't raised the dead, animated any skeletons, or cast a single kill spell. For me, that was an achievement. After all, I was a Grand Mistress Necromancer turned farm girl...And I loved my new life.

Mostly.

Sometimes.

All right. In complete honesty, I was dying to cast a silencer spell right now. The reason was simple—Gail and Lizzie Dunkel had joined me for a wagon ride into town.

"Who do you think we'll meet in the village?" asked Lizzie brightly. She and her twin sister flanked me on the driver's bench. The pair both had big blue eyes, tanned skin, long blonde hair, and curvy figures. They even wore matching green gowns. I was their opposite: long dark hair, brown eyes, porcelain complexion, and slim build.

"Perhaps the widow Feyer or the Hartmann boys," replied Gail. The two went on to list other farm families we might encounter. Their chatter was high-pitched and soothing, like a pair of happy birds. Still, I ached to cast my spell. Why? Without it, the sisters would eventually ask me to join their conversation.

In my life, magick came easily. But small talk? Not at all.

My horse Smokey took a familiar turn into an orchard. Bright morning sunlight gleamed off the trees.

"What beautiful apples," sighed Lizzie.

"They look delicious," added Gail. She rubbed her stomach. "How I'd love to stop and try one." She stared at me pointedly. After all, I was holding the reins to Smokey.

Even so, we weren't stopping. The fruit looked too waxy and perfect, which meant this orchard had been hit with freeze blight. Sure, the apples looked gorgeous. But once you bit in, you'd find the colorful shell was filled with foul white goop. Yes, there was still an apple in the milky slop, but it wasn't anything you'd want to eat— more of a small, gray and disgusting lump. Most decidedly not delicious. I gently flicked my reins so Smokey would move a little faster.

Lizzie fluttered her lashes at me. "Can't we please stop, Elea?"

I pretended not to hear her question.

Gail nudged me in the ribs. "You do talk, don't you?"

I straightened my spine. What was I afraid of, exactly? Not so long ago, I rode through far more dangerous woods than these, all in the hopes that bandits would attack me. Plus, I raised thousands of Necromancers from the dead. I even exiled none other than Viktor, a fearsome mage who could wield the hybrid magick of both Creation Casters and Necromancers. Back then, I feared no one—I was a Grand Mistress Necromancer on a mission. Now, I was merely an ex-mage trying to chitchat with some other farm girls.

Small talk. How hard could that be?

"We aren't stopping." I nodded to the trees. "Those are covered in freeze blight."

The girls began gasping and waving their arms in panic.

I ground my back teeth. As it turned out, small talk was rather hard.

"Freeze blight," cried Lizzie. "Oh, no! It couldn't have hit our shire."

"This is terrible," added Gail. "There will be no food this winter. We're all going to die."

Lizzie gripped my upper arm. "You're just teasing...Aren't you?"

A long pause followed in which I silently cursed my friend Philippe. This had all been his idea. He'd urged me to transport the

Dunkel sisters in what he called his Elea Stops Frightening The Locals plan. I'd tried to argue my way out of it, but for some reason, it was impossible to win a verbal battle with Philippe. Now, I was stuck answering Lizzie's question.

I kept my features carefully level. My Necromancer training taught me to mask my emotions. "I'm sure we'll all be fine." Mostly I said this because I could always cast spells that would kill the blight and speed the harvest. But I'd only do that if things got really dire. One rotten orchard wasn't enough to break my vow against magick.

Here was my issue. My parents left me Braddock Farm. It was all I had to remember them by. I wanted to honor their legacy and become a farm girl once more. My best chance to do that was in giving up on magick altogether. "Perhaps we should talk about something else?" I asked.

"I love this idea," said Lizzie. "How delightful that you wish to join our conversation." Lizzie looked so please, I almost felt guilty for not wanting to chat with her. Almost.

"Let me think." Gail tapped her tiny pointed chin. "Ah, I have it. Elea, what's your favorite way to bake a barley loaf?"

Barley loaf? That's a thing?

"I don't bake."

Lizzie stared me, slack jawed. "Surely you've made apple tarts?"

"No."

"Bran muffins?"

"No."

"Spiced pie?"

"No." How many things did most farm girls bake? For my part, I ate whatever Mabel and Sam had ready. The pair had been watching over my farm while I was out adventuring this past year. They'd stayed on after I returned, mostly because they were excellent farmers. Mabel kept a perpetual pot of stew over the hearth.

"What about porridge?" asked Gail.

Relief washed through me. I was about to answer that, Yes, I know how to make porridge, when Lizzie elbowed her sister in the rib cage. "Hush, Gail. Everyone knows how to make porridge." She leaned forward on the driver's bench in order to catch my eye. "What do you make that's special?"

"Nothing you'd like to hear about, I'm afraid." I was trying to keep my stories about Necromancer spells to a minimum. My tales tended to frighten everyone except Philippe.

"Please," said Gail. "We know you aren't a witch these days."

"I've never been a witch," I said slowly. "I'm a Grand Mistress Necromancer."

"Right," said Lizzie. She and Gail shared a long look. I got the feeling I'd made a social blunder somewhere along the line, but I couldn't think where. No self-respecting Necromancer tolerated being called a witch. Witches were hacks who performed black magick at travelling faires. Mages like me spent years mastering our skills, and we never used our powers for evil.

"Well," said Gail. "Tell us what things you made as a Necromancer."

My mood lifted. Fine. If they want the truth, they'll get it.

"I'm quite good at animating skulls."

Lizzie popped her hand over her mouth. "Skulls."

The shocked look on her face was just too precious. "That's right. And I always cover mine with gemstones. It makes for a nice effect, especially when the eye sockets glow while they're talking."

More silence. I may have pushed that too far. It was all part of my Zuchtlos nature, which was what Necromancers called someone who was impetuous. I decided to steer the conversation onto safer ground. "Philippe said nice things about both of you, by the way. I'm so glad he suggested we spend time together."

Another long and meaningful stare passed between the sisters. I almost wanted to offer to let them sit side by side. After all, they had to lean forward to gawk around me.

Lizzie's eyes narrowed. "Do you fancy Philippe? Is he courting you?"

I should have seen that question coming and been prepared for it. But I didn't and I wasn't, so I blurted out the truth. "I don't fancy Philippe and we aren't courting."

"Are you certain?" asked Gail. "He's awfully sweet on you."

Gail wasn't exaggerating. Philippe often proclaimed his undying affection for me, but I had other suspicions. Namely, I thought Philippe would rather be living with his sister, Amelia. However,

Amelia had recently been reunited with her lost friend Veronique, a woman that Philippe detested. So he was hiding out nearby until Veronique took off.

"Believe me," I said. "I have no designs on Philippe as anything other than as a friend."

"If you say so." Gail giggled, and it reminded me how she and Lizzie were nineteen, which wasn't much younger than my twenty-two years. Still, our ages felt centuries apart. I hadn't giggled in years.

Lizzie fanned her face dramatically. "Most girls would die for a chance at that man."

"You're not wrong," I said. In fact, Philippe was exactly the kind of fellow that I should fancy. He was handsome, charming, and kind. Unfortunately, my heart was still set on Rowan, the man who was engaged to Philippe's sister.

What a disaster.

I decided to close out this topic. "If you doubt me, we can settle the issue once we get to the village. I'll stop by the tavern where Philippe is staying. He can explain things directly."

Gail squirmed. "Visit Philippe alone? But we've no chaperones to protect our reputations."

"Don't worry. I can kill almost anything, including Philippe."

Lizzie and Gail stared at me yet again, wide eyed. I was going for some kind of record here: Most Social Mistakes By A Necromancer.

"Wh-what?" asked Lizzie.

Obviously, I needed to change the subject once more. I cleared my throat. "But that's enough about Philippe. Do you have any news about this weekend's faire?"

The Dunkel faire was an annual tradition. It always took place on the fields behind their main house, and the next celebration was this Saturday. This was yet another potential social catastrophe which Philippe had manipulated me into.

Gail beamed. "Oh, the preparations for the faire are coming along quite well. We already have set up the tables and—"

All of a sudden, a wave of energy coursed over me, caressing my skin into gooseflesh. The rest of Gail's words were lost to my consciousness.

Someone is casting magick nearby.

The spell felt like hundreds of embers searing my skin. That could only mean one thing. A detection spell from a Creation Caster. Interesting.

All Creation Casters knew magick, but most could only perform a handful of low-level spells. Senior Casters were extremely rare. Sadly, an evil mage named Viktor had transformed most Senior Casters into Changed Ones, which were part-animal mages that could cast hardly any spells. Rowan and I had sent Viktor into exile; most Changed Ones were thrilled with that accomplishment.

A handful still served Viktor, though.

A sinking feeling crept into my stomach. Something told me this new mage was one of Viktor's followers. Not good.

I pulled the wagon to a stop and scanned my surroundings. We'd passed the orchard some time ago. Now, tall stalks of green barley lined either side of the road. The shadows within them seemed too dark for daylight.

Something was wrong here.

And because I was Zuchtlos, that wrongness felt absolutely exciting to me. My shoulders squared. The world came into clearer focus. An evil Creation Caster was definitely close by. A battle of wits and magick could start any second now.

For the first time in ages, I giggled with joy.

—*The End*—

∽

*To find out more about CHERISHED, visit:*

**http://monsterhousebooks.com/books/beholder/cherished**